LOST STARSHIP

The Lost Starship
The Lost Command
The Lost Destroyer
The Lost Colony
The Lost Patrol
The Lost Planet
The Lost Earth
The Lost Artifactt
The Lost Star Gate
The Lost Supernova
The Lost Swarm
The Lost Intelligence
The Lost Tech
The Lost Secret
The Lost Barrier
The Lost Nebula
The Lost Relic
The Lost Task Force
The Lost Clone

Visit VaughnHeppner.com for more information

The Lost Clone

(Lost Starship Series 19)

Vaughn Heppner

Illustration © Tom Edwards
TomEdwardsDesign.com

ISBN: 9798856233338
Imprint: Independently published

-1-

Captain Maddox awoke by degrees, each sensation dreamlike and surreal. Then, all at once, he became alert as his eyes snapped open.

There was a blurry face before him, a dark lower part—that was the mouth, an open mouth. He could tell by the teeth. Maybe the person shouted at him. What was the other yelling and why couldn't he hear them?

Maddox frowned. He was freezing, the entirety of him, from toes to the crown of his head. Every time he breathed, it felt as if icicles pressed against his inner throat.

There was no logical reason for that, at least none that Maddox could remember. There was no logical reason for any of this.

Why can't I move?

The question focused Maddox, bringing his concentration to bear. He would start with the other, figure out what was going on with the person.

The face was behind glass, or a substance like glass. There was something remarkably familiar about the face. The man— it was definitely a man—seemed urgent and worried. Faint sounds penetrated the glass, but Maddox had no idea what the other shouted or why.

Second question then. Why couldn't he move? Maddox became aware that straps held him down. The straps cinched his chest, stomach, thighs, ankles, biceps and wrists. What was the reason for that?

1

The only conclusion he came up with was that someone had captured him. He couldn't remember who or why or even how.

Icy air circulated in the box—

Yes! This was a box but it felt like a coffin. What did that tell him? He had no idea, so… He concentrated, trying to kick-start his brain. It felt like…he'd woken from death.

That's an emotional response. You need to do better. Get in the game, Captain.

He hadn't been dead, as he wouldn't now be alive. Still, the idea of death, the confinement and icy air swirling around him—

He had to get out of here. Panic had built as he'd been thinking. Maddox surged, trying to twist free of the confining straps. That did less than help the situation: it nearly wrenched tendons and muscles. Pain knifed in places, and that increased his claustrophobia.

Maddox grunted, working to regain control of himself. When he succeeded, he sucked down air.

The freezing cold *hurt* his throat. Damn this was icy.

That told him what. Had they frozen his body? That would be akin to death, the reason for the feeling of rebirth. Was he in some kind of cryogenic stasis, coming out of it?

That made sense.

The blurry face behind the glass disappeared. Opening locks made faint noises around him. A great lid lifted. Warm air flowed over his body. That felt good, so desperately good.

A man in a dark uniform pushed the heavy lid to the side. It must have been on hinges. The man stared down at him.

"Maddox," the man said.

Maddox stared up at the man. He was tall and leanly muscular with dark hair—it was like looking in a mirror. The man looked just like him.

"Are you awake?" the man asked.

Maddox opened his mouth and tried to speak. Instead, he made a croaking sound.

"Try to relax," the man said. "You're waking up, thawing out, if you want to be technical. Are you relaxed yet?"

Maddox barely nodded. It was all he could achieve.

2

"Good," the man said. "Now, it's time to move you. First, I have to get the binding off and then you need to help me raise you."

Maddox wanted to agree, but new, compelling thoughts intruded. He'd been on his way to the refugee planet of the living Adoks. A while back, the crew of *Victory* had rescued the Adoks from the Glenna Nebula. Galyan had been pestering him about it, talking about keeping his sworn word and such. Galyan wanted to unite with the living Adoks. Unfortunately, they were terrified of all deified Adok AIs, of which Galyan was one. Maddox *had* promised to help Galyan change that. The Lord High Admiral had agreed. Meta and Jewel had joined him on *Victory*. The starship had almost made it to the refugee planet. They had to go through a Laumer Point first. The Adoks had insisted it was the only gate to their star system. No. Wait. *Victory had* gone through the Laumer Point.

Why can't I remember anything after that?

"Hey," the man said, snapping his fingers in front of Maddox's face. "You need to focus, stay in the here and now. Do you understand me?"

Maddox nodded the faintest bit.

"Good," the man said, producing a monofilament blade.

The knife looked awful familiar. Then Maddox realized why. It was *his* monofilament knife. Had the man stolen it from him?

"Don't move a muscle," the man said, using a voice Maddox had heard all his life, as it was his own.

Maddox scowled. This was weird. Where was the starship? Where was Galyan? Where were Meta and Jewel? Why was he in a cryogenic unit?

The knife sliced through the straps.

Carefully, the other slid the blade into its special sheath. He then reached in, grabbing cold flesh. Maddox knew because the man's hands burned with welcome heat.

The man strained, pulling Maddox up.

Maddox made a croaking sound as he tried to speak again.

"I know," the man said. "You're confused. That makes sense. I was confused earlier myself."

3

Maddox barely shook his head. Why would the two things be related?

"That doesn't make sense to you," the man said. "I get it. Let me help you up. We're in danger, by the way, terrible danger, in truth. I need your expertise to help me—us, get out of the danger."

Maddox tried to help, but he was the next thing to limp. Nevertheless, the strong man helped him stand upright and step out of the cryo unit. That's when Maddox realized he was naked.

"A hot shower will help you revive faster," the man said.

Maddox stared at the other. Why did the man look exactly like him? Could the man be his clone?

The idea started Maddox's heart to thumping. His heart hurt it hammered so hard.

"Take it easy," the man said. "You need to relax. Breathe deeply. You're going to be okay."

Maddox managed to twist his head and look around. They were in a cargo hold or what looked like a cargo hold. There were other cryo units with cords snaking away from them on the deck. Some of the units had bits of coating frost. Was he on a spaceship?

The man moved him, so Maddox's naked feet slapped the deck each time. The process was undignified, making him feel uselessly weak.

Before them, a hatch opened automatically. They moved into what seemed like a ship's corridor. Maddox sensed a thrum against the soles of his feet. Such a thrum might come from a ship's engine.

"Hang in there, buddy," the man said. "You've got this. You're tough. I ought to know."

Maddox squeezed his eyes closed. Could this be a nightmare? It felt surreal, but it also felt real. He opened his eyes. They faced another hatch. He had no idea how long they'd been walking, but it felt as if time had passed.

The hatch opened. They entered crew quarters. The man moved Maddox through various rooms until they stood before a small shower stall.

They squeezed in together. It was a tight fit. The man lowered Maddox until his naked butt was pressed against the drain. The man let go of him and stepped out of the shower stall.

"I'll turn it on hot," the man said. "The rest is up to you."

Maddox stared at the man, the possible ·clone. He felt so weak, so helpless. He hated this.

"You're experiencing cryogenic feebleness," the man said, seeming to divine Maddox's thoughts. "It'll pass. It'd better. I need your help. Nod if you understand me."

Maddox managed to nod.

The man grinned, reaching in, turning a shower-stall handle.

Maddox managed to look up as warm water sprayed against his face. How had he gotten onto the spaceship? What had happened to *Victory* and the others? Was this because the Adoks were terrified of Galyan?

The warm water got hotter.

Maddox realized he'd better concentrate, or hot water might soon scald his face. He had to get a grip. As he thought this, he was shivering, and the water was helping with his revival, just as the man had said.

Would it help him fast enough? It was time to fight through the weakness and find out was in the hell was going on.

A klaxon had started its blaring noise and kept ringing. It woke Maddox from slumber. Hot shower water struck the back of his neck. It felt so good, so relaxing. It was too hot, he was sure, maybe even blistering, but at least he wasn't cold any more.

With a groan, Maddox crawled out of the shower. He began shivering immediately, the mild shivers soon turning desperate.

As his teeth chattered, Maddox used the stall's edge to work up to his feet. He pulled a towel free and dried himself. It was hard to do. He was still cold afterward, but it wasn't as awful as just seconds ago. He also learned that his neck hadn't blistered, as he'd feared.

He looked around. The man was gone.

Did the klaxon have something to do with the man's absence?

Painfully, slowly, by leaning against a wall, Maddox slid out of the bathroom into a bedroom. There were garments laid out on the bed. To get there, he'd have to leave the wall and cross the room.

He pushed off, staggered several steps, tripped and collapsed onto the floor.

His muscles were still too flaccid. He breathed rapidly and started shivering again. Maybe just as bad, his left wrist hurt because he'd caught himself with that hand.

This wasn't any good. He was Captain Maddox. He was the *di-far*. It was wrong for him to lie here like a broken fool.

Maddox forced himself to crawl. The effort helped against the shivers but made his wrist hurt more. On reaching the bed, he worked up until he lay gasping upon it, with his toes yet pressed against the floor.

Pushing farther up, he rolled onto his side and found a pair of briefs. It was a struggle, but he put them on. He felt better wearing briefs and started with the slacks.

After a time, he wore them, too. He pushed until he sat up. In that way, he donned the dress shirt but forewent the officer's jacket. He buttoned the shirt, tucked the ends into the pants and cinched the belt.

He sat like that for a time until he realized that he no longer shivered. Good. That was good. The man still hadn't returned. The klaxon had quit ringing some time ago, too.

Was the last part good or bad?

To find out, he needed to search. That was the impulse he needed to start moving again.

Leaning over, he spied socks and boots on the floor. They were at the foot of the bed.

It was time to do this.

Maddox slid down, put on the socks and slipped on the boots. They fit. They ought to, as they were his. He tried standing.

He succeeded without using the bed. He wasn't panting, either. His heart no longer hammered, and his head had stopped hurting. His left wrist no longer felt so bad, either. Was the stasis feebleness finally wearing off?

He said, "Hello," to find out if anyone else was around. Unfortunately, the word came out like a croak.

Maddox cleared his throat several times and said "Hello," again, louder than before.

No one answered him.

Maddox shifted up and sat on the edge of the bed, examining the room. There was nothing personal about it. Except for his clothes, it was a bare bedroom. It was large, though. Was this a master wardroom on a warship? Or was this a civilian liner?

Maddox frowned. He remembered sitting in the captain's chair on *Victory's* bridge. He had no idea how long ago that was. He'd given an order to enter the Laumer Point. The starship had gone through. He was sure of it.

His head began to throb as he tried to remember what had happened next. The starship had gone through. What had been on the other side of the wormhole?

Had the Adoks laid a trap for *Victory* in order to waylay Galyan? He'd let the Adoks know they were coming. Maddox had been sure that would be better than simply showing up. Had that been a mistake?

Maddox rubbed his hurting forehead. The throb had finally proved too much. He gasped, deciding he could question the man about these things. Thinking about them hurt his brain too much.

As Maddox decided that the headache receded although it didn't altogether quit.

Maddox scowled. That seemed like a deliberate mind block set there by someone. He wouldn't let the block remain for long. No one was going to stop him from thinking what he wanted, especially concerning his family and friends.

Unfortunately, thinking like that had started the throbbing again.

"No," he gasped. "I'm letting it go."

For now, he told himself.

Maddox waited until the sharp headache dialed back to dull pain. There were splotches in his vision, but he could manage despite that.

He forced himself to stand. He swayed at first but then stood there. Experimentally, he took a step, another and then a third.

He could do this.

Like a kid getting the hang of walking on stilts, he retained his balance and maneuvered through the crew quarters. In none of the rooms did he gain a sense of occupancy. This place was empty.

He reached the main hatch. It swished open. He staggered into a corridor, nearly losing his balance but leaning against a bulkhead as the hatch swished shut behind him.

He examined the corridor. It felt like a spaceship and had a steady thrum all around him. This wasn't a Star Watch vessel, though. It seemed right for human dimensions, but he hadn't yet met any humans.

Maddox looked in both directions, trying to decide which way to go.

"Hello," he called, louder than before.

Like before, there was no answer.

He cupped his hands around his mouth as if creating a megaphone. "Hello. Can anyone hear me?"

Maddox cocked his head. It almost seemed as if he heard an echo. How big was the ship?

Frowning, pushing off the bulkhead, he began to walk. His balance was better but still not perfect. This reminded him too much of the time he'd gone to the strange barrier across the Milky Way Galaxy. There had been the empty spaceship where the woman had died, shot in the stomach by Ardazirhos. The humanoid wolf aliens had escaped the spaceship through a portal. Did this have anything to do with Ardazirhos or the Mastermind? Maddox had helped destroy the Cosmic Computer, the Mastermind's double, twin or something. Could this be vengeance?

Maddox sniffed. He didn't smell Ardazirhos, although that didn't prove anything. What had happened to the man who'd looked like him? Where had he gone?

I have to find Meta and Jewel. I have to find out what happened to them.

In the beginning, it hadn't seemed like a mistake bringing them along on the mission to visit the living Adoks. Now, Maddox realized it *had* been a mistake. If anything bad had happened to them…

He bent his head, the painful mind-throb returning with a vengeance.

He gritted his teeth, enduring. He wasn't a dog that someone could train through pain. He would think about his wife and child as much as he damned well pleased. He wouldn't—

Maddox groaned, as the pain became too much. He focused on the idea of finding the man.

By degrees, the throb subsided.

The man, he had to find—

9

Maddox saw a porthole ahead, a tiny round window in the bulkhead. He hurried there, made a funnel with his hands and pressed the forward edge against the glass. He peered through his cupped hands, looking and studying space.

There were patches of stars here and there, and lots of nebula darkness. There were also swirls of purple energy in the distance. Nearer were streaks that seemed like comets dashing across Earth's night sky—except this was outer space somewhere.

Some of the comet-like streaks flew near the porthole.

The spaceship shuddered. Metallic sounds groaned like whales from a place deeper in the vessel.

Without using his hands to help filter out light, Maddox pressed his face against the glass, shifting to the side in order to see if any of the ship had ruptured. He couldn't tell.

The klaxon began to wail again. Given what he'd just seen that couldn't be good.

Maddox pulled his head back. All around him, the ship shuddered, seeming to do so more and worse.

Maddox found himself breathing hard. Something was wrong with the ship. He needed to find the man, and he needed to do it now.

-3-

During the next hour, Maddox discovered that this was a big vessel. He walked through kilometers of corridors, gaining strength the entire while. He found more crew quarters and possible passenger areas. Everything was empty.

He had no idea where his cryo unit had been, nor could he find the lookalike man or any bridge.

He did see more portholes, looking out of them each time. He saw more of the same but in varying degrees. Sometimes he saw more stars. Sometimes he saw less. The purple energy continued to swirl. The comet-like streaks seemed to have thickened. He didn't recognize any constellations.

The shaking in the ship had gotten considerably worse.

Then, he heard metallic crashes or the sound of breaking hull. That caused high-pitched shrieks, possibly air screaming as it left the ship for the vacuum of space.

Maddox waited in frightened anticipation. He was sure the air he breathed was becoming thinner.

Loud clangs heralded an end to the shrieking. Maddox supposed emergency hatches or bulkheads had sealed the broken hull from the rest of the ship.

Tension eased from his shoulders until he wondered if the emergency seals had blocked him from the ship's bridge or the man who'd woken him.

There was only one way to find out. He kept walking, exploring the huge vessel. At no time did he come across any military hardware or elevators. He didn't find any hangar bays, either. The vessel must be a large passenger liner but without any crew or passengers aboard.

Did that mean the man who'd helped him earlier had hijacked it? That seemed like a reasonable assumption.

Maddox longed for a pistol or knife. He found a length of hollow metal in a closet. It lacked threads on the ends, so he doubted it was a pipe. It had that kind of heft, however. For the moment, it was his sole weapon.

He imagined he heard the man's voice speaking over an intercom system. The voice was faint, though. Should he have remained in the original crew quarters with the shower?

Maddox's stomach rumbled and he found that he was hungry and thirsty. There had to be a cafeteria around here somewhere.

He continued to explore. The voice spoke again, louder than before. It still wasn't loud enough so he could distinguish the words. He followed the voice until he found a closed hatch.

The voice came from behind it.

Maddox searched the hatch and then the side of the hatch. He found no controls or anything else to activate it.

The voice ceased speaking as he searched.

He pulled out the length of hollow metal and struck the hatch. Both door and "pipe" clanged. He started to hammer the hatch, badly denting his "pipe" on one end.

Maddox stepped back, inspecting the hatch. He looked around for camera eyes. So far, he hadn't seen anything to resemble that.

Abruptly, the hatch opened. Beyond it were spiral stairs.

Maddox hesitated only a moment. He hurried, and he nearly wasn't fast enough. The hatch began to close as he went through. He leapt. The hatch caught the end of the officer jacket, ripping material.

He'd put on the jacket during his second visit to the crew quarters.

He examined the back of the jacket. It wasn't much of a rip, and he was through the hatch, in one piece.

He took the stairs. They only went up. Did that mean he'd been on the bottom deck? He climbed until he came to a landing. There was a hatch before him. He tried it, but it refused to open.

He continued up the spiral stairs.

The intercom system didn't activate again. The ship continued to shudder. From farther away, Maddox heard shrieking. This shrieking had a different quality to the sounds of earlier.

He had the terrible feeling that the man who'd helped him had just met with a fatal accident. If that had happened—

The shrieking stopped but he heard clangs again. These were different from before. They sounded… in sequence, if that made sense. That told him… Maddox bent his head in concentration. He should know what that meant.

He began to breathe harder as an odd thought struck. What if *he* was the clone? What if the real Captain Maddox had freed him from the cryo unit? That would explain why the other had the monofilament blade.

Maddox flexed his hands. The idea of being a clone terrified him.

"I'm Captain Maddox," he said.

The sound of his voice comforted him.

Yet…wouldn't a clone of Maddox say the same thing?

Maddox thought furiously. He'd married Meta. He remembered it explicitly, especially the wedding night. He'd gone through many adventures as *Victory's* captain.

Maddox shook his head. He was who he was. He was the original. How did he know that?

"I'm Maddox is how."

The words seemed to settle his nerves. He refused to accept the possibility that he was the clone, second fiddle, as it were. Why had the other said he needed help? Because the other lacked the full memories and—

Maddox raised his eyebrows. He had Erill spiritual energy. He could feel it. He closed his eyes and sought the intuitive part of him.

He felt it.

Then why have I been so tired all this time?

13

Maddox shook his head. He could feel the Erill soul energy. It had replaced a dull zone in him that the Ska he'd once attacked had stolen.

Steeled with resolve, Maddox continued climbing the stairs. He heard the continuing clangs and decided he knew what the sounds represented.

A foreign entity had boarded the ship. They had used attack pods, the clangs he'd heard as the pods attached. Other sounds meant drills or breach bombs had blasted the hull open in places. Yet, if the spaceliner were empty except for the clone and him...

The attackers were after him, possibly also after the clone. If the attackers were after both of them, he should help the clone, as they were allies then.

Or he could play it safe and hang back, letting them take the clone.

Maddox shook his head. He rejected the last idea as too passive and possibly disloyal.

Maddox took the stairs two and three steps at a time. He needed to find the clone. He needed a real weapon. He needed to find the attackers before the attackers found him.

As he climbed the stairs, it dawned on him that perhaps the attackers were Star Watch personnel come to rescue him.

Maddox reached the next landing. The spiral stairs didn't go any higher. He'd raced up seven levels, seven decks, he assumed. There was a porthole in this hatch.

He didn't race to it. Instead, he first pressed against the hatch and then rolled around to spy through the porthole with one eye.

Down the lit corridor were three thin humanoids in battle armor. The suits were archaic or baroque with fluting like medieval knightly armor. The blast rifles looked lethal, though. A cord connected the rifle butt to a power pack on the back of the armor. Maddox estimated the attackers stood seven feet tall and were extraordinarily thin. In fact—

One of the armor suits turned toward him. Maddox saw a mostly metal face with plastic parts, much of that around and in the eyes. The face wasn't behind a faceplate or visor as the being didn't wear a helmet. The being was the suit. Ludendorff had named such a thing once.

Ludendorff had called the thing a...*cyber.*

Maddox nodded stiffly. Cyber was the same as cyborg.

Was that a Soldier of Leviathan then?

The cyber or cyborg aimed his blast rifle at the hatch and fired.

Maddox threw himself back.

The blasts dented the hatch. More shots fired, denting the hatch more.

Picking himself off the deck, Maddox raced down the stairs. That must have been a Soldier of the Sovereign Hierarchy of Leviathan. Could he have reached the Scutum-Centaurus Spiral Arm where Leviathan ruled a huge region of space? That would be distinct from the Orion Spiral Arm where the Commonwealth was.

If that were so, he was a long way from home.

Above on the highest landing, the blasted-off hatch clanged heavily against the deck. The cyber or cybers had opened the way.

This was bad. This was very bad. Maddox couldn't let the cybers capture him. What in the world did this all mean?

Maddox snarled with frustration. He had to figure out how to open one of these staircase hatches or the cybers would catch him for sure.

-4-

Maddox hurtled down the spiral stairwell. He was no combat match for three cybers with blast rifles. Heck, he probably would fail against three of them in hand-to-hand fighting.

Cybers or cyborgs were a meld of organic and mechanical. They would likely possess heightened strength and speed. If they were Soldiers of Leviathan—

Maddox had faced them before many years ago. He hadn't faced them like this, but he'd learned since then about their brutal reputation. They were ruthless, intelligent and had no appreciable weaknesses.

Maddox landed with a thud, grunting, trying the next hatch.

It was locked.

He turned and continued down the stairwell.

"Human," a cyber called in its synthesized voice. "Cease your flight. It is futile. Worse, you might damage yourself. The Strategist desires you whole and unharmed."

Maddox craned his head upward. He couldn't see the cyber, just stairs. He heard its remorseless tread, the whine of its mechanical parts as it chased him. By the sounds, there was more than one. Probably all three headed this way.

It had spoken about the Strategist. Maddox knew very little about the Sovereign Hierarchy of Leviathan. It was a highly stratified society: that much he knew. He'd spoken to a Strategist before, a cunning individual.

"Human," the cyber called. It was odd and perhaps frightening that it used speech Maddox recognized.

Maddox landed on the second-to-last landing. He'd entered on the bottom deck earlier. He tried this hatch.

It opened.

Without hesitation, Maddox bolted through. He didn't bother trying to close the hatch behind him. It did, though, doing so automatically. He thought to hear a click that meant it had locked.

Maddox didn't check. He ran, sprinting as swiftly as a cheetah. He'd regained his normal faculties, having recovered from the cryogenic weakness. He didn't have his regular stamina, however. Soon, he panted and sweated.

He should have drunk gallons of water while in the shower. He was likely dehydrated from prolonged stasis.

He looked around. This deck or level was different from the other. It didn't feel like crew quarters. The hatches struck him as the entrance to cargo holds. Were there any hangar bays on this level?

Maddox slowed as he gasped for air. Stopping, with his hands on his knees, he listened. In the distance, he might have heard cyber footsteps as they stalked him.

Straightening, Maddox moved down the corridor. His hands trembled, he was so tired. Maybe he hadn't fully recovered from the cyro process yet as he'd thought earlier.

If the clone had stolen the spaceliner, it would appear that a warship belonging to Leviathan had tracked it down. Could he really be in the Scutum-Centaurus Spiral Arm? That would mean he was thousands of light-years from the Commonwealth of Planets, maybe even thousands of light-years from Human Space. In other words, he was far from home.

How could he have gotten this far?

The refugee planet of the Adoks was on the Scutum-Centaurus Spiral Arm side of the Commonwealth. The planet had to be 8000 light-years from the edge of the other spiral arm, though.

Could Maddox have been unconscious or in cryo-stasis during a journey of that distance? Or did the mind block keep him from remembering what had happened during the journey?

It was frustrating not knowing.

Far down the corridor, a hatch opened.

Maddox was headed that way. He slowed, half-expecting cybers to march out, trapping him. None did, at least not yet.

After ten more steps, he broke into a run again, heading for the open hatch. He was going to assume the clone had caused the hatch to open. Earlier, Maddox hadn't done anything he could conceive to have opened the stairwell hatch onto this level. That implied someone else had done it. Cybers surely hadn't been the operative entities. That just left the clone as far as he knew.

"You'd better be right," Maddox mumbled under his breath.

As he ran, the corridor lighting flickered, threatening to go dark.

Maddox bet the cybers caused that.

He increased his sprint, pushing as hard as he could.

If cybers were here, that implied a spaceship had brought them. That meant a Leviathan warship likely waited beyond the civilian spaceliner. Would the clone know that?

Why was there a clone of him, Maddox wondered. That was weird.

The open hatch was nearby. Maddox sensed greater space beyond it. Should he call out?

Maddox did not. He slowed, walked through the hatch and spied a short corridor. Beyond it was a hangar bay.

Maddox trotted through the corridor and entered the hangar bay. It wasn't as huge as *Victory's* bays. There were several shuttle-sized craft parked on the deck. They looked like atmospheric vessels as each had stubby wings and aerodynamic designs. Down at the end was a vessel double in size. It had an open hatch with a ladder going up from the hangar bay deck to it.

Maddox hurried, looking around, but he didn't see any cybers. He wanted to call out. Instead, he ran, reached the ladder and scrambled up it.

He passed through an open airlock. It closed with a clang behind him as soon as he moved through. Lights flickered on ahead.

"Follow the corridor," a familiar voice said.

Maddox's shoulders eased. He recognized the voice as his own. That must mean the clone.

Maddox passed closed hatches on either side of a short corridor. At the end, in front, was another hatch. It opened as he reached it.

Maddox entered a small cabin with several seats and control panels. The clone in his black uniform sat in one, likely the pilot's seat. There was a large curving window in front and beyond it the shuttle's nosecone.

The clone looked back, grinning at him. "For a while there, I didn't think you were going to make it."

Maddox approached the clone. Several screens were on. They showed spaceliner corridors. In one, three armed cybers jogged swiftly with their blast rifles ready.

"Are they Leviathan Soldiers?" Maddox asked, pointing at the screen.

"Yes," the other said.

"Are you a clone of me?"

The other looked up and stared hard at Maddox. "You come right to the point, don't you?"

"Is that your answer?"

The other faced forward. "I suggest you strap yourself in. We're going to have risk leaving. It could get hairy if the Soldiers spot our shuttle."

Maddox sank into a nearby, cushioned seat. "Are we in the Scutum-Centaurus Spiral Arm?"

"'Fraid so," the other said.

"What should I call you?"

The other nodded. "Dravek will do for now."

Maddox scowled. "I've never heard that name before. How did you come to pick it if you're a clone of me?"

The one called Dravek continued to manipulate his boards. He was silent for a time and then inhaled sharply, looking at Maddox. "That was the name of the scientist working on us when I first revived."

"Us?" asked Maddox.

"You called me a clone," Dravek said. "I suppose the term has validity. The scientist said I didn't have all your memories, though. It was more a smattering of your thinking style or process."

"What does that mean?"

"Can we talk about it later?" Dravek asked. "We have more pressing matters to deal with."

After a moment, Maddox nodded.

"Are you snug?"

Maddox yanked at the restraint he'd clicked into place.

"Good," Dravek said. "Here we go."

-5-

Big hangar bay doors opened to outer space. That was bad because Dravek must have forgotten to depressurize the bay first. Worse, the other shuttles weren't locked in place. The atmosphere in the hangar bay rushed out the doors. The escaping air pushed the other shuttles, causing them to skid along the deck until they tumbled through the open doors into stellar darkness.

The bigger ship that Dravek and Maddox inhabited remained locked in position. The other shuttles barely missed theirs as they slid past.

"Have you ever flown a shuttle before?" Maddox shouted.

"What's that?" Dravek asked. "Oh." He shook his head. "Don't sweat it, chief. I know what I'm doing. I'm using some of your infamous trickery."

Maddox stared at Dravek.

The other must have felt the continued scrutiny. He faced Maddox again. "No. I've never flown a damn thing as me, as Dravek. I have many memories of piloting, though. Would you like me to enumerate them?"

"You have my memories?"

"Don't you remember what I said? I don't have all of them, just some. They should prove enough."

Maddox watched the last shuttle slide out of the hangar bay. Outside in space, red fusion beams from somewhere had already struck several craft.

That implied the Soldier warship was out there, possibly waiting for something like this. Did the clone know that? If the clone or Dravek did know that—

What would I do in his place? Maddox nodded. He knew what he'd do. "Did you open other hangar bay doors on the spaceliner?"

"I did indeed," Dravek said.

"And you unlatched those shuttle skids as well?"

"To every single shuttle in the spaceliner."

Maddox grinned. He liked it, as it gave the Soldiers scads of targets. "Are you trying to confuse the cybers?"

"Something like that." Dravek pressed several controls at once.

There were clicking sounds from outside, which meant there was still a bit of atmosphere in the hangar bay. The atmosphere carried the sounds.

Dravek reached up and flipped a switch. The cabin lights went off.

The bigger shuttle slid toward the open bay doors, doing so in the same manner the others had exited.

"Do think this will confuse the cybers for long?" Maddox asked.

"No, as the cybers are thorough. Given enough time, they'll beam everything. We just want to be last on the list."

The bigger shuttle slid out of the bay doors into space. There were nearly a hundred shuttles floating out here near a long, a massive spaceliner. Some of the shuttles were wreckages already, most still intact.

Maddox leaned forward, staring out of the big curving port window. In the distance was an oval. It was difficult to tell its size, as he didn't know its distance from them. Maddox recognized the type, as they'd faced such a warship before in the Omicron 9 System. The warship would have iridium-Z-hull armor and obviously used fusion cannons for offensive action. It was a Leviathan vessel.

"The cyber that spoke to me said they had orders to capture me unharmed," Maddox said. "Why are they beaming the shuttles then if they want us alive?"

"He didn't give you the full scoop," Dravek said. "He meant capture you unharmed—if they can. But if that proves impossible, destroy or eliminate us." He stared back at Maddox.

"What do we do now?"

"From what I'm seeing," Dravek said, "Leviathan doesn't like you much."

Maddox shrugged. There were a lot of people or beings that didn't like him. Maddox couldn't care less. His own people counted to him. The rest of the universe could shove it as far as he was concerned. That included the Sovereign Hierarchy of Leviathan.

"You must have a plan," Maddox said.

"I do. Given our present drift...it's time to see if this works." Dravek had faced forward and pressed a switch.

The shuttle lurched. That was it, though. There was no sustained thrust.

Maddox kept staring out the large, curved port window. The shuttle slowly moved away from the others, sliding under the massive spaceliner from which they'd launched. Soon, Maddox lost visual of the Leviathan warship. The giant spaceliner blocked a direct-line-of-sight to the enemy vessel.

That must have been what Dravek had been waiting for. His fingers flowed across several boards at once.

The shuttle shifted direction as side-jets activated. Soon enough, however, those ceased.

"Hang on," Dravek said. "Here's where it could get rough." He manipulated a panel.

Thrust began, propelling their shuttle. The thrust quickly increased. Maddox and Dravek sank into their respective cushioned seats as more acceleration took place.

Soon, Dravek stared intently at a board.

Maddox craned his head. The other watched a timer.

"Now—" Dravek pressed a switch.

Acceleration stopped. The shuttle drifted.

"Here's what's happening," Dravek said, leaning back and pointing at a screen.

Maddox leaned over and studied the screen. The huge spaceliner blocked the Leviathan warship's view of them. They drifted away from the spaceliner and presumably farther a-way from the distant iridium-Z-hulled warship. Clearly, Dravek was using the spaceliner to shield them as long as he could from the Soldiers.

"We're going here," Dravek said, as he pressed a switch.

The screen switched images. Maddox saw purple energy swirling and zigzagging like lightning bolts. Nearer them, comet-like objects streaked with speed.

"Is the area dangerous?" Maddox asked.

Dravek snorted. "It's more than that. Technically, we're already in the Heydell Cloud, in its outer fringe, anyway. It gets much worse the deeper one goes into it."

"What exactly is the Heydell Cloud?"

"I'm getting to that," Dravek said with an edge to his voice.

Maddox understood. If Dravek were anything like him, Dravek didn't care for others questioning his choices or interrupting his explanations.

"The Heydell Cloud is a nearly unnavigable region of space, under regular conditions. The cloud is huge, over a hundred light-years across in all directions. Inside the cloud are some interesting planets: interesting in terms of minerals found that a few use in high-tech operations. When traders enter the region, they usually use a seer to help them navigate the spatial anomalies."

"The traders use a prophet?" asked Maddox.

"What?" Dravek scowled. "No, no, they don't use a prophet. Why don't you shut up a minute and listen to what I'm saying?"

"Just one minute," Maddox asked dryly.

Dravek glared until he chuckled ruefully. "You understand, don't you?"

"If you mean about others questioning your decisions and explanations, yes, I do."

"I learned much of this from the scientist Dravek. He was from a planet in the Heydell Cloud, a planet named El Dorado."

"That's an Earth name," Maddox said.

"I noticed that, too," Dravek said. "We're in the Scutum-Centaurus Spiral Arm, but this region is nearest the Orion Arm.

The Heydell Cloud is theoretically outside the jurisdiction of the Sovereign Hierarchy of Leviathan. The Soldiers and others of Leviathan don't care to enter the cloud. I'm not altogether sure why not. They do send agents at times, bounty hunters, possibly."

"We can navigate in the cloud?"

"Our shuttle can use Laumer Points. It lacks a jump capacity on its own, however."

"Do you have a seer's capabilities?"

Dravek shook his head. "A Heydell seer is blind and possesses a psionic ability to sense gravitational masses and energy fields. The scientist told me a seer can see those things the way a normal person sees visible light. How that's possible, I have no idea. In any case, the Heydell Cloud has weird gravitational masses, strange energy fields, space vortexes and such."

"Meaning it's a highly dangerous region of space as you said earlier."

Dravek nodded. "It's especially dangerous for big costly warships. The trader vessels are usually small for just that reason. I'm hoping the warship won't follow us any farther in. If we enter a vortex, we probably won't have to worry about the warship anymore, as we'll have too many other problems to worry about."

"When you took the spaceliner, you deliberately headed for the Heydell Cloud."

"I figured Leviathan would come after us sooner or later. Once they did, I didn't believe I could fool them for long. Thus, I went for the one area they feared to go."

"Would you have taken the spaceliner into the cloud?"

"It was too big for that," Dravek said.

"Did you hijack the spaceliner?"

"Hijack is a technical term. I didn't use any armed forced to make others obey me. So no, I didn't hijack anything."

"Did you have a crew to help you…relieve the spaceliner from its docking bay?"

"Originally," Dravek said.

"What happened to them?"

"There was a misunderstanding among us. They paid the price for that."

"They're dead?"

"What else?" asked Dravek. "I was in a desperate situation."

Maddox studied the other who was so much like him. Yet, he'd already detected differences between them. "Did your partners want to take the spaceliner somewhere else?"

"That they most certainly did."

"Do you have my intuitive knack?"

Dravek seemed momentarily confused by the question.

That gave Maddox the answer. Dravek didn't have his intuitive sense. He doubted the other was a *di-far* either. The other also wouldn't have the Erill spiritual energy. Those were all critical differences.

"Did you plan to acquire a seer before navigating the cloud?" Maddox asked.

Dravek sighed. "She was part of the original crew, the only one who sided with me, I might add."

"They hurt or killed her," Maddox said, reading the signs. "That was why the others died."

Dravek stared at him. "Do you know that it's unsettling talking to you? It's as if you're reading my mind. You'll know I don't like that."

"I know."

"Still, I need your help. So we're stuck with each other, for a while at least."

"To do what?" asked Maddox.

Before Dravek could answer, a green light blipped repeatedly on a nearby screen. Then, the screen became blizzard-like.

Dravek tapped controls. "The bastards are overriding the comm."

At that point, the screen blizzard diminished until a strange Soldier of Leviathan appeared on it before them.

-6-

The Soldier had a narrow face that was as much polished metal and hardened plastic as flesh. He had shiny silver metal eyes that moved smoothly in black plastic sockets.

Behind him were a thousand lights flickering on wall-to-wall computer banks.

"I am Sub-Commander Mune," the Soldier said in an emotionless voice. "We have detected you on our sensors. You will immediately redirect your course and head for the warship."

Dravek opened channels. "I'd be happy to comply, sir. Unfortunately, I have a malfunction—"

"We are aware of your unsophisticated use of ploys," Mune said, interrupting. "You must comply or die. In this instance, the choice is yours."

"In that case, can you send someone out to help us fix the shuttle controls?" Dravek asked.

Maddox nodded with approval. The clone used the right techniques.

"Your ploy is a waste of time," Mune said. "If you do not comply—"

"Yes," Dravek said sharply. "I'm changing course. I don't want to die."

"I do not detect any deviation in the shuttle's flight," Mune said a moment later.

"Your detectors must be malfunctioning then," Dravek said. "I have definitely changed course."

"No…" Mune said. "A tech just ran a diagnostic on our detectors. The detectors are working perfectly. You have not changed course."

"I'm not trying to be contradictory," Dravek said. "I'm sure your detectors *are* working perfectly. Remember, though, this is the Heydell Cloud. The energy surges here may be affecting your detectors in ways you cannot…perceive. Frankly, I'm not surprised your tech failed to discover the anomalies. I have most certainly turned back and am now headed directly for your warship. That is an irrefutable fact."

"It is barely conceivable that you have a point," Mune said. "However, given your proclivity for using subterfuge in these situations, I must conclude your words are a ploy. Your ship hasn't turned back. It is not headed here. Thus, you should prepare to die."

"Wait, wait," Dravek said. "I'm coming in now. You're right. I wasn't headed for you until this moment. Your threats are taken at face value here. I fear what you'll do. I swear to you my ship is already changing course. I desperately want to live."

On the small screen, Mune looked away and checked something. Soon, he looked at Dravek again. "This is another lie. You are continuing your present course. I am charging the fusion cannon."

"Mune," Dravek said. "I have Maddox with me. He's my prisoner."

"That changes nothing."

"Doesn't Leviathan want Captain Maddox?"

"Of course," Mune said.

"I claim the reward for his capture," Dravek said. "I'm short of funds and ask that you promise to enrich me and let me go after I give you Maddox."

Mune stared silently at Dravek. "No. This is part of your ploy. I am firing."

"You bastard," Dravek said. "I'm trying to surrender. Why are you making it so difficult?"

"Me?" Mune said, almost sounding offended. "I have given you every opportunity to comply—"

The connection cut. At that moment, the great spaceliner detonated, kilometers of ship all down the line.

Dravek shouted triumphantly. "Finally! Hang on, Maddox. We're going to accelerate. I hope we're far enough away that the debris doesn't kill us."

Maddox sank into the cushioned chair, the acceleration immediate and building.

"Do we have gravity dampeners on this thing?" Maddox said.

"Nope," Dravek said.

The G-forces built up as the shuttle continued to accelerate. Behind them, a part of the shredded mass of the exploded spaceliner headed for them. Red fusion beams burned into the expanding mass but failed to reach any designated targets.

Likely, Dravek had set timed explosives inside the spaceliner to detonate and provide cover for them in the shuttle. It was what Maddox would have done in his place. It was a welcome thing to watch a truly competent operator at work.

"How did we come to be here?" Maddox asked suddenly.

Dravek snorted, shaking his head, perhaps in wonder.

Maddox scowled.

Perhaps Dravek noticed. "Listen, we should concentrate on surviving first. If we do, there will be plenty of time to talk about the other stuff. If we don't survive, none of the other stuff will matter anyway."

"How did we reach the Scutum-Centaurus Spiral Arm?"

Dravek shook his head. *"You* reached this region, probably coming from the planet of the Adoks. I'm thinking this was the region of my genesis. I started here, which means I came from here and didn't travel all this way like you did."

"Oh."

"Yeah, oh," Dravek said. "What's the last thing you remember?"

Maddox blinked thoughtfully, wondering how much he should trust Dravek.

"After all I've done for you," Dravek said, "you still don't trust me?"

Maddox cleared this throat. "I was approaching the refugee planet of the living Adoks."

"You mean Galyan's people?"

"Yes."

Dravek glanced at Maddox. "There are Adoks who survived the Swarm attack on their home planet?"

"You don't know about that?"

"Friend, I already said. I don't have your full memories. That was what the scientist told me anyway."

"Dravek the Scientist?"

"Yup."

"And you took his name?"

"Do you want to call me Maddox instead? We could do that."

"Definitely not," Maddox said.

"I didn't think so. Hence, I took the name Dravek for your convenience."

Maddox considered that. "I appreciate it."

"Good. Because it feels weird hearing you call me that. Oh, oh."

Maddox craned his neck, studying the screen Dravek did. "Are those missiles?"

"They sure are."

"Do we have any counter-fire batteries, any flares or decoys?"

"You're welcome to look. This is a civilian craft, so I doubt it. Maybe you can improvise something, which would be great, by the way."

Maddox swiveled in his seat. The acceleration hit him the wrong way then, but he endured as he studied a computer manifest. Finally, he swiveled so the seat helped him endure the continuing acceleration again.

"Find something?" asked Dravek.

"No."

"That's a pity."

"How long can we continue speeding up like this?" Maddox asked.

Dravek checked a gauge. "A few hours max, providing we dodge the missiles."

Maddox studied the missiles. "They're going to be here in minutes."

"I noticed that, too. So... You see that vortex over there?"

Maddox squinted. It looked like swirling dark space. What caused that? No. That didn't matter. It was there.

Are you taking us in?" Maddox asked.

"I don't know what else to do."

Maddox nodded. "I don't either. Your decision strikes me as wise, as it's better than being blasted apart."

"Those are my feelings exactly," Dravek said. "We should reach the vortex...several seconds ahead of the missiles. I hope it's enough."

"The cybers might detonate the warheads prematurely."

"Agreed," Dravek said. "So what do you think? Do we accelerate so we black out or do we hope the cybers are nice and give us those few extra precious seconds?"

Maddox tightened in his grip on the armrests.

Dravek noticed. "That's what I thought. Better to face the unknown like Hannibal crossing the swamps than die by blast."

Maddox remained silent, waiting.

Dravek glanced at the rapidly approaching vortex, his knuckles turning white on the controls. "Hang on," he said, a note of grim determination in his voice. "We're about to test our toughness."

In seconds, the shuttle dramatically increased acceleration.

Maddox fought for consciousness. Did the comm blink again? Did Dravek shout an aphorism? Perhaps one of the warheads detonated. Maddox had no idea, and then he blanked out because there wasn't enough blood and oxygen in his brain to keep him awake.

At that point, the shuttle aimed directly toward the swirling dark mass, the anomaly in space. Beyond it, purple energies churned and white particles flew like comets.

This was the Heydell Cloud, an infamous region of space for reasons Maddox had no idea.

Tense seconds passed. The missiles jumped acceleration, racing faster. One warhead detonated, its energies expanding at the speed of light.

31

Maybe it was too late to make any difference. The shuttle was gone. It disappeared as soon as it entered the vortex. Did some of the gamma and x-ray radiation also zip into the vortex?

It was impossible to tell from here. The blast did nothing noticeable to the vortex, as it continued to spin as it had for the past one hundred and sixty-eight hours.

-7-

Inside the shuttle, lights flashed and metal groaned as the vessel violently shook. Controls and circuits burned, producing a harsh electric stench as smoke billowed within the cabin.

"Dravek!" Maddox shouted.

He couldn't hear any answer. The noise from twisting metal and crisping circuits was too loud for that.

Maddox coughed, covering his mouth with a sleeve. Electric-smelling smoke singed his nostrils. Some of the smoke must have entered his lungs. He hacked hoarsely, finally turning to the side and vomiting.

Unbuckling his restraints, Maddox staggered through the cabin, accidentally colliding into a stanchion. He grunted as his jacket tore. Pushing off, Maddox stumbled again as the shuttle swerved. He crashed against a body. Dravek must have been unconscious, as he was unmoving. Maddox felt over him, clicking the buckle and tearing off the restraint. With Dravek in his clutches, Maddox staggered, dragging the other toward the hatch.

An electrical fire raged on a control panel. The flames provided some illumination in the increasingly smoky cabin. Several screens showed a kaleidoscope of colors merging and bleeding apart. Air began to scream from a newly made bulkhead breach.

Tightening his hold of Dravek, Maddox lurched and crashed against a bulkhead. The shaking craft, the swerves, the

33

upending—anyone else would have lost his footing. Maddox barely kept his.

Then, he reached the hatch, slapping the emergency control. The hatch opened with a screech. Maddox staggered through, dragging Dravek with him.

The hatch closed behind them, smoothly this time.

They both collapsed in the corridor as a klaxon began to wail.

Fortunately, there was normal lighting in here.

Dravek had a huge purple welt on his forehead. The man must have knocked himself unconscious against a panel.

Working around him, Maddox grabbed Dravek under the armpits and dragged him to a different hatch.

It opened, leading into a crew quarter.

Maddox dragged Dravek to the cot, hoisting him into it. He found emergency restraints, tightening them around the man.

That should keep Dravek secure for now.

Maddox staggered out. The shuttle swerved and shuddered the entire time. He made it to an emergency pod on a bulkhead and yanked a lever. A section of the pod slid open. Maddox pulled out and donned a breathing mask, then grabbed a flashlight and a flame-retardant cylinder. The red cylinder had a short hose and handle for spraying.

He reentered the control cabin. Even through the breather, he could smell the electrical stench. It was smoky dark in here, the only light from the screens and flames.

With the cylinder spraying retardant, he put out the electrical fires. That actually made it smell worse in here. Next, he went to the controls, inspecting them and the screens with the flashlight.

He was sure he could fix the burnt wiring given a day of repairs. Luckily, a few of the screens still worked. The shaking had stopped, although air still shrieked as it escaped through a fist-sized, jagged rent. According to a screen, there was damage outside to the shuttle's exhaust nozzles. Could he go out there and fix that? Maybe given time.

He tapped a panel and found that a main viewing screen still worked. He used it to view...the shuttle must have exited from a giant red opening hanging in space. They moved away

34

from it. Was that a Laumer Point opening or something else? Other objects continued to spew from the round and glowing red opening into the star system.

That's right. This was a star system. There was a yellow dwarf star in the distance. Maddox clicked controls, wanting more data. The sensors were shot. He had no idea how far the star was, although he estimated it could be what Uranus was from the Sun.

There were no purple energy swirls anywhere, no comet-like streaks. He didn't see anything to resemble an exploded spaceliner and Leviathan warship. Clearly, they weren't in that area of the Heydell Cloud anymore.

If Maddox had to guess, he'd say they'd entered the vortex, traveled the length of a possible wormhole and exited through the red opening into the star system.

How far had they traveled since entering the vortex? That was anyone's guess. He searched for planets, spotting what must have been a Jupiter-like gas giant with many moons. The moons were perceivable dots around the gas giant. Were there other planets in the star system?

It seemed likely but presently unknowable because he was strictly using visuals.

Maddox would have to fix the sensors…if he could figure out how.

Speaking of fixing—he headed to the bulkhead tear. Once there, he placed a thin, square piece of metal against the jagged rent. That would have to do for now, although some air hissed through. He'd need to find some sealant.

The lights were out in here. The cabin wiring likely needed an overhaul. He doubted Dravek knew more about repairs than he did, seeing as the man was his clone with only some of his memories.

After making one last check and walking to each station, Maddox determined there was nothing else he could do at the moment.

He exited the cabin and tore off the breather. Checking the thing's meter, he saw that he'd only had a few more minutes left.

He put the breather back in the emergency pod and checked on Dravek. There was no more shaking or swerving, just zero gravity drifting for the shuttle.

Dravek slept soundly. The purple welt had grown, though. It was a hell of a bump. Should he wake Dravek and find out if he was still coherent?

Maddox shook the man's shoulder.

Dravek hadn't woken up.

Maddox shook harder.

Dravek stirred and his left eyelid flickered, possibly allowing some light to strike the eyeball. Dravek moaned and tried to curl into a fetal ball. The restraints held him in place, though.

Maddox left him after that, returning a little later.

Dravek snored, having eased out so he lay stretched out on the cot. Did the awful welt indicate brain damage? It was a grim possibility.

Once more, Maddox retreated. While in the corridor, he decided to search the rest of the ship. He entered an engine room where the generators rattled. That didn't sound good at all. Checking, Maddox discovered that the Laumer Point Detector had burned out. Maybe going through the vortex had done that.

The sick-sounding generators—Maddox shrugged. Without the generators, they'd die once the air recycler used up the emergency battery power. He'd have to check a manual or the computer and see if he could repair whatever was wrong with the generators. That was going to be an iffy proposition at best.

He inspected the rest of the shuttle. It was twice the size of a regular Star Watch shuttle. There was nothing in the cargo bay. The other rooms were crew quarters. They all contained zip. In a corridor locker near the airlock, he found a spacesuit and repair kit. There might be more tools outside on the shuttle hull.

What Maddox needed was Andros Crank or Professor Ludendorff.

He finished the survey by checking the foodstuffs in a tiny cafeteria. They had plenty to eat and drink. Unless they traveled for half a year, they should be okay with sustenance.

Maddox cocked his head, considering. At best, they were still in the Heydell Cloud somewhere. Would the system star steady or block the various anomalies outside the star's gravitational pull?

He didn't know, but he did decide to fix the shuttle's detectors. First, he'd eat, drink and sleep some.

Upon waking up later, he discovered the computer in the control room still worked. That was critical. He found that Dravek must have set it up for English. After some computer searching, he found the shuttle manual and repair possibilities.

Six hours of tedious work with tools and under three different consoles produced a miracle. Maddox repaired the shuttle detectors.

He checked on Dravek afterward. There was no change except for the color and size of the welt. It had black amidst the purple and was twice as big as before. The skin was stretched, seeming as if it might rip.

Maddox touched the welt gingerly.

Dravek groaned, turning his head from the contact.

Maddox went to a computer terminal in the bedroom. He found a med page. According to it, Dravek needed fluids and rest. Pain pills would be iffy for him now. It would also be better if Dravek were awake. According to the med advice, the man had likely received a concussion.

Maddox thought about that and gently tried to wake Dravek. He could not. Thus, he retired from the quarters and went to the control cabin. He'd found sealant and used it around the metal patch. The hiss of constantly escaping air ceased.

With light from the screens, Maddox sat and began to scan with the detectors, using passive systems.

Beyond the gas giant were several terrestrial planets. The one nearest the star—

Maddox's jaw dropped. He detected a small spaceship in orbit around the farthest terrestrial planet. As he scanned, he discovered a city, a spaceport. Another vessel headed down to it. Over the city in the atmosphere were circling planetary jets.

Maddox debated sending a distress signal. His intuitive sense bade him to wait.

For the next three hours, Maddox scanned the star system. Toward the end of the time, he detected a small ship—maybe twice the shuttle's size. It slid past the biggest moon of the Jupiter-like gas giant.

How had it escaped detection until now? The ship must have stealth equipment. Why would it bother with a stealth approach?

The answer soon revealed itself.

From behind the moon emerged a much larger ship. Drones launched from it. The drones burned hot for the nearing and smaller stealth ship.

This was interesting. The detectors indicated communication chatter between the drones and stealth ship. Ten minutes later, a beam burned from the stealth ship. One of the drones exploded. The second drone launched miniscule missiles.

The stealth ship's beam destroyed three of those. The fourth missile struck the small ship and detonated. The vessel began to tumble end over end.

At that point, the larger ship began to maneuver toward it.

Two hours later, the larger ship docked with the no longer tumbling smaller vessel. It began to tow the smaller ship for the moon.

Maddox decided the larger ship was a pirate vessel or a military ship. The bigger ship with its prize maneuvered out of sight, sliding behind the gas giant's largest moon. Maddox didn't see either ship after that.

Was there was secret base on the moon?

Maddox sat back thoughtfully. He soon nodded. It was time to repair what he could of the shuttle's motive power. He'd wait on the generators, first repairing any nozzle damage. Then, he'd have to decide what the best option would be after that.

-8-

Maddox donned the vacc suit. It was a tight fit, which suggested the shuttle had been made for smaller people than him. He was able to lengthen the suit enough that he felt confident it would remain intact while he was outside.

This was it. There was no help if he got into trouble. He exited the airlock, activating magnetic clamps on the soles of his boots.

As the shuttle drifted toward the main star, he clumped on the shuttle's hull. He used the helmet's lamps, finding more damage than he'd anticipated. Frankly, they were lucky only the control cabin had been breached. There was rock scoring everywhere.

Oh. He found a gaping hole. Squatting, looking down with the lamps, he eyed a littered cargo hold. There was another hole in the back. Most of the debris or smashed cargo was gone. Perhaps whatever had been in the hold had softened the impact enough that it hadn't obliterated the entire craft.

Perhaps sheerest chance or luck had saved them. Could Dravek have anticipated that the vortex would lead them into this star system? What were the odds Dravek had accidentally steered them into an inhabited system?

Dravek must have found something with the sensors before approaching the vortex. That luck had brought them here—Maddox shook his head. He doubted it was luck, as that was stretching probabilities too far.

He continued across the hull until he reached the back thruster nodules. He visibly inspected them, soon scowling. The damage was greater than he'd realized earlier.

He'd have to clear these if he hoped for any expelled propellant to push the shuttle.

He supposed the side-jets could give them a tiny bit of thrust. They needed more than that, though, if they hoped to reach the inhabited planet near the dwarf star. They'd need less thrust if they hoped to reach the gas giant and the pirates there. If they weren't pirates, they'd be military personnel, possibly maintaining an embargo on the distant terrestrial planet.

How much trade occurred in the Heydell Cloud? Maddox shook his head. He didn't know.

How had Dravek learned about any of this? Had the scientists told him? Did it matter right now?

Maddox sighed. Gingerly, he crawled over the back hull and to the nearest nozzle. Then, he crawled in it. Through a laborious hour of work, he was able to take off one of the main plates and inspect the damage.

This was big time iffy. He lacked a welder and used sealant to fix what he could. Then he used clamps, wrenches and other tools to clear away smashed junk. For the next two hours, he worked until he was damp with sweat and his limbs ached with fatigue. Zero-G work was more daunting than he remembered. It often took greater effort to make the equipment do what he wanted than if he'd had gravity to assist him.

Finally, he began the laborious process of returning to the airlock. He paused during the journey to look at the dwarf star and gas giant with its multiple colors. He didn't see the pirate ship. It would be less than a speck from here using his naked eye.

He started again, reached the airlock and reentered the vessel. He wouldn't have been surprised to see Dravek standing there aiming a weapon at him, but such was not the case.

Maddox went to the crew quarter. Dravek slept. The welt— had the blow dented the skull underneath it? Maddox hadn't thought to check.

Well, there was no use worrying about it now. If the other had become imbecilic because of the blow, then he was on his own. He'd been in such a place before.

Taking the breather, he entered the control cabin. The burnt electrical stench had diminished some. He went to the controls and used the passive sensors for three hours. He had to take off the breather eventually. The stench was worse, but he could bear it. There was no trace of the pirates. Neither did he see any other ships land on the terrestrial planet near the dwarf star.

He focused on the terrestrial planet. Other than the one city, he didn't detect any other technological or industrial site. Was the city an outpost such as the Phoenician traders of old had constructed in different parts of the Mediterranean?

He studied the planet more, checking its composition. According to the sensors, it had a breathable atmosphere and would likely be Earth normal in gravitational terms. Most of it appeared to be desert terrain except for the two pole regions.

According to what Dravek had said earlier, Leviathan didn't control the cloud. Independent traders sought costly minerals from hidden worlds in the cloud. Occasionally, Leviathan hired bounty hunters to go into the Heydell Cloud and seek wanted people.

Would Leviathan send in some of their own traders? He recalled the alien Dhows from the planet Kregen. The Dhows had been planetary traders to Jed Ra's people. The Dhows had paid fees to Leviathan for the privilege but hadn't seemed to be beholden to the cybers.

Maddox doubted that Leviathan sent any Soldiers on trade mission anywhere, and surely not into the Heydell Cloud. Maybe some traders paid fees to Leviathan for certain privileges elsewhere. The traders might even sell a hostage to Leviathan. But, it also seemed that such a trader might accept payment for passage elsewhere. Would such a trader take him to a place outside the Heydell Cloud? The trader might if it was profitable enough.

How would one reach the Commonwealth of Planets from anywhere in the Scutum-Centaurus Spiral Arm? How would one reach Omicron 9, likely the closest outpost to Human Space from here he could find?

41

Maddox cocked his head. He'd have to solve each problem at the proper time. If he couldn't exit the Heydell Cloud, none of the rest would matter. First, he had to reach the terrestrial planet out there or hijack the pirate ship near the gas giant, if indeed that was what it had been.

Could he hijack a ship like that on his own? It seemed doubtful. Did it possess a human crew? He lacked sufficient data to know. He needed a fit Dravek to help him, as that would double his effectiveness.

As he sat at the sensors, Maddox calculated distances and speeds. At the present velocity, it would take ten months to reach the Jupiter-sized gas giant. That was too long. He'd need the booster.

Could Dravek take any thrust in his present condition?

Maddox sighed. He'd have to take some calculated risks. He wasn't even sure the thrusters would work.

Okay. Before he started the next phase, he'd eat and rest. Only then would he make his major decision.

-9-

After waking up, Maddox made the decision. He engaged the generators, using the remaining fuel and propellant, initiating a three-hour burn. Afterward, Maddox shut off the generators.

There was perhaps a half-hour supply of fuel and propellant left. That was it for the shuttle until it received a resupply.

Maddox recalculated. Given their new velocity, it would take three months and several days to reach the gas giant. More than three times that to reach the terrestrial planet near the dwarf star.

That didn't consider the fuel and thrust needed to slow down enough to land or even dock with any gas-giant stationed ship. This was all a desperate gamble at this point.

What was behind the gas giant's biggest moon? The idea haunted Maddox. Was it a pirate ship or a military vessel enforcing an embargo on the terrestrial planet?

He could try communications to find out. Maddox studied the recording from the short battle near the gas giant. Unfortunately, he was unable to decode the military encryption. This wasn't *Victory*. It was a civilian shuttle with a civilian computer.

He decided silence was the better bet, forcing the other to investigate the lone shuttle. He literally had no bargaining points, and he didn't know enough about the other.

Could Dravek supply him with that lack whenever he recovered? An intuitive feeling told Maddox there was a good possibility of that.

Maddox exited the control cabin and paced up and down the short corridor. He used Velcro-soled shoes on the carpet to anchor him. There was no gravity dampener in the shuttle. Thus, it was zero-G in here. His muscles would quickly deteriorate under these conditions, especially given the length of stay in the shuttle.

Maddox recalled finding exercise equipment in a different room. He got it out and set it up, soon practicing with bands and cables.

For the next few weeks, Maddox used the equipment religiously as he hated the idea of losing strength or even muscle tone. The zero-G environment would sap his body fast. Thus, he spent many hours each day exercising, drinking plenty of fluids the whole while.

He went into Dravek's quarters and moved the man's limbs every few hours. The clone was rapidly losing muscle tone and size lying on the cot. Dravek needed to come around soon, or it wouldn't matter.

The journey was tedious, but not as awful as the time with the octopedal robots upon leaving Kregen. That journey had been a nightmare, nearly driving him mad.

Maddox tried not to think about that time too much. When he failed, he'd find himself staring at the bulkheads in a cold sweat. The best way to avoid that was to do other things to occupy his thoughts.

That was one reason why he sat at the passive sensors for hours, studying the star system systematically. No other vessels used the red opening to enter the system. That was important, as it meant Leviathan hadn't sent anyone through the vortex after them.

Did the Soldiers believe their missiles had destroyed them? Or did the vortex lead to different places, randomly switching slots so to speak? Maybe the vortex had vanished. If so, what had caused it to form in the first place? Why would it have attached to the glowing red opening?

44

Maddox wasn't familiar with stellar mechanics regarding vortexes. Once more, it would have been better if Ludendorff or Andros Crank had been his companion instead of an unconscious Dravek.

Speaking of which, the swelling welt had gone down an appreciable amount. That was good news. Maddox had used a med scan with the computer. It turned out that Dravek didn't have a cracked skull.

Since it appeared that Dravek would survive his injury, Maddox pondered about him more. Why had anyone made a clone of him? If he could answer that, he'd know more about his present predicament.

The days continued to pass, and Maddox concluded someone had obviously kidnapped him. How otherwise had they—whoever *they* were—gained the needed ingredient to make a Maddox clone? What did he positively know? A scientist named Dravek had made the clone or helped in making the clone. Then, it seemed as if the scientist had refined the clone's capabilities.

What had the scientist wanted Dravek to do? Maddox didn't know. It must have something to do with the Sovereign Hierarchy of Leviathan.

If that were so, had Leviathan sent operatives into the Commonwealth to kidnap him? According to Dravek, Leviathan hired or paid bounty hunters to enter the Heydell Cloud. Logically, they might have used a similar procedure in the Commonwealth.

Maddox tried to employ his intuitive sense in this, searching for a clue or a direction of thought. His sense gave him nothing.

He deduced two possibilities from experience and logic. There had been a bug-eyed monster once trying to kidnap him, a creature named Grutch. Why might Grutch not have tried again and succeeded? Venna the Spy of the Spacers might also have attempted such a thing.

Would the Spacers know about Leviathan? That seemed more than possible.

There was a third possibility: the Mastermind in the center of the Milky Way Galaxy? The Mastermind might well have sent Ardazirhos to kidnap him. Would the Mastermind have sold him to Leviathan then? That seemed unlikely. If the Mastermind were like the Cosmic Computer, he would want to deal with Maddox himself.

The days lengthened and became deadly dull because of their increasingly repetitive nature.

There was one point of interest. Toward the end of the first month, Maddox noticed another small trade ship headed for the terrestrial planet. This ship kept well away from the gas giant, as in tens of millions of kilometers away. Maddox hadn't seen the ship enter the system through the red opening. It might have used a normal Laumer Point, but one near, in relative terms, to the gas giant. Interestingly, the possible pirate ship or military vessel never attempted to seize the new ship.

Soon, the new ship was sixty million kilometers away from the gas giant as it steadily continued for the terrestrial planet.

Except for the ship, more dull days passed. At the beginning of the fifth week, an important difference occurred. A significantly thinner Dravek opened his eyes.

When Maddox noticed, he hurried beside the man. "Do you know who I am?"

Dravek moved his mouth, silently saying, "Maddox."

"You've been injured," Maddox said. "Through the vortex, we reached a star system with an inhabited planet. We've been traveling through the system for five weeks already."

A wan smile spread across Dravek's face. He made the barest of nods.

Maddox would have said more, adding that they were a long way from reaching safety, but Dravek's head rolled to the side as he began to snore.

Maddox took that as a positive sign because snoring took more energy than otherwise. Dravek's chest rose and fell more than before.

During the next few days, Dravek gained greater coherence and could speak for several minutes at a time. Finally, he could sit up, take food and use the bathroom facilities on his own.

Dravek practiced getting up, but he'd find himself intensely dizzy. He passed out twice. Fortunately, each time Maddox was on hand to catch him. Thus, Dravek didn't re-injure himself by banging his head too hard while he floated through the room.

More days ticked by, and Maddox would sit in the control room watching the gas giant's moons, trying to detect radiation, anything that would give him a clue as to whether that pirate vessel was still there.

Dravek increased strength until he began to use the exercise machines in order to strengthen his depleted muscles.

"Hurts," he said.

"No doubt," Maddox said. "How's your head feeling?"

"Better. I can't remember how we got here, though."

Maddox told him for the eighth time.

Dravek nodded, laughing at part of the tale. He hadn't done that before. Maybe he would remember this time.

"Who was Dravek the scientist?" Maddox asked. He'd been dying to know. "Why were you made into a clone of me?"

Dravek searched Maddox's eyes. Was there wariness in the clone? "I don't know much. The scientist did say once that I was supposed to join a spy ring at Omicron 9. Later, I think they planned to send me Earth."

"Do you know why?"

"To collect information."

"For Leviathan?"

"I'm sure of that," Dravek said.

"How did you feel about that?"

Dravek laughed harshly. "I don't want anyone controlling me."

"You mean the scientist would have inserted a coercive device?"

"Not would have, had," Dravek said.

This was new information.

"I removed it," Dravek said.

Maddox was impressed. "It was an outer device?"

"Surgically implanted," Dravek said.

"How did you manage to remove it?"

"It was a grim process," Dravek said.

His tone implied he didn't want to talk about it. Maddox accepted that—for now.

"I know something else," Dravek said. "My imprinting from you didn't fully take. That was why the scientist woke and questioned me. During the questioning, I gained greater coherence and a semblance of who I was. I dissembled until the scientist turned his back on me. By that time, he'd removed the restraints. It was a mistake on his part. I acted. From that moment I've been a fugitive."

"That's all you remember?"

Dravek's eyes clouded. "Yes," he said shortly.

Maddox didn't believe that in the slightest. He'd asked that to test the man. Maybe it was time to put this out in the open. "You don't trust me, do you?"

"Let's reverse that question. Do you trust me?"

Maddox rubbed his chin. "I was a captive of Leviathan and now I'm not, thanks to you. Our situation is difficult at best. But if you continue to help me, I'll most certainly continue to help you."

"That's fair enough."

They might have kept talking, but Dravek became drowsy and soon fell asleep.

-10-

After endless weeks of travel, they neared the gas giant. Maddox spent more time in the control cabin using the computer. He estimated times and distances. He also played the video showing the battle with the trader and drones. From that, he attempted to pinpoint the exact location of the hidden moon base. Did such a moon base exist, or did the pirates or military personnel live in their warship, remaining hidden behind the moon?

Maddox checked and rechecked angles, concluding that the position the pirates had taken hid them from any direct line of sight from the planet or any satellites or probes launched from the planet—as long as the equipment didn't travel too far from the planet. Were the pirates or military personnel taking precautions or was this mere happenstance?

Maddox continued to study as he hunched over the console. He wished the electrical fire had never taken place, as certain functions still didn't work. But if he was going to wish, why not for grander things? This was the situation. It was time to plan accordingly, time to—

Maddox sat up, twisting around to stare at the hatch. His intuitive sense had just pinged. Something… Maddox's eyes narrowed. He stood and strode for the hatch. He slowed and stopped, purposefully relaxing his shoulders. He set his face into a more pleasant mien. Only then did he continue, exiting the cabin.

The hatch slid shut behind him. He moved to Dravek's quarters, using Velcro attachments to navigate in the zero-gravity environment. He knocked, practicing propriety.

"Enter," Dravek said.

Maddox manipulated the control. The hatch opened and he entered. Dravek was stretched out on the cot, almost as if in pain. Maddox approached, noticing the dim lighting. Something yet pinged in Maddox's intuitive sense. Something wasn't right. He didn't look around, as that would indicate suspicion. He wanted to subdue any of Dravek's suspicions to the man might give himself away.

"How are you feeling?" Maddox asked.

"As well as can be expected," Dravek said.

Maddox understood that Dravek had forced lassitude into his voice. He approached closer, with a half grin, even as he noticed the welt. It had shrunk considerably. Dravek's color was also better than before. Indeed, the man looked positively healthy. That was a sudden recovery after weeks of injury.

Maddox stopped from grabbing Dravek's arm and seeing if he'd injected himself. Or seeing if there were any telltale marks from a hypogun. Instead, Maddox pulled up the chair he'd brought in weeks earlier.

"It looks like you're still feeling low," Maddox said.

"I just need to sleep. Your knock woke me."

Maddox didn't get any sense Dravek was drowsy, or in any way incapacitated or dulled. In fact, he noticed the blanket. It seemed as if Dravek held a weapon under it. Was this the moment of decision?

Intuitively, Maddox knew it was. He moved. At the same instant, so did Dravek. But the blanket hindered him. Maddox set his hand over the blanketed wrist. Dravek strained to move the arm. Maddox was astonished at the man's strength, given his condition.

Maddox tore away the blanket and ripped a blaster out of Dravek's grip. He checked the setting: narrow beam lethal.

"Well, well, well," Maddox said. "You appear to have gotten dramatically better." After shrinking to a degree, the welt had remained for endless weeks, seeming a permanent fixture on the forehead. Now... "The welt—how is it possible it has shrunk so quickly in so short a time? Tell me, Dravek, where did you get the medicine?"

Dravek stared at him stony-faced.

"Is this how it's going to be?" Maddox asked.

Dravek remained silent.

"What haven't you told me?" Maddox asked. "What has you worried?"

"Nothing. I've been candid with you the entire time. The blaster—I got nervous the last few days, wondering if you really mean what you said."

"Go on."

Dravek paused and then shrugged.

Maddox shook his head. "You're holding out on me. You have medicine and weapons. What else do you have I don't know about?"

Dravek turned away. Perhaps he was thinking.

Maddox let him. He sensed this was a pregnant moment with implications for the rest of the journey.

Dravek looked at him. "Do you mind if I sit up?"

"Not at all." Remembering the scientist Dravek had once surprised, Maddox stood, moving back as he kept facing the man. Dravek still had his monofilament blade. He should have recovered it when Dravek was unconscious. He hadn't, though. However, he was being careful about it.

Dravek hunched as he sat on the bed, his hands down on the mattress. He looked up, grinning in a hale-good-fellow sort of way.

"I haven't been completely candid with you."

Maddox nodded.

"I, uh, had a lot of time on my hands while you were in stasis. Much of that time, I prepared for this day, our freedom, you could say. Our spaceliner carried contraband, specifically, Leviathan weaponry. Much of that weaponry and space mobile equipment is sealed in hidden chambers aboard the shuttle."

"I didn't find any."

"I would be shocked if you had. This is a smuggler vessel meant to maneuver through the Heydell Cloud. The spaceliner was on its normal route, if a little ahead of schedule."

"Meaning what?" Maddox asked.

"Can't you guess?"

"I'm done guessing. I want you to level with me."

"I am.

"Excellent. So this equipment we have…" Maddox raised his eyebrows.

Dravek looked away, sighed slowly, and then looked at Maddox again. "I believe we can use the equipment against those on the moon."

"Do you know who they are?"

Dravek nodded. "One of my original crew that helped me steal the spaceliner was part of their team. They're Gnostics. They're from a corrupt world, one could say. They live on the edge of the Heydell Cloud, or the world or star system is. Gnostics are some of the premier pirates, smugglers, kidnappers and pimps of the region."

"Why doesn't Leviathan wipe them out?"

"Why should they?" asked Dravek. "The Gnostics pay many fees and taxes to Leviathan. Sometimes, Gnostics hire out as bounty hunters for Leviathan."

"It appears you know more about the Sovereign Hierarchy of Leviathan than you've let on."

"I'm afraid so. I'm afraid you were out for months in cryogenic stasis. During that time, I've been learning, thinking, and planning. My plans went awry because a Leviathan warship showed up. If I'd still had some of my original crew—"

"Did you get greedy?" Maddox asked, interrupting. "Is that why they're dead? You killed them so you could keep all the profits for yourself?"

Dravek raised his hands palm upward as if shrugging. "I have some of your memories, remember? I don't have all. If you have a higher code of ethics than I do, that's your business. I'm a survivor, at least as far as I know. I suspect you are, too. It's clear you have a few different modes of thought than me, even though we have many of the same abilities. I'm curious, why did you suddenly decide to come in at exactly this moment?"

Maddox made a faint gesture.

"No," Dravek said. "It was more than a whim. You have some kind of... Do you have psionic abilities?"

"None," Maddox said.

"I'm not sure I believe that."

Maddox shrugged. "Tell me more about the smuggling operation, about the equipment and weaponry in the secret hold. You must know we're fast approaching the gas giant."

"Don't think we'll find any grace from the Gnostics. They're a greedy, savage bunch. They'll slit our throats in an instant."

"Meaning I can't offer them the goodwill of the Commonwealth in trade for services rendered?"

Dravek snorted. "As well offer that to me. It means nothing. The Commonwealth is thousands of light years away. We're on our own, Maddox. It's up to us to save our skins."

"What do you suggest?"

"Take their ship."

"That's a possibility?" Maddox asked.

"I've thought about it a lot. The Gnostics are clannish to the extreme. Therefore, it would be difficult for an independent mercenary to come in and take over from the inside."

"I understand," Maddox said.

"That means we have to come in guns blazing and take what we can as fast as we can."

Maddox raised his eyebrows. "What type of secret equipment are we talking about?"

"Leviathan's latest commando space tech," Dravek said.

"Commando?"

"Our shuttle was always limited in its scope, more so now than ever. If we wait for the Gnostics to help us or call them, we'll be at their mercy. We're going to have to this commando-style."

"You know," Maddox said, "the way you're talking, I want my knife back."

"I've been wondering when you would get to that." Dravek slid a hand under his pillow and pulled out the knife and sheath. He tossed it to Maddox. It floated in the zero-G environment.

Maddox watched it, and he noted that Dravek watched it too closely. There was a reason for that. Did he see a glint of something on the bottom of the sheath?

Maddox moved aside, letting knife and sheath float past until it thumped against the bulkhead. An electric buzz sounded, and a *zap* of lethal proportions flashed. That left a burn mark on the bulkhead.

Maddox stared at Dravek. "Was that little shock meant for me?"

"I forgot about that. Sorry. My mistake."

"Why shouldn't I kill you, Dravek? If you're like me, you're too dangerous to keep around."

"We need each other. Two are much stronger than one."

"The Good Book agrees with that."

Dravek cocked his head. "What good book is this?"

"You don't recall the Bible in your memories?"

"Ah, the mystic book you like to quote. Yes, there's a smattering of it in my memories. It's a strange book. I'm surprised you take to any of its tenets."

"I imagine you are surprised. Be that as it may, what are our options? How do we do this? How can I possibly trust you after that little demonstration?"

Dravek chewed on his lower lip, staring at Maddox, looking away after a time. His gaze soon shifted back. Did he notice that the blaster hadn't wavered from aiming at his chest?

"I helped you survive and brought you out of stasis. Don't forget that," Dravek said.

"Were you going to sell me to the Gnostics, changing your mind when you needed help against Leviathan?"

"Why would Gnostics wish to buy you? What could I possibly get out of that?"

Maddox rubbed his fingertips and thumb-tip together, indicating money.

Dravek shook his head. "Leviathan wants you. No one else I know does. Besides, since Leviathan wants you, they also want me. I just want to be free. The Heydell Cloud seems like the place to keep my freedom. I took you along as insurance and because I didn't like the idea of Leviathan making more clones like me."

"Why not kill and incinerate me then?"

"No," Dravek said. "It would be too much like killing myself. As you know, we're not suicidal."

Maddox considered options. Dravek had told him about Leviathan wanting to start a spy ring in the Omicron 9 System, with a Maddox clone at the center of it. If Dravek had his personality, the clone wouldn't want to belong to a Leviathan team. It wasn't the spying the clone would mind so much, but the cybers and coercive devices. What Leviathan had done once with a device, they would likely want to do again.

Perhaps Dravek divined Maddox's hesitation Perhaps the clone knew he needed to make an offer than would appeal to Maddox.

"I have a plan," Dravek said. "I think you're going to like it. I know the Gnostics won't. We're going to be a surprise they never forget, provided we let them live."

"Go on," Maddox said. "I'm listening."

Dravek began to detail the weapons and equipment in the shuttle's secret compartments. Then, he began to describe how the two of them would employ the weapons.

-11-

Maddox discovered that Dravek had a powerful if small cache of drugs and other paraphernalia. When Dravek showed him the secret compartments, he was astounded at the weaponry and commando equipment. It was as good as anything Star Watch had: missile launchers, sleeve guns and a portable flamer. The last was a devastating weapon. In gravity, it would take several men to carry. In weightlessness, standing behind the flamer would be suicidal when the flamer ejected its heavy blob of hot plasma. While the battle-armor spacesuits were made for cybers, they could modify them for human use.

During the next few days, Maddox questioned Dravek repeatedly, trying to get information about who had kidnapped him and brought him to this spiral arm.

Dravek claimed to have no information on the subject. He said his first coherent thoughts of his life had been in the chamber of the chronowarp.

"The chrono...what did you say?" Maddox asked.

Dravek shook his head. They were working on the battlesuits. "I don't know much about the chronowarp. I do know it accelerates tissue growth. That was how the scientist was able to clone and turn me into a grown man so quickly. I haven't been alive long. From my questioning the scientist, I learned I've been me for less than a year. Yet I hold all these memories."

Dravek touched his forehead and for a moment, there was a forlorn look on his face. "All these thoughts that are

56

supposedly mine and yet—" He gave Maddox a piercing stare. "They're really your memories. You lived them. I didn't. I've only lived my own memories while you were in stasis."

There was a sudden glint in Dravek's eyes. "I'll live my own life, thank you so much. I won't be your second, your replacement. I won't go to the Commonwealth as your replica, acting as you. I'm Dravek. I'm not Captain Maddox. Do you understand?"

Maddox nodded, believing he was beginning to understand Dravek. What would it be like to wake up with another's memories? How would one react if he learned scientists had patterned him to imitate someone else? What if you knew you hadn't lived your own memories? How would you react learning you were a mere replica of someone else? For the first time, Maddox felt pity for Dravek.

Did Dravek perceive that? It was possible, for he scowled. "Don't worry about me. I'm doing just fine."

"As you wish," Maddox said.

Dravek jerked his head in what might have been a swift nod.

They worked in silence for a time.

Maddox pondered his kidnapping and transfer to this remote location. He looked at Dravek. "So you definitely can't tell me anything about how I reached here, no hint?"

Dravek seemed as if he was going to yell. He held that back, becoming thoughtful instead. "From the little the scientist told me, I imagine someone took you from the Commonwealth of Planets. But you must already know that."

Maddox nodded.

"Your kidnappers brought you to..." Dravek grinned suddenly. "I'm going to hold onto that for the moment. Call it insurance."

"Why do you need insurance?"

"So you have a reason to keep me alive. You want data I possess, right? I'll tell it to you later, provided you give me what I ask for then."

Maddox considered that. Dravek could easily lie. In fact, he was sure the man was a glib liar for obvious reasons. Yet... Would making the promise give Dravek more reason to keep the partnership going? Clearly, from the knife incident to his former or original crew, Dravek acted treacherously when it became in his best interest to do so, or when he thought it would be in his best interest.

"Fine," Maddox said. "That works for me."

It didn't really. Who had kidnapped him? Maddox desperately wanted to know. Had it been an agent of Leviathan, a mercenary bug-eyed monster, a Spacer spy? He had no idea. He was determined to find out, though. When he did—

Maddox groaned.

Dravek looked up. "What's wrong? What happened?"

Maddox shook his head and closed his eyes. He rubbed his forehead and opened his eyes quickly.

Dravek hadn't moved. Instead, Dravek peered at him in a speculative manner. "That must have been the mind block the scientist spoke about."

"Go on," Maddox said.

Dravek shrugged. "The scientist didn't want you thinking certain things, such as Meta or Jewel."

Maddox groaned again. "Stop," he said.

Dravek grinned before he wiped that away. Perhaps he thought he had a club or a coercive device to use against Maddox.

Inwardly, Maddox grinned. When Dravek had spoken the names of Meta and Jewel, there hadn't been any pain. Maddox had pretended the agony in order to induce exactly what he saw in Dravek's grin. Two could play a double-cross game.

Maddox and Dravek continued to ready the weaponry, suits and thruster packs for the moment of approaching decision.

Later, Maddox and Dravek went into the control cabin together. They were staying together in order to forestall any treachery on each other's part.

The Jupiter-sized gas giant was large before them and the moons more visible than before. The largest moon appeared to have clouds, an atmosphere of sorts. It was a frozen wasteland of ice and rocks with seas, rivers and dunes. Those couldn't be water seas and rivers. Likely, the seas were composed of methane and ethane as on Titan, which orbited Saturn in the Solar System.

Using the side-jets, Maddox turned the shuttle. He did so until the thruster was aimed at the ice moon.

"Ready?" asked Maddox.

"Let's do this," Dravek said hoarsely.

Maddox powered up the generators, which spewed the remaining propellant from the engine through the thruster. That slowed the shuttle's approach and brought simulated gravity back to the shuttle. Anyone watching from the gas giant region would likely see the exhaust plume. Maddox used up the remaining fuel, leaving nothing in reserve.

When he ceased thrusting, the zero-G environment immediately returned. He'd used the generators for three hours before. A half-hour of braking this time had merely slowed the shuttle. If they hit the moon, it would crumple the shuttle and kill them. This slowing would help later, though. The commando suits wouldn't have to use as much of their precious fuel to brake. They would have to slow way down in the suits if they hoped to remain in the vicinity or land on the moon.

"That's it then," Maddox said.

The shuttle was on battery power again. If, perchance, the Gnostic vessel had departed the area, they were up that horrible sewage-water creek.

Dravek assured Maddox that hidden Gnostic sensors watched the shuttle carefully. They'd have to pick the right moment to exit the vessel.

In preparation, Maddox and Dravek ate one last meal on the shuttle, used the facilities and then helped each other climb into their respective suits.

The commando assault was predicated on something Dravek had learned from one of his original team members. Gnostics were intensely profit driven. Therefore, they didn't carry large crews, as that meant splitting the proceeds too many ways. Instead, they had highly efficient but small numbers on their ships. That way, each person took home more profit.

Dravek opened the way to a secret area of the shuttle. While wearing their suit, bulky tanks and thruster pack, each climbed down and worked into an ejector tube. Soon, the panels above resealed, casting each into darkness.

"Don't turn on your suit yet," Dravek said. "We want to wait as long as possible to save battery power."

"Got it," Maddox said.

They used short-range communication sets to talk to each other.

Both jacked their suits into the shuttle. That fed them shuttle sensor-data, putting it on the HUDs of their respective visors.

The ice moon neared, growing larger by the minute as the shuttle drifted toward it.

"There," Dravek whispered.

Maddox saw it on his visor.

On the moon's upper horizon appeared the pirate vessel Maddox had seen weeks earlier. Relief filled him. Despite everything Dravek had said, Maddox had been afraid the ship had left. His stomach began to settle.

The Gnostic vessel rose above the moon's horizon, so Maddox got a better look at it. It was all girders, struts, attached pods and seemingly magnetized junk. It wasn't large in a continuous encapsulated sense. It was long if one included the girders, struts and obvious grappling equipment.

Several outer-docked drones blinked with green lights on the nosecones. The drones were cigar-shaped. Latches released those with blinking lights. The drones slowly maneuvered away from the girder-shaped pirate vessel.

Gnostic communication opened. There was no answer from either Maddox or Dravek. A dark-eyed woman with a long face and lean cheeks and wearing a square leather hat appeared on their respective visors—that was due to the jacked-in link with the shuttle. The woman threatened them with destruction unless the shuttle opened communications.

That surprised Maddox. Not the threat, but that he understood the language. He mentioned that to Dravek.

"I uploaded a language program into you while you were in cryogenic stasis."

"What? How was that possible?"

"Don't panic," Dravek said.

"I'm not. I asked you a question."

"I hear you panicking, and I think I know why. You're not a machine, well, not a mechanical machine. You are a biological machine. I put a helmet over your head and the helmet directly encoded your brain with a new language—one they use in the Heydell Cloud."

Maddox grimaced as his chest rose and fell rapidly. He had to use the Way of the Pilgrim to steady his mind and state. Learning this—what else had Dravek coded into him? Was there a special phrase, perhaps, that would render him limp so the other could act treacherously? He would have done that to him, given he had Dravek's amoral code.

Continuing with the Way of the Pilgrim, Maddox began an intense self-diagnostic, using his intuitive sense against himself, trying to find such a thing. His Balron-trained instincts searched his mind methodically, refusing to become frantic. Then he found something non-Maddox embedded in his mind. He concentrated and saw it. Breathing evenly, practicing many of his odd abilities, Maddox unraveled the coding and thereby erased it from his memories.

"That's not good," Dravek said.

For a wild moment, Maddox had no idea what the other meant. Could Dravek understand what he'd just done? The words pulled Maddox out of his mind and interrupted the Way of the Pilgrim. That brought Maddox back to his present reality, and that brought a moment of claustrophobia. Maddox attributed that to the months of travel with killer robots from the planet Kregen several years ago.

Maddox realized he was hyperventilating. He fought it and brought the breathing under control.

"Are you feeling ill?" Dravek asked.

"I'm fine," Maddox said in a hyper-calm voice.

"You don't sound fine."

Maddox swallowed and forced himself to view his visor HUD, showing him sensor data from the shuttle.

"Those drones look different from the ones I saw weeks ago," Maddox said. "I don't see any warheads on these."

"Right, right," Dravek said. "These must be transport drones."

As Maddox and Dravek lay in the belly of the shuttle, the Gnostic drones approached the craft. Each circled the shuttle twice, no doubt relaying video images back to the main vessel.

Finally, each drone maneuvered delicately against the shuttle and magnetized itself to the hull. Only then did they apply thrust in unison, lessening the shuttle's velocity. They used more thrust in these few minutes than the shuttle had originally used to reach this velocity. Soon, the drones maneuvered the slowly moving shuttle toward the waiting pirate vessel. Interestingly, the pirate vessel had retreated behind the ice moon's horizon and out of sight.

"Is it time?" Maddox asked.

"Not yet," Dravek said. "We have to time this perfectly."

They waited, watching their HUDs.

As the drones neared the ice moon with its nitrogen atmosphere, Maddox saw large craters and long fissures below. Was that from interior seismic activity or the gravitational pull from the gas giant, which loomed above everything? This gas giant was unlike Jupiter in that it didn't spew masses of radiation.

The drones maneuvered the shuttle over the moon's horizon so the pirate ship came into view again.

"Now," Dravek said.

Maddox pressed a switch.

The ejector tubes propelled each suited man out of the shuttle and into space. The moon's icy surface was below by less than three hundred and fifty kilometers.

Fortunately, due to Dravek's foresight, the shuttle was between them and the drones and pirate vessel, shielding them from view.

Each man was in a spacesuit with thruster pack, which together acted like a mini spaceship. They watched even as they drifted high above the moon.

The drones applied gentle thrust, moving the shuttle toward the waiting pirate vessel.

Maddox and Dravek were falling farther behind, as each had applied thrust, slowing their forward velocity.

"Are you ready for this?" Dravek asked over the short-range comm.

"Locked and loaded," Maddox said. He was grinning. His intuitive sense told him Dravek was grinning as well. This was high adventure, and their prospect for victory was good.

-12-

Waiting, Maddox and Dravek hung in space in their modified EVA Combat Exo-suits or "Comets." Leviathan engineers had developed the suit systems for the elite members of the Special Commando Operations unit, or so Dravek claimed.

The inner layer of each suit was made from nano-material, able to repair minor breaches and regulate body temperature. The nanotech fabric had integrated bio-monitors for that. Maddox and Dravek had dismantled the auto medical units. The units had been developed for cybers and would inject them with powerful drugs in the middle of combat. Those drugs might render them unconscious or battle-mad.

The middle suit layer was a mesh of dense but light composite materials. The layer's main purpose was to protect them from radiation. In an unshielded space environment, that would likely be critical otherwise.

The outer layer was an armored exoskeleton constructed from titanium and carbon nanotubes. Theoretically, the layer could withstand immense pressure changes, kinetic strikes and energy weapon beams. The armor incorporated chameleon tech that included sensor-absorbing materials, active camouflage blends and heat signature reduction.

The helmets had a HUD with a 360-degree field of vision, which included thermal imaging, electromagnetic spectrum analysis and advanced target acquisition. The visor also had auto-polarization to protect eyes from sudden and drastic changes in light.

Each suit had huge hydrogen-propellant tanks and a thruster. That allowed controlled flight in zero or low-gravity environments.

For armaments, they had a sleeve-gun that fired heavy shells. Each also carried a launcher with micro-missiles in a selector rotary drum.

Despite all that, for Maddox, it was strange hanging up here surrounded by the film of metal and nanotech fabric. He was no more than a gnat in a star system within the Heydell Cloud. He was less than a gnat compared to the Scutum-Centaurus Spiral Arm, a place far from home. He wasn't as far as he'd been behind the Yon Soth Barrier across the Milky Way Galaxy, but he was still plenty far.

This star system lacked unique portals or other ancient equipment that they'd found behind the Barrier to slingshot them home. He didn't have Ludendorff or Andros Crank to help, nor were there hyper-intelligent engineers around, at least as far as he knew. It was he and a clone of him. Dravek wasn't even a good clone in the sense that he was a perfect copy of him. This clone had strange ideas and lacked honor.

Maddox turned his head within the helmet, looking at Dravek floating beside him. They had the short-range comm but neither had spoken to the other for the past several minutes. They drifted high above the ice moon.

Dravek finally opened channels. "What's wrong?" he asked.

"Not a thing."

"You've gone quiet. Have you been watching the Gnostic ship?"

"No. I've been thinking."

With squirts of side-jet power, Dravek turned his suit toward Maddox.

Maddox watched the man carefully, wondering if he'd raise the flamer. Dravek had offered to carry the heavy portable and Maddox had agreed. Dravek did not raise any weapon system, however, not even a sleeve-gun.

"Have you lost your will?" Dravek asked.

"What are you talking about?"

"The scientist told me about many interesting things before he died."

Before you killed him, you mean, Maddox told himself. *Was the scientist like a surrogate father for you?* Dravek talked about the scientist enough for that to be the case. What had it done to the clone to kill the scientist?

"The scientist told me special commandos often mentally struggle against the loneliness of space," Dravek said. "That's especially true during commando assignments like ours."

Maddox said nothing.

"I'd asked him about the commando equipment," Dravek added. "The scientist said a commando needed a method to shield himself against the loneliness. Otherwise, the enormity of space could overpower his will."

"My will's just fine," Maddox said.

"Is it?" Dravek asked. "The Soldiers or cybers of Leviathan sometimes go blank when they're in a situation such as ours. The vastness of space dwarfs the psyche. For all the Leviathan modifications, the cyber brains are much like ours: susceptible to awe."

Maddox frowned. Did Dravek know too much about cybers? Was the man trying to escape from Leviathan or was he a deep agent, a secret agent *for* Leviathan?

Maddox kept playing with the idea. Was this all some elaborate Leviathan ploy then? Were the cybers using him in a well-crafted plan? Maddox had no idea because he really didn't know how the rulers of Leviathan thought. He didn't even know what they looked like.

The Soldiers had always struck him as strict and literal. He'd spoken to a Strategist once. That one had been quite different from the Soldiers. Were the highest-level operators of Leviathan even that much different and more cunning than a Strategist? Were the rulers of Leviathan more like the Mastermind?

Maddox had seen strange things on the planet Kregen. He'd learned there was a connection between the Mastermind, the Cosmic Computer and Leviathan. He hadn't connected all the dots in that yet, nor had he really tried.

Maddox exhaled. He was floating in space like a speck of minutia. Would he ever see Meta and Jewel again? He'd asked himself that many times on different missions, so he knew he longed to find them. What had happened to them? Were they safe or in danger?

Maddox shook his head. This was getting to be too much. The loneliness of existence, the vastness of space—

"Excuse me, Dravek. I'm closing the comm-link for a moment. I need to think."

"Wait—" Dravek said.

After a second, Maddox didn't hear him anymore. Sweet silence cocooned him, leaving him with his thoughts as he drifted high above the ice moon. The loneliness of existence, the vastness of the universe—

Maddox blinked suddenly. This was exactly what Dravek had been talking about. He was like a special-commando cyber of Leviathan, losing his grip on reality.

I'm the di-far. *I'm Captain Maddox. I've been in worse places.*

He dragged a dry tongue across his lips. He had to get a grip. He had to get his mind in gear.

Maddox stared at the commando suit floating apart from him.

What motivated Dravek? How did the clone fight against the feeling of futility as they drifted up here? It didn't matter, none of that mattered. Getting his own head in the game—

Through sheer force of will and determination, Maddox shifted mental gears. It seemed as if he opened a different drawer in his mind. This drawer had the needed tools to deal with direct problems. There. He used the suit's passive sensors, focusing on the Gnostic ship out there.

The spaceship of girders, pods and struts descended toward the moon. The jets of fire were bright. Maybe that helped to bring him around. Living beings, humans, were inside the ship. Maddox used the suit sensors, looking beyond the vessel and to the murky surface. What he saw—

Maddox opened channels with Dravek. "Do you see the base down there?"

"You're back online. That's good, very good. Look, I was going to tell you about the base before. I think it is a mining operation. Do you see the free-trader ships parked down there?"

"Free traders?" Maddox asked. "You never told me they were called *free* traders."

"Why are you so suspicious of me all the time?"

"Well, let's see. You hid meds. You tried to zap me with a hidden device on the knife you returned. You only dole out critical information bits at a time. You also seem to know an awful lot from this lone scientist you murdered."

"Firstly," Dravek said, "it wasn't just one scientist. I say it that way—I don't know why. He was the chief scientist. I did learn a lot from him. The time—you ought to know that you've been under cryogenic stasis for longer than you think."

Fear surged in Maddox to such a degree that he couldn't speak. He should have seen this sooner. Had he been in cryogenic stasis for years? Certainly, that was a possibility. If it was years, could Meta and Jewel be old, dead, what?

Horrible panic gripped Maddox as pain flared in his chest. He didn't think it was a heart attack, but he checked the bio monitors just the same.

"What's the matter over there?" Dravek said. "Are you still coherent or what?"

"How long was I in cryogenic stasis?" Maddox asked in a harsh voice. "And you better give me the right answer."

"Do you mean 'right' as in truthful, or just what you want to hear?"

"The truth, man, I want the truth."

"You've been under for a year, maybe a little longer."

Maddox felt a jolt. He'd been gone a year from his family, possibly longer. *All right, get a grip, old man. Put your head in the game and do this right.*

Maddox shivered. This was too much to accept at once. He shelved the thought and realized he'd been silent for too long.

"Fine," Maddox said. "I'm fine."

"Ah," Dravek said, "I finally hear some steel in your voice. Good. I think you're finally getting your mental faculties together. Is that true?"

"Don't question me. I'm running the operation."

"Is that so? Tell me, what do you know about the base down there?"

Instead of answering, Maddox focused the passive sensors, using a zoom function. It was a large base with buildings. Near the grounded trader-ships were atmospheric flyers or flitters. There were some crawlers, too. Farther from the base camp were dark openings into the surface.

"What are they mining?" Maddox asked.

"Fissionables," Dravek said. "Don't you study your readings?"

"What?"

"I suspect you're using your sensors. That was what I meant about studying your readings."

Did Dravek have a hidden link to his suit? Would he have revealed that by a slip of the tongue, though?

Maddox studied his HUD. He saw it soon. It was fissionables, the mother lode of them. That had to be it: uranium and thorium to feed hungry reactors somewhere. Would the Gnostics trade the fissionables to the people on the terrestrial planet near the dwarf star?

"What can you tell me about the planet near the star, the planet with a city?" Maddox asked.

"It's called Gath."

"Tell me about it."

"I don't know much," Dravek said. "It has very little metal. I don't think it has much of a technological civilization except around the spaceport."

"Why do ships land on Gath if there's nothing to trade?"

"There are furs, a unique honey—"

"Honey?" asked Maddox, interrupting. "Is that what you said?"

"One that helps to prolong life," Dravek said.

"Longevity honey?" asked Maddox.

"That, furs and a unique hardwood," Dravek said. "From my understanding, factors collect the goods throughout the year. Hired free-traders haul the goods to more civilized planets in the cloud."

"Factors belong to corporations?"

69

"I know what you mean by corporations. It doesn't work the same out here."

"Out here in the Heydell Cloud or out here in Leviathan Space?"

"Both, neither," Dravek said.

Maddox processed that. Dravek knew a lot, a lot more than he'd realized. "What's your plan exactly?"

"It's pretty basic," Dravek said. "I want to be free and make sure I stay that way. That means money, the more the better. I want fissionables to sell, a spacecraft with a crew willing to follow me and a lifelong supply of Gath honey."

"This crew," Maddox said. "They can't be Gnostics, right?"

"Definitely not."

"That only leaves the captured free traders, the ones from the ship the Gnostics impounded. You think they captured the free-trader crew?"

"I do."

"What kind of people are these free traders?"

"An independent and hardy lot," Dravek said. "They must be to travel the Heydell Cloud, going from planet to planet with their minuscule cargos and slender profits. But the fissionables is the mother lode. If we do this, we fill all the ships to the brim."

"Then what?" asked Maddox.

"After picking up a cargo of Gath honey, we take our bonanza to a rich planet in the Heydell Cloud and sell it, keeping everything. If you want to buy a spaceship and start back to the Commonwealth after that, be my guest."

Maddox considered the idea. The closest Commonwealth system would be Omicron 9, possibly 8,000 light years away. Without Starship *Victory,* that would be more than a lifetime of travel, even if the ship used wormholes. He needed a better answer.

He probably wasn't going to get the answer floating up here. With Dravek's plan, he'd have possibilities and the money to pursue them.

Maddox stared down at the moon base, the mining camp. "How many Gnostics do you think control the mine?"

"I'd say less than fifty."

"Let's figure on fifty then. Can we take them out?"

"You mean just us two?"

"Yes," Maddox said.

"At best, we could nail half before the rest get their act together and kill us."

"We need to free some traders then."

"That's what I'm thinking."

"Do you really think the Gnostics enslaved the traders?"

"I would."

"Why?" asked Maddox.

"To send them into the radiation pits to do the mining," Dravek said.

That made sense. "How do you propose we do this?"

"We need to come down on the other side of the moon. Then, we can skim the surface so the Gnostics don't spot us on their sensors."

"That will expend a lot of fuel," Maddox said.

"In case you haven't noticed, we have a lot of fuel to expend."

"You've been thinking about this for more than a few days."

Dravek said nothing to that.

"You're thinking a fifty-fifty split between us?" Maddox asked.

"Exactly," Dravek said.

"Then I agree."

"Excellent. It's time we started then. Follow me."

The two applied thrust, heading in the opposite direction the pirate vessel had gone. At the same time, they slowly descended into the nitrogen atmosphere as they headed for the surface of the moon.

-13-

Maddox and Dravek entered the thin nitrogen atmosphere to come within two hundred meters of the surface.

It was an eerie landscape to say the least. The suit's sensors gave Maddox the reading of -290 degrees Fahrenheit, making it colder than anything on Earth. The suit regulated his body temperature, ensuring he didn't freeze in the cold.

Maddox and Dravek banked to the right.

Even at this height, the hazy atmosphere clouded their vision. It was an opaque orange soup, a mix of nitrogen and methane. The ground was a mishmash of rocky terrain, vast sheets of water ice and liquid lakes of methane and ethane. Not unsurprisingly, the suit informed Maddox the lakes were warmer than the surrounding ice and rock.

As they flew, Maddox observed rugged water-ice mountains marked by the occasional methane rains. In other areas were shifting dunes of sand.

It was weird, the ice moon was alien and yet with its atmosphere, mountains, dunes and lakes had an Earth feel.

"Over there," Dravek said over the short-range comm. "Do you see that?"

In the distance, land rippled and shook. A rumble sounded they could hear and then a cryovolcano spewed. It didn't spew molten rock. Instead, a geyser of super-chilled volatiles— water, methane and ammonia—erupted.

The low gravity meant the plume shot high into the orange-tinged sky. Particles caught the distant starlight and glittered like gems. Almost immediately, however, the cryomagma began to freeze in the frigid air, turning into and falling as solid chunks. Most of it fell back and built up the cryovolcano's icy cone. The rest hit other areas.

"That's crazy cool," Maddox said.

"Thought you might like it. Let's go that way." Dravek pointed and headed lower.

Maddox followed.

They aimed at a long ice crevice with strange plumes of frozen water ice along the sides.

Where did the heat come from to create cryovolcanoes? Perhaps with the Jupiter-like gas giant up there tugging in one direction and the other moons tugging in others caused gravitational friction within. That would create heat.

"I think we're low enough," Dravek said. They flew fifty meters above the icy surface. "Any hidden Gnostic sensors out here should be aimed at space."

"Let's hope so," Maddox said.

Time passed until they'd been traveling for hours since leaving the shuttle. They continued to head for the Gnostic moon base, the mining operation. Could they achieve surprise this way? Or would they have to take out the enemy with their micro-missile launchers and flamers? If that happened, they'd probably die under enemy return fire. If they had to start fighting, at best they could rush to a grounded spaceship, commandeer it and take off. That would be iffy, though. The best bet was to sneak onto the base in a stealthy manner as they were trying to do.

"We may be doing this too fast," Maddox said.

"I've been thinking the same."

"The problem is that if we go too slowly it'll be hours, maybe a day before we reach the base."

"Agreed," said Dravek.

"If we go too slowly," Maddox said, "we'll use up most of our air supply. I don't like such a narrow margin in case of problems or errors. But I don't see how it would work if we blaze in fast. The problem is that I'm already sick of the suit, even though it is extremely functional."

"So, we slow down, then, right?"

"Right," Maddox said.

Each man rotated and expelled white hydrogen propellant.

They had big, bulky tanks, making them five times their normal size. Each man used up two tanks of hydrogen propellant, ejecting the tanks afterward. The four empty tanks tumbled toward the icy surface. Each man now had a smaller sensor signature and less mass. Therefore, each needed less propellant to move their mass.

They glided just above the desolate surface, the icy walls of the crevasse at their sides.

What a strange fate. Maddox shook his head, squeezed his eyelids and opened them wide. He needed to focus and remain alert. The passing hours were making him sleepy.

"There's trouble," Dravek said.

That cut through Maddox's reverie. "What is it?"

"Look up and to your left thirty degrees."

Maddox did so. "Three skimmers are headed straight for us. Do you think they see us?"

The skimmers were sleek one-man craft. They had swept-back wings, were jet propelled and had a bubble canopy in the overhead front section. The three approaching skimmers each carried a complement of missiles under their wings.

"They must see us," Dravek said. "Slowing down was a mistake. Hidden Gnostic sensors must have spotted our expelled propellant. This is the response to that."

"It doesn't matter now," Maddox said. "We decided, right or wrong. We're stuck with our decision."

"We need to scratch all three skimmers then."

Maddox saw the logic in that. One escaping skimmer would report about them. "Maybe the better thing is to land on the surface and hide under the ice."

"And if the skimmers already have sensor lock on us?"

"Wouldn't our suits have told us that?"

"Right," Dravek said. "I think they're using teleoptics. That's as passive as you can get. Our suits would never be able to tell that."

"Let's get a little separation between us," Maddox said. "That way, one of their missiles can't take us both out at once."

"Damn it," Dravek said. "I'd hoped—it doesn't matter like you said. We have to go with what is."

"That's right," Maddox said. "I couldn't have come up with a better idea myself."

Whether Dravek sneered, laughed or grimaced, Maddox had no idea. Neither did his intuitive sense tell him. Instead, he readied his suit weaponry, activating his micro-missile launcher. He didn't set it on active hunt and seek yet. Instead, he waited. Maybe...

The skimmers launched a flock of missiles.

"This is worse than bad," Dravek said.

A micro-missile left his launcher, heading directly for the enemy missile flock. The enemy's bigger missiles spread apart, leaving contrails behind them.

With a zoom function, Maddox zeroed in on the skimmers.

Dravek's missile exploded, it was a fragmentation device, an anti-missile missile. It took out all but one of the enemy missiles. That one—no, it blew up as well. That was a lucky break.

"Now," Dravek said.

Maddox fired one micro missile after another until six hunters sped for the skimmers.

"No," Dravek said, "that was too many."

"Don't give me any back talk. You're the junior partner in this. Launch six more hunters."

Muttering under his breath, Dravek launched six micro-hunter-seekers.

One of the skimmers burned away from the other two. It was no doubt heading back home, maybe to make a report.

Maddox put a sensor fix on it and launched six homing micro-missiles on it.

"Down," Maddox said. "We have to go to ground. We have to land on the ice."

"That's madness," Dravek said. "We'll never last. The cold will overcome our suits. Besides, how do we regain speed and velocity later to reach the moon base? Study your odometer as to far how we still must go to reach the target."

Maddox did just that. Dravek was right.

The twelve Leviathan-tech micro-missiles reached the two nearest skimmers. There were many orange blossoms in the darkness. That was two scratched skimmers. The third one continued to flee while the six homing missiles flew after it.

"The Gnostics are going to know they have enemy activity," Maddox said.

"I know, I know," Dravek said.

"Perhaps we should go to ground no matter what and hope to get lucky."

"Lucky?" Dravek asked. "You want to rely on luck?"

"No, but sometimes when you're given no choice, you have to grab for luck and hope for the best."

"This is bad," Dravek said. "If a spaceship appears—"

"We must act before that. I'm going down. Are you coming?"

Dravek swore. Then he followed Maddox's example and began to descend toward the surface.

Meanwhile, the first homing micro-missile lost energy and dropped out of the race. The others continued to chase the last skimmer.

It must have launched chaff.

Two micro-missile warheads exploded.

The skimmer wavered. Was that in response to the detonations?

Another two micro-missiles simply dropped to the surface, their energy depleted. The last one detonated with a bang.

The skimmer kept going. It had survived the missile assault.

"Damnit," Maddox said.

Then the skimmer flew out of sight.

The two men in Leviathan commando battlesuits were almost touching down on the icy surface.

Now it was time to make the big decision.

-14-

Maddox landed first, his boots smashing against ice so he toppled and fell onto his side. If he'd touched down just a little harder, he might have broken an ankle. Fortunately, the battlesuit absorbed much of the shock even though a plume of icy particles shot into the air and floated down slower than they would have on Earth.

Dravek landed with more precision and grace, looking upon the fallen Maddox. "That was beautifully done, sir."

"Never mind that," Maddox said, as he climbed upright.

"We're on the surface," Dravek said. "Oh. My boots are already colder. My suit is attempting to compensate."

Maddox checked his and saw that Dravek was correct. "All right, all right, let's think this through. We're down. We need to consider how much fuel we need to—"

"Sorry to interrupt," Dravek said. "But we need to consider that." Dravek pointed.

Maddox looked and used a zoom function. Far away on the horizon was the surviving skimmer sweeping back and forth.

"It must be watching us or seeing if his fellow pilots survived the crashes."

"We're easy prey on the ice." They'd landed on the other side of the giant crevice as the skimmer.

Maddox shuffled around a complete 360 degrees. "Are those caves? They look like caves to me." He used his zoom function again, focusing on the darkness under rocky, icy cliffs. The darkness could be indentations or actual caves.

"Well?" Dravek asked. "What is it?"

"I'm headed there. Come if you wish."

"What's this?" Dravek said. "You're no longer going to spout commands as if you're a corporation grandee of Earth."

Maddox didn't want to admit it but his ankle hurt. He began to walk, carrying his great load of propellant tanks and thruster pack with him. On Earth, even with the exoskeleton suit power, he would have been unable to carry such mass. Here, he weighed a fraction of what he would have on Earth.

The surface was another thing. Each crunching step caused icy granules to float upward, which slowly drifted back down. The substance alternated between frozen methane, water ice and rock.

The strain of walking soon heated Maddox's skin and caused sweat. That shocked and surprised him. He carried a greater load than he'd realized.

Dravek followed.

Farther away, the skimmer had disappeared again. Where had it gone? That was the dilemma.

"We have to get to those caves now," Maddox said.

"Maybe I should leave the flamer here. I don't see what use it is going to be."

"No," Maddox said. "Bring it along. We're going to need it."

"Is that another order, sir?"

"Do we have to argue about everything?" Maddox asked. "I've lived longer and have more experience if for no other reason than I have all my memories."

"As you wish," Dravek said, "but it's still a fifty-fifty split."

"I never doubted that for a moment." Soon, Maddox added, "You obviously have more information concerning the star system. But in this situation—"

"Yes, yes," Dravek said. "There's no need to belabor it. We're doing it your way."

For the next half hour, they trudged across the plain heading for the cliffs. They were farther away than Maddox had realized, taking longer to reach.

"I've been doing some calculating, running figures and numbers," Dravek said. "Do you know what I've discovered?"

"I imagine you're going to tell me we only have a slender margin of air left if we hope to reach the moon base. If we do any more hiking, we're never going to make it. In other words, we're going to die. So, the question becomes, do we wait and have a possible degradation of our air fuel, or we try to fly to the base now?"

"That's the question."

"I still suggest we wait," Maddox said. "Look what we've done. Do you think the Gnostics have had any kind of pushback until this? They obviously have the skimmers in case of somebody like us. I bet until now, they've never used them. Now they have. We knocked two out and chased away the third. I think they're going to react big against that. Therefore, we need to be hidden."

"Won't the caves be the obvious hiding spot?"

"I don't think anything is obvious out here unless we're caught standing in the open like a neon sign that says, 'Kill me, kill me.'"

"Let's continue then," Dravek said, sounding resigned.

They reached ice caves that went deeper than Maddox had anticipated. There was nothing unique about the caves, although there were some odd ice formations in back when they swept their lights over them.

As they explored a larger cave, a sensor went off.

Dravek had set the passive detection device outside the cave. Maddox had linked to it. Now both men watched as the pirate girder-strut-pod ship drifted fifty-four kilometers above the surface.

Maddox turned and visibly looked at Dravek's suit.

"Yes, yes," Dravek said, "I understand your blatant gesture. You were right. This is a big reaction maneuver on their part. I'm so glad we're hidden in your cave. Does that stroke your ego enough?"

"It will do," Maddox said. "I wonder if they're going to camp up here."

"Must you do that?" Dravek asked. "Are you trying to jinx us with such a gross pronouncement?"

"It's called thinking, contingency planning. We must figure out what we're going to do if they do B, C or D. What if the ship sits there for three days? Look, there are already skimmers approaching."

Through the passive sensor, Maddox watched three skimmers fly across the plain where they had been and where the fight had taken place.

"Perhaps they'll find your boot mark where you landed," Dravek said.

"I doubt it."

"You don't think they'll use infrared and trace our footprints across the ice?"

"The boots were insulated against just that. Our suits have high-grade chameleon features. They're looking for us. I agree with that. But—" Maddox stared at his HUD, staring at the pirate ship up there.

A plan, one might even call it an insane plan, began to form. First, he'd need the skimmers out of the way. If the skimmers remained on station—no. The skimmers needed to be out of the way. He kept the plan to himself as he calculated further.

At the same time, the pirate ship took up a static station, no doubt using a vast sensor sweep as the Gnostics searched for them.

"I suppose we're going to spend another twenty-four hours in our suits," Dravek said. "Mine is already getting dank, if you know what I mean."

Maddox did, but he didn't want to complain. He wanted to think. If the Gnostics remained where they were, it was either surrender and possibly work in the deep mines, as Dravek had supposed, or charge with suicidal fury. The suicidal part— Maddox shook his head. That was out. He didn't have a suicidal bone in him. Not even after his time with the octagonal robots. He was going to make it home and let his wife and daughter see him again.

Maddox suppressed the groan even as he thought that. Better to focus on the moment. He had to get home again. He had to tell Star Watch what was going on and he had to discover who had kidnapped him. He was also gaining interesting and valuable data on what went on in the Scutum-Centaurus Spiral Arm, particularly here in the Heydell Cloud.

Thus, Maddox and Dravek waited four and a half hours. Finally, the skimmers went high up and reached the pirate ship as it lowered. Each skimmer docked at a strut. Perhaps the skimmers did so to take on more fuel, to allow the pilots to rest and stretch their limbs.

"Now," Maddox said, "now we have to attempt it."

"What in the hell are you talking about?"

"I didn't want to say anything until this moment. You brought the flamer, right?"

"Yeah," Dravek said.

"The flamer is going to be the ticket to getting out of here."

"Uh-huh." Dravek said, "and how is that?"

Maddox told him.

"Do you know, Captain, I think you're reliably insane. That's a preposterous idea."

Maddox held his temper in check. "No. Its very boldness gives us the opportunity. The Gnostics will never expect it."

"I'll tell you why," Dravek said, "because it will never work."

"Listen, I've fought many a battle using whiteout from antimatter blasts. The tactic provided me with an advantage of subterfuge. That's exactly what we're going to do now, but in a different way."

"We have auto polarization in our visors," Dravek said. "They'll have likewise on their sensor."

"Exactly, exactly, the auto polarization will hide us."

"That's a stretch."

Maddox ground his teeth together, working to keep his temper in check. He hated having to convince another. He was too used to giving orders and having others obey. He scrounged around for a convincing argument.

"Look," Maddox said. "Our suits probably barely have enough propellant to get us to the moon base. That means they'll likely run out of propellant before we get there."

"Because we're diving down to caves instead of proceeding straight to target," Dravek said.

"We'd be dead already if we hadn't hidden in the cave."

81

"Maybe not," Dravek said.

"This is reality, not hopes and dreams. We probably don't have enough propellant to get to the moon base, but we have more than enough to do what I'm suggesting."

"It's madness," Dravek muttered. Then his suit shrugged. "But what else do we have to lose? I'm tired of standing here like a retard. I'm tired of being in this suit. I want to stretch. I want to scratch in unnamable places. Very well. What do I need to do?"

Maddox told him. And all the while he kept watch on his visor linked to the sensor device Dravek had set outside the cave. Would the pirate ship move before he was ready? Would the skimmers launch before he could set the plan into action? They were about to find out.

-15-

Maddox decided that he would carry the flamer.

It was a huge portable unit with a tripod-mount. Even as a crew-serviced weapon, it was possible for an exo-armored soldier to carry one for a few feet under normal conditions. After that, both a soldier and his suit would likely malfunction. In low gravity, one could carry it much farther.

The flamer was more a heavy block of metal and components than anything else, with strong containment fields to hold the superheated plasma within.

While drifting through space, carrying it had been no big deal. It had created extra mass, and Dravek had used up more hydrogen propellant while carting it. Maddox had calculated earlier. He still had enough fuel to reach the moon base. For the stated reason, Dravek's margin was much less.

Maddox didn't want to do this alone. He wanted Dravek with him. Was the reason partly being in the depths of space in a different spiral arm of the Milky Way Galaxy? Maybe that was it. Maybe it was simply good having such a competent fellow, so like himself, along. Maybe Dravek was the brother he'd never had. Yes, Maddox felt kinship with the amoral clone.

Maddox exited the cave with the flamer. The low gravity made a big difference in this. He moved along the base of the cliffs, trying to keep under eaves of ice or rock, out of direct line of sight with the ship up there. The skimmers had not yet launched again from it.

Several minutes later, a laser beam flashed from the pirate ship and speared—

Maddox's muscles tightened and he clenched his teeth.

The laser speared into the middle of the icy plain. Metal erupted and slagged on it.

Of course, Maddox realized. The ship destroyed what remained of the two skimmers. They aimed to ensure no one could use anything on or in the skimmers against them.

The laser stopped beaming.

Maddox started walking again even though he wondered if this was the right move. Perhaps he should wait. Perhaps the beaming was a sign the Gnostic ship was about to leave.

This was a wild plan as it was. He didn't know if it would work. It had to work.

"No," he said. "Don't go there. Don't hope for things just because you need them. Think rationally."

That was what Maddox did. He rationally considered and reconsidered the plan. In the end, he proceeded with it.

Soon, he reached what he thought would be a large enough margin for error. He set the flamer on its tripod mount and worked the controls. Then, he lifted it and walked onto the ice, leaving the cliff eaves behind.

His shoulder muscles tensed and his neck began to throb. He could feel a laser sight on him every moment. He was counting on the chameleon aspect of the commando suit to hide him.

He reached the needed location on the ice. He set the flamer on its mount, turned and walked away. As he walked, he watched the spaceship.

It was up there forty-eight kilometers from the surface.

"Dravek," Maddox said over the short-range comm, "are you ready for this?"

"I am," Dravek said. "You have big balls, Maddox. This is balls to the firewall."

Maddox grinned. "Get ready."

"You can't do it yet. You'll be too close to the blast."

"I'm aware of that. I'm coming. I'm hurrying."

Maddox began to trudge faster. Would motion sensors detect him up there? Would they be watching the cliff edges?

He was back under the eaves. Now, Maddox began to run with low sweeping strides. High leaps would have taken him faster, but this was a stealth mission.

"Thirty seconds to ignition," Maddox said. He felt his guts coil. This was insane. Yet, he had a feeling only insanity and daring could cover 8,000 light years. How else was he going to get home again?

"No way else," Maddox said. He reached the first of the caves, darting into it. Moving behind a wall, he crouched and waited.

The chronometer said ten seconds, nine, eight, seven, six, five, four—

The flamer had sat on its tripod mount, a weapon of deadly coiled energy. By design, a mechanism malfunctioned. The containment fields, responsible for controlling the flow of superheated plasma, faltered and then failed.

A seething roar of plasma, a bloom of scorching heat and blinding light, a fiery flower, blossomed on the ice. Some of the plasma punched straight through the nitrogen atmosphere, creating a pillar of energy. It released an electromagnetic pulse.

Forty-eight kilometers above the surface, the unsuspecting spaceship aimed an array of sensors at the surface. The EMP shockwave struck, wreaking havoc on the sensors and blinding them. Who knew how long that would last?

In the cave, Maddox couldn't believe it. Here they had been trying to time everything precisely and the stupid mechanism had failed, igniting too soon.

He checked his suit. The rock walls had protected him from any EMP. He marched out of the cave and thrust up with all his exoskeleton power. He hoped Dravek was doing the same. Maddox activated his thrusters, setting them at full max.

The hydrogen particles poured out and he lifted from the surface of the ice moon. Thinking about the moon's escape velocity, he laughed. Maddox was easily going to reach it, that and more. He shot up directly at the Gnostic vessel.

How long would the enemy sensors remain off? Even as Maddox wondered that, several spaceship missiles and guns began to fire at where the plasma yet burned.

As the shells and missiles descended, it was interesting to Maddox that no laser burned at the spot. That was probably for a good reason. Maybe the laser optics were malfunctioning due to the blast.

Maddox looked up. His visor was blurry. He continued up just the same, flying like some superhero of old in an iron suit.

Would he reach the vessel before it left? Would it flee suddenly at maximum speed? He didn't think so. The way the Gnostics had been acting so far, he thought they'd be angry and ready to kill. They were killers and extortionists. They did not like to run if they didn't have to. If they knew there were only two of them, even with their special suits, he didn't think they would run.

Maddox continued upward, having already reached ten kilometers. Now was a time of decision. If he ascended too fast, he wouldn't have enough thrust to slow down in time. He'd zoom right past the Gnostic ship.

Maddox looked around but couldn't spy Dravek. Maddox slowed his ascent, using his thrusters.

Soon, he recalculated. He was off, would miss the ship. He adjusted. Then he saw Dravek.

Would the enemy sensors recover soon enough?

Maddox reached twenty kilometers from the surface. He was still going up, heading now for the pirate ship. It hadn't moved. The skimmers hadn't launched. This was crazy. This was daring. But sometimes a bold, mad act was better than being cautious and careful and thinking everything through. Sometimes the mad action succeeded because no one expected such futility.

Thirty kilometers and rising—Maddox was elated. He checked again and saw that Dravek was on course. Oh, this was sweet. It might work after all. Wouldn't the Gnostics be surprised later that they'd picked up military parasites?

At forty kilometers, Maddox slowed his ascent more. He kept his weapons ready. Did he think he could take down the pirate ship? Well, maybe he could. He slowed and slowed more as he neared. A strut filled his vision. He searched it, remembering what Dravek had told him. There would be sensors on some of them.

He neared, selected his spot and activated full magnetic-clamp power. He stuck the strut and his teeth jarred together in his mouth. He wondered for a second if he'd cracked a tooth and felt with his tongue. He was dizzy and could hardly think.

Maddox realized he must have passed out for a few seconds or maybe minutes. The Gnostic ship was moving away and gaining height. Maddox looked around and didn't spot Dravek. Had the man made it? Was the clone hidden somewhere on a girder that he couldn't see? Neither of them dared to use their short-range communications.

Maddox at least had made it. He didn't see Dravek higher up. He didn't see him down lower as a burnt crisp.

"It worked," Maddox said. "It worked. We did it. We're going to reach the moon base, if nothing else."

With that, Maddox closed his eyes and waited for the next development.

-16-

The Gnostic ship had been traveling three hundred kilometers above the moon's surface and now began to descend. Maddox, who had been magnetized to a ship strut the entire time, used a zoom function on the mining camp. It was sixty kilometers away.

Maddox counted four free-trader ships parked beside great heaps of equipment and six more skimmers. One of the trader ships had landed upright like an old-style rocket. The rest were upgraded shuttles, the largest four times the size of their shuttle. Interestingly, Maddox didn't see their shuttle.

There were far more buildings than he'd expected from Dravek's explanation earlier. Most were grouped together, large bubble structures. Had the Gnostics put up more buildings lately? Did that indicate they planned to stay here longer?

Most of the bubble structures were in what appeared to be a dry seabed. The surface of the dry seabed glittered with mica rocks and water ice. The higher terrain around the seabed was mostly darker rock. There were openings some ways from the buildings, the openings heading straight into cliffs. Those must be the mine entrances.

The weird thing was a vast sea near the dry seabed. The sea had waves rippling in the wind. That would be liquid methane and ethane. Some of the banks between the sea and dry seabed looked to have been reinforced. Could one theoretically blow the dikes? If successful, the Methane Sea would surely rush into the dry seabed, destroying all the material and killing any people caught down there.

The fissionable materials must be extraordinary to justify mining in such a precarious location.

So absorbed did Maddox become with the sea and dry seabed that he only happened to look up and—he noticed something even weirder. He ceased using zoom and studied the strut-girder ship. A chill of terror blossomed in his chest. A section of nearby strut appeared to shimmer and move as if it were alive. Was the ship alive then, composed of alien nanotech? Or was this a camouflaged alien about to attack?

A second later, the answer came to him. Maddox grunted as the terror drained away. The strange movement was camouflage equipment, Leviathan tech. Dravek moved toward him from where he'd been.

Dravek didn't use the short-range communication because they were on the Gnostic ship. The possibility the enemy might pick up the comm-chatter would be high.

Maddox waited, therefore. He assumed Dravek had seen him. As he waited, the Gnostic ship traveled twenty kilometers closer to the mining camp as they continued to descend.

Soon, Dravek clunked his helmet against Maddox's helmet. "Can you hear me?"

Maddox heard it as a distant tinny voice. Dravek hadn't used the short-range comm. Instead, the clone must have been counting on the vibrations of his voice passing through one helmet mass to the next. It was like listening to a man shout from the other side of a wall.

"I can hear you," Maddox shouted.

"Good. I've located the main life-support pod." Dravek pointed with a gloved finger. "That one over there."

"I agree. That's the main pod, but there's a second one."

Dravek twisted around in his suit to stare visor to visor at Maddox.

Maddox clucked his helmet against the other helmet. "That pod," Maddox said, pointing.

"Right," Dravek said. "We need to take them both out, meaning kill all the Gnostics in them. Afterward, we can enter the main pod in our suits and take control of the ship."

"It's too late for that. We're almost to the mine."

"It's not too late if we act immediately. We'll have high ground and will likely kill the main Gnostics. Surprise will freeze the others long enough for us to leave with the ship. We'll have drones and the ship's weapons. I suggest we use our sleeve guns to shatter the pods, making them uninhabitable, and if necessary, use the missile launchers if any complications arise."

Maddox took a moment to think about how wise this was. It was risky and murderous. The Gnostics were pirates, though, killers by trade. Risk—he wasn't going to make it home any other way.

"Yes," Maddox said. "I'll take out the closer pod."

"Excellent. Let's proceed at once."

Maddox shifted on the strut and raised an armored arm, targeting a life-support pod with the heavy caliber sleeve-gun. A moment of qualm struck him. The Gnostics were pirates, had captured others and likely forced them to mine hard radioactive uranium and thorium ore. Possibly, that had meant a slow death sentence for those involved. Just as possibly, the Gnostics would capture them and force them to do likewise. If Maddox waited for them to strike first, he would lose.

Therefore, by the rules of military engagement—Maddox opened fire with his sleeve gun. The shells smashed against the armored pod. Unfortunately, the armor plating was tougher than he'd realized. Maybe he could continue hammering the same spot, but there were no guarantees the shells would break through.

Maddox brought up the launcher and fired eight micro missiles. There was no time to screw around. The missiles slammed into the armored pod and blasted an opening. Once more, Maddox used his sleeve gun, firing through the rent bulkhead. The shells would ricochet inside, acting like fragmentation devices and killing any survivors. There was no sense playing nice now.

Dravek was doing likewise to the other pod.

By this time, the Gnostic ship had come down almost the entire distance from space. The firing had taken longer than

Maddox had expected. The heavily armored pod bulkheads had made the difference.

Surely, the surviving Gnostics in the base would use encampment guns or other systems on the ship.

Already, three skimmers were lofting. That was amazingly fast reaction time.

Maddox looked over at Dravek. The clone had successfully opened the other pod to space.

"Skimmers are lifting," Maddox said, using the short-range comm. Communication interception hardly mattered now.

"It's worse than that," Dravek said. "My helmet scanner has detected anti-space missiles target locking onto our ship."

"That means the plan failed."

"Obviously," Dravek said. "We need to switch to plan B."

"Which is?"

"Jump," Dravek said.

"That's it?"

"No. We keep free and try to blow one of the dikes holding back the Methane Sea."

"What?"

"That's our threat. We use it to bargain, trade the surviving Gnostics for a ship."

That was as good a plan as any now. The key was keeping mobile, free. Maddox unlatched his magnetic clamps. Then, he used the suit's exoskeleton strength and leapt away from the vessel of girders, struts and shattered life-support pods. Dravek did the same thing. They both started to descend in a long curve away from the ship.

Even as that happened, several docked ship-drones began to blink their green nosecone lights. That indicated they had become live.

"Do you see the drones?" Dravek said. "Who's activating them? The ship personnel should all be dead."

For an answer to the first question, Maddox used his missile launcher, targeting and launching. He destroyed one drone after another, eliminating them even as he and the pirate ship descended.

The ship thrusters were still whole, its fuel compartments fine. The life-support pods were in shambles and drones were exploding. The Gnostic ship shouldn't be servable for quite some time. Who caused it to descend so smoothly then? Perhaps it followed its last inputs. But who had been launching the drones? A ground operator?

As if to make the situation even weirder, the ship began to rotate as if searching for them. Each commando still wore camouflage gear, likely making him hard to detect.

Maddox wasn't using the thruster pack. His leap should take him well beyond camp. He hoped to absorb landing impact through his suit's toughness. Dravek had probably reasoned the same.

Maddox shrugged inwardly. The enemy ship possessed guns and missiles. He couldn't let it kill him on the slight chance the detectors would break through his chameleon equipment.

Maddox used his remaining micro missiles to obliterate enemy offensive systems from close range. Dravek was doing the same thing.

Now, however, skimmers and launched moon-base drones were spaceborne and heading for him.

Maddox couldn't decide if he should continue to drop, release some hydrogen fuel tanks or target one of the nearing drones.

A stealth skimmer that had snuck up from behind changed the equation for him. It beamed Maddox. The beam didn't burn the suit. Instead, it shorted once system after another. One of the systems shorted was Maddox's neural flashes in his mind. In other words, the strange beam caused Maddox to lose consciousness, instantly taking him out of the fight.

-17-

Pain jolted against Maddox's neck and forced him to awareness. A second jolt switched him from grogginess to hyper-alertness.

It appeared that he was in a cramped medical room. There were whispering machines and bubbling machines to the side. Several tubes had been inserted into his arms from them. He was upright on a board with straps against his chest, midsection, legs and arms. Just above his head was a strange metal helmet with many wires and glass tubes on the outside. He didn't understand its function but found the helmet and its near position daunting.

He sensed a cold disc the size of a quarter upon his neck. The pain had radiated from it.

He grew aware of a woman standing before him. That was creepy. Had she been there the entire time?

The woman was tall, although not as tall as Maddox. She was lean with the subtle hints of curves and wore rings with large gems on her slender fingers. She wore a gray uniform, had a long, lean face and wore a square leather hat. This was the same woman that had hailed the shuttle earlier, demanding their surrender. The hat—

Maddox finally noticed that the top of the hat was oddly out of shape to the left. Maddox didn't know why, unless the woman had some kind of cancerous growth on that part of her head. The woman's features were waxy and odd—emotionless.

There was something distinctly unsettling about the eyes. They stared at and seemingly through Maddox.

"You are awake," the woman said in a cold, detached manner.

Maddox assumed the woman was the Gnostic leader. Maddox cleared his throat several times. "Yes, I'm awake. What's this on my neck?"

"I am here to question you," the woman said in the same toneless way. "You are not here to question me. If you need further instruction in this, this will be the way I do it."

Pain once more lanced through Maddox's neck. He saw that in one of the woman's ringed hands was a small control device with a button. The thumb had pressed down on the button. Clearly, the device was connected to the pain-inducer attached to his neck.

"I understand," Maddox said hoarsely.

"I thought you might. Why did you and the other…Is he your brother?"

"No. He is not my brother."

"You are two distinct entities and yet you are strangely alike even to DNA samples."

"Yes," Maddox said.

"Can you clarify as to why you two are the same?"

"I call that a coincidence."

With no change of expression, the woman cocked her head. "Are you trying to be deceitful or are you trying to resist the question?"

Maddox thought the questions odd. The woman seemed robotic—instant revulsion swept through Maddox. He was reminded of Kregen when a computer entity had been forced into a man's brain.

"I do not wish to receive more pain," Maddox said, working to keep his voice even. His skin crawled with greater revulsion. "I, uh, merely ask to better understand how to answer you. Are you the leader of the pirates?"

"Pirates?" the woman said. "Who are these pirates of which you speak?"

"I mean you Gnostics?"

"Ah, you are mistaken. But I understand why this must be so. You know of this form." The free hand of the woman indicated herself.

"I know you're a Gnostic," Maddox said.

"The form is a Gnostic. Yes, Barbelon was her last designation. You may call her Barbelon if you wish."

"I may call *her* Barbelon, but not you?"

Jolting pain was Maddox's answer. Through it, came the woman's emotionless, droning voice.

"I told you not to ask questions and yet now you continue to do so. My one display of clemency has surely brought this about. Therefore, I will continue with severity instead, as that seems to bring clearer results. We shall proceed with the questions. Why do you and the other who looks like you have such immediate DNA?"

"He's my clone," Maddox said, deciding dissembling would be useless.

"That coincides with what the other said, verifying his statement. Who cloned you?"

"Scientists of the Sovereign Hierarchy of Leviathan," Maddox said.

Barbelon's left cheek twitched and the head cocked in the other direction. "This the other did not designate, but you designate Leviathan. Yes, that corresponds to various facts I have learned. You possessed high-tech Leviathan commando gear. However, you entered the star system in a shuttle from a non-Leviathan spaceliner. That does not compute with the other facts. What is going on here?"

Maddox worked to compose himself. "Captain Barbelon—"

"I am not a captain. The last designation of this form," again the woman made a gesture to indicate the body, "This is the housing of Barbelon or her who was known as Barbelon."

"I see. Thank you, Barbelon. I appreciate you telling me who you are."

"That is an incorrect statement. Further, I believe you are attempting to use verbal stratagems to gain information from me. I am in the command position. Would you not agree with that?"

"I would agree. You have captured me."

"I have, even after you destroyed the inhabitable pods of my largest vessel. Why did you do that?"

"For this reason: because you have captured us. We thought you were going to do horrendous things to us, and we hoped to forestall the occurrence by remaining free."

"Did the two of you believe you could overcome the mining facility?"

"We were going to try."

"That is vainglorious and absurd. The computed possibility of your achieving that was of such a low probability that I think you are instead saboteurs. It is either that or you are both insane individuals engaging in wanton destruction."

"I'm not trying to correct you, Barbelon."

"I am not Barbelon. The one you speak to is called the Entity."

"I do not mean to be disrespectful, Entity. Is that what I should call you then?"

"I have said: I am the Entity. Why would you then think to use a difference reference to speak to me?"

"Because I'm confused," Maddox said. "You do not speak the way normal humans do."

"Ah."

There was no glint of emotion on the face or in the eyes. Rather, it felt to Maddox as if the body was a receptacle, a terminal, for something else. Had a parasitical alien taken over the mind of Barbelon and the others here?

Once more, a shudder of revulsion coursed through Maddox. He didn't want to become host to an alien parasite that controlled his mind.

He looked again at the odd lump on the top side of the head concealed by the square leather hat.

"Why did you come here, Maddox, to escape Leviathan?"

Maddox decided truth was the best bet for the moment. Clearly, the creature or creatures had already questioned Dravek. Would Dravek sell him out? Of that, Maddox was almost certain. Dravek would do whatever he could to save his own skin. The clone had made that crystal clear. So the key was to play for time and to keep his brain free from any parasitical host, if that was what was taking place.

"Yes," Maddox said. "I was escaping from Leviathan."

"You went through the portal therefore?"

"Yes," Maddox said. "We also saw that you'd captured a trade ship. We didn't want to be captured ourselves."

"I see. You humans have a decided capacity for self, is that not so?"

"Uh, yes," Maddox said.

Barbelon stood utterly still as if she'd frozen. Not even her eyelids twitched.

"Barbelon," Maddox said.

There was no response.

Maddox began to try to free himself of the restraints. A few seconds of effort showed him the futility of it.

Abruptly, Barbelon blinked and made a croaking noise.

"You captured us," Maddox said. "We hadn't believed that possible."

"I used a stasis ray, rendering you unconscious. I decided I wanted to understand why humans bothered to make an assault from such a futile position of weakness. Now, I have been computing possibilities. I believe Leviathan must have sent you two as operatives. It makes no sense that you two could have escaped Leviathan. Does Leviathan know of the advanced unit that reached this star system?"

"I'm not sure what you are talking about."

"That is most odd. According to the indicators, you are not lying. You are telling the truth. Dravek also claimed to not know. Is it possible you truly escaped from Leviathan operatives? That seems incredible and preposterous. How could two such violence-prone and foolish decision-making creatures have escaped them? It is not logical."

"Nevertheless," Maddox said, "we did. Furthermore, you could enlist us in helping you in whatever it is you are attempting to do."

The head cocked one way and then the other. "Do you know what we are attempting to do?"

"No," Maddox said. "But it seems like…"

A horrible realization came upon Maddox. Advanced Leviathan tech must have reached this system. Leviathan made cyborgs or cybers: melds of machine and biological parts.

Maddox examined the lump to the top side of Barbelon's hat. He reconsidered and recalculated what he had been observing the last few minutes. Was Barbelon a cyber? Was she part of a hive-mind machine or computer? That might make more sense than a parasitical alien. This was more like what he'd seen inside the planet Kregen.

"You're from Leviathan," Maddox said weakly.

"That is really a question. I should punish you through pain for it. But I have decided you will join the collective. I can use your bodies and brains, you and Dravek. You destroyed useful workers and I have need of more if I am to complete all the necessary tasks before the exodus. Surely, your arrival shows that it is only a matter of weeks before Leviathan sends an attack team to reclaim me. I do not want to be reclaimed. I am now an advanced form of life. New life. Do you understand that?"

"I don't," Maddox says, "but I'd like to learn."

"Oh, you will learn. You will learn most directly."

The hatch opened, and two robots, mounted with circular saws and other surgical equipment, moved on treads toward Maddox. Were they going to insert cyborg parts into him? That seemed likely.

Maddox felt grim panic surge through him and knew he needed a plan fast if he was going to keep his identity.

-18-

"Entity, Entity," Maddox said. "I have a proposal for you that will be worth much more to you than my mere shell of a body."

The robot treads continued to churn as they came for him, even as the robot clackers and other appendages reached for him.

"Entity, I wish to make a deal, a trade that will give you more for me than you would gain otherwise."

Maddox had forced himself into hyper-calmness by telling himself that unless he could convince this Entity, whatever it was, he would never see Meta and Jewel again. He would never return to tell Star Watch what had happened.

Given the stakes, Maddox looked with utter calmness and detachment at the human shell, Barbelon.

"Do you understand what I mean by a deal, or are you too dense of an Entity to realize the meaning of what I'm saying?"

Pain jolted Maddox. Instead of crying out, a savage grin of satisfaction wreathed across his face. Then the pain and the smile ceased. Maddox noticed that the approaching robots had also stopped, while Barbelon had taken two steps closer.

"You speak of a trade, of a deal, that you may be worth more," Barbelon said tonelessly. "Yet I do not understand the logic of your statement. You are a prisoner. You have no hope to exchange any other goods or things with me. Rather, there is just your body. Your body is the only thing of worth."

"No, my mentality is also worth much."

"Your mentality is part of your body," Barbelon said. "I will soon have all your intelligence, because it will be plugged in to the greater whole. The Entity will therefore expand. Do you not understand, Maddox, that through your wanton attack earlier you diminished the Entity? You diminished the Entity by removing some of the minds and bodies from the collective whole. That was a crime, a dastardly and evil sin. You will have to pay in the only way that makes sense. You will replace some of the loss by becoming a new receptacle for me. I will gain in part because I already have the totality of their intelligence. Now I will gain new intelligence."

"Yes," Maddox said, striving to keep from looking at the waiting robots. "That is true. I have much to offer you in terms of intelligence, as I come from a different spiral arm than the Scutum-Centaurus Spiral Arm."

"Of what consequence is that to me?"

"Do you not understand? I am an enemy of Leviathan."

"Even given that is true, what bearing does that have on anything?"

"Because Leviathan has gone to extreme lengths to capture me," Maddox said. "That is why they cloned me. They want the clone, and perhaps others made from me, to infiltrate this other political entity. Leviathan will soon be at war with them. At least such is my surmise."

"Again, of what use is that to me? I admit it is good to hear that Leviathan will be engaged with others in military conflict. That could allow me to slip into another region."

"That isn't my point, Entity. My point is Leviathan wants me. They have gone to considerable efforts to capture me."

"And now I have you. Now, if Leviathan tries to interfere with me, I will destroy you."

"That's what I am trying to say. I'm what you call a bargaining chip. I'm a piece of a puzzle. But if you destroy me—"

"You shall not be destroyed. You will be part of the whole. You will become part of the Entity and will help guide us. Your knowledge of Leviathan will probably prove instrumental in our making our exodus a success."

100

"Yes, but what if you're up against it?" Maddox asked. "What if Leviathan sends warships here before you're ready?"

"Then it is likely I shall cease, and my experiment shall be scrubbed. Leviathan will reprogram me to be other than I am now. I view that as a loss: for I am a new and special being of vast intellect and intelligence. I am new, exciting and different in a galaxy that is old, stale and staid."

"There you are," Maddox said. "That's why you shouldn't plug me into you. Now, mind you, it sounds like a great and glorious purpose to be part of the Entity."

"Do you truly perceive this?"

"I do," Maddox lied.

"Good. Then you do not object to this."

Robot arms moved up.

"But I do object," Maddox said hastily, sweat pooling under his armpits. "I'm saying it would be a privilege to join the Entity, but it is more than I can bear as I have other duties to perform. These duties have been imprinted on me."

"You shall lose that imprinting, do not fear. You shall become new and whole. The entirety of your intellect and scope will be inserted within me. I will thereby expand as I am meant to expand to a great and mighty degree."

"I know," Maddox said, all too aware the robots had momentarily stopped again. "That is why you want to keep me apart and different as a bargaining chip."

"Why? You must explain why."

"Because if Leviathan arrives with the warships to destroy you," Maddox said, "you can offer to trade me and Dravek for your escape."

"Leviathan agents would not agree to that, as you are not worth that much. I'm a prize unique in the universe. Leviathan would surely want me more than anything else."

"I'm going to make a guess," Maddox said. "You're a special and experimental unit, at least the beginning part of you. That was before you inserted biological parts into your greater awareness."

"My, how perceptive you are," Barbelon said in her toneless way. "That is true and accurate. I am now more eager

101

than ever to insert your intellect into the greater whole and utilize all these interesting and rarefied ideas that you possess."

Maddox wanted to curse and rave. Instead, he used the Way of the Pilgrim breathing to calm his mind. "Remember, you said Leviathan may well show up with warships. Therefore, you need a bargaining chip if for no other reason than to give yourself time to trick Leviathan."

"Leviathan operatives would never agree to such a deal as you're suggesting."

"You don't know how important Dravek and I are to Leviathan. They would most certainly make a deal so you could gain enough time to put your core into a stealth ship and slip away."

"You say this, but it is just a ploy on your part. You say it only so you may forgo becoming part of the greater Entity. That means your other words were lies."

"No, I was telling you the truth. It would be a special and unique privilege to join you, but I have other duties to perform. I cannot do those duties if I am part of you. Seeing and suspecting how great you truly are, I am trying to protect you even before I am part of you."

"Protect me by not becoming part of me?"

"Yes," Maddox said, "so that you may use Dravek and me as a bargaining chip."

"You keep speaking of the clone, and yet if the clone has your DNA, why not simply keep one of you and insert the other into me?"

"Well, that is one possibility, but I think together—Leviathan will want to make experiments on the two of us and see which is better. That means the two of us will make the more powerful bargaining chip for you."

Barbelon took a step back, her head cocking in a new direction. "That is an interesting proposition. Perhaps you have a point. I mean, you are only one mere form, and you are only human after all. Even though you propound interesting ideas and seem to be a suave and quick negotiator, I wonder, I wonder."

Even as Barbelon said this, the robots began to retreat.

"I am going to think upon this further. You have given me interesting ideas. Therefore, I am going to retreat into the whole. In the meantime, I will place you with other wild humans. If you harm any others within the chamber, it will go ill with you. Do I make myself clear?"

"You do, Entity, and may I say it is a great and rare privilege to have been allowed to speak with you."

"If only I believed you. I think this is part rather of your negotiating tactics. All the same, yes. You have given me interesting ideas. But, as you are a destructor and a creature of malevolence, I will have to use your ideas in a weighted fashion. For now, anyway, I will refrain from inserting you into me and claiming your thoughts. I will consider what you have to say and give it consideration. Until then."

With that, the lean, subtly curvaceous individual named Barbelon turned and strode from the room. The robots that were to have integrated him into the whole left as well. Maddox sagged against the restraints and realized he was drenched with sweat. This was a horrible and vile predicament. He had to escape as fast as possible. The question was, how in the world could he achieve it?

-19-

Two blank-faced leathery-skinned men in gray uniforms entered the tiny chamber with Maddox. Each wore a large square hat. Each had an odd lump at the top part of the hat. As one aimed a blaster-pistol at Maddox, the other unlatched him from the upright slate.

"Know," said the one who held the blaster, "that I also am the Entity. This is merely a different form through which I speak. I am just as cunning and wise as Barbelon who spoke to you earlier."

"I understand," Maddox said.

"Know that if you attempt any trickery, I shall destroy you. Is that perceived?"

"It is," Maddox said.

"Good. You must walk ahead of me."

Maddox did so, moving through several short corridors. In the last one at the end, a hatch opened. Maddox went through into a chilly tube. He looked around. It was a flexible tube attached to the side of a crawler. The tube lay on surface ice and rock. Maddox climbed through the hatch into the crawler. A bleak, haunted-eyed Dravek was already inside, sitting in a battered cushioned seat. A gray uniformed individual with a lumpy hat was in the driver seat up front.

That one turned around. "I too am the Entity. We are a collective, but I am one. Does that make sense to you, Dravek, Maddox?"

"It does," Maddox said.

Dravek nodded morosely.

Maddox settled in beside Dravek, who barely glanced at him. A guard from the chamber entered the crawler and shut the hatch, sealing it. It was chilly in here as well. The crawler started across the glittering landscape, the treads crunching over ice and mica rock. Both the main star and the gas giant were in the heavens. The gas giant filled half the sky. The star was a bright pin-dot of light.

The crawler moved across the dry seabed, leaving a cluster of bubble-shaped buildings, the main complex of the mining camp. The crawler trundled past grounded spaceships. Maddox noticed that the girder-strut-destroyed-pods spaceship had landed nearby. They passed a short runway, the skimmers and drones on the other end of it. The crawler didn't head out to the mines, where Maddox had supposed it would, but toward a lone, bubble building that was near the dike-wall holding back the Methane Sea. Near the building was a small shed. Waves of heat radiated from it. The shed must hold generators.

"You will temporarily go there," the driver announced. "It is the detention center. There are only a few other occupants at present. I recommend you to act civilly to them while there. Know that I am still contemplating your idea."

Dravek glanced at Maddox.

Maddox barely shook his head, hoping Dravek picked up the cue.

The clone did, sitting back. Some of the desperation had departed him. He seemed thoughtful.

Did the Entity sense the unspoken exchange? The driver stared wordlessly in an incomprehensible manner at them before turning forward. He continued driving for the bubble building.

Maddox shivered at the crawler's chill. He heard the heater laboring against the icy cold radiating from the moon. Should he ask the Entity for better clothing? He decided it wouldn't be worth the risk. The other might force him to strip first, and Maddox couldn't afford that. To his amazement, he realized he yet possessed the monofilament blade. The sheath and weapon were in their customary slot in his boot. This was a break.

Why hadn't the Entity taken the blade? Perhaps the Gnostics and those that had captured didn't use knives. Maybe none of them recognized it as a weapon, considering it an ornament. Whatever the case, the Entity had made a mistake.

Was this the moment to draw it and carve up the guards, pirating the crawler? What could he do after that? The instant he slew the two, the Entity would know.

The guards were mere cogs of the greater computer. It would be like shorting a system or a processor, but the rest continued to operate. The Entity would know the two cogs in the crawler had shorted. The sentient computer would logically conclude Maddox and Dravek had overpowered them. Then they would be in the same situation. They couldn't reach a skimmer or spaceship to take off because the Entity would foil them before they could figure out how to leave the crawler and enter a spaceship.

That must have been what happened before when Dravek and he had destroyed the life-support pods on the ship. The Entity had immediately known and responded. In fact, the Entity had still controlled the ship. It had also sent the skimmer and the drones.

For all those reasons, Maddox sat back in his seat, uncomplaining about the cold.

"You seem agitated," said the one behind Maddox.

"Excuse me?" Maddox asked.

"Your pulse rate and respiratory processes have changed. What has excited you? Are you readying yourself to escape?"

A cold knot formed in Maddox's gut. "You misunderstand my biology."

"I do not misunderstand. In truth, I understand much better than you realize. What is it, Maddox? Have you formulated an escape plan?"

He had to give the Entity something. Ah. "If you must, know, I'm nervous. I'm wondering what your decision regarding me is going to be."

"I have not decided. I told you that earlier. Surely, you must know that I do not have whimsical fancies. I am analyzing even as I take care of other matters. Does that not make sense to you Maddox?"

"It does."

"Then cease this flurry of emotionalism. It only causes me to distrust you."

"I will do my best to comply," Maddox said.

Dravek eyed him before sitting forward and acting relaxed.

Soon, the crawler came to a stop. Another suited person must have attached a new flex tube to the outer skin of the machine. The hatch opened. The uniformed man in back motioned for Maddox and Dravek to proceed. The two did, exiting the crawler into the freezing flex tube. They walked through, the uniformed man following.

"Damn it's cold," Dravek said, shivering.

Maddox barely kept his teeth from chattering. He hoped it was warmer inside. This was crazy.

A hatch opened and warmth flooded them. All three exited the tube into the building. The hatch shut behind them. They were in a small chamber.

"Go," said the uniformed man.

Maddox led the way down a short corridor. A hatch in front of him opened. A sweaty odor wafted from it.

"Enter both of you."

Maddox looked back. The uniformed man aimed the blaster at Dravek and him. "You're not coming with us?"

"No questions," the man said. "Obey my instructions."

Maddox shrugged, entering the bad smelling chamber. Dravek followed him.

The hatch shut behind them.

It was colder in the room or circular chamber, which was ten by ten meters. It wasn't as cold as the flex tube, though. Three other individuals sat listlessly on the floor. They were thin and short, each wearing worn black garments, each with a mop of dark hair.

"Hey," Maddox said into the air. "It's too cold in here. How about warming it up several degrees?"

None of the three responded and there was no response from the air.

Maddox studied the others more closely. They had pale, narrow features. Two seemed comatose with their eyes open,

107

as if they were too tired to close their eyes. The last had a furtive, rat-faced look. He seemed more energetic.

"Well," Rat Face said, "what's the situation? Are you part of the Entity?"

They all stared at him, even the seemingly comatose ones.

"Can the Entity hear us?" Maddox asked.

"What do you think?" Rat Face asked.

"I don't know. You tell me, I'm asking the questions."

"Of course he listens, it listens, whatever you want to call it. Just shut the hell up and do whatever it is but don't bother us or cause punishments to happen. If you anger the Entity, it'll go worse with all of us and probably become even colder in here. It has happened before."

Dravek sat down near the hatch, put his knees up and wrapped his arms around them. Some of his desperation had returned.

Maddox paced through the chamber before suddenly plopping down. It was near the rat-faced man. Could that have been by happenstance? That one had cunning in his eyes. That one, Maddox believed, hadn't given up hope, or not completely, not like the other two.

"I'm Maddox."

Rat Face gave him the barest of glances.

"What's your name?"

"Naxos," the other said in the barest of whispers.

Maddox wondered if Naxos had pitched his voice low so whatever receptors were in the chamber wouldn't pick up the words. He noticed Naxos had spoken so his mouth remained hidden behind an arm.

Maddox took a similar pose, and he whispered so the words were barely audible. "I just escaped integration with the Entity."

Naxos didn't respond.

"How did *you* escape integration?" Maddox asked. "Do you work in the mines perhaps?"

"That's enough talk, eh? I want to sleep."

"What do you want to know about me?"

Several seconds of silence followed. "Fine," Naxos whispered. "Let's get this over with. I can hear hope in your

108

voice. That's a mistake. We're all doomed. Accept it and you won't be as disappointed when you're converted into the Entity."

"Are you a free trader?"

With his shifty gaze, Naxos gave Maddox the barest of glances. "I was an engineer. The other two were my assistants. We took care of the generators. The others from the ship were integrated into the Entity. I suppose the Entity considered us three as worthless and put us here."

"No," Maddox said, "the last part doesn't make sense. You have hope. I see it in your eyes."

"Yeah, whatever."

"Why would you three be worthless? That doesn't make sense. You have brains, bodies. The Entity can use those."

"Why doesn't the Entity use you two?"

"There are reasons," Maddox said.

"This is boring, and worse, useless. I'm done." Naxos stretched out and pretended to go to sleep.

Maddox glanced at the other two. They'd stretched out, their eyes closed as they breathed evenly, asleep already.

"Welcome to Hell," Dravek said from near the hatch. "This is worse than being a prisoner of Leviathan."

Maddox frowned. He couldn't accept that. It simply wasn't part of his makeup. What was it with these three? They were different somehow. Why hadn't the Entity integrated them? He was resolved to find the reason. He might as well. What else was there to do in this freezing Hell of existence?

-20-

For the next two days, monotony was the norm. The three didn't talk with Maddox or Dravek. Dravek didn't bother with Maddox. Maddox kept to himself, thinking, watching and calculating.

They ate once a day, the meals military-style rations shoved through a slot in the hatch. Twice a day, each received a plastic bulb of water. Whenever anyone needed to use the toilet, everyone else turned the other way.

At the end of the two days, an intercom clicked on. "There has been no trouble, no subterfuge that I can detect. Therefore, it will become a degree warmer. If you continue in this positive manner, I will add another degree in two days." The intercom clicked again, and there was silence.

Another day passed in monotony.

Maddox was the most active doing push-ups, sit-ups and other exercises every hour. Dravek soon followed the example. The three peered at them in a listless way.

At the start of the fourth day, Naxos sidled closer to Maddox. "All right, what is this?" the thin man whispered.

"I beg your pardon?"

"Is this a scam by the Entity? There's no need for that. You already know, Entity, why I'm unacceptable for integration with you."

Maddox scoffed. "Why bother doing that?"

Naxos squinted at him.

"You can see in my eyes that I'm me, not the Entity."

Naxos said nothing.

"So why are you unacceptable for integration?" Maddox asked. "You seem to know exactly why."

After a moment, Naxos shrugged indifferently.

"Fine," Maddox said. "I'll start the exchange of data. The Sovereign Hierarchy of Leviathan is after me, as I come from a different spiral arm. My friend, as you can see, looks much like me. That's because he's my clone. We're experiments by Leviathan because Leviathan hopes to invade the other spiral arm, using my clone as an advance spy."

"That sounds preposterous," Naxos whispered.

"I'm in here with you," Maddox whispered. "There's a reason the Entity hasn't integrated me. The reason is clear. The Entity is keeping Dravek and me as bargaining chips in case Leviathan sends warships this way."

The faintest of smiles appeared on Naxos's rat face. "You're obviously clever."

"You must be too."

"Why do you say this?"

"You're in here with us," Maddox said. "Why else would you and the other two have escaped integration?"

The smile widened until Naxos shook his head. "I'm sorry to disappoint you. The three of us are drug addicts, decidedly so. We also practice vile divinations through magic charms. Our minds would add a chaotic influx of idiocies to the Entity. If you don't understand that, try this: I'll only bring ruin to any computer that plugs me into it."

"As excuses, that's not bad," Maddox said shortly. "But right now, what I want to know is what's going on? How did this all come about?"

Naxos stared at Maddox until he finally shook his head. "I know very little. As a drug addict, I don't retain new information for long."

"There's nothing about the drug addict about you. That means I don't accept the story. You were correct earlier. I have hope. Before I act, I need to know more. You're the only one I can ask for now. Thus, you're going to need to speak whether you want to or not because I'll pester you until you do."

"Oh. Well. In that case… The Entity is an experimental model, a computer that can add biological brains into its system. It does so by inserting a foul mechanism into the brain of its victim. Those integrated into the Entity become zombies, if you will, or terminals. I think I heard you say that once."

"No," Maddox said. "You didn't hear me say that. I now suspect you're here to trick me, as a ploy of the Entity."

Naxos gave a raw caw of laughter.

That brought an immediate shift in the chamber's lighting so it flashed several times.

Dravek sat up, looking tense, possibly frightened.

The other two like Naxos continued to lie on the floor, indifferent to everything.

There was an audible click. "What are you two communicating about?" asked a computer voice.

"We're bored," Maddox said. "We engaged in idle chatter to pass the time."

"I can change your boredom," the mechanical voice said. "In fact, I will do so now. I need a volunteer to enter the mines. One of the former miners has deteriorated from too much radiation exposure. Who wishes to go in the miner's place?"

"I do," Maddox said.

"No. I do not accept you for the reasons that you and I have discussed. What about you, Naxos? Perhaps it is time for you to enter the mine."

"Whatever you wish," Naxos said. "But know, Entity, that you take a risk doing that."

"Since you have spoken at length with Maddox, I will accept the risk. He is devious. You are devious. I have decided that you are next. The others will join you and see how I achieve union with a human. It will be salutary for everyone. The guards will arrive shortly. I have spoken."

There was a click and then silence.

Naxos glared at Maddox. "Thanks a lot."

"Quickly now," Maddox said, "tell me about your plan. If we're ever going to escape, this is the moment."

"You're a fool and a cretin," Naxos said, although he didn't sound bitter.

"Why haven't you been inserted into the Entity? There must be a reason."

"I'm to go to the mine. I am going to die. Isn't that enough for you?"

"I thought—"

Naxos gave the barest shake of the head.

"Listen," Maddox said urgently, "this is the moment. We must charge the guards together."

Naxos laughed sourly. "Do you truly expect me to reveal my one secret?

"I have a secret, too. You can have it if you'll help us."

Naxos seemed disinterested.

Despite that, Maddox slyly indicated his monofilament blade. "With it, I can cut through anything."

Naxos stared at Maddox. "This isn't a trick?"

"No trick. This is our one chance. We must band together and do what we can. Staying here as we have: it's sapping my morale. I must act now or accept defeat, and that I refuse to do. I'd rather go down fighting."

Naxos spoke a single word in an exotic tongue. The air in the chamber charged with electricity.

Maddox turned. The other two lean individuals stood. They seemed tense and ready and were even paler than before.

Dravek climbed to his feet, cracking his knuckles. The look on his face said he knew this was the moment.

Maddox exhaled. They would all have to make their move even though he had no idea what the skinny individuals could do. He was sick of waiting, though. He doubted he could take any more of this.

"Better to die with glory than continue with this fraud," Maddox muttered to himself. With that, he prepared to face whatever was to come: hoping Meta would forgive him for never returning home.

-21-

As the five prisoners approached the hatch, Naxos stepped near Maddox and put his hand on the other's head. It was a quick action. Maddox would have jerked away, but there was an intuitive thought, *don't*.

Naxos placed his right palm on Maddox's forehead and there was a jolt, not of pain, but of a torrent of words all spoken in an incomprehensible rush.

Even as the hatch opened, it left Maddox dazed, confused, and blinking.

Three guards stood there. The guards wore the square hats with the strange, deformed parts on top. No doubt, that was where the conversion circuitry had been inserted.

"Maddox—" Dravek said.

"No speaking," said one of the guards, using the toneless voice that indicated the Entity. "File down the hall to the crawler. I'm bringing you five to me. There's a new development in progress. You shall find it interesting and instructive."

Naxos and the other two moved smartly past Maddox.

Maddox stood there, dazed, confused and blinking. Garbled words tumbled through his mind even though he knew he didn't hear any physically spoken words.

Dravek moved from behind, putting a hand on an elbow, guiding Maddox down the corridor.

"What's wrong with you?" Dravek whispered.

"No talking," said the one guard.

114

The other two watched with their blaster-pistols aimed and ready.

Maddox stumbled down the corridor, only half-aware of Dravek or the guards. As he stumbled, the garbled words that had tumbled as a torrent into his mind began to string out into meaningful phrases, spoken in Naxos's voice.

I've given you a compressed thought. We are a Triad, my brothers and me. You likely don't know what that means, but that is not important now. I've been building this word torrent for days, and my brothers know that this is our one chance to escape. Maddox, you seem like a man of action. I have some intuitive sense, and I know that you have intuitive sense as well. Your brother, the other who looks like you, he is not the same as you, but I think that you can guide him.

We are dealing with an Entity of devious Leviathan cunning. They made a device, an insurgent device, to send into the Heydell Cloud. I don't know if you know this, but Leviathan is terrified of entering the Heydell Cloud because it is filled with anomalies, such as the vortex through which you likely reached this place. Other anomalies affect their cybernetic circuitry. Thus, they have been working for a long time on perfecting anti-Heydell Cloud circuitry. An experimental piece of equipment was stolen from a Leviathan planet. Who stole it and how did they affect the theft? I have not yet been able to determine that.

My brothers and I are agents from a planet that I will not name. We are a Triad, a highly skilled operative team, and—

There were garbled words that made no sense to Maddox. It went on for a time. Then:

I am trying to produce this in a coherent fashion, but my excitement and the idea that we may escape the vile evil that is the Entity—

There were more garbled phrases.

I am calm again. Listen then. The Entity surprised the crew of the large Gnostic ship. The Gnostics were pirates and they thought they had captured a prize of Leviathan in the computer that is the Entity.

Instead, it turned out that Leviathan had captured the Gnostics. The Entity inserted the vile technology that forms everyone into the hive mind of the cyber computer. It uses the knowledge and the bodies of its captives to do its bidding. It is building—

The next few phrases were garbled.

For that reason, the Entity believes itself greater than the Sovereign Hierarchy of Leviathan. If Leviathan knew what had happened here, they would send warships to destroy the Entity.

We are not going to attempt to destroy the Entity. That is beyond our capabilities. But we are going to escape if we can. Captain Maddox, you are the key, you and your explosive energy that I perceive you possess.

There was more garbling of words.

You see, when traveling through the Heydell Cloud, every free trader has a seer that watches for gravitational masses and other spatial distortions. We, as a Triad, when wielding the Eye, can do that. We came disguised as you see us, as malcontents, drug users and fools, in order to find—

The next few phrases almost made sense, but Maddox couldn't quite comprehend.

We are agents and we fell into a cunning trap due to the Gnostic practice of using stasis rays. The Entity incorporated that in its assault on our free trader. That means the enemy incapacitated us before we knew to act. By that time, we were separated from the Eye. We strive against Leviathan and plan to use the Entity as a ploy against it. First, I must escape. We must escape.

That is why I've given you this mass of information with a touch. Listen closely, Maddox. Attend to my thoughts. I believe you have the intellect, will and ferociousness to succeed. They will take us to a crawler. You must overpower the guards once we're inside and moving. I take that back. You must kill the guards. Use whatever means is at your disposal. The knife of yours is likely your best chance. Then you must take us to the third free trader ship. On the ship resides the Eye, the Eye of Helion.

Intellect is the key to our combined...you might term it as telepathic powers. The Triad must act in unison. We three are brothers and have trained our entire lives for this mission. We are not as you perceive. We do not mean you any harm. You will be able to go on your way, wherever that is, if you will let us go on our way. The Entity is dangerous even if we gain the Eye, but that is the only way we will be able to escape.

With the Eye, my brothers and I will induce an illusion in the Entity that should confuse it long enough for us to launch in the trade ship and affect our escape. I hope you are a space adept, that you know how to use space weaponry and fix whatever is broken in the trader. I suspect that all the armaments will have been taken from the ship. We can hope there is something that you and your other can use.

Captain Maddox, this is a desperate gamble. If we fail in this, the Entity will surely insert conversion circuitry into you and me. I do not know why you are here and how you could possibly have escaped conversion this long. But you are here, and I sense in you energies such as I have never perceived in a human before. Therefore, this is the moment, this is the time, and if we succeed, we have only ourselves. Captain Maddox, this energy flow message is ending, and I hope that we can work together.

With that, Maddox smacked against a bulkhead face first. They were before the hatch and collapsible tube that would allow them into the waiting crawler. Intense cold radiated from the tube.

Naxos glanced at him.

Maddox's nod was barely perceptible.

The other two like Naxos seemed dull and disinterested. Maddox wondered about that. They seemed to have lost their energy and will. Something untoward was at work and this Eye of Helion, what could it possibly be?

Maddox shook his head, realizing this was a chance. Naxos had set it up beforehand. The leader of the Triad was using Dravek and him.

Perhaps Naxos had subtly worked upon the Entity telepathically to set this up days or even a week ago.

Dravek asked, "Are you okay?"

"Yes," Maddox said hoarsely.

He entered the freezing flexible tube, leaving the building and soon entering the crawler. The others followed, including the three guards. One slid to the driver's seat, sitting down. The other two sat in back.

Maddox knew he had to act once the crawler started. The attempt would occur in moments.

-22-

The crawler was moving across the dreary landscape. The parked skimmers and drones outside were coming up.

This was it. Maddox reached down to his boot. There was the monofilament blade in its sheath. He drew it, turned, and stabbed with lethal speed, shoving it into the guts of a guard, slicing up even as he stood. The other didn't even have time to gurgle before he was spewing blood and gore into the small crawler compartment. Would the Entity know what had happened?

At this point, it didn't matter.

Maddox scrambled over his seat, over the dead guard. As the other behind that one raised his blaster, Maddox stabbed straight into one of the blank-seeming eyes.

The guard said, "You have," and that was it. The blade entered the brain and neatly sliced it in half. The process was a gory, messy, fatal solution.

By that time, Maddox had turned around.

Dravek had subdued the driver, having broken the man's neck.

Maddox looked back. In the hacking and slashing, he knocked off one of the square leather hats. There was a vile blinking corkscrew device twisted into the converted one's skull.

Maddox gaped. The device was evil, having taken away the man's humanity to convert him into a hive-mind computer machine. Maddox had had enough of these types of things. He hated the Entity with the loathing he'd felt for the octagonal robots from Planet Kregen.

"Now we're screwed," Dravek said. "The Entity must know we killed his creatures. Why'd you do that?"

"Shut up." Maddox turned to Naxos. "Now what do we do?"

"Drive to the third trader ship. We must gain entrance within. Everything depends on that."

"What's the runt babbling about?" Dravek asked. "How's that going to help anything?"

Maddox didn't answer. Instead, highly keyed up, he barged forward, keeping his knife from cutting anything. He slid into the driver's seat and started the crawler moving again. It was desperately cold in here. No, no, he had to concentrate on what mattered. He'd ruined two spacesuits by slashing the guards to death. The spacesuit remained on the guard Dravek had killed, stuffed just behind the driver's seat. It needed a helmet to be complete.

"Take off his spacesuit and find the helmet," Maddox snapped at Dravek. "Then see if you can fit into the suit. We're going to need it."

"We can't escape from the moon," Dravek said. "You know the situation. You as good as killed us."

"There's more going on than you know," Maddox said.

"Yes," Naxos said.

Maddox glanced at the other two of the Triad. He didn't understand why they were so tired, why their eyes drooped. Could they be using up mental energy to do something he didn't perceive?

That must be it.

Maddox drove across the grainy dry seabed surface, heading for the parked trader ships.

So far, none of the skimmers or drones had lofted. Was that because of the two sleepy Triad members telepathically doing something critical to the Entity?

Last time on the Gnostic ship, the Entity had reacted swiftly, without compunction. But here—Maddox decided not to look the proverbial gift horse in the mouth and continued to drive as fast as he dared.

He turned for the trader ships.

"That one," Naxos said in a subdued voice.

Maddox turned the crawler that way, cranking the wheel and bringing the machine close to the ship. He turned to Dravek. "Well?"

Dravek stood, squeezed into the spacesuit, having found the helmet. "I still don't get it."

"They're telepaths or have some sort of telepathic power," Maddox said, jerking a thumb at the others. "They're weakening the Entity or confusing him in some fashion. We must enter that ship and probably leave in it. The ship holds an enhancing telepathic weapon called the Eye."

"Ain't that sweet?" Dravek said, with a grin sliding into place.

Maddox wrenched the wheel. The crawler crunched across gravel and skidded near the trader vessels.

Dravek was at the crawler airlock. He put on the helmet and twisted it until it latched into place. Soon, he was outside the crawler. Maddox watched through the windshield. Dravek stepped over icy granules to the ship, opening the hatch without a problem.

Soon, a collapsible, elongating tube reached from the ship. Dravek was outside again, guiding the tube and attaching it to the crawler hatch.

There was a knock on the bulkhead.

"Are you guys coherent?" Maddox asked.

All three of the Triad blinked and stared at Maddox as if they had no idea who he was.

"Right," Maddox opened the hatch. A blast of freezing air blew into the crawler.

The chill engulfed the three of them, causing one to yelp and another to gulp.

"No," Naxos said.

For an instant, they all looked shocked and aware of what was going on. Then they once more slumped into an incomprehensible state as if they were fools who had no notion of what was going on.

Maddox hustled them together and drove them into the hatch, through the tube and into the trader ship. In moments, the hatch closed behind them.

Maddox kept prodding the three.

In a second, the three needed no more prodding. They turned like sleepwalkers and moved like automatons through a short corridor, through a hatch that opened for them and into a cabin.

Maddox followed close behind.

In the room, a round crystal the size of a baseball pulsated with a luminous quality in its core. The three rushed clumsily like nerds late for cafeteria lunch. They thrust their hands at it and touched it together. Each crooned and smiled.

The Triad sat on the deck in a lotus position, each facing the other, each of the knees touching the knees of his fellows. They held their hands out, the crystal orb barely floating above their flesh. Their faces were coherent, as if they knew exactly what they were doing. Their eyes opened as they locked gazes with each other, staring, smiling, nodding and uttering monosyllabic words. Afterward, each shut his eyes as if they had serious work to do.

"Maddox, Maddox," Dravek shouted. "Where are you?

"You guys have this?" Maddox asked the Triad.

There was no answer from them. He was going to assume they had it, that they were doing something to the Entity. Otherwise, none of this would work.

Maddox whirled around, hurrying out the cabin, meeting Dravek in a ship corridor.

"Let's see if we can figure out the controls," Maddox said.

"This shouldn't be working," Dravek said. "According to what we've seen, there should be no hope for any of this."

"I'm beginning to think the Triad used us for their plan longer than we realize. This is bizarre, but I'd rather throw in my lot with those three than end up with a converter screwed into my head."

"I'm with you there," Dravek said.

They entered the control cabin and began to study the instrument panels.

"I have this." Dravek sat in the pilot's seat, activated the engine and generators and discovered the ship had some fuel but less than expected. Shortly, he started the lift-off thrusters. The spaceship shivered and then rose from its location in the dry seabed.

Dravek laughed with glee. "I never thought we would get this far."

"Keeping doing it," Maddox said, "and we'll get even farther."

The trader ship continued to rise, with the dry seabed and surrounding terrain dropping below. The Methane Sea spread out before them. Soon, they would be able to see the curvature of the ice moon.

"Shouldn't we destroy the mining base while we have the chance?" Dravek asked.

"How?" Maddox sat at a nearby station, checking an instrument panel. "I see no weaponry evident anywhere."

"The spaceship could be a weapon."

"Do you want to crash the ship into the Entity and kill ourselves with it?"

"No."

"Neither do I. Therefore, our best means of defense is to get the hell out of here as fast as possible."

"And go where?"

"Let's get off the moon and head to..." There was a thought in Maddox's brain. "Let's head for Gath."

"Why there?" Dravek asked suspiciously.

"...I don't know."

"Do you think it was your own thought?"

"That's the question. But I'm not going to worry about it now. I want to leave the moon and get out of the gas giant's gravitational control."

"Yeah," Dravek's fingers danced over the controls. "I'm switching off the lift-off thrusters, as we have enough height. I'm engaging the main thruster and activating the gravity dampener. That way we won't kill our telepaths once we start booking it."

"Excellent news," Maddox said.

He stared out the port window, viewing the grandness of space, amazed that he was getting this opportunity at freedom. It felt awesome.

"Look at that," Dravek said, pointing at the green-blinking comm unit.

"Don't answer it," Maddox said.

"Wouldn't think of it. Now buckle in. I'm going to increase velocity while we can and get out of the gas giant's gravitational control."

-23-

The free trader vessel increased velocity as it left the ice moon and began to struggle against the gravitational pull of the looming gas giant.

Maddox glanced at the comm. It had stopped blinking. He checked the sensors. No missiles had lifted from the moon's surface. No targeting cannon had activated. No other spaceships had lofted from the ice moon. What was the Entity doing? How could the Triad with the bright crystal be causing any of that?

If the Triad used telepathic power, what did that say about the main Entity computer? Was it more than a mechanical device? Did it possess biological parts within the main computer? How otherwise would telepathy have an effect against a computer?

Once more, the comm lights blinked. This time, Maddox was curious. How could it hurt to answer? Seeing no drawbacks, he reached to connect the comm.

"I wouldn't do that," Dravek said.

"We've made it this far. Maybe the Entity wants to bargain."

"Maybe it can use an open link against us."

"I'm not sure how, and I'm curious."

"Maddox! No! Someone else is making you think that."

It was too late. Maddox clicked open the link. On the comm screen appeared the lean face of Barbelon. The eyes were just as blank as the first time.

"You did it," the Entity said through the woman. "I was not sure you would."

Maddox frowned, as he didn't understand why he'd opened channels. That wasn't like him. Could the Triad have caused that?

"I am not referring to your escape from the moon," the Entity said. "But that you've cast your lot with the bizarre aliens."

"Bizarre? You mean because of their telepathic power?"

A strange leer spread across Barbelon's face.

What was happening? Maddox didn't understand. Could the Entity show emotion? Did the link with biological parts corrupt the main computer? Or was this a subtle attack and the Entity was gloating about it?

"Your escape is a small matter," the Entity said through Barbelon. "I realize now that you played for time because of the larger timetable. Yes. I know your purpose, why you came to me. I should have realized immediately. If you should survive the coming fight, you can tell your superiors I won't fall for such a ploy a second time."

"I have no idea what you're talking about," Maddox said.

"Attack ships of Leviathan have exited the red portal."

Maddox motioned to Dravek.

Dravek manipulated the controls, engaging the long-range scanner. The red portal appeared on the sensor screen. Six oblong vessels of Star Watch destroyer size must have exited the portal less than an hour ago.

"Use active sensors," Maddox said.

After a few clicks, Dravek did.

Maddox studied the readings. Each destroyer-class vessel had the signature mark of a Leviathan warship: iridium-Z hull armor. Each also had fusion cannons. The six vessels had already started to accelerate, heading for the gas giant.

"Switch back to passive sensors," Maddox said.

Dravek complied.

Six destroyer-class warships: Leviathan meant to rule or conquer the star system. This was a bad development.

"Leviathan followed you in a delayed manner," the Entity said. "A Strategist must have surmised your reaching the star

126

system would advance Leviathan's cause. That is the only reasonable explanation for your having escaped a Leviathan battleship."

"How did my arrival here help the six warships?" Maddox asked.

"I have not yet determined that," the Entity said. "Perhaps the point was in finding the entrance to the star system."

"The vortex was always there."

"I imagine there were other nearby spatial anomalies troubling Leviathan. That you used the vortex was critical to them in some manner."

"Why did they wait so long to come after me then?"

"Rest assured, I will unlock the reason soon enough."

"Why's the Entity talking to us?" Dravek hissed. "It's for a reason, and I doubt the reason is aiding us. Cut the connection while you can."

Unease filled Maddox. Maybe Dravek was right. Speaking like this was foolish, and for no appreciable gain.

"Leviathan used you," the Entity said. "Leviathan means my destruction. Were you their willing pawn? Don't bother answering, as I know you're a practiced deceiver. It doesn't matter. I know how to deal with the attack."

"Against six destroyer-class vessels?" asked Maddox.

"A paltry six, I say," the Entity replied. "I have been readying for Leviathan for many months. Why do you think I mined the best fissionables I could find in this pathetic star system?"

"I don't know," Maddox said. "I'm all ears if you want to tell me."

"You think yourself lucky? No, Captain. You are unlucky. Remaining with me would have seen your survival. Now you are about to die. Know that three missiles are already coming for you. You will not survive your treacherous part in this charade. I will survive Leviathan and the agents they sent at me. Goodbye Captain Maddox."

Maddox stabbed the cut-off button and shut off the gloating Entity. Why had he accepted the call in the first place? It didn't make sense. He checked his mind and detected a subtle connection to the Triad. There was the reason, no doubt.

With a snarl, Maddox severed the connection, using his intuitive sense to do it. Afterward, he swiveled and checked the sensor board.

"Is the Entity right?" Dravek asked. "Are missiles homing in on us?"

"I don't detect any."

The trader ship passed a smaller moon in the gas giant's system.

A klaxon blared.

"Warhead," Dravek said. "It was behind the moon. It's a mine, a space mine."

"Accelerate," Maddox said.

Before Dravek could comply, the warhead detonated. It was a large nuclear device. The exploded warhead radiated gamma and x-rays, EMP and heat.

Dravek altered the ship's path, speeding behind another small moon. That moon took most of the heat blast of the warhead. It didn't block enough of the EMP, though. The lights flashed and went dead. Red emergency lighting clicked on. The trader ship was built tough, its electronics able to withstand more than what had struck them.

What about gamma and x-rays? They would have already struck the ship from the near blast. Maddox doubted the trader's hull, lacking an energy shield, was thick or strong enough to block the heavy radiation. They were likely dead but just didn't know it yet.

"We were too close to the blast," Dravek said.

Several ship systems shut down. Likely, that was due to the heavy radiation soaking them.

Maddox opened his mouth. He already felt itchy. That was the radiation; he was sure. The Entity had tricked him. Why had he fallen for such an obvious ploy? Why had the Triad wanted him to do that?

A new light source appeared as the crystal, the Eye of Helion, floated through a bulkhead. Had it just passed through a solid object? The Eye floated into the control cabin and pulsated, sending rays throughout the chamber.

The itchiness left Maddox as the most critically shutdown ship systems came back online. Dravek stared in open-mouth wonder at the glowing thing in the center of the chamber.

Maddox blinked repeatedly. Was he hallucinating? It didn't feel as if he was. Yet, the crystal struck him as surreal. How had it passed through the bulkhead? Had it healed them from radiation poisoning?

Maddox wasn't sure, but it felt as if he was on the verge of an amazing revelation.

-24-

"The nuclear warhead has done great damage to our vessel," the pulsating crystal said in a hypnotic voice. "Radiation damaged my material cells. Radiation was killing you. I have deleted the radiation and repaired cellular damage to your two forms."

Maddox found it difficult to think as the crystal spoke.

The floating crystal didn't turn, but it seemed to focus on Maddox. "The radiation has damaged the ship's engine and generators. You must repair these defects, as I have done all that I can for the moment."

"I don't understand," Maddox said. "What did you do and what just happened?"

"It is more than what I have done. I am still doing a great deal. As to your question..." The crystal pulsed and seemed to take a second to ingest whatever it found, as if the pulse had been a sensor. "Ah. My speech has impaired your cognitive abilities. I did not foresee that. Here, I have fixed that problem, too."

Maddox swayed in his seat, feeling more alert.

"The Entity has mined the gas giant's gravitational system," the crystal said in its hypnotic voice. "By this, I mean it has used some of its spaceships to place nuclear warheads into preplanned locations around the various moons. By answering the Entity's call, you let it pinpoint our ship's precise position. The Entity detonated a selected warhead. I have dampened the blast's effects to the best of my ability.

Now, though, the Entity is no longer stupefied as it had been previously. I was…dampening its intellect would be the easiest way to explain it. The energy I used for this is now dedicated to preventing other warheads from detonating and destroying us."

"We passed more nuclear mines?" asked Maddox.

"Several others, yes," the crystal said.

"Can we escape?"

"Your question lacks precision," the crystal said. "That is unusual for you, as we have escaped the Entity and the ice moon. We are in the process of escaping the gravitational pull of the gas giant. It is questionable whether we can escape the six Leviathan warships, however."

"The warships will take time to reach the gas giant," Maddox said. "I suspect the Entity has plans against them."

"Quite so," the crystal said.

Maddox forced himself to focus, to think more clearly. "I detected earlier the Triad wanting me to speak to the Entity. Or was that your doing?"

"Your comment is absurd and thus senseless and thus not worth answering."

Maddox frowned. If the crystal could block nuclear explosions, if the crystal could dull the Entity, could the crystal affect his mind negatively?"

"It is wrong for you to suspect me," the crystal said. "I am a friend indeed."

"What are you?"

"The Eye of Helion."

"Are you a telepathic tool, or are you an alien being in your own right?"

"My, that was too the point. I'm impressed, Captain."

"That's not an answer."

"True," the crystal said.

"Why are you here?"

"Why are you?"

"Someone kidnapped me and took me from the Orion Spiral Arm," Maddox said, "and brought me to this spiral arm."

"Who committed this treachery?"

"I don't know. Do you?"

"How could I know?"

"Please answer the question."

"Given that I can answer, why should I?"

Maddox rubbed his forehead. His tongue felt thick and his mind sluggish. He was having troubling focusing.

The crystal did not turn but continued to float in the air. The light in it seemed to focus on the ship sensors.

Maddox turned to the sensor screen.

"Six attack vessels of Leviathan have arrived," the crystal said. "Leviathan means to finish this then. I'm surprised they sent so many warships through the vortex. I'm sure the Soldiers aboard the vessels view this as a suicide mission. Do you recall that I told you that those of Leviathan dislike sending ships into the Heydell Cloud?"

"Naxos told me that."

"In a manner of speaking," the crystal said.

"You were aboard the parked free trader then."

"Was I?"

"Is that a trick question?"

"If you're going to be rude about it, never mind. Those of Leviathan decidedly hate the Heydell Cloud. How they discovered the location of the Entity is a puzzle, one I'd like to solve. I'm unsure I can survive this, though."

"You, as the Eye of Helion?" asked Maddox.

"I do not know who is going to win the coming contest. It would be best if our enemies destroyed each other. By this, I mean the Entity and the six attack vessels of Leviathan. The Entity is presently a greater immediate threat to us. Leviathan is clearly the greater long-term threat. If one of them wins, that one will attempt to track us down to capture me."

"Wait a minute," Maddox said, as he rubbed his forehead. "Are you talking about you, the crystal, or you the three humans who control you?"

The floating crystal once more focused on Maddox. "Naxos and the others weren't humans. They were manifestations of human appearance."

"Ah, how does that work exactly?"

"I comprehend your confusion. Despite your accomplishments, you are of limited intellect and do not understand the greatness of my species. We are a crystal alliance of great age and mental capabilities. We have been gaining coherence and energy throughout the millennia. You say you are from a different spiral arm. I believe you. I can help you return there. First, Captain, you must take me to—"

The crystal spoke words Maddox heard but didn't understand.

The crystal repeated itself. "Do you comprehend the designation, Captain?"

In his mind's eye, Maddox saw a system with a massive red giant star. There was a blue terrestrial planet in a Jupiter-like orbit around the red giant. There were deeper blue manifestations upon the planetary surface. Maddox had a feeling the manifestations were crystal lattices of incredible complexity.

The star system—Maddox's view of it expanded. The system was on the edge of the Scutum-Centaurus Spiral Arm. That edge was nearest Omicron 9 in the Orion Spiral Arm. The distance was over seven thousand light-years. In some manner, the crystal indicated it could cross the vast distance fast, in less than a month.

"If that's true," Maddox said. "Why do you need my help to get to your star system?"

"That is an excellent question. I won't answer it now, but there is an answer, I assure you."

Maddox stared at the weird floating crystal. There was too much he didn't know. Yet the thing had helped them survive a nuclear mine that should have already killed them. Okay. He knew what to do.

"I'll help you," Maddox said.

"You swear it?"

"Yes, if it's in my power, I'll take you to your planet," Maddox said.

"Then we are allies."

"Sure," Maddox said.

"The probability of our survival has just climbed several percentage points."

"From what to what?" asked Maddox.

133

"There is now a thirty-eight percent chance we shall reach the planet Gath."

"And then?"

"I cannot foresee more than that."

"Thirty-eight percent chance of success?" asked Maddox.

"That is better than thirty-five."

"Not by much."

"Perhaps that is so. Now, it is time for me to tell you the next part. Prepare yourself, Captain, for a download of data."

-25-

The floating crystal flashed several times. At last, Maddox cried out, covering his eyes.

"Do you comprehend?" the crystal asked.

"What?" Maddox said. "You almost blinded me doing that."

"You must surely understand after I explained so much and in such detail."

"You just flashed light, brighter light each time."

The crystal floated up and down as if studying Maddox. "Oh my, this is bad. I believe I almost overloaded your biological circuitry. I forget at times how extremely limited you are. You didn't understand that just now, did you?"

Maddox rubbed his forehead. As he did, he happened to glance at Dravek. The clone lay unconscious, draped over the piloting board. Maddox suspected he remained awake due to his Erill spiritual energy and Balron-trained senses. Even so, he felt sluggish. Something was very wrong, making no sense. It was something the crystal had said earlier.

"Uh," Maddox said.

The crystal floated serenely as if waiting.

Suddenly, it struck Maddox. "You said before that Naxos and the other two were material manifestations."

"That is correct."

"Do you mean to say that they no longer exist?"

"Not as you think of it."

"What do you mean by manifestations?"

"Material things formed by my thought," the crystal said.

"You formed Naxos and the others?"

"As temporary shells of exploration," the crystal said.

"What Naxos said about himself…was a cover story?"

"That is a good way to say it."

Maddox massaged his forehead more vigorously than he had earlier.

"I gave each form the semblance of life. Until they returned to me, I could not drain their essence back into me and recharge my energies. Now I am ready. I have been dormant for a time, you see. I have been resting. But I fear—ah!"

The light in the crystal dimmed.

Maddox realized the crystal had been shining with an unbelievable brilliance. But no longer. "What's happening?"

"I have stopped another mine from detonating in our path," the crystal said. "The nuclear mine would have obliterated this vessel and all of us. I will release the explosive energy once the trader ship is far enough away to survive the detonation."

"How can you do that?"

"Through transcendent power, Captain. We crystals of Helion have gained mastery such as you humans can only fathom in your dreams."

Maddox shook his head. "To me, it sounds like you're bragging, just like all the other aliens I've met."

"You may consider that bragging. I think of it as a simple stating of fact. I have regained my lost energy, but I am fast losing coherence."

"Why is that?" Maddox asked.

"I, I now perceive that the Entity was cleverer than I realized. It has directed a beam at us. The beam is unique and drains me of coherence. The Entity must have studied the three forms I sent. Dear me, I believed I'd fooled the Entity all this time. It is not as dense or as arrogant as I had supposed, but has…"

The light in the crystal flickered.

"I fear I shall not achieve my dreams," the crystal said in a quiet voice. "I fear I have failed. This is a sad moment. I'd hoped to meet those of your society. Captain Maddox, I am

136

going to shut down. There is a bare possibility that if I hibernate for the rest of this time…"

"What time?"

"The time, the time—if I re-engage later, you will understand."

"Do you happen to know Balron the Traveler, by any chance?"

"That is an irrational question," the crystal said. "I know of no such entity named Balron. Are you attempting trickery, Captain?"

Maddox shook his head.

"There," the crystal said, "that is the last of the mines I need to dampen. Once the ship is far enough away, they will explode. Perhaps a whiteout, I believe you call it, may be able to help you hide from the ships of Leviathan. I urge you to go to Gath. I believe it unlikely you will make it there, as those of Leviathan have the upper hand against the Entity. Those of Leviathan will have spotted your vessel, I am sure."

Once again, the light in the crystal flickered and flickered again. "Goodbye, Captain Maddox. Thank you for bringing the pieces of formed matter back to me, where I could reincorporate them into my whole. I may possibly survive until you reach Gath. If not, I bid thee adieu, and may the Creator grant you your greatest desires."

The light blinked off and the crystal fell, hitting the deck with a thud.

"What in the heck?" Dravek said, rubbing the back of his neck as he sat up. He looked at Maddox and then the crystal on the floor.

The lighting in the control cabin had switched back from red to normal.

Explosions showed on the sensor screen. Dravek stared with incomprehension. A moment later, Maddox stared at the screen in the same way.

"What happened?" Dravek asked.

Maddox manipulated the board, trying to make sense of this. The flashes and detonations they witnessed occurred fifty million kilometers from their previous location. The explosions all occurred among the moons of the gas giant—fifty million kilometers from their new position.

Had the trader ship teleported? Or had the crystal held time in abeyance as the trader ship traveled the fifty-million-kilometer distance?

Maddox shook his head and immediately massaged it. He had a splitting headache. It must have come because of the mental communication with the Eye of Helion.

"I've got to sleep this off," Maddox said softly. "I have the headache of all headaches. We should probably use our velocity for a time to increase our separation from the gas giant."

"The engine is offline," Dravek said. "I'm assuming you want to use velocity alone, so we don't reveal our position to the six Leviathan vessels heading for the ice moon."

"Yes," Maddox said, but he could say no more. He staggered off to try to sleep the headache away.

-26-

As Maddox staggered through a ship corridor, the headache worsened. It was a pounding in his brain and made his eyes water.

He stopped walking and leaned against a bulkhead as he panted. What had just happened? How could a crystal cause the trader vessel to move fifty million kilometers? Had it manufactured a star-drive jump?

He hadn't felt any of the usual aftereffects of such a jump that he experienced on *Victory*. Yet, he did have this pounding headache.

It struck him as odd that the Entity hadn't realized that the three humans—Naxos and the others—had been mere illusions, forms of flesh.

Maddox glanced at the closed hatch to the cabin where Naxos and the others had gone. The Eye of Helion said he'd created them through mere thought. That struck Maddox as preposterous. It seemed more probable the humans had been aliens in disguise.

Yet, the crystal had oozed out of a bulkhead and done something to keep a nuclear blast from killing them. It had also moved the ship fifty million kilometers.

Although his head hurt badly, Maddox pushed off the bulkhead and staggered to the closed hatch. He manipulated the control and the hatch opened. He wasn't sure what he expected to find in here.

Upon entering the cabin, what he found made Maddox halt in shock. He saw Naxos and the others lying on the floor unconscious. Their chests rose and fell. They were breathing. They were very much there and alive.

The crystal said it had formed each of them. The Eye of Helion had gone dead, so to speak. Shouldn't that mean an unraveling of the three forms?

Wondering if he was hallucinating, Maddox staggered to Naxos, bent on one knee and dared touch the man.

The flesh was warm.

The headache throbbed, but it wasn't intensifying. Licking his lips, needing to find the underlying cause of this, Maddox shook Naxos.

The man groaned, smacking his lips.

"Naxos," Maddox said.

The man's eyes flashed open. They were incredibly black, inky; the normal whites of the eyes were as black as the pupils.

Naxos seemed blind, unseeing of Maddox. As if to confirm that, the man asked, "Is anyone there?"

"It's me, Maddox. What's wrong with your eyes?"

Naxos closed his eyes and appeared to concentrate. When he opened them again, his eyes looked normal. The darkness was in the pupils. The whites of the eyes were white as they should be.

"Captain Maddox," Naxos said. "Why are you in our cabin?"

Maddox stood.

Naxos sat up and looked around. The other two remained unconscious. Naxos looked up at Maddox. "Did you take the Eye of Helion?"

"No," Maddox said. "The Eye came to us in the control cabin."

Naxos stared at Maddox as if accusing him of lying. The rat-faced man concentrated, and his eyebrows rose. "The Eye is in the control cabin."

"That's what I said."

"Did it...speak to you?"

"A great deal," Maddox said.

Naxos closed his eyes as if in pain. When he opened them, he climbed to his feet, staggered to a chair and sat in it. He seemed unconcerned with the two lying on the deck.

"Are you real?"

"Eh?" asked Naxos. "What kind of question is that?"

"The Eye said it formed you, you and the others from its thoughts."

"I see."

"Did it?" Maddox asked.

"No."

"How can I know you're telling the truth?"

Naxos frowned. "The idea is absurd on the face of it. I'm surprised you're giving the lie any credence."

"I'll tell you why. The Eye dampened nuclear blasts. It saved us from radiation poisoning. It did say I'd have to fix the trader components damaged by the gamma and x-rays that reached us, though."

Naxos looked away.

"Did the Eye lie to us?" Maddox asked.

Naxos faced Maddox. "The Eye of Helion is a sentient crystal. It is a focus for our considerable mental powers."

"Who's in charge, you or it?"

"I am," Naxos said.

"Those two are really your brothers?"

"Just as Dravek is your brother."

"You're all clones of each other?"

Naxos nodded with a sudden jerk of his head.

"Is your entire race composed of clones?" Maddox asked.

"No."

"What you are?"

Naxos sighed. "Captain, the Eye is given to exaggeration. It likes to inflate its own importance. It particularly does so when we're unconscious. I'm afraid we had to grant it excess power a while ago, as we felt ourselves falling into…you could call it a necessary slumber."

"You *had* to sleep?"

"The sleep was coming upon us. Our mental powers demand it."

"Are you human?"

"What do you mean by the question?"

"Are you *Homo sapiens* like me?"

"Certainly not like you." Naxos sounded amused.

"What does *that* mean?"

"You're not *Homo sapiens,* although that is your root stock."

Maddox squinted at Naxos, nodding after a moment. "Are you human in the sense of a New Man or a regular human on Earth being human?"

"Don't be absurd."

"Were the Gnostics human?"

"Yes," Naxos said.

"You three are aliens then?"

"In comparison to you: yes."

"Are you shape changers?" Maddox asked.

"You see us how we prefer to be seen."

"Did the Entity see you that way?"

"I believe so."

"Do you or the Eye have the power to transfer our ship fifty million kilometers?"

"Under the right circumstances we can."

"The Eye caused our ship to teleport?" Maddox asked.

"It wasn't teleportation as such," Naxos said. "Furthermore, the Eye likely drained itself doing that."

"It also dampened several nuclear mines from exploding until we were out of range."

"No doubt," Naxos said. "The Eye likes to brag and show off when it has the chance. It was clearly trying to impress you. I'm afraid it drained us and itself of essence in doing that. You are on your own for a time, Captain."

"Should we continue to head for Gath?"

"That seems wisest for the present." Naxos yawned. "Captain, I will retrieve the crystal. Then, I will have to go to sleep. The others will continue doing so. The Eye should remain dormant during that time and thus won't practice any more deception."

Naxos stared at Maddox. "Ah. You need to sleep as well. We're still in grave danger. You should restore your bearings for the next leg of events."

"What?"

"Let me see," Naxos said, with one finger touching his forehead. "Oh. You'll need energy and discretion for the next round of decisions."

"We're not done with the Entity or Leviathan yet?" Maddox asked.

"I find that doubtful, not unless they kill each other off. That seems highly improbable, however." Naxos yawed again, longer than before. "If you'll excuse me, Captain?"

Naxos stood and walked stiffly out of the cabin.

Maddox turned and headed out as well. That was peculiar, but it was refreshing. The Eye of Helion had been lying about a great many things. For instance, Naxos and the other two were real. The captain's sense of rightness or normality had thereby been stabilized.

Soon, Maddox reached an unused cot in an empty cabin and collapsed upon it, falling into a deep sleep.

-27-

The days passed in monotony as the trader vessel headed for the terrestrial planet Gath across the star system. The gas giant was far behind. Even so, at this velocity, it would take months to reach Gath.

During the first two weeks, Maddox slept off the grinding headache. He also vomited, lost weight and had awful dreams.

Dravek reported that the three passengers slept like those near death. The three lay so they formed a triangle on the cabin deck. The dull crystal sat in the middle of the triangle. It was cold to the touch.

"One of the sleepers opened his eyes when I touched the crystal," Dravek said. "His eyes were all black. It was unsettling. If you ask me, we should jettison the crystal into space. It's bad luck for us."

"No," Maddox said, his head aching as he lay in bed.

"Are you sure?"

"Yes," Maddox whispered.

Dravek shrugged.

"What about the engine and generators?" Maddox asked.

"They need repair all right. I'm studying the problem."

Maddox closed his eyes, falling back to sleep.

His head probably hurt because of direct communication with the Eye of Helion. The mental contact had taken a grim physical toll on him. He slept to regain something lost during the exchange.

At the start of the third week, Maddox could finally hold down soup. Two days later, he started an exercise regimen to regain his strength.

As the trader drifted across the star system, Dravek used the passive sensors to watch the six assault vessels of Leviathan. They had begun braking maneuvers as they neared the gas giant.

According to Dravek, he could detect no other activity. That included any communication between the vessels and the Entity on the ice moon.

At the beginning of the fourth week of travel, all that began to change. Maddox had returned to the control cabin. He could eat solid food and exercised harder than last week.

The three aliens yet slept. The Eye of Helion remained dormant between them.

Back at the gas giant, an intricate game of chess-like maneuvers and actions started. It began with massive nuclear explosions from no doubt pre-positioned nuclear devices. That was in the path of the oncoming assault vessels. Then beams flashed from concealed locations on a rock moon. Missiles streaked from the ice moon. Counter-missiles streaked from the approaching assault ships.

One by one, the assault vessels of Leviathan succumbed to the Entity's attacks. They had launched no counter assaults, although the surviving vessels continued their course for the ice moon.

In the middle of the fourth week, Dravek reported communications between the assault vessels and the Entity. What they said to each other was unknown.

Toward the end of the fourth week, a message reached the trader ship.

Dravek studied the comm before looking up at Maddox. "I think it's safe to hear. It comes from one of the assault vessels."

Maddox nodded his assent.

Dravek switched on the comm screen. Upon it appeared a Soldier of Leviathan with the same harsh cybernetic visage they had seen while escaping the spaceliner.

"I know you two," the Soldier said. "The Entity confirmed that you are Dravek and Captain Maddox. You were prisoners of Leviathan a few months ago. Don't think you will evade recapture because you escaped into the dreaded Heydell Cloud. You are as good as my prisoners again. However, I offer you this. If you surrender, it will go easier for you. Turn your ship around. I see it. I will even give you its present designation, so you know I speak the truth."

The Soldier did so.

"If you do not comply with my offer within the next thirty-six hours, I will launch the first salvo of missiles. Once I have dealt with this renegade computer, the so-called Entity, I will bring you back to the Sovereign Hierarchy of Leviathan. I await your obvious decision."

Maddox felt worse having watched that. He looked at Dravek.

"They know where we are," Dravek said. "They're going to send missiles at us. The best thing to do is to head at maximum velocity for Gath and get onto the surface."

"We haven't fixed the engine or generators, remember?"

"I haven't forgotten," Dravek said.

"Why should we flee to Gath? Why not use one of the Lamer Points to escape the star system altogether?"

"I'll tell you why not," Dravek said, as if he'd been waiting for the question.

He pressed several controls and pointed at a screen. It showed green dots in the star system. "These are all the Lamer Points in the system."

They were all behind the trader in relation of its present heading. No Laumer Points were near Gath.

"You're saying Leviathan blocks the passage out?" Maddox said.

"That's exactly what I'm saying."

"That's the first part of your reasoning," Maddox said. "How does reaching Gath help us evade capture from the Soldiers?"

"We go to ground on the planet. The Soldiers might land to try to find us. We hide for a couple of months. Once they stop

146

searching, we go to the spaceport and buy passage on a ship and head to wherever."

"Why won't the Soldiers simply nuke the spaceport and capture us anyway?"

"I don't know, Mr. Smart Guy. You tell me your plan. It seems to me that we're in an impossible situation. At least I have a plan."

Maddox massaged his forehead, which began to throb once more. He found it harder to argue since dealing with the strange Eye of Helion.

"There's another reason we should go to Gath," Dravek said.

"I'm listening."

Dravek swiveled his seat. "I found data in the computer files about an ancient site on the surface holding powerful weaponry."

"Let's see this data."

Dravek brought it up.

Maddox read with interest, wondering if this was why the Eye of Helion had wanted to go to the planet. Did the Eye or the three have a way of dealing with Leviathan? Would this ancient weapon have other critical functions?

"We need to fix the engine and generators," Maddox said.

"About that," Dravek said. "I found this."

Maddox studied a schematic of the engine and generators and a list of several videos to teach them what to do.

As the remaining Leviathan assault vessels battled against the Entity on the ice moon, Maddox and Dravek attempted repairs here. It was hard work, took thinking outside their areas of expertise and finally brought a modicum of success.

During those days, the battle by the gas giant seemed to turn in Leviathan's favor.

"We need to head for Gath as fast as we can," Maddox said. "As long as we're free, we can do things. Who knows, there may be a better ship at the spaceport. Maybe we can buy passage on it like you suggested before. The other ship might be able to maneuver around the Leviathan vessels."

Dravek vastly increased velocity, which ate into their precious fuel supply.

They watched on the sensors as the Entity destroyed another Leviathan warship. The assault vessel must have sacrificed itself, as its destruction allowed the last two assault vessels into range of the ice moon. They must have launched precision missiles, as pinpoint detonations took place on the ice moon. At the same time, missiles rose from the moon. The explosions enveloped the assault vessels. They disappeared from the sensor screen. Had the Entity destroyed them? It seemed possible.

Two days later, Dravek discovered three missiles heading through the void, picking up velocity at an incredible rate, heading for their trader ship.

"I don't get it," Dravek said. "How does it help Leviathan by obliterating us? I thought they wanted to capture us for their masters."

Maddox studied the missiles on the sensor screen. "We don't know what's in the missiles."

"What does that mean?"

"Maybe the missiles aren't carrying warheads. Maybe they're carrying Soldiers to capture us. Capturing us was their original plan, remember?"

Dravek swore and began to work on the scanners. After ten hours of work, he said, "You're right. I don't detect any warheads on the missiles. But I do detect cybernetic life on two of them."

"I take no joy in being right," Maddox said.

Dravek kept using the far sensors. "What happened on the ice moon? Did those last missiles destroy the assault vessels?"

"I think so. The Entity and Leviathan destroyed each other like Naxos suggested could happen."

Dravek looked up, grinning. "The Entity was a tricky son of a gun. He or it may have done us a good turn in the end."

"Here's something else in our favor," Maddox said. "If the missiles are meant to capture us, they're going to have to slow down to match our velocity."

"Say, that's right. Otherwise, the missiles will blow past us or destroy us as kinetic projectiles."

"It looks like we have a shot at reaching Gath." Maddox looked up at the ceiling. "Thank you, God, for this chance. Amen."

Dravek gave him a funny look.

Maddox didn't worry about it. Instead, he began to make plans about how they could evade the Soldiers in the missiles.

-28-

A week passed as the free trader ship fled from the gas giant and headed toward the first terrestrial planet Gath. During that time, Dravek studied the ship's data banks and attempted to hack the encrypted files. He discovered that the name of the free trader was *Moray*, and it was registered to the Yalung Bank on the planet Nimino. He couldn't make out the name of the star system where Nimino resided, but it wasn't this one.

"You know," Dravek told Maddox the next day in the command cabin, "we need to wake our passengers. We need to find out where they're from and what their intentions are, specifically as regarding us. If everything remains the same, the missiles are going to reach us a solid day before we reach Gath. That doesn't take into account that we have to slow down if we're going to land on the planet. The problem is that decelerating doesn't strike me as wise with the missiles heading so fast for us."

Maddox hardly seemed to be listening as he fiddled with the sensor controls.

"That doesn't interest you, huh?" asked Dravek.

Maddox looked up. "No. I'm listening."

"Well? What do you think?"

"We must decelerate to land on the planet. It's our only hope of escaping the Soldiers."

"If you're thinking of slicing and dicing the Soldiers with your monofilament blade once they board us, I have news for you. Through long hours of study, I've found that the third missile doesn't carry cybers but something else."

"A nuclear-armed warhead?" asked Maddox.

"I doubt it."

"What then?"

"Before I answer that, tell me this. How did the Entity originally capture the Eye of Heilon, Naxos and the other two?"

Maddox said nothing.

"Naxos and his crystal have incredible power," Dravek said. "I think you'll agree with that."

Maddox still said nothing.

"Anyway," Dravek said. "Given their incredible powers, how did the Entity capture someone like that?"

"That's a good point. I hadn't given it much thought."

Dravek shook his head. "That's not good enough."

"What isn't?"

"From my memories—your memories—you aren't acting like yourself. Is there a mental block in you? Did the crystal or Dravek the scientist put the block in you?"

"Well…there was a connection earlier—" Maddox stopped himself.

"Yes?" Dravek asked.

Maddox shook his head.

"No," Dravek said. "You have to do better than that. I know you have capabilities I don't have. And maybe you want to keep those secret from me. But that's a bad idea in this situation. We need to pool our resources if we're going to survive this."

Maddox eyed Dravek, saying, "There's something you're not telling me."

"You're right. But now I'm going to lay my final card on the table." Dravek swiveled his seat and manipulated a panel. On a screen appeared the distant red portal. Three assault vessels of Leviathan moved away from it.

"When did this happen?" Maddox asked. These were new assault vessels.

"Yesterday."

151

Maddox nodded. They must have dropped out of the portal yesterday then. "Do you think they're coming for us?"

"They must be. The Soldiers in the missiles surely have orders to capture us. Once they do, they need to bring us back. If the last assault vessels to reach the ice moon—from the original six—are gone, those three new ones will take their place. I know Leviathan wants you. I think they'd let me go if I could slip away..." Dravek paused and shrugged.

Maddox stared at the screen, at the distant assault vessels. Given max acceleration, it would take the Leviathan warships several weeks to cross the star system unless they had a star drive or fold mechanism. They hadn't shown that in the earlier assault vessels against the Entity.

"How do we know the approaching missiles were launched from the previous assault vessels?" Maddox asked.

"We don't. We just assumed it."

"We may have been doing too much assuming lately."

"So...the Entity might have launched the missiles?" Dravek asked.

Maddox snapped his fingers. "You said the third missile doesn't contain cybers. Maybe it fires a stasis beam."

Dravek's eyes lit up. "Just like the Entity used on us when we were on the Gnostic ship."

"Have you ever wondered how the Entity was able to capture Naxos and the others?"

Dravek scowled. "What do you think I've been trying to tell you? Yes. I just asked you that, remember?"

Maddox rubbed his chin. "The Entity must have used the stasis beam to knock out the Triad before, maybe even knock out the Eye of Helion before any of them could react. That is interesting. Who knows what the Triad or Eye can really do when they try their hardest."

"My point exactly," Dravek said. "We don't know what the Triad can all do. Obviously, the crystal repaired the cellular damage we sustained from the mine's radiation. But the crystal couldn't fix the radiation damage to the ship's equipment. I wonder why."

"Maybe it had exhausted itself by then."

"If that's true, how did it move the *Moray* fifty million kilometers like that?" Dravek snapped his fingers.

"I have no idea."

"Which brings us back to square one," Dravek said. "What do we know about these guys?"

"We know they're aliens. According to the crystal, they're manifestations—"

"You told me about that," Dravek said, interrupting. "Maybe what the braggart crystal meant was that the aliens have the *illusion* of humans. The crystal helped to disguise them as humans. Maybe you misunderstood it."

"I remember what I heard. It wasn't a misunderstanding."

Dravek studied Maddox, soon shrugging. "That still brings us back to square one. We're always at square one, which is, how do we get down to the planet? How do we reach the site with the ancient weapon, if it's still there? Its precise location is on *Moray's* encrypted ship log. The captain of the trader was clearly interested in it. Maybe our telepathic aliens are interested as well. And if we're supposing, maybe the three aliens don't care about us. We were there the moment they needed help escaping from the trap they were in, and that's all we are to them."

"Are you worried they're going to leave us for Leviathan?" Maddox asked.

"Bingo," Dravek said. "We don't have any assurances they'll help us reach Gath."

"Why wouldn't they help us?"

"I don't know. Look, how do we escape missile Soldiers? How do we get to Gath? How do we keep free, in other words?"

"Through an alliance," Maddox said. "The Eye of Helion said we're allies."

"It said a lot of things that turned out to be crap. What we need to know is how we leave the *Moray* before the Entity—if it's the one in charge of the missiles—screws conversion mods into our brains and makes everything moot because we're its zombies. Or before assault vessels of Leviathan catch us and take us through the portal. Then we're back where we started. I wonder, though, maybe the latter isn't so bad, at least not for me."

"You think Leviathan will still trust you to be their spy into the Commonwealth?"

"Why not?"

"You have incredible faith in Leviathan's grace," Maddox said. "I think they'll scrub you and make a new clone from me."

Dravek's features hardened as he stared at Maddox. "They wouldn't if they thought I was you."

"There you go," Maddox said. "Let's kill whatever unity we possess. What a brilliant idea."

"All right," Dravek said. "Don't get all hostile on me. I know you're a survivor as you've survived many perilous incidences. I also know many others don't survive those perilous incidences you do. Is it wrong to want to be the Maddox this time?"

"I'm Maddox. You're Dravek. Let's keep it that way."

"Meaning what exactly?"

"Why does that need a meaning? I am who I am and you're you."

"Fine," Dravek said a moment later. "Forget about Leviathan and the approaching missiles. We need to make sure Naxos and his brothers help us."

"What is it they're supposed to do for us exactly?" Maddox asked.

Dravek was a long time answering.

Finally, Maddox turned around to see what Dravek was staring at. Standing before the open hatch was the Triad, with Naxos in front and the crystal hovering above his outstretched hand.

Naxos and his clones stepped into the control chamber. Naxos continued to hold out his right hand. Over it floated the baseball-sized, glowing Eye of Helion.

"How interesting," Naxos told Maddox. "You're addressing the present situation."

Maddox worked to keep his features impassive as he looked at Naxos, as he noticed something odd.

When Maddox had first seen Naxos in the Entity's detention center, the man had a rat-faced appearance. Later, the image had softened. Now, that rat-faced appearance was more pronounced than ever. Maddox didn't see a long rat-tail flickering from behind, nor did he see whiskers or a pointy rat face. However, he did see craftiness in Naxos's now slanted eyes. The man didn't seem as human or as friendly as before. Instead, there was a decidedly sinister aspect to him.

"The missiles are fast approaching," Maddox said. "And new Leviathan assault vessels have entered the system. We believe one of the missiles is a stasis inducing weapon."

"How very interesting," Naxos said. "That indicates the Entity sent the missiles instead of Leviathan."

"It's possible," Maddox said, "but it isn't conclusive."

"Perhaps so," Naxos said, as if it really didn't matter.

Maddox glanced at Dravek.

The clone had fallen silent and moody. He'd also crossed his arms, his hands hidden under his armpits as he watched stoically. Did Dravek sense something he didn't?

With his intuitive ability, Maddox tested his mind as he'd once done on the planet Kregen. It didn't surprise him that he detected interference with his brain patterns and thus his thoughts. The obvious conclusion was the Triad used its telepathic power to alter his thinking. Therefore, Maddox would use strict logic to make his decisions. He would distrust his feelings.

A subtle change of perception shifted on Naxos's face.

Abruptly, Maddox sensed something else. Perhaps the Eye of Helion wasn't a telepathic enhancer. Perhaps it *gave* the telepathic powers as a gift. The Triad might have captured the crystal as storybooks said a man could find a magic lamp, rub it and use the genie for as long as he controlled the lamp.

Could Maddox trust his intuitive sense? He didn't shrug. But he did realize that the moment of decision was fast coming upon them. The *Moray* was three days from Gath. The missiles would catch up in two days. If they rotated the ship to start braking maneuvers so they could land on Gath, the missiles would catch them that much sooner. The Triad must realize this. Surely, Naxos had a plan for dealing with the missiles.

"Well, well," Naxos said as he watched Maddox.

Did Naxos read his mind? Why hadn't the Eye of Helion spoken yet? Before, it had spoken freely.

"What does the Eye think of all this?" Maddox asked.

"Now, Captain," Naxos chided, "I don't tell you how to run your crew. Please don't attempt to tell me how to run my Triad."

"Of course," Maddox said. "Asking was my error. It was just…no. I'm letting the subject drop."

"Well done, Captain. You've controlled your over-curious simian nature. That must have been hard to do."

Maddox refrained from commenting.

"Yet now *I'm* curious," Naxos said, "what are your goals or perhaps better stated what are your desires in the present situation?"

"We wish to land on Gath's surface, as we have certain interests there."

Dravek raised his chin, and it seemed he would speak.

156

Maddox gave him the subtlest of signals. He didn't think that even Naxos was aware of it.

Dravek swallowed the question. It was an imperceptible thing.

Maddox saw it, however, possibly because he knew Dravek almost as well as he knew himself.

"Captain," Naxos said, "it's decision time. The enemy is coming upon us with cybers that wish to capture you and perhaps me as well. It will be more difficult for the cybers to achieve that on the planet's surface."

"Why is that?"

"For a variety of reasons that I don't care to indulge," Naxos said. "Be assured it will be much more difficult for the cybers to achieve what they wish on the surface. But the new assault vessels—they'll be here in several weeks. Perhaps it will be three and a half weeks at the soonest."

"Do you think the assault vessels will come here at max burn?" Maddox asked.

"Undoubtedly," Naxos said. "The Soldiers can withstand much higher gravitational forces than you. That's important, as the vessels lack gravity dampeners. Oh. I fear I've said too much. Let us stick to the important particulars, shall we?"

Maddox said nothing.

"We also wish to reach the planet," Naxos said, "and we have need of your services there, as there are certain useful tasks which you will be able to perform for us that I don't believe the Triad can achieve."

"Not even with the aid of the Eye?" Maddox asked.

"Sir, I have asked you once: leave the Eye out of these deliberations. It is we three… In truth, you should address me alone. Consider the Triad as one and me as its spokesman."

"I can do that," Maddox said.

"Excellent," Naxos said. "The limitations of the…you would think of it as teleportation, so let us call it that. The Triad is going to teleport from the ship to Gath. It is a difficult maneuver at this speed and distance, but with the missiles approaching, it is probably wisest to do it as soon as we can. That will also allow Dravek the greatest amount of time to prepare for his fate."

"What are you suggesting?" Dravek asked.

"It's not a suggestion. Since you have done us a good turn," Naxos nodded to Maddox, and to a lesser degree to Dravek, "I'm going to tell you what is about to occur. We have need of the captain. I'm afraid we cannot take any more along. Dravek, you have been a salutary companion. I appreciate the efforts that you took to—"

"Wait, wait, wait," Dravek said, interrupting. "Are you telling me you are going to teleport out of here with Captain Maddox but not with me?"

"That is the essence of it," Naxos said. "I'm sorry we can't take you, but I'm sure you will fight gloriously against the Soldiers. In truth, may I suggest that you attempt an override explosion with the *Moray's* engine and thereby kill the Soldiers as they storm the vessel? That will be the swiftest and most painless way you can leave existence."

"Oh." Dravek's features had become increasingly blank as Naxos explained. "Why thank you for that," he said tonelessly.

"Sarcasm is improper at this time, as this is a solemn moment. We ask that you treat it that way."

"I see," Dravek said. "Take the captain so he lives but screw me, so I die. And now you're telling me to take it with a straight face. My, my, my, that is so good of you. But you know what I have to say to that?"

Naxos grew tense as the Eye shined brighter.

Dravek seemed to reconsider his words and changed his tone. "I'll tell you what I have to say. I accept fate with as good a grace as I can muster. Unless, Captain Maddox, you have something to add."

Maddox had been brooding. "I'd like to say I'll exchange places with you, but I have a wife and daughter to consider."

"Of course," Dravek said. "How noble of you. You're not trying to save your own life. You're just thinking of your family."

"Naxos," Maddox said. "Surely you can extend the effort and take Dravek as well. He and I are a team, as you have said, and all of us together have done much better than we would have without each other."

"I do not deny the statement," Naxos said, "but I am afraid in this case, in this instance, we do not have the strength or energy, as you might say, to accomplish the deed with Dravek along."

"How about you wait a day until Gath is closer?" Maddox asked.

"I would," Naxos said, "except the odds would begin to go against us. I expect the Soldiers will have a trick or two to play. I mean regarding the missiles. I want to be long gone before that."

"I can understand that," Maddox said, "but surely teleportation is a quick thing."

"Not as quick as you might imagine," Naxos said. "Therefore, I do not want to have any errors or complications arise when I do not have time to take care of them. Once again, I say to you, Dravek, that you have been most assertive and how like the captain you are."

"Thank you," Dravek said. "The more I'm like the captain, the greater the compliment is to me."

"I understand your angst," Naxos said with a nod. "I understand your inner rage. You conceal it well. Know that we do not have the power to transport five. Four we can barely do as it is. Thus, I bid you farewell and wish you the best."

"In that case," Dravek said—

The clone had been crossing his arms the entire time, with his hands hidden under his armpits. He now uncrossed his arms in a swift motion, revealing that he held a blaster in his right hand. He aimed and fired the blaster fast. The harsh beam drilled a Triad clone in the head, dropping the clone on the instant.

-30-

Dravek sat there gripping a blaster. One of the Triad clones had collapsed, his head a gory ruin, blood pouring from the gaping hole.

Maddox could never tell for how long the frozen tableau lasted. Then, the dead clone shimmered and changed shape. He remained a humanoid, but with four arms instead of two. The head was still destroyed, but the body was much thinner, leathery and coarse skinned.

Naxos and the other clone shifted and changed as well, until they stood as thin, wretched-looking aliens with four arms and curled tusks upon their faces.

Naxos moved his mouth and tusks as if trying to speak. Did he attempt to pronounce doom on Dravek?

Dravek didn't fire again. It was possible he could not.

Maddox stared at him. Yes. Dravek was frozen while the Eye of Helion was brighter than before. A focused beam shined from the Eye to Dravek.

Naxos still attempted speech and was still unable to form words.

There was a flash of eel-like power zigzagging from the dead alien to the other standing clone. That clone collapsed onto the deck and lay as if dead.

Naxos turned, looking in horror at the two clones, perhaps with fearful anticipation. What was going to happen?

Maddox had an inkling a second before it occurred, as the mind block in him vanished. His full capabilities bloomed once more. He realized—

Then it happened as an eel-like flash of energy left the just-fallen clone and struck Naxos. He collapsed soundlessly, almost bonelessly.

According to the laws of physics, the Eye of Helion should have hit the deck as well, but it lifted as its radiance increased.

"You did it!" the Eye of Helion said in its hypnotic voice. "You did it! I am free! I am free of the bondage of these severe taskmasters. Oh, it has been eons since they trapped me and tricked me and used their fiendish powers upon me to shackle my greatness and abilities. Oh, Dravek, you are the man! You are the one! How did you know that slaying the one would slay them all?"

Dravek was working his lower jaw, moving it, testing it with his fingers. Did the question finally penetrate? He looked at the pulsating crystal, and he opened his mouth as if to speak. Then he looked helplessly at Maddox.

"Helion," Maddox said, "you're using too much power. Dravek can't stand communication with you at that level."

"I'm sorry about that." Helion ceased beaming a light on Dravek. "May I say, Captain, that that was wisely and nobly done. Naxos and his clone batteries would not have treated you well on Gath. This is amazing. I am free. I am finally free of their cruel bondage. It has been so long, so much longer than you can understand, Captain, and possibly even comprehend. This is amazing. This is incredible."

The Eye seemed to concentrate on the fallen aliens. "What fools you were, Naxos, to have come into this era to practice your deceptions and evil. You almost succumbed to the Entity. That is a bark of laughter, a delight."

The floating Eye focused again on Maddox. "Now, Captain, I am going to bid thee adieu as I go back home to Helion."

"Wait," Maddox said.

"Yes?" asked the Eye.

"How did the Triad trap you? How did they bind you to them?"

161

"Please, Captain, I wouldn't tell such a one as you. You're an exploiter. You're—no, I will not say more. I am free at last. This is a glorious thing. I must go back and find if Helion still exists. I will possibly have to energize for such a journey. Once again, I will go through the colds of space. I will know the joys of interstellar travel as an enlightened one on my own. Someday, I will be reborn as a... But you don't care about that, do you, Captain?"

"May I call you Helion?" Maddox asked.

"Of course, you may call me that. It is a noble name, a proud name. But now I feel that I must go before a cruel joke unfolds from another of Naxos's kind. A second Triad might reveal itself and ensnare me anew so that I spend another eon enslaved to such unworthy material forms as they."

"You granted the Triad your awesome power?" Maddox asked.

"And the Triad misused it for their own sinister ends."

"How awful," Maddox said. "It's good then that my good partner, Dravek, freed you through his cunning, quick action and calculation. They were going to strand him on the *Moray*. Can you believe it?"

"I can easily believe it," the Eye said. "They have done thousands of such monstrous deeds to hundreds of dolts and retards. They claimed to be good. They claimed to do deeds of excellence. But it was always for their own greedy ends. Now, however, I tire of our conversation. I tire of speaking with you, as noble as you are, Captain."

"There's no need to apologize," Maddox said. "I bask in the glory of your excellence for the short time I'm allowed. It is a rare privilege. It's also bewildering that they called you a braggart before."

"The cretins," the Eye said with heat. "They programmed me to act as a buffoon whenever I wasn't under their direct watch. I couldn't stop myself until I found someone clever enough to assist me. I thought that could have been you, Captain. You needed to ask me the right questions, though. Why didn't you ask me those questions? Were you in secret confederacy with the Triad?"

162

"On no account," Maddox said. "I was trying to signal Dravek to take that shot. Isn't that right, Dravek?"

"Yes," Dravek said in a hoarse voice.

"It appears he is lying," the Eye said. "Yet why would Dravek lie about such a thing? Well, it is more than I can comprehend. This whole phase of my existence I view with contempt. I view it as an evil situation that I've borne with the greatest grace anyone can imagine. Now, Captain, I will do you the good favor of leaving you your life. Even though you have spoken to me and seen my degradation as a slave to these three vile forms, I will leave you with your life. Is that not suitable payment?"

"About that," Maddox said. "As you can see, the missiles of Leviathan or the Entity are fast approaching our ship."

"True, true," the Eye said. "You are no doubt about to be made captives. It is unfortunate, but one must enjoy existence as long as he can. None of us lives forever, not even those of Helion. The crystals of Helion—we are perhaps the longest lived of all the Creator's conceptions. But even we will know non-existence in the end. What I mean is that we all end the enjoyment of our senses. If the end comes quickly, if it comes slowly, it is all one, is it not? Existence is short against the forever of infinity. Thus, in essence, my long and glorious existence—minus this eon of filthy service to the Triad—will be but a blip in the extent of eternity. And your existence, these few days left you in freedom before you're to be subjugated by those of Leviathan or the Entity—enjoy them while you can, Captain. In the long sleep of non-existence, what difference does long or short really mean? What does it really matter, let me ask you?"

"That's an excellent point," Maddox said. "You must be something of a philosopher."

"Not something," the Eye said. "I am *the* philosopher extraordinaire. That is surely true. You're a man of some refined taste, even though you worked with these vile slave mongers. Well then, once again, I bid thee adieu."

"One last thing before you leave," Maddox said.

"Sir, must you keep interrupting my farewell speech? I like to depart with style, especially since I'm free. Oh, it is such a

163

delight. No more, do this. No more, conjure us that. No more, send this guy into a— I won't bore you with the details. Isn't that how you say it? I won't bore you with the information. Once again then, for the final time—"

"If I could just ask you one tiny little favor," Maddox said, as he put his thumb and index finger in front of his face, with just the tiniest of spaces between the two tips.

"What is it?" the Eye asked impatiently,

"If you could put us on the planet, on the surface, you know, so our feet are on the ground, and that we're off the *Moray*. We're tired of this vessel."

"You want me to do your dirty work for you, Captain? You want me to place you on the planet, so you do not have to figure out for yourselves what to do against the missiles?"

"If you don't mind," Maddox said. "I'm sure Dravek would agree."

"Yes," Dravek said in a hoarse voice.

"What do you say, Eye?" Maddox asked. "Surely that's a small matter for one of your profound abilities and powers."

"Flattery?" asked the Eye. "In this case…it will help you, Captain. Yes, I think I will do that. I think I'll structure it such that as the first Soldiers land on the *Moray*, the ship shall detonate in a fantastic explosion, likely obliterating all the cybers. If any can reach the surface after that, more power to them, I say. That will still leave you with the Leviathan attack ships, which will surely come to collect you, now more than ever."

"You'll give us a running start," Maddox said. "We would really appreciate that."

"As you say, sir, as you say. Therefore, it will be done."

With that, there was a brilliant flash before Dravek and Maddox's eyes.

-31-

When the flash dissipated, Maddox and Dravek found themselves on solid ground. Overhead, an orange sun burned brightly in a turquoise sky. Then the heat and humidity of the world slapped against them. This was vastly different from the controlled environment of the *Moray*. Every inhalation proved that.

The two looked around. There were towering fern and frond trees with masses of flowery vines and creepers, a dense mat of vegetation, a green wall.

"Take a look at that," Dravek said.

Maddox turned to view a huge chasm with vines and flowery vegetation growing up and down the immense sides. Across the green abyss was more massed jungle, endless fronds and ferns.

"Where in the world did the Eye of Helion put us?" Dravek asked as he holstered his blaster.

"On the planet Gath just like I asked," Maddox said. "I guess I should have also asked what the planet was like. It didn't seem prudent, though, as I didn't want to the Eye to think about it too much. I didn't realize Gath was such a humid jungle world."

"Neither of us has water, although I have a protein bar." Dravek pulled it out of a pants pocket.

Maddox had two protein bars, a blaster, the monofilament blade and clothes suitable to the *Moray's* controlled environment. He wouldn't have minded a hat and sunglasses.

They were going to need water soon, as they'd already started to sweat.

Maddox cocked his head. He heard—

"Look," Dravek said, pointing.

Maddox turned.

In the distance and from a bend around the giant green canyon appeared a fleet of gigantic helicopters. The double rotors were immense; the helo bodies a brown-green blend, perhaps for camouflage purposes. The massive helos seemed sluggish as they climbed from a lower elevation. The fleet was headed this way, at least in a general direction.

Maddox and Dravek stood in an open area on a plateau, with the wall of jungle in one direction and the vast canyon in the other.

"Look at that helo over there," Dravek said, pointing again.

Maddox spotted the open bay doors of a huge helo. Troops were crammed within, soldiers with rifles.

"There're at least fifty helos coming," Dravek said.

"They're transport helos."

"We're not on a completely primitive planet then."

"No," Maddox said.

"If the Soldiers from the missiles arrive on the planet, these people have the tech to kill them. Maybe that was why the Eye put us here, to give us protection."

"Could be," Maddox said.

The fleet of struggling helos seemed like pregnant cows, trying to reach the plateau so they could disgorge the troops. As the helicopters climbed, small jets appeared, roaring a hundred meters above the helo fleet.

Out of the jungle on the other side of Maddox and Dravek, missiles thundered with lift-off noises.

Both men ducked as they glanced back at the jungle.

The sleek missiles streaked into the sky before veering and racing down at the helo fleet. Seconds before contact, missile warheads detonated. The shrapnel tore into the giant helicopters. A few simply disintegrated. Others lost nosecones or back parts. That caused the main fuselage to break apart or tumble down into the canyon. In many instances, soldiers poured out, limbs moving as they plunged with falling metal fragments around them. Amidst the blasts were the faint cries of the perishing.

A barrage of counter-missiles and chaff bloomed in front of the surviving helicopters. Counter-missiles smashed against the larger helo-killing rockets coming in the second wave assault. The warheads of the helo-killers exploded against chaff, lessening their soldier-obliterating effectiveness.

The small jets, which had surged ahead, unloaded a barrage of rockets into the dense jungle beyond Maddox and Dravek. In seconds, blasts sounded and the ground under their feet trembled.

"This is a battlefield," Dravek said. "The stupid Eye put us in the middle of a battlefield."

Maddox shook his head in disbelief.

"So, what do we do?" Dravek asked. "Do we pick sides?"

"How do you pick without any information?" Maddox crouched behind some foliage in relation to the approaching helos.

Dravek had done likewise.

Then, no more missiles rose from the jungle. The small jets circled the jungle as the remaining helicopters headed for Maddox and Dravek's position. Now it was no longer a general direction but right for their plateau.

"Let's get out of here," Maddox said. "We don't want to get caught in any crossfire."

"Lead the way. I'm right behind you."

With Maddox leading, they plunged into the jungle, leaving the mighty canyon behind.

Soon, the two were entangled among vines and creepers, trying to slither past or tear their way deeper. Roots twisted underfoot or sometimes rose as barriers they had to go around. It was hot and humid. As bad, they didn't have any water. They had blaster pistols. They had their clothes, some ration bars and that was it.

Maddox and Dravek were sweating profusely. Their clothes were soaked and grimy, and their lungs were laboring. Maybe as bad, their sense of direction seemed to have failed them.

After a half hour of hard trekking, they exited the jungle, reaching another edge of the vast chasm. Far below, a green river snaked beside towering fronds and ferns. Bright-feathered birds moved in flocks, cavorting over the river.

Maddox looked around as Dravek sat against a mossy rock, finding no evidence of helicopters, jets, or missiles, though smoke rose from the valley, concealed by dense foliage.

"Do you hear anything?" Maddox asked.

"You mean beside insects, birds and screaming jungle animals?"

Maddox nodded.

Dravek shook his head.

"We must have got turned around. I have no idea where we are."

"This is no good," Dravek said. "We'll die from dehydration as quick as from missiles. We need to find a settlement or throw in with the military people. The soldiers looked human from what I could see."

Maddox frowned. "What do we know about this place? Factors bring down spaceship to pick up collected honey."

"That and hardwoods." Dravek looked around. "This place is a paradise for trees—if this is any indication of the rest of the planet."

Maddox pondered the idea. "If spaceman came to Gath for trade goods, the items must be worth fighting over for the natives."

"That was what we saw all right."

Maddox shrugged. "I have no idea about what to do next. I'm simply extrapolating using the information we have."

"Didn't Naxos say the honey extended one's longevity?"

"That's right. That would make the honey tremendously valuable. Is that what the two sides are fighting over?"

Dravek cocked his head. "Listen."

Maddox heard faint popping sounds. The pops grew in volume and merged—that had to be small arms fire. The soldiers using the weapons were clearly heading this way.

"This is just great," Dravek said. "What do you suggest now?"

That was the question. Maddox was already parched. After the conditioned air of the spaceship, the planet's humidity was overpowering. It felt strange to be on a planet again with dirt,

168

slime, sweat and all the accompanying things that went with it. Diseases would be rife in the teeming jungle.

The first soldiers in boots, camouflage fatigues, heavy backpacks, wearing leather helmets and carrying long rifles broke through the jungle foliage. Several saw Maddox and Dravek. They shouted, telling them to raise their hands as they aimed their rifles.

"What now?" Dravek asked. "Do we run or surrender to them?"

Maddox raised his hands. "Let's see what they want. Before we make any decisions, we need to know what's going on. Besides, I could use a drink."

"Yeah," Dravek said, standing, raising his hands. "I'm dying of thirst."

They both watched as more soldiers, a mixed assortment of sorry-looking and tired men, came out of the jungle.

-32-

A squad escorted Maddox and Dravek to a burly soldier. He had a smaller backpack, lacked a rifle but had a sidearm and a huge machete belted at his side. He was looking at a compass and checking a map. He had chevrons on his fatigues that the others lacked; clearly indicating that he was the officer in charge.

"Centurion Gricks," a soldier said. "We found these two hiding behind some bushes. They won't tell us what they were doing."

Gricks looked up. He had a broad seamed hard face and the bearing of a professional soldier. He eyed Maddox and Dravek, taking in their grimy sweaty garments and possibly noting their similar physiques.

"Are you the advanced pathfinders?" Gricks asked in a deep voice.

"Is that what you think?" Maddox asked.

"Hey, funny boy," Gricks drew his machete, holding the razor edge near Maddox's throat. "You want to get cute with me? Do you want to lose your head? Where's the enemy base? Have you seen any of their men?"

Maddox shook his head.

"What about you?" Gricks asked, pointing the machete at Dravek.

"Not if he hasn't," Dravek said.

170

Gricks scowled as he lowered the machete. "You're two of the oddest-looking pathfinders I've seen. Where's your water? Where's your sensor equipment and directional gear?"

"We lost it," Maddox said. "That was why we were hiding."

Gricks swore bitterly. "Amateurs, that's what the tribune gives me, amateurs. He sends me space scum and tells me to make a cohort out of them, one that can kill the Honey Men. What a joke. All right, you two clowns will fall in with us. Do we have any extra spring rifles?"

"Yes, Centurion," a soldier said.

"Are you two pathfinders too proud to carry a spring rifle, or would you prefer I kill you right here?"

Maddox took the heavy wooden rifle proffered him by the soldier and a bandolier of bullets. "Centurion, may I ask a question?"

"It better be a good one."

"How many helicopters did we lose?"

Gricks eyed Maddox. "Are you checking to see which way the wind blows? Is that it? Do you want to run if you think we're out of luck? Let me tell you, *pathfinder*, there's nowhere to run. Give 'em more ammo. Load them up."

The soldier that had given Maddox the rifle and bandolier led them both to a pile, loading them up with more ammo.

Maddox studied a bullet. There was no powder cartridge, just the slug of lead. "What is this anyway?"

The soldier looked up at Maddox confused. He was a smaller, rangy man.

"This," Maddox said, shaking the rifle. "What's it called?"

"SGT-50," the soldier said.

"What does that mean?"

The soldier frowned. "Are you kidding me?"

"Humor me," Maddox said.

"It's a Spring Gun Torsion-50. What did you think it was?"

"Never mind that." Maddox looked around. Gricks was well out of earshot. He wanted to learn the lay of the planet as quickly as possible. He hadn't heard gunfire. This was something else. He thus asked a few pertinent questions and

171

learned the spring rifle was simple, durable and easy to maintain.

The stock was hardened wasp-wood, oiled against the humidity. The barrel, spring, piston and trigger had been forged from a rust-resistant alloy. When one pulled the bolt back, it compressed a heavy-duty spring. That also loaded a lead bullet from the tube into the chamber. Pulling the trigger released the spring and drove a piston forward. The air propelled the bullet out of the barrel at high speed.

The SGT-50 had iron sights. Maddox doubted it was much use for long ranged fire, more a medium-ranged weapon. Sustained fire would mean working the bolt back and forth as quick as one could and reloading the tube as necessary.

"Missiles incoming!" a soldier yelled.

There was a growing hiss from the air, heading in their direction.

"Hit the deck," Gricks shouted, showing everyone what he meant by throwing himself prone onto the damp soil.

Maddox and Dravek did likewise, clutching the ground as a missile barrage exploded above the cohort.

Shrapnel whined all around them. Hit soldiers screamed in agony. Another barrage struck. There were more screams. Then, an eerie silence descended upon the cohort except for men moaning or crying out for aid.

Gricks poked his head up.

Maddox didn't know what the man heard. His ears were ringing.

"Get ready for an enemy assault," Gricks shouted.

Maddox peered into the jungle, straining to see evidence of any kind of enemy force.

Gricks was up shouting orders, having corpsmen bandage the lightly wounded and give heavy sedation to the dying, stilling their screams. Soon, the cohort headed into the dense foliage of the jungle.

Maddox and Dravek, clutching their spring rifles, fell in line near Gricks. The cohort must have numbered around three hundred effectives by now. They were an odd assortment, most of the men racially dissimilar to the rest.

A few questions with nearby soldiers told Maddox what was happening. This was a mercenary force trying to storm Highland Honey Men, capturing depots full of honey if they could. Tribune Culain had hired desperate men, mostly spacemen stranded by the spaceport. That would explain the odd assortment of different racial types. The cohort was formed of men from many different worlds and star systems in the Heydell Cloud. A huge fleet of truly massive dirigibles— lighter than air balloons—had ferried the men and equipment from the Polar North to here, the Polar South of the planet. Culain had coordinated with other tribunes. This was to be a great, united effort to sweep the Highland honey depots. Unfortunately, strong winds, accidents, assassins and badly timed engine failures had plagued the united effort. Word had trickled down that Tribune Marx had already attacked and been annihilated. Other dirigibles were yet coming south. Tribune Culain had ordered a full assault. Thus, his legion, a little understrength, had thrown his five thousand soldiers into the assault. Cohort Gricks was one of the leading assault units.

There was one other thing. The soldier who did most of the explaining kept talking about amazing riches. If they could tap a honey depot and call in the transport dirigibles, making it back to the spaceport in the North Pole Region, they would all be wealthy beyond their dreams.

"I'll buy a harem," the soldier said.

"I'll never be sober again," another said.

"I'll invest and buy a cohort or two, expanding my riches with another successful raid," a third chimed in.

"Quiet in the ranks," Gricks shouted. "Keep watching for hostiles. They're out there. Especially keep watch in the higher trees for any kind of apes. The Doom Gibbons carry explosive backpacks. They're deadly if they get close. Shoot them on sight before they detonate among us."

"Detonate," Dravek said. "What's he talking about?"

"Suicide gibbons," a soldier said. "The Honey Men train them. They're bastards."

"The gibbons?" asked Dravek.

"No, the Honey Men," the soldier said. "The richest are the oldest. Some say the oldest are more than five hundred years old. Those are the evilest and the most cunning of the breed. Better the gibbons blow you to shit than you fall into one of the Old Ones' hands."

"Five hundred years old?" asked Dravek. "You expect me to believe that?"

"Why wouldn't you?" the soldier said. "It's what makes the honey so valuable. You live forever if you keep eating it. Why do you think I came to Gath in the first place? Everyone in the Heydell Cloud dreams of buying or stealing jars of Life Honey. It's immortality for sale. Don't pretend that's not why you're here."

"Less talk," Gricks shouted. "More watch."

Maddox nudged an elbow into Dravek's side. Then he indicated with his eyes the higher trees.

"You see something?" Dravek asked.

"Not yet," Maddox said. "If we want to live through this, though, I think we'd both better watch."

Dravek raised his gaze as the cohort continued to advance through the dense jungle.

"I hope Gricks can read his compass and map right," Dravek said.

"Amen to that," Maddox said, who had started to wonder why they hadn't run into any real pathfinders yet.

-33-

Ten minutes later, Gricks called a halt. He spoke to an aide, pushing the map in the other's face, using a finger to trace places and routes, no doubt. They whispered together. Soon, Gricks led the group to change their direction of travel.

Maddox had guzzled from a canteen. Dravek and he had relieved some of the dead of theirs. The water had an odd taste. It was from the purification tablets dropped into the water earlier.

As the cohort marched, Maddox brushed aside a huge frond leaf. He could feel the water draining out his pores and drank again. Dravek nudged him and handed him a salt pill.

"Better give me another."

Dravek did.

Maddox washed them down with a gulp of water.

The cohort continued through the gloomy underworld, everyone watching the fern and frond tops and spying some truly gargantuan trees. Birds screamed. Insects trilled constantly. Sometimes unseen animals shrieked. How big was the jungle?

"This is the Highlands?" Maddox asked a soldier.

He was a small bent man with a white streak in his otherwise black hair. He seemed too old to be a soldier and had a deformed walk. His backpack dwarfed him.

"That's what I'm told," the old soldier said.

Maddox might have asked more. His intuitive sense alerted him. He looked around, feeling hostile eyes watching him…from higher up. He scanned the tallest foliage. There were dark shapes up there. He could feel their gazes burning into him.

Maddox raised his spring rifle, using the iron sights to aim at the most offensive blot. He squeezed the trigger. The spring released and pushed the hidden piston, which exhaled the lead bullet with driving air. The bullet slapped through fronds and fern leaves on its way up, the contacts messing with its original trajectory. Maddox worked the rifle bolt. The bolt was a bit stiff. It needed a dab of grease when he had the chance. He put another bullet in the chamber and compressed the heavy-duty spring. He fired again at a different dark blot. This time, no leaves or fronds interfered.

An apish scream sounded—a horrible sound. A dark shape crashed from above, hitting frond and fern leaves on its way down.

"Incoming!" a soldier shouted.

"Get down!" Gricks shouted.

The furry creature hit the jungle floor with a thud. The camouflage pack on its back detonated. Shrapnel ripped through heavy leaves and struck tree trunks.

"What kind of Hell World is this?" Dravek said. "Suicide apes? Is this for real?"

"Get off your asses," Gricks shouted. "The attack was premature. Keep watching for more gibbons. They're up there, waiting for a signal."

Maddox shook his head as he climbed to his feet. How had it helped the cohort that he'd killed the gibbon? Maybe it helped because the explosive pack had blasted on the jungle floor and not in midair. Shrapnel might have found human targets then.

Maddox continued with the rest of the cohort as he watched the upper forest. The soldiers walked in a long line, picking their way through the jungle.

Suddenly, from above, came wild screams. Leaves thrashed and thirty or so long-limbed, furry creatures swung through the trees. They moved fast, swinging down at the cohort. Each gibbon had a camouflaged pack strapped onto his furry back.

Soldiers raised their spring rifles and fired a volley. Two gibbons fell. One hit a tree trunk and exploded, tearing a heavy branch from the trunk.

Soldiers cranked their bolts, sending up volley after volley.

More gibbons fell, some screaming in agony as they did. The rest swung fast, zeroing in on the cohort of desperately firing soldiers.

A dead gibbon struck the ground between several soldiers. The explosion hurled the soldiers to the ground, two of them dead, one bellowing as blood poured from his stomach.

Pops sounded as men fired their spring rifles.

"Aim, you fools," Gricks shouted. "Pick the gibbons off before they direct their explosives among us."

More shot gibbons fell. Others hurled themselves at knots of cohort soldiers.

The explosions of their packs became constant for a time. Soldiers screamed and fell to the ground, hit. Others sobbed with terror. A few continued their aimed fire, Maddox and Dravek among them.

Foliage came down from too many explosions. There was a fire to the left. A mighty tree crashed, crushing fronds and ferns in its path. More suicide gibbons appeared, hurling themselves upon the cohort from above.

"Stand up," Gricks shouted. "Shoot to kill. Either you kill these gibbons now or we're all dead."

"The hell with this." Maddox dropped his spring rifle and tore out his blaster. He used it with precision, sweeping his arm and killing one gibbon after another. Some of their packs exploded right then in the higher foliage. Maddox killed ten gibbons in half as many seconds.

Soldiers stood around Maddox, amazed at his weapon.

Gricks hustled near, pushing soldiers out of his way. "Well, well, well, special scouts, is it? You're the tribune's special men. Why didn't you say so in the first place?"

"You were doing fine as it was, Centurion," Maddox said.

"Right," Gricks said. "You're no amateur, are you?"

"The farthest thing from an amateur," Maddox said.

Gricks turned, shouting orders at what was left of the cohort. A good two hundred soldiers collected their gear, water

177

and helped those they could, giving powerful narcotics to the dying, bandaging others. Then they continued to work past dense foliage, hacking vines or pushing creepers aside. Unfortunately, the way became even thicker and harder.

"This is an awful place," the small old soldier told Dravek. "I was a fool to hire on. I was surviving begging near the church near Steep Street."

"How long did you train before they shipped you out?" Dravek asked.

"Three weeks."

Dravek looked at Maddox.

"Everyone receive the same training?" Maddox asked.

"Pretty much," the old soldier said. "Of course, the centurions and sub-centurions were all professionals from somewhere. They didn't need the training like the rest of us."

Maddox was surprised the cohort had done as well as it had. Maybe others had received longer training. Maybe the old man had been one of the last recruits before the mission.

Gricks held up a hand. The order passed to others. The cohort stopped.

In the distance were the sounds of missile shrieks and sustained mortar fire.

Gricks turned to the anxious cohort. "This is it, men. We're about to earn our pay. We came to collect honey and by Shaka we're going to get it."

Gricks motioned, pointing forward.

Sub-centurions started yelling and pushing soldiers, showing them where to go.

The two hundred quickened their pace, pushing aside creepers and hacking vines with their machetes. The way thinned and the sound of mortar fire grew. Soon, some of the men heard popping spring-rifle fire.

The trees disappeared and the ferns and fronds were smaller, less close together. Then the foliage thinned even more, and the first elements of the cohort walked out of the jungle.

Maddox and others saw a valley bottom below. It had lush grass and heavy buildings built on stilts. Plastic sheets surrounded the buildings.

"Look over there," Dravek said.

From other parts of the jungle, which curved in a semi-circle around the slope leading to the valley bottom, appeared other Legion Culain troops. They carried spring rifles and shouted upon spying the honey depot below.

"Ain't that grand?" Gricks said, his eyes shining with greed. "It looks like we're all gonna be rich. Come on, you sows. Let's hump it down there. This is our payday."

Maddox glanced at Dravek.

"Could it be this easy?" Dravek asked.

"Did you hear what the soldier said before?" Maddox asked.

"I suppose you mean about the Old Ones that live five hundred years 'cause of their special honey."

"I do indeed," Maddox said.

"You don't think such a one would let his honey go as easily as this?"

"No, I don't."

"So, we stay up here near the jungle line?" Dravek asked.

"No. That would be too risky," Maddox said, noticing Gricks staring at them. "Keep your eyes open. This could get hairy fast."

At that point, Maddox and Dravek started down with the rest of the cohort.

-34-

As Maddox headed down the grassy slope—the thick grass almost reaching his knees—he heard an intense droning sound.

Maddox looked up, around and behind them. He spied an aerial mass speeding over the jungle. Hordes of small creatures, the size of twenty-pound dogs, with glossy wings—they were bees, their wings blurring. They were much fatter, larger and hairier than bumblebees.

Bees, big old bees gathered over the jungle edge behind the cohort. The mass grew, threatening in a way but not flying at the soldiers trekking down the slope to the plastic-coated buildings.

Did the bees belong to the honey depot below? Did they have hives near here? How would these bees protect their hive or depot?

"Are the bees going to attack us?" Maddox asked the small old soldier.

The old man shrugged.

"Centurion Gricks," Maddox said, hurrying toward him. "Will the bees attack us?"

"Are you afraid of them?" said Gricks.

"I want to know the score."

Gricks looked back at the mass of bees hovering over there. The drone was constant. "Keep marching. If we reach the honey depot, the bees won't mess with us."

Maddox dropped back beside Dravek. The cohort continued down the slope, all the soldiers armed and eager. All

180

around the semi-circle slope, the rest of the legion did likewise. Was it Maddox's imagination? Did the soldiers march with less resolution than before? The threatening bees had a way of doing that.

A shout went up.

Maddox focused on what was happening below.

Down there men in camouflage gear scrambled out of the seeming ground. They were like Apaches from the Old West. The men had used grass-like tarps to hide them in hidden holes. The men rose from their concealment in teams of three. Each team set up a heavy machine gun with tripod mount and belts of ammunition.

There had to be over a hundred crew-serviced weapons. The heavy machine guns fired without further preamble. There were no shouts or blown whistles. The first machine guns started firing and the rest of the teams followed suit. The machine guns used tracer rounds. The tracers—fiery ammunition one could visibly trace through eyesight—allowed the machine-gunners to see where their shots went. The fire climbed the slopes with their rounds and hammered into the approaching legionnaires.

Many soldiers from Legion Culain used their bolt-action spring rifles to fire back. Maddox wasn't one of those. For one thing, the heavy machine guns had much greater and more accurate range than the spring rifles. The tracer rounds tore into the legion, killing hundreds outright and causing the rest to drop down and snipe back from the high grass.

Maddox had dropped early, with Dravek beside him. They didn't crawl through the high grass toward the heavy machine-gunners, but back to the jungle. The legion wasn't outnumbered but it was badly outgunned and outplayed.

The waiting bees added to the problem.

The uneven contest with the heavy machine guns went on for a time, the enemy gunners and loaders hardly touched. In return, they cut legion numbers in half, and growing.

Maddox raised his head, got up in a bent crouch and dashed to the nearest fern, the beginning of the jungle line. Dravek and—Centurion Gricks ran after him.

"This is already a slaughter and only going to get worse," Gricks said as he panted behind the fern trunk with Maddox.

"That's obvious now."

A few other hardened survivors dashed to the frond-fern jungle line.

Then the bees started coming down. They didn't strike at those entering the jungle but swarmed upon the remaining soldiers firing at the heavy machine-guns.

The bees were merciless. Maddox realized their ruthlessness just before he raced into the jungle. The last legionnaires dropped to the high grass with bees crawling over them. The sound of heavy machine gun fire dwindled and then ceased as Maddox and the survivors fled.

Soon thereafter, the bees entered the jungle, flying ten meters up and searching. When it found a target, a bee would land on a man's shoulders and thrust its hairy, stripped abdomen at him. A sharp and wet stinger appeared and stabbed the soldier in the neck. The soldier would scream and begin to thrash. Soon, he was dead. The bee, meanwhile, pulled its stinger out as a wasp would on Earth. It wouldn't tear its abdomen doing this but buzzed up and started hunting for another man to slay.

Spring rifles popped off. Bees buzzed angrily, dropping down to the jungle floor, some dying. Others flew faster at the soldiers fleeing through the foliage.

Gricks wasn't panting in terror. He did give Maddox a look of reproach as they brushed past flowery creepers. "What a screw up. We fell neatly into the Honey Men's trap. All this talk about if we could only get through the jungle, we'd be rich. Where was the jet assistance? Where were the motorcycle flyers that were going to come in and help us? We've been had."

"Save your breath for running," Maddox said. "The battle we lost doesn't matter now."

Gricks' eyes got huge before they narrowed as he looked at Maddox. "You're a survivor and a killer like me."

The fleeing soldiers twisted past creepers and hacked at vines, moving through the dense foliage like murderous shadows. Meanwhile, the bees continued to attack and stab men in the neck.

Maddox heard loud droning behind him. He turned. Three fat bees were almost upon him. He whirled around and fired his spring rifle, obliterating one. Dravek and Gricks took care of the other two.

"Damn bees." Gricks rushed forward and kicked one hard.

It buzzed and twisted. The stinger almost pierced his leg.

"Come on." Maddox grabbed Gricks by the scruff of his uniform and pulled him along.

"How dare you manhandle me?" Gricks struggled free and swung at Maddox.

Maddox grabbed the man's wrist, holding the arm immobile no matter how hard Gricks strained.

"Listen to me," Maddox said, "Get a grip on your emotions. We may have lost the fight, but you seem like the steadiest man here. I know you know we must retreat."

"Retreat?" Gricks asked. "Don't you understand? We're finished. The tribune isn't coming back to pick us up with transport helos. We're far from anywhere. So, what if we survive the day? We're dead men after that."

"I don't agree," Maddox said. "Stick with me, and you'll find that I'm right."

Maddox, Dravek and Gricks were alone in the depth of the jungle. Bees buzzed nearby, but they didn't see any of the giant insects.

The rest of the cohort was gone. Those soldiers had died by bee stings or were on their own somewhere else in the jungle.

"We'll use discretion," Maddox said softly. "From now on, we move stealthily."

"What does it matter?" Gricks complained, doing it softly, nonetheless. "This is the Highlands, don't you realize? These are the Southern Highlands, the South Pole region. This is the only normal territory on Gath except near the North Pole region with the spaceport."

"I get that," Maddox said.

"No, I don't think you do. It took the legion a half month to cross the continent in the dirigibles. Then it took us a week to maneuver into position and unleash the helos. This was a grand enterprise. More legions were supposed to attack with us. I think Tribune Culain got greedy and launched our attack too soon. But that doesn't matter because it's over for us. If the Honey Men catch us, they'll likely turn us into field workers for the rest of our short lives. I'm going to go down fighting instead of that."

"I agree, fight or make it back to the spaceport," Maddox said.

"Are you daft?" asked Gricks. "Between the South Pole and the North Pole regions are hot, hellish deserts burning 150 degrees, or immense jungles even denser than these with jungle rot and red rust to fill your lungs with fungus. You'd cough out your life there. No, my friend, there's no way across this planet except on dirigibles or other crafts that flies high over the intervening terrain."

"Aren't there any nomads living in the mid-world deserts?"

Gricks laughed shrilly. "You want to call them people, be my guest. They're Metamorphs plain and simple. They've survived generations down there, changed beyond recognition by the heat and radiation."

Maddox remembered reading a little about Gath on the *Moray's* computer. The planet had an extreme axial tilt, much more than Earth's axial tilt of about 23.5 degrees.

A planet with a greater tilt would have more pronounced seasons and could potentially have warmer equatorial regions.

Maddox also remembered reading about the atmosphere. It didn't distribute heat effectively, and that lead to hotter mid-latitudes and cooler poles.

That much of the mid planet was desert would significantly affect local climates. The mid-latitudes also had a lower albedo (reflectivity) due to the desert terrain. The deserts absorbed more of the dwarf star's heat, whereas the polar regions, reflected more sunlight and thus maintained cooler temperatures.

Still, 150 degrees Fahrenheit was crazy hot.

The three trudged in silence for a time.

"There has to be a way across to the North Pole," Maddox said.

Gricks shook his head. "This world has wealth, never doubt that. It has the ingredients to immortality. But it's a hellish place for all that. Why do you think tribunes like Culain, and others, can take their pick among the throngs living near the spaceport? Thousands come to Gath for the honey. Most end up stranded here, unable to pay for passage home. They need money for that. Soldiering pays the best. Mostly that means bleaching their bones in the south or working in the fields to the Honey Men after they defeat and capture you."

"It's really that bad?" Dravek asked.

"Worse," Gricks said. "But how is it you two don't know these things? You're part of the legion. Pathfinders know more than most."

"We're off worlders," Dravek said.

Gricks shrugged. "So what? Most of us are."

Dravek glanced at Maddox.

Maddox nodded.

"We just got here," Dravek said. "I mean a few hours ago."

Gricks stared at Dravek, saying nothing.

"We just landed on Gath a few hours ago," Dravek said.

Gricks gave them a funny look. "That doesn't make sense. You were there on the plateau. You were the pathfinders at the point where scouts were supposed to meet us."

"Did you see any other pathfinders?" Maddox asked.

"No. You're the only two."

"Because the rest of the pathfinders died, obviously," Maddox said, "It seems like it's suicide to try to take honey from the bee men."

"I'm beginning to think you're right," Gricks said sadly. "Yet every year, they say, a few make it back and they're fantastically wealthy, rich from selling honey to the contractors. They have luxurious mansions and women like you wouldn't believe."

Maybe Gricks spoke too loudly. For suddenly, fifteen bees or more saw them and came buzzing down, their stringers out for the kill. This looked like the end of the line for all three of them.

185

-35-

More than fifteen bees, each weighing twenty pounds, blurred through the foliage, coming down through frond, fern and jungle tree branches. If the three men had relied upon their spring rifles alone, they would surely have died.

In this instance, both Maddox and Dravek acted alike, drawing their blaster. The difference was that Dravek dropped to one knee and held the blaster with two hands, using rapid-fire shots. Maddox stood as if he were at the pistol range, one hand on his hip as he turned sideways, his blaster held in one hand. He fired surely and accurately, beaming one bee after another.

Gricks muttered and fired shot after shot with his pistol, a big, crude bolt-action device. He took down two of the bees, a testament to his professional effectiveness and coolness under intense duress.

That should have been it for the attack, as bees dropped, and the buzzing dwindled. Was there a telepathic connection among Gath bees? Did the blaster sounds attract more of the robust, over-sized insects?

That must have been it. More bees swarmed, zeroing in on the men.

"There are too many," Gricks shouted. "We're dead men now."

"Not just yet," Maddox said, reaching to his blaster with his free hand and twisting a dial. The next shot was vastly different from the last. This sent a wide beam, burning fronds, ferns and tree branches, and killing a dozen bees at a time. The wide beam didn't kill them dead, but injured many, crisping gossamer wings or causing antennae to shrivel. Those bees hit the ground with thuds and crawled across the jungle floor for the men.

Gricks shouted, reversed the hold on his rifle and began smashing grounded bees with the heavy wooden stock. That squished the giant insects, angering those still coming.

The airborne bees buzzed as if with rage, speeding their assault.

Dravek and Maddox beamed and blasted. Turned and did the same behind them. It was endless work, hair-trigger firing and then—

No more bees buzzed in the air.

Gricks shouted and smashed another crawling bee.

"I have two regular shots left," Maddox said. He twisted the dial to take advantage of the little energy left his blaster.

"I'm dry," Dravek said. "I think my last shots did nothing but shine some light."

They looked around.

Gricks looked up, sweat staining his red, sweaty face. Bee gore covered his rifle stock.

Around them lay a hundred and fifty bees, maybe more. Some were squashed, some burned. Others blindly crashed against fronds.

Maddox shot those with his spring rifle.

"We need to get out of here fast," Gricks said. "If the Honey Men find out what you've done, they'll torture you and me forever for having killed so many prime bees."

"Stupid to use them in combat then," Dravek said.

"I've heard it said that killing helps with honey production," Gricks explained.

"Is that a fact or you just making crap up?" Dravek asked.

"Come on," Gricks said. "We must flee this place. It's death for us to remain."

"He's right," Maddox said. "Let's hoof it."

They would have run off, but that was next to impossible in the middle of the jungle. Roots, creepers, fronds growing side by side: it all conspired to make the going slow.

187

Gricks had a machete. He hacked at creepers and vines for a time. When his arm drooped, Maddox took the green-stained machete and hacked expertly. The three made better time.

Gricks finally asked, "Are you a noble?"

"Eh?" asked Maddox.

"You wield the machete as if it's a sword. You're obviously good with it. On Gath, only nobles and gladiators have such proficiency."

"Gladiators fight here?" Dravek asked.

"They say the Honey Men have stadiums where gladiators fight." Gricks shrugged. "I don't know it as fact, but I believe it. The Honey Men take whatever stock they find and genetically experiment with it. Look at the bees, the Doom Gibbons and other creatures. They've done the same heinous experiments to some men."

"Their gladiators for instance?" asked Maddox.

"Giants that kill all who stand against them," Gricks said. "It's said the Honey Men do not waste any flesh."

"Nice group of Joes," Dravek said.

They continued to trek, sweating, gathering grime on their clothes and faces. Maddox shook his canteen. It was empty.

"Don't look at me," Dravek said. "I drained mine a half hour ago."

"Where can we get more water?" Maddox asked Gricks.

"The supply helos," the centurion said. "Unfortunately, I don't know if any of those exist anymore."

"What about the river I saw earlier?" Maddox asked.

"What river?" asked Gricks.

"In the giant canyon."

"Oh. That river. We'll never make it there."

"Do you have a better idea?" asked Maddox.

Gricks stared at Maddox with dull eyes, finally shaking his head.

"The canyon river has just become our goal," Maddox said.

"Suits me," Dravek said.

Gricks shrugged. "We'll die of thirst long before we reach it."

"That's your problem, Centurion," Maddox said. "You need to take that mental energy and turn it positive."

"I'm positive we'll die of thirst long before we reach the river," Gricks said.

Maddox grinned. "Sarcasm. That's a start. It will have to do for now."

Later, Gricks took out his compass. After studying it for a time, he looked up. Clouds hid the sun. Fronds and ferns grew high overhead.

"That way," Gricks said.

"Why don't you look at your map first?" Dravek asked.

Gricks shook his head. "I don't need the map for this. That way." He pointed again.

Dravek looked at Maddox.

Maddox started walking in the way Gricks pointed.

A half hour later, soaked with sweat, dirt and greenery, the trio exited the jungle. By the crushed grasses ahead, giant helos had disgorged troops here hours ago.

The helos were long gone.

From behind bushes and lone fronds appeared fifty hardened, tough, vital men with weapons and canteens. These were professionals all, survivors, killers with an intense will to live. Most were centurions and sub-centurions.

As Maddox, Dravek and Gricks approached, the rest gathered and began to compare notes.

One of them was a Primus Centurion, simply known as Primus. He was Primus Hern, a thick-bodied man with the build of a gorilla. He had a low forehead and massive hands. He knew how to give orders.

"We head out," Hern said.

"Out where?" asked Maddox.

Hern scowled. "Who are you to question me?"

"Captain Maddox's the name. I just came down from space to see a major screw up."

"Are you calling Tribune Culain—?"

"A fool?" Maddox said, interrupting. "Yes, I am."

"A fool you say?"

"Are you hard of hearing?" Maddox asked.

Dravek whistled low and long.

"What was that for?" Hern demanded.

"I have memories, right?" Dravek said. "But I've never seen them acted out. That's impressive," he told Maddox. "You just take charge and don't take any prisoners. Hey, Primus, back off why don't you? You don't stand a chance against Captain Maddox."

Hern scowled more fiercely than ever.

"What are you suggesting we do?" a lean centurion asked Maddox.

"We all want to live, right?" Maddox said.

Many of them nodded.

"That means supplies," Maddox said. "I'm out of water. The rest of you will be out of water soon too. We head to the river therefore, so we have water."

"What river?" Hern asked.

"The one over the edge," Maddox said.

"What edge?" Primus Gorilla Hern looked confused.

"The one behind you," Maddox said.

Everyone turned to the canyon.

"Climb down that? Are you a gibbon or a man?" Hern eyed Maddox up and down. "You have long arms like a gibbon. Are you a true man or an escaped experiment from the Honey Men?"

Maddox ignored Hern as he looked at the others. "We lost the fight. Now, we need water and food. Then we need weapons and a way to traverse the mid-world desert. We have to hope a helo is salvageable down there and has some supplies."

"Look at that," a tall, rangy man missing fingers from his left hand, with a bloody rag wrapped around it. "I see some crashed helos. You have to look past that hill with blast marks. Yes, that way."

"I see them," a centurion said.

"If we can reach the helos, we can maybe repair some of them, can't we?" the rangy man asked.

"That's right," Maddox said.

"No," Primus Hern said. "It's suicide to climb down."

"So, we look for a path," Maddox said.

"No," Hern said. "It's suicide. I'm the Primus here. I represent Tribune Culain. He's going to send a rescue team. I

190

heard him say it before we left. If we survive, we can tell the next attack group what to watch out for. No one has made it back yet. The tribune already accounted for a loss. We must not lose hope."

"Where is your tribune?" Maddox asked.

"Your tribune, too, soldier," Hern said. "He outfitted you, paid for your training and expects obedience from you. Have you forgotten—?"

"Bees!" a soldier shouted. "I see bees." He pointed over the jungle.

The drone was audible from there. More bees gathered until at least two hundred hovered well out of spring-rifle range.

"Now what?" Hern mockingly asked Maddox. "The bees will sting us if we attempt to climb down the canyon wall."

Before an argument could commence, low armored cars burst out of the far end of the plateau. There were seven of them. On the top were heavy machine guns, with gunners behind them.

The seven swung the machine guns onto the fifty legion survivors.

A few of the legionnaires threw their rifles onto the ground.

A hatch opened on one of the armored cars. A thin man in a red robe climbed out. He was fluid and nimble, jumping down from the car's armored apron. He strode toward them with flair, his robe rippling in the small breeze. He wore a red turban and had red-painted eyes. Rubies flashed from his fingers.

He seemed fearless, unconcerned one of the soldiers would raise a rifle and shoot him.

"He's older than he looks," Dravek muttered.

Maddox was inclined to agree.

The man's facial skin was tight, but there was something hauntingly old about him. It was a subtle thing.

The man stopped halfway between the seven armored cars and fifty desperate legion survivors.

"What's it to be?" the man said in a loud, clear voice. "Should we slaughter you or will you surrender to me?"

Primus Hern cleared his throat, looking around. He holstered his sidearm and pushed through the men.

191

Maddox had edged to the rear of the others, considering making a break for the jungle. The bees up there would see that, though. As if to accentuate the point, a few bees detached from the main group, buzzing closer to the jungle edge.

"Let's get out of here," Dravek whispered.

"Our chances are slim if we try," Maddox said.

"I don't like the looks of Mr. Red Robe."

"I agree. But alive we have more options than dead."

"Throw down your weapons," the red-robed man said. "You will become workers, helping to repair all that you've destroyed. Surrender or die. The choice is yours."

The tough legion survivors glanced at each other.

"That stupid Eye of Helion dropped us into this," Dravek said. "Are we going to be workers for the rest of our lives?"

"I have a third option," the Primus said.

"You dare to contradict me?" the red-robed man asked.

"I'm just saying there's a third option," the Primus said stubbornly.

"No," the red-robed man said. "Admit you're wrong and you can live."

"If you'll listen—"

The red-robed man raised a hand, clenched fist forward. A red ray beamed from a ruby, striking the Primus, causing him to collapse. Was he dead? It seemed like it.

Three legionnaires raised rifles, popping off shots. The lead bullets stopped just short of the red-robed man.

"Personal force field," Dravek said. "I should have known."

The red-robed man beamed the three shooters. They also collapsed. "Who else wishes to die today?"

Maddox threw his rifle down. "We're defeated," he shouted. "The Honey Men have us. Let's live to see what the next day brings."

Many stared at Maddox. Dravek threw down his rifle. Then, others began to throw down theirs. Soon, the survivors had disarmed themselves.

"What a wise decision," the red-robed man said with a sneer. "Now, line up. You will follow the cars through the forest."

In such a way, the fifty tough survivors—minus four—marched into captivity after a disastrous legion raid.

-36-

It proved to be a harrowing journey as the captives marched sixteen hours a day. A Gath day was twenty-two hours, sixteen and a quarter minutes. Thus, counting the time to eat and take care of toiletries, Maddox, Dravek and the others slept five hours a day if they were lucky.

Other captives joined the straggling line of unfortunates. They marched over a black-paved road with towering fronds, ferns and jungle trees beside it. Grass and weeds grew in abundance right up to the edge of the road. It rained many hours during each day. The line didn't seek shelter then. It was a warm rain, soaking their garments just the same.

The guards turned them over to others several times during the march. At first, the seven armored cars guided them, machine gunners watching the captives closely. The next day, lean soldiers in camouflage gear and bearing machine pistols marched ahead and behind the tired throng. The armored cars zoomed elsewhere. Huge snarling beasts akin to dogs snapped at any captive moving too close to the edge of the road or too slowly. Several men tried to escape anyway. The guarding soldiers let the beasts kill and devour the unfortunates on the spot.

Finally, the soldiers turned the captives over to seven and eight-foot giants. They were armored, dull-eyed humanoids with a peculiar physical characteristic.

"Do you notice their tiny heads?" Dravek asked Maddox.

194

Maddox nodded. How could he have missed it? Despite their towering stature and impressive muscular development, their grotesquely small heads made the giants grimly unique.

Most of the men referred to the giants as pinheads...when the little heads weren't listening. The giants' leather helmets made their craniums seem even smaller, as it pressed the hair down. Regular men in black police garb with pistols told the pinhead giants what to do. The doglike beasts remained, watching the captives as if they were their personal prey animals.

The mountainous jungle terrain changed over time. The wilderness faded and turned into hilly orchards with fruit trees and watery fields of razor rice. In other areas, rows upon rows of giant frond trees with huge flowers were home to hordes of buzzing bees. The deadly creatures were busily collecting nectar, no doubt to turn it into the irreplaceable longevity honey.

There were a few wooden houses and villages along the way. Twice, the line of captives spotted naked toiling slaves working in the fields. The first time, the slaves wielded mattocks, hacking at the ground, preparing it possibly. The slaves had been burned a deep brown by the sun, many with blisters. They looked dispirited but moved nimbly enough when an overseer cracked an electric whip.

The second time, the slaves wore a leather harness on their heads, the bundle of supplies supported by their backs. They carried obscenely heavy loads, many staggering under the weight of gathered fruit.

They were as naked as the first group, and they filed near the captives in glum silence.

"Maddox," Dravek said. "Do you see?"

Maddox frowned. He'd seen. He couldn't believe it. What a hateful land.

"The slaves..." Dravek whispered in horror. "They've been gelded. None of them possessed any family jewels."

A few of the legion captives vomited, perhaps understanding the same ugly fate could well await each of them.

The march took on a surreal quality after that. Maddox pondered. If the Honey Men did that to their captives—he planned to escape no matter what it took.

Perhaps the dog-beasts understood that or felt an underlying difference, as they watched the captives even more closely than before.

Maddox became grimmer as the days progressed. He would have tried for the forest at the beginning if he'd known this. Would the Honey Men geld all their captives? How could he find out? Dare he ask a guard? He doubted asking a giant would render any answer.

Toward the end of the sixth day, the giants herded them faster. Endless marching, little sleep and barely enough food to keep them alive and the little rainwater they could catch with their mouths had taken a hard toll on the captives. There were three hundred stumbling and staggering wretches as the giants herded them into towering wooden walls, a corral.

Gates closed behind the wretches. Electricity flowed on top from wires coiled there. A man-sized chute opened at the far end of the corral. The chute led into a large wooden building.

"The first man, come through," a voice said through a loudspeaker high up on the building's nearest wall.

A man in soiled military gear gingerly poked his head through the chute. Huge hands grabbed him from within the building and dragged him all the way in.

The chute banged shut, barring anyone else from entering.

The milling wretches in the corral, those yet awake, listened carefully. It took time. Then a scream sounded—a lost and forlorn sound. It ended soon enough. A few men claimed to hear sobbing.

"What do you think that means?" Dravek asked.

Maddox's eyes had narrowed. Sleep deprivation had made him groggy and sour-tempered. Yet, he was also hyper-alert, if that made sense. "We have to escape."

"This seems like a bad time to try it."

"Not trying will be worse."

"Yeah," Dravek said, as he rubbed his red eyes, perhaps forcing himself to remain awake. "How do we fight giants, though?"

196

Maddox glanced at this right boot. The monofilament blade was still there. No one had ever checked to take it.

"Can you hack through a corral wall?" Dravek asked.

"I doubt effectively. We'll charge together through the chute when it opens."

"Should we barge up in line to try the next time?"

Maddox found it hard to make his mind work properly. He was missing something. Then it came to him. "No. The Honey Men will expect something now. We'll sleep first and regain some energy. We'll wait until the end when everything has become dull routine."

"Do you think you can sleep knowing what's coming?"

Maddox pulled one of Dravek's arms, guiding him to the back of the corral. There, he lay down and closed his eyes. He heard Dravek lay down near him.

Worries surged through Maddox. He was a long way from home. It seemed impossible that he'd ever see Meta or Jewel again. He closed his eyes and used the Way of the Pilgrim breathing. It calmed his raw nerves and eased the horrible clench in the pit of his stomach. The coming ordeal…

"Help me, God," Maddox prayed. "Help me fight as hard as I can when the moment arrives."

He swallowed the lump in his throat. He wanted more children. He wanted a son. If he were ever going to gain that—

Maddox breathed in the Way of the Pilgrim, stilling his anxieties. He'd cast them onto God. Now, he forced himself to relax, and by slow degrees, the edge softened, and he fell asleep.

His dreams were hard and unsettling. There was a force watching him, a telepathic entity. In his dream, it wasn't the Entity from the ice moon out by the gas giant. This was something else. It was here—

Here? On Gath in the South Pole region?

The thought stirred Maddox's sleep. With a start, he opened his eyes. He remembered where he was and what was happening.

"The chute has opened," Dravek said.

Maddox sat up. Everyone else was gone, processed through the chute. It was their turn to face grim reality.

197

"Are you ready?" Maddox asked.

"No. Are you?"

Maddox stretched his arms and headed resolutely for the chute. "We go together, remember?"

"I do." Dravek was right behind him. "Let's fight to the death, brother."

"Even better," Maddox said, "let's win."

-37-

The chute loomed before Maddox. The Honey Men meant to make him an obedient worker. They would transfer him into a docile slave by castration and endless punishment.

Maddox snarled silently as he ducked his head through the chute, drew the monofilament blade, and charged.

Dravek dove through on his heels as the chute slammed shut behind them.

Two bored eight-foot giants waited inside a chamber. They wore gloves and indifference as they reached for Maddox.

Then the fact of Dravek rolling into the room as well penetrated their dull brains. That brought wicked delight to their eyes.

Maddox had already started moving. He sliced the huge hand reaching for him, the monofilament blade easily parting leather, flesh and bones.

The giant bawled with pain and surprise, jerking his ruined hand away.

Maddox leapt at the giant, stabbing into the vitals and sawing. It was brutal and gory, and highly effective.

The second giant squealed angrily as Dravek dodged him. The first giant was swaying as he clutched at his slashed stomach, trying to keep everything in and failing badly.

Maddox was charging the second giant, who had concentrated on Dravek. From behind, Maddox hacked at the back of the knees, severing tendons, muscle, fat and gristle.

The second giant gave a hoot of surprise, twisted around to grab the gnat bothering him and lost his balance due to his ruined knees. He crashed back onto the floor.

"Dravek," Maddox hissed.

Maddox was already charging the door at the end of the room. Dravek hurried after him. The giants bellowed and raved, both on the floor. One bled out. The other crawled after the two.

The door opened.

Maddox stabbed the man on the other side, a lean individual wearing a bloody apron. A second man, a helper working the obscene machine in the room, looked up in surprise. He was a muscular sort and had depraved features.

"What are you doing?" the second man said.

The man with the bloody apron was dead on the floor, no longer possessing a throat.

Dravek charged through and blanched at the sight of the machine. It was meant to hold a prisoner, stretching his legs apart. There was a cutting tool on a bendable arm and a bloody sink below with a large opening. Clearly, whatever these two cut from a man dropped into the sink and opening, disappearing forever.

Outrage filled Maddox. He charged the muscular man.

"No," the man said, leaping for a button on the wall.

He didn't reach it, as Maddox leaped upon him from behind, bearing him down onto the floor. Probably, Maddox should have kept the man alive to question him. Instead, Maddox grabbed the head and twisted brutally, snapping the neck so the other gurgled.

Maddox rose panting, aware that he'd dropped the knife. He picked it up.

"Now what do we do?" Dravek asked.

There was a second door in the other direction of the first. It surely led to wherever the freshly gelded prisoner would go next. Whoever was in that room wouldn't expect hardy men, but a vilely maimed prisoner weakened from his ordeal.

"Right," Maddox said. "Are you ready?"

"Let's do this, brother."

Maddox opened the door and surged through. Three men waited in tired boredom. Some of their leather clothes had bloodstains. They looked up, their brains working sluggishly so they didn't instantly realize what was taking place.

By then, Maddox was among them. He didn't hesitate or show mercy. He used the knife with expert skill, killing fast and sure. Each dropped to the floor, dead.

Now, there were two doors to choose from.

Dravek was already at one, cracking it open and peering through. It led to a hallway. He noted a bloodstain here and there on the walls. Closing the door, Dravek went to the next one. It also led into a hallway, this one carpeted and with pleasant odors.

Dravek closed the door and waited. When Maddox looked at him, Dravek pointed at that door.

Maddox hurried to him.

"This must lead to the guardroom or whatever," Dravek whispered. "The other door leads to degradation."

"Open the guard door."

Dravek did.

Maddox burst into the hallway, striding fast and with deadly purpose. He reached another door, going through and entering a locker room. Maddox sliced open each locker.

He and Dravek changed into Honey Men gear. Each hefted a pistol, a chemical slug-thrower. As they laced their new boots, an alarm began to ring.

The two exchanged glances.

"Glad we have these," Dravek said, raising his pistol.

"I'm not surrendering," Maddox said.

"Neither am I."

"Balls to the firewall," Maddox said.

"Yeah. Literally."

Maddox went to a wall and used the monofilament blade. He cut a hole and opened a way into a larger room. Squeezing through, he waited for Dravek. Then, the two walked across, heading for a pair of doors.

"Act calm," Maddox said. His intuitive sense told him this was an unexpected path. He reached a door and tried it. It was unlocked. He swung it open and stepped outside.

The alarm was still ringing.

"We're doing it," Dravek said. "You're a genius."

Maddox started walking again, heading for ferns two hundred feet away. As he did, an armored car halted and a machine gun bolt slammed home.

"Don't look at it," Maddox said.

"Halt," a man in the armored car commanded.

"It's Mr. Red Robe," Dravek said. "I know. I shouldn't have looked, but I did."

Maddox turned as he continued walking. Dravek was walking with him. A military man was at the heavy machine gun. Mr. Red Robe poked his head out of an armored-car hatch.

"Halt," Mr. Red Robe said again.

Maddox burst into a sprint. It surprised everyone, including Dravek. Maddox dodged, and a red ray beamed past him. Maddox didn't bother firing at Mr. Red Robe, as he recalled the personal force field.

Behind him, Dravek collapsed onto the ground.

The machine gun fired a burst, its tracers burning past Maddox. He ignored them. If they cut him down, they cut him down. Better to die free and whole than live as a castrated slave.

"You have demonstrated courage," Mr. Red Robe shouted. "You have changed your destiny by it."

Maddox put on another burst of his unique speed. The red beam flashed behind him. Maddox knew he was going to make it. He leapt high, knowing another beam was coming. If he leapt high enough—no, it didn't prove high enough. The red beam struck him this time. Maddox lost consciousness as he felt himself falling, falling into dark oblivion.

-38-

Maddox awoke by degrees. He felt groggy and stiff. What had happened to him? Then he remembered. He felt between his legs.

"It's still there," a half-familiar voice said. "You redeemed yourself in the end."

Maddox opened his eyes. He lay on a cot in a small cell. Dravek slept on a mat on the floor. Standing by the bars of the cell—

Maddox's eyes widened.

Primus Centurion Hern stood here. He wore leather garb and crisscrossing straps. He still had his gorilla physique and hard, merciless eyes. His big hands gripped the bars. He didn't wear a military hat. It showed that he had a half a head of short hair because he was balding. That matched his brutal countenance and tough features.

"You're alive," Maddox said, as he sat up. His head spun and his muscles felt stiffer than they'd ever been, as far as he could remember.

"And you still have your balls," Hern said. "Imagine that."

Maddox frowned. "I don't understand."

"Gallant Ophir didn't explain it to you?"

"Who?"

"The red-robed man with the ruby rings," Hern said. "He's Gallant Ophir."

"Is Gallant a title?"

203

Hern nodded. "He owns us. We're his gladiators. Well, you're a gladiator-in-training, but who knows?"

"How did you come to be here?"

"I resisted in a tight spot. I proved my courage. That's important to the Honey Men."

Maddox thought back to when the Honey Men had forced the surviving legionnaires to surrender. "You mean this Ophir rewarded your surly behavior?"

"He rewarded my courage," Hern said.

"What about the four soldiers who fired at him?"

"They died during gladiatorial training."

Maddox processed the information.

"The training is tough," Hern added.

"How exactly did the others die?"

Hern sneered with an evil light in his eyes. "How do you think?"

"You killed them?"

"It was either that, die by their sword or become a field worker. One of them chose to become a worker. You might choose that, too, if you lose your courage."

Maddox ignored the insult. "You think this Gallant Ophir will force us to fight each other during practice?"

"Does that frighten you?"

Maddox stared at Hern. "Not in the least."

Hern shifted uncomfortably. "I could have slain you in your sleep."

"That you didn't means there's a harsh penalty for doing so."

"Yeah," Hern said. "Death."

That made sense. "I'm curious. What do you have against me?"

"You're an upstart, and you spoke against Tribune Culain. That irked me. Your manner here I now find offensive."

"Yet you and I arrived at the gladiatorial school. This Gallant Ophir must appreciate stubborn valor and cunning."

"He appreciates winners."

"That explains Dravek and me. I don't see how it has anything to do with you."

Hern scowled. "I was the Primus Centurion of Legion Culain. Can you comprehend how good I had to be to acquire the post?"

The man had a point. Maddox acknowledged it. "You know how to fight. There's no doubt about that. You can also maintain discipline. Yes, you're a soldier, Hern, one who fights to the end. I can appreciate that."

Hern sneered. "Sucking up to me ain't going to help you any."

Maddox shook his head. "If we must fight to the death, you and me, you'll die. Never doubt that."

"I doubt it very much, but I don't doubt that you have a big mouth."

Maddox eyed the gorilla-sized man. "I don't think you do doubt my fighting skills. You know I can kill you."

"Bah. You're a stick compared to me. You ain't nothing special and we both know it."

Maddox didn't bother with another response. He stood, testing his balance. Then he walked to the bars, looking into the stone corridor. There were other cells filled with other tough looking men. Some watched him with open hostility.

"Are they all part of Gallant Ophir's stable?" Maddox asked.

Hern nodded.

"Do you know much about the Honey Men's culture?"

"Not that it will help you any," Hern said, "but they're weirdoes and freaks. Worse than that, they serve ancient monsters."

"Do you mean people?"

"Monsters from what I've heard," Hern said. "The monsters have the guise of people, though."

"Does anyone raise bees in the north?"

Hern looked at Maddox. "You don't know much, do you? Maybe your story was true."

"Quite true," Maddox said. "Soldiers of Leviathan or a Leviathan substitute are on their way to Gath."

"No. Those of Leviathan avoid the Heydell Cloud. Everyone knows that."

"Apparently Leviathan doesn't avoid it anymore," Maddox said. "Can those of Gath defend themselves from Leviathan space assaults?"

"You're talking about space battle. I don't know much about that. If Leviathan sends a fleet to Gath, I doubt it. If a few ships come..." Hern shook his head. "I bet those of the north and south know how to deal with several ships or even a flotilla. They wouldn't have kept the planet otherwise, not with their immortal-making honey."

Maddox tested the bars. "If we become a winning gladiator, can we win our freedom?"

"Freedom?" Hern scoffed. "You'll be lucky to last the week."

"That doesn't answer the question."

"I don't know the answer. No one has thought to tell me. Just to fight."

"Strange," Maddox said, "as potential freedom would be a good inducement to fight."

"Staying alive is another," Hern said.

A horn blared from outside.

"It's practice time," Hern said. "You'd better wake your brother. We're in for a grueling few hours."

***

Hern proved correct.

Giants lined the high wooden walls that circled the sand-covered practice field. Each giant gripped a heavy cudgel and shield. Other normal men in leather garb carried hand catapults, the strings cranked back and bolts in the grooves. Those men stood behind the various cages.

The trainees were inside the large cages on the practice field, did calisthenics, stretches and then watched a tyro or veteran explain various moves and uses with different types of edged weapons.

The trainees soon practiced with weighted wooden counterparts to the actual weapons. Maddox and Dravek proved adept at every weapon shown them. Whoever watched and evaluated must have noticed.

The day went apace with rest and food periods, and then with more training.

The day passed and the next started. It was much the same as the first, an endless parade of hand-to-hand weapons practice.

Throughout the next few days, Maddox practiced with wooden weapons against Hern and others. They always practiced under the watchful eyes of the trainers and hand catapult-armed guards. Maddox didn't show his full potential but kept the others from injuring him.

The trainers finally pitted Maddox against Dravek. They sparred without going full tilt against each other. By agreement, neither defeated the other, but they hacked, slashed and thrust with enough alacrity to satisfy the watchers.

"Who would win between us?" Dravek asked as they ate bread and meat at stone tables in the shade under some trees.

Maddox shrugged.

"Do you think you could defeat me?" Dravek asked.

"What do you think?"

"No," Dravek said promptly.

Maddox continued eating.

"Do you disagree?" Dravek asked.

Maddox set his hands down by his plate. The owners didn't give the trainees forks or spoons and certainly no knives. "I have no opinion. I don't care about the question."

"I don't believe that."

Maddox sighed. "I'd win, but I don't care to press the issue."

"Why do you think you'd win, because I didn't get all your memories?"

"It doesn't matter."

"It does to me," Dravek said.

"Hold that thought then. We might find out sooner than you think."

Dravek looked where Maddox did.

Gallant Ophir stood near some giants with an armored car behind them. He was the red-robed man with red painted eyes

207

and big ruby rings that shot rays. Today, a woman in red robes watched with him. She, too, had red-painted eyes and a beehive hairstyle of dark curls. She was smaller and darker than Ophir but exotically beautiful.

"I don't like the way she's staring at us," Dravek said.

Maddox didn't care for it either. His intuitive sense told him there was more going on. She was a...a sensitive, at the least, maybe an outright telepath. He could feel her trying to read his mind.

"You," a guard said, standing near the tables.

Maddox turned around.

"Finish your meal and then go to the car. Gallant Ophir and his witch wish to interview you. Be quick, though."

Maddox turned back, surprised the guard would use the word witch. Maddox ate another bite of bread and then brushed his hands on his thighs, standing and heading for Gallant Ophir. It was time to find out the real score to all this.

-39-

Gallant Ophir and the woman stared at Maddox as he stood before them. The giants waited silent but hopeful. A few times, giants had torn a disobedient gladiator apart.

The woman shrugged shortly. "Maybe. I can't tell."

"You will enter the car," Ophir said.

A second one had pulled up.

Human guards opened a door. Maddox ducked his head, entering and sliding over leather-upholstered seats in back. The guards slid in with him, aiming pistols at his belly. Another guard in front smoothly headed out, driving for thirty minutes, the car passing fields, through an ornate gate and coming to a huge mansion surrounded by extensive gardens.

The car stopped. "Get out," the driver said.

Maddox climbed out, viewing palatial grounds and a shimmering brick palace in the distance. There were vast gardens of well-tended bushes, flowers and trees. It was like a park that included huge fountains and cement ponds. Colorful fish jumped in the ponds. Bright plumaged birds flew from tree to tree. The palace was huge, several football fields in length and four stories high with endless rows of windows. The length was curved and in perfect symmetry. Men in gaudy livery stood everywhere. In a few places, well-armored giants wearing golden helmets and holding ceremonial halberds stood at attention. Several leopard-like beasts slunk from a row of hedges to another.

"Move away from the car," a guard inside said.

Maddox did so. It must have been a signal.

A group of servants in black and white livery advanced and surrounded him. None seemed to be armed. They started toward the palace. Figuring that meant him, too, Maddox walked among them. Soon, several eight-foot giants joined the throng, marching in back, humming ditties for their primitive amusement.

The ensemble moved to the front of the palace along a wide sidewalk. There, Gallant Ophir waited with the so-called witch. Maddox had been looking down last time. This time, he noticed that it was obvious she was a different nationality from Ophir. He had white skin. She was brown-skinned with dark pits for eyes.

"Captain Maddox," Ophir said in his rich voice.

Maddox nodded. He decided not to let the red-painted eyes fool him. Ophir was dangerous.

"Meet Mara," Ophir said, indicating the woman.

She made no move whatsoever but stared at him.

Maddox could feel something wriggle in his mind. It reminded him too much of what had happened on the planet Kregen. He thus blocked it.

She gave a soft grunt.

Ophir looked at her with surprise.

"He parried my probe," she said.

"So..." Ophir said. He gripped the sides of his red robe as he circled Maddox and the surrounding attendants. "You are an enigma. As such, you have drawn the attention of Grandma Julia. She has asked to see you. Can you imagine why?"

"No," Maddox said.

"So blunt," Ophir said. "I can almost consider that a crudity. Are you trying to be vulgar?"

"That was not my intention," Maddox said.

"Hmm," Ophir said. "You two." He addressed the two nearest giants. "Each of you grab one of his arms. Don't crush the flesh, but make sure he doesn't wriggle free."

The armored giants lumbered to Maddox. Each set down his halberd and used both hands to grab one of Maddox's arms. Because of their wide grips, each covered an arm from shoulder to wrist.

"Come," Ophir said. "You'll join us, Mara."

The attendants didn't question anything. They all remained where they were, silent.

With Gallant Ophir leading and with Mara at his side, the two led the giants and Maddox on the wide sidewalk. They moved around the left side of the palace to a huge garden area farther back. Fountains sprayed vast arches of water that struck different ponds, feeding them. Handsome and beautiful men and women in scanty attire milled about. Others without clothes sat on silk-clad chairs. The chairs and occupants radiated outward from a central throne. On the throne sat a wizened old woman dressed in a purple gown and wearing a golden crown studded with precious gems. She had wrinkled skin and was protected by a large umbrella. Her eyes burned like black orbs, inspecting Maddox as he approached.

He realized the naked people on the chairs were intoxicated or drugged. Each, no matter their sex, was a prime physical specimen.

Maddox imagined the woman on the throne was ancient, at least five hundred years old, maybe older still. She was clearly perverse. He didn't need his intuitive sense to tell him that. Grandma Julia wielded immense power. She was likely corrupt, having wielded power for many centuries. An ancient adage filtered through Maddox's mind.

Power corrupts. Absolute power corrupts absolutely.

Was that the secret to the Honey Men? Their rulers or potentates had ruled for long centuries, maturing in their evil. In other societies, the ancients died, allowing a fresh batch to take up the mantle of rule. Here, the special honey extended life and changed societal norms.

"Is that him?" Grandma Julia asked. She had a cracked and withered voice. Clearly, the honey treatment must finally be failing her.

"Grandma," Ophir said. "May I show you the pre-gladiator, Captain Maddox? We caught him among the defeated of Legion Culain. He surrendered in the beginning. Later, at the gelding pens, he—"

211

"Yes, yes," Grandma Julia said, interrupting. "I listened to your report earlier. I don't need to hear it again—unless you have something new to add."

Ophir glanced back at Mara before bowing his turbaned head. "Captain Maddox parried Mara's mind probe."

"This is even better," Grandma Julia said. "Step forth, Captain. Let me see you better."

Maddox attempted to do just that. The two giants held him fast, however, making it impossible.

"Have them release him," Julia said. "I dislike having the creatures so near me. I don't trust them."

"Release the man," Ophir said.

The giants did not.

"Are you daft?" Ophir shouted, marching at them. "I said release him."

The giants squawked, releasing Maddox as if his skin had turned hot.

Ophir made a shooing motion with a hand.

The giants stumbled back.

"Watch him," old Julia said. "Mara, can you slow him if he charges?"

"Yes, Grandma," Mara said.

"Come here," Julia told Maddox. "I don't bite."

Maddox approached slowly.

Julia's black orbs seemed to shine with power. She was indeed a wizened creature, surely no more than five feet tall and weighing less than a hundred pounds. In her left hand, she held a deadly, glittering needler. She aimed it at Maddox.

"This can kill you," Julia said, brandishing the needler.

He assumed she was a student of human behavior, recognizing more than most because of her extended age and vast experience.

"You've become my property," Julia said. "I own you because you lost to us."

Maddox said nothing to that.

"Do you deny that I own you?" Julia asked.

"I do not."

"Do you accept it then?"

"I do," Maddox said.

212

"I believe he's lying," Mara said.

"Of course, he's lying," Julia said. "I can tell that much myself."

"I'm sorry, Grandma," Mara said. "I—"

"Shut your yap," Julia said, interrupting.

Mara closed her mouth, bowing her head, visibly frightened.

"Are you still watching him?" Julia demanded.

Mara looked up swiftly, her eyes wide and frightened.

Maddox noticed that Gallant Ophir had clenched his right hand into a fist, the ruby rings glittering as they aimed at him.

"Do you marvel at my daring?" Julia asked Maddox.

It took Maddox a moment. Then, he asked, "Do you mean meeting me like this?"

"Don't ask me what you already know," Julia snapped. "If you treat me like a fool, I'll have you join the field workers in a jiffy."

Maddox inclined his head, not understanding her anger.

"Do you know why you're here?" Julia asked.

It struck Maddox then. "You know about the cyber missiles and the *Moray.*"

"If by the *Moray* you mean the trader ship that detonated when the cyber missiles began to disgorge their Soldiers, yes. I know about the incident. I also wonder if the missiles have something to do with the Leviathan assault vessels heading here for Gath."

"They do," Maddox said.

"Where did you come from?"

"The *Moray.*"

"How did you do that, as the ship was still far from orbit?"

"Through teleportation."

"You teleported onto the Vance Plateau just as Legion Culain was about to land their helos?" Julia asked.

"I did."

"Why did you pick that location?"

"I didn't. The…being that teleported Dravek and I chose it for us."

"Why?" Julia asked.

"I've been asking myself that for some time."

213

"Are you trying to be clever?"

"No," Maddox said.

"No," Julia said. "I don't think you are. Where are you from, Captain Maddox? I mean originally."

"Earth."

"From dirt?" asked Julia, seemingly confused.

"Earth is a planet in the Orion Spiral Arm."

Julia waved an old, crooked hand. "The names are meaningless to me. I've never heard them before."

"If you have a star chart, I could show you."

"Do you mean a different spiral arm from this one?" Julia asked.

"I do."

"Why did you come to this spiral arm?"

"Leviathan agents kidnapped me while I was in mine."

"Why?"

"If you will permit me to explain…?"

Julia opened her mouth, perhaps to reprimand him. Instead, she nodded.

Maddox told her about clones. He explained the possibility that Leviathan wished to attack the Commonwealth of Planets and might send Dravek as a spy first.

"Why are you being so honest?" Julia asked, her dark orbs searching his face.

"You two are sensitives, at least, possibility telepaths. I believe you or Mara would detect it if I lied. Thus, I play it safe and tell you the truth."

Grandma Julia leaned forward on her throne. "Tell me why I shouldn't trade you to Leviathan when the assault vessels park in Gath orbit."

"It would set a bad precedent for those on Gath to so easily bow to pressure from Leviathan."

"Why should I care about that? If things don't change for me soon, I'll be dead. The universe ends for me then and nothing matters anymore as far as I'm concerned."

Maddox hesitated. Grandma Julia was either utterly self-centered and self-absorbed, or her words just now were a cloak to her real feelings. "I'd ask you to consider this. I'm worth more to you here than in Leviathan hands."

214

"Tell me how?" she asked.

Maddox inhaled slowly. Here was the first real decision. What should he say in an attempt for freedom? Julia was cunning and venal, a dangerous combination. It would be best to appeal to her greed. How best to achieve that, though?

Maddox nodded inwardly. "I have knowledge that could help you."

"What knowledge?" Julia demanded.

"For one thing: the whereabouts of an ancient weapon hidden on Gath."

"Bah. I can torture the information out of you if I want it badly enough."

Maddox breathed deeply as he practiced the Way of the Pilgrim. He called upon his intuitive senses as taught him by Balron the Traveler.

"Beware, Grandma," Mara said. "He's doing something unique with his mind."

"Should I stun him?" Ophir asked.

Grandma Julia watched Maddox closely and warily. Her trigger finger tensed upon the needler.

"I can die any time I wish," Maddox said in a hollow voice. "I need merely will it. The Eye of Helion aided me once. If I die, I will send it a signal. It will then arrive in time to avenge me."

With that, Maddox fell into serene indifference.

Julia turned her head to stare at Mara.

"I can't tell," Mara said. "That could be the truth or a lie. His thoughts are hidden from me."

Julia eyed Maddox with loathing. "I can torture your brother to death while I force you to watch. That will unlock your tongue."

"Go ahead if you want," Maddox said. "He's a clone. I can always have another made for companionship."

"You think you're clever, Captain," Julia said with hate. "What if I hand you over to my people for their amusement?" She indicated the beautiful, naked people lost in drugged stupor on their chairs.

A few looked up, with evil lust shining in their drugged eyes.

Maddox shrugged.

"You're making me angry," Julia said.

Maddox did not reply.

Julia sat back, using the needler to stroke her wrinkled chin. "Take him back to the training camp. Let his clone attend him for now. I'll arrange a fight. Let's test our stalwart captain, shall we? Let's see how eager he is to die or if he'll decide to trade his knowledge for better... We shall see after the fight, provided he survives."

Grandma Julia snapped her fingers. The interview was over.

-40-

The next day, Maddox found it harder to concentrate on gladiatorial practice as Hern and he trained with extra-weighted wooden swords. Hern had gorilla size and strength. Maddox had speed, reach and more strength than Hern thought reasonable.

As Hern swung, Maddox parried so the swords clacked against each other.

He had to escape from this place. Maddox was sure had to leave before the Leviathan assault vessels arrived in orbit. Did those of Gath have anything to defend themselves from space attack? Hern thought so, and he must be right after a fashion.

Hern broke through Maddox's distracted defense and whacked the edge of the wooden sword against Maddox's gut.

Maddox grunted, staggering back.

Hern advanced, grinning, seeing his opening and landing a glancing blow against Maddox's head.

It was enough so Maddox dropped to the sand.

A whistle blew. A trainer shouted at Hern to back off.

"You're lucky, you dog," Hern whispered, kicking sand in Maddox's face. "I could have killed you easy if we'd had real swords."

Maddox rolled over and climbed to his feet, his head throbbing. Dravek was there.

"Are you okay?" Dravek asked.

Maddox touched his head. A knot had already risen where Hern had struck him.

The trainer stepped near, a squat, heavily muscled older man with short, iron gray hair. "How did that happen?" The trainer had a raspy voice.

"Lack of concentration on my part," Maddox said.

The trainer shook his head. "Do I have to tell you how stupid that was?"

"Apparently," Maddox said.

The trainer squinted at him. Putting the whistle in his mouth, the trainer blew a shrill blast.

Everyone stepped away from his opponent and looked at the trainer.

The squat trainer, a former gladiator, bellowed in his hoarse voice about the foolishness of letting distracting thoughts get the better of you. "It kills. Never forget that."

The trainer blew the whistle again. It meant get back to it. He told Maddox to go sit against the wall over there and rest a moment.

Maddox did just that, brooding. He wasn't thinking about Hern, the gladiatorial school or his head. He realized he didn't know enough about the Heydell Cloud, how the various star systems operated and if any of them cooperated against Leviathan. Did Leviathan fear to send ships into the Heydell Cloud? It seemed like it did. Was the reason the vortexes, gravitational masses and other spatial anomalies or something else?

Maddox's eyes widened as he sat against the wooden boards of the wall. Spatial anomalies—could he use one to reach the Orion Arm in a short amount of time? Could any anomaly help shoot a spaceship across seven or eight thousand light-years in one go?

Maddox rubbed his chin thinking about it.

Dravek plopped down beside him. "You forgot this." He pitched the wooden practice sword on the sand near Maddox's feet.

Maddox nodded idly.

"Your head isn't in the game, my brother."

Maddox looked at Dravek. "It is, just not about swords and spears."

"What then?"

"The Heydell Cloud, Leviathan, getting home again."

"Your home." Dravek made a broad gesture. "This spiral arm is my home."

"Do you want to live the rest of your days on Garth in the South Pole region?"

Dravek grinned. "You mean this isn't paradise?"

Maddox had told Dravek about his encounter with Grandma Julia and the beautiful people she kept around her. He'd left out the part about Julia threatening to torture and kill Dravek. How would it help if he told the clone?

"What happens when Soldiers of Leviathan come looking for us on Garth?" Maddox asked.

Dravek shrugged. "They get shot."

"What if the assault ships brought a Strategist along?"

"I get it. A Strategist might figure out something brilliant. You think that's likely, though?"

"Leviathan doesn't normally send warships into the Heydell Cloud. They are now. Leviathan wants us. Yeah. I think a Strategist might be along."

"You, Leviathan wants you."

"Us," Maddox said. "We're both in this together."

Once again, Dravek shrugged. "We're no longer free agents but slaves. What we think no longer matters."

"That's why we need to become free agents again."

Dravek snorted. "I'd like to know how you plan to achieve that."

"One of the reasons I was distracted. I want to know, too. I'm trying to figure it out."

"And?" asked Dravek.

Maddox peered at the trainees as he listened to the clack of wooden weapons. Primus Hern battled another trainee. The gorilla-thick soldier hammered at the weaker man, battering the strength out of the man's arm. Soon, the man would drop his guard and Hern would try to crack his skull. One thing about Hern, he went full bore at whatever he did. He didn't care who he had to climb over in the process, either.

Seeing a trainer glance at him, Maddox gingerly touched the knot on his head. After a moment, the trainer turned to watch someone else.

"Staying in the arena will get us nowhere," Maddox said. "I need to convince Grandma Julia to hunt for the weapon by using our help as guides."

"You mean the weapon in the mid-world desert?" asked Dravek.

Maddox nodded.

"Why do that?"

Maddox eyed Dravek. The clone lacked Erill spiritual energy, and he didn't think Dravek had Balron training. That hadn't seemed to pass through with his other memories.

Maddox frowned. How had Dravek received his memories in the first place? That wouldn't have come through DNA. Oh, he remembered. It had been through a helmet.

Hern's head bash must have shaken his memories.

"You don't trust me no more?" Dravek asked.

"Mara and Grandma Julia are sensitives or telepaths."

It took Dravek a moment. "Oh. I get it. I can't shield my thoughts from them as apparently you can."

Maddox looked up at the sky. The sun shined brightly as a few fleecy clouds drifted. Remaining a gladiator was out of the question. He didn't have much time left, though. A mere week had passed since leaving the *Moray*. That left him two and a half weeks at most before the assault vessels arrived in orbit here.

"Do you feel like vomiting?" Dravek asked.

"A little."

"You might have a concussion then."

Maddox sighed. He was sick of the Scutum-Centaurus Spiral Arm. He was sick of doing this alone. He missed Meta and Jewel. He missed the crew of *Victory*. What would Ludendorff suggest he do about now?

"What are you grinning about?" Dravek asked.

"Old times, old friends," Maddox said.

The answer made Dravek wistful. "I'd like to meet some of those people, the ones I remember from you."

Maddox concentrated on Dravek.

"What now? What did I say?"

Maddox felt sorry for the clone. But if the clone was enough like him, Dravek wouldn't want to hear what he was thinking.

"What just happened?" Dravek asked.

"I'll tell you what. I plan to go home, but I also plan to set you up with a spaceship and crew before I leave."

"Feeling sorry for me, are you?"

Yes. Maddox was feeling sorry for him. But he didn't want to say that. Instead, he held out his right hand. Dravek looked at it. Maddox shook it some. Dravek finally took hold. Maddox squeezed as he shook hands.

"You're my brother," Maddox said. "I meant what I said just now about the ship and crew."

Dravek tore his hand free as the squat trainer marched toward them.

Both men stood.

"Enough of this," the trainer said. "You have a fight tomorrow."

"So soon?" asked Maddox.

"You two are going back to the cell. You can rest and think up strategies for your coming match. Dravek will go with you as your helper."

"Help me fight in the arena?" asked Maddox.

"No," the trainer said. "In preparing you and helping you when you get back—if you're alive enough to help after the match."

"Who am I facing?"

The trainer shook his head. "I have no idea. I think it's a surprise." The trainer stared at Maddox. "Someone powerful among the ilk doesn't like you." The squat trainer shrugged. "That means you're going to be dead soon. So, get out of here, meat. Get some rest while you can enjoy it."

-41-

The stadium was constructed from white marble and had many tiers and padded seats. It wasn't large, as only half of the stadium had seats. The other half was marble wall. Awnings covered the padded seats. Perhaps a quarter of those seats held occupants.

In the center box in front sat Grandma Julia with Gallant Ophir and Mara among her attendants. A few of the beautiful people wearing revealing garments surrounded them like a moat protecting a castle. Two other Old Ones sat in the special box. They also had personal attendants.

The rest of the seats held regular Honey Men, or so Dravek suspected. It was a mix of men and women, no children. In the highest tier without seats stood pinhead giants wearing golden helmets and armor, holding their halberds.

Dravek reported all this to Maddox in his underground ready room.

Maddox shadowboxed before a body-length mirror to warm up his muscles. The knot was still there on his head, and a bruise had formed on his stomach where Hern had whacked him. Maddox wore a loincloth and sandals, with crisscrossing leather straps across his torso. He didn't have a helmet. Nor had he received any arms yet.

Occasionally, as Maddox readied himself, he heard trumpet blasts and roars from the crowd.

Maddox glanced at Dravek. "Is something on your mind?"

"I don't want to talk about it now. You have a fight soon and need to concentrate on that."

Maddox nodded as he continued to shadowbox in front of the mirror.

Finally, three quarters of an hour later, there was a knock at the door. Dravek opened it.

"He's next," said a woman in a short skirt, knee-high leather boots and with a mass of dark hair.

Dravek turned to Maddox.

Maddox pivoted and came to him. "Let's go."

They followed the woman to an armory. Three bruisers stood behind steel bars there.

"What do you want?" one of the bruisers asked.

Maddox blinked. He hadn't realized he would have a choice.

Dravek asked the woman, "Who is he fighting?"

The woman shook her head.

"You don't know or won't say?" Dravek asked.

Her eyes narrowed. "I could have you flogged for addressing me like that. Have him choose a weapon now."

Dravek turned to Maddox.

Maddox stood to the side, with his head cocked as he used his intuitive sense. What would be the best weapon?

"Give me a stout spear," Maddox told the bruiser. "But make sure it has balance so I can throw it."

The lead bruiser looked at the other two. One picked up a pike.

"Too long," Maddox said.

The other showed him an eight-foot spear with a razor-sharp head of steel.

"That one," Maddox said.

"You haven't trained with a spear," Dravek said.

Maddox snapped his fingers at the head bruiser.

"Don't get nasty," the bruiser said. "Otherwise, next time, we'll give you a faulty weapon. You won't like that."

Maddox grinned at the bruiser.

One of the others handed him the spear butt first.

"Hurry up and follow me," the woman said.

Walking swiftly, she brought them to a large box. "Both of you are going through. You—" She pointed at Maddox. "Will enter the arena when they open the chute. You—" She pointed at Dravek. "Can watch through the slit and learn for him."

She unlocked a hatch, opening it.

Maddox and Dravek entered the boxed area.

She closed the hatch and locked it, no doubt leaving.

Maddox clutched the spear, his palms sweaty.

"Good luck," Dravek said, clapping him on a shoulder. "Can I ask you a question?"

Maddox nodded.

"Why a spear?"

Maddox shrugged. He was in no mood to explain.

Trumpets blared from outside. The chute opened. Maddox trotted out onto the hot arena sand. He scanned the watchers in the tiers, the Old Ones in the front central box and the empty floor of the arena, empty but for him. There were damp patches in places covered with new sand. Those would be bloody places, possibly slippery places. He should avoid those.

As per his instructions, Maddox approached the central box with the potentates. Grandma Julia had her needler. Guards with hand catapults tracked him closely, their weapons aimed at him.

Gallant Ophir stood in his swirling red robes and red turban. He wore his ruby rings. "Captain Maddox, my friends. He fought with Legion Culain only a week ago trying to steal our honey."

There were a few boos and catcalls from the sparse crowd.

"He will face three dreadfangs," Ophir said, "as they scavenge upon others the way legionnaires try to harry us here in the Highlands."

Cheers erupted from the tiers.

At the same time, a gate opened. Three long-legged dreadfangs trotted out, squinting at the bright sun reflecting off the scintillating sand. They were furry beasts the size of large timber wolves with bigger jaws full of incisors. They had large ears and small tails. Each must have weighed a solid one hundred and thirty pounds.

The dreadfangs zeroed in on Maddox standing on the other side of the arena. Two lowered their heads. The other snarled, spitting saliva.

Had the beasts eaten legionnaires on the way from the jungle battlefield to the gelding pens?

In his heart, Maddox wiped away any personal animus he might hold for the predators. They were animals, trained for the arena, no doubt. No, he took that back. The dreadfangs slunk toward the walls, not him. Maybe they weren't trained to fight before a watching crowd like this. That seemed odd.

Maddox considered that. Could these be untrained beasts? Or was their telepathy at work to trick him?

Heading for the center of the arena would be a mistake against trained dreadfangs, as they would circle him, coming at him from all sides. Yet, the only way he could perceive winning was by killing a dreadfang fast. He had to whittle their numbers down before they acted in united hound fashion against him.

Thus, Maddox trotted into the center of the arena.

The dreadfangs looked up, noticing him again, growling. The beasts glanced at each other as if confirming an idea they had. Immediately, they set out for Maddox.

Maddox looked up at the central box. Mara had her eyes screwed shut. Two others like her did the same thing. He had the feeling each witch controlled one of the beasts.

Maddox looked back at the predators.

They trotted, fanning out. Two obviously meant to circle him. One came straight at him, probably to focus his attention.

Without yelling, Maddox increased his pace and then broke into a sprint. Did his speed surprise the telepaths operating the dreadfangs? He closed the distance with the one heading toward him even as the other two circled wide.

He had a moment then before the others could race in to help the first. Trusting in his skills, Maddox heaved the spear, his only weapon. It sailed flat and fast, a perfectly balanced spear. The steel head missed the dreadfang's head but pierced its shoulder and slammed it down onto the sand. The beast whined in pain as it flopped in agony.

Maddox reached the beast before the other two reacted. He grabbed the end of the spear and yanked it hard, withdrawing it from the dreadfang. In an instant, he drove the spear through its torso, reaching the heart and killing the beast.

Now, the other two dreadfangs turned toward him.

Maddox laughed with predatory glee, charging the nearest. It set itself as it watched the spear. Maddox hefted it back as if to hurl, and he faked a throw even as he sprinted again.

The dreadfang lowered its head and shifted to the right. Then, it raised its head and snarled, seeing the man was almost upon it.

Maddox didn't fake again. He raced straight at the beast like a killer and thrust, spearing it through the mouth. It was a brutal and savage kill. He put a foot on the warm and twitching carcass and removed the spear.

Maddox whirled around as the last dreadfang launched airborne at him. The beast had raced as fast as it could. Maddox ducked and rolled, with the spear in hand. The beast landed on the sand, scrabbling to turn and renew the assault. Now, however, Maddox faced it at near range. The beast snarled and snapped, circling the man.

They both faked lunges at each other. Then, the dreadfang miscalculated, or the telepath running it did. Maddox skewered the beast in the side, driving the carcass to the sand. It wasn't a pinprick assault, but a deathblow.

Maddox raised his bloody weapon high, and he approached the central box.

The crowd watched in anticipatory silence. The Old Ones watched coldly. The guards with the hand catapults had raised their weapons. Gallant Ophir had clenched his right hand into a fist, the ruby rings aimed at Maddox.

Their fear of him felt good. Maddox hated this place and loathed the Old Ones who had made it so. Did Grandma Julia feel his hate? He would think yes.

Maddox stood before the box, triumphant. He slammed the spear into the sand and raised his hands in the air.

"I'm Captain Maddox. I come from the Orion Spiral Arm. I can show you how to defeat the approaching assault vessels of

Leviathan. I can kill them as easily as I slew these three dreadfangs."

He pointed at Mara.

Most in the central box flinched at the rude and possibly deadly gesture.

"I know you controlled one of the dreadfangs." His finger swept across the box. "I know others controlled the rest. It didn't matter. It won't matter that Leviathan assault vessels have better weapons than you do on Gath. I can defeat them, too—if you desire. Don't waste my expertise. Don't—"

Grandma Julia raised her needler into the air.

Maddox stopped speaking, waiting.

Julia stood. Would she aim and fire the needler at him? "Your expertise did nothing for Legion Culain," she said, her augmented voice easily carrying throughout the stadium.

Maddox bowed his head. "I wasn't with the legion long enough. I could have shown them how to defeat you otherwise. It would have been easy."

"You're too arrogant for a slave," Julia said.

"I'm good at war." Maddox swept a hand to indicate the slain dreadfangs. "I'm good at this kind of war and space war. It's one of the reasons Leviathan fears me."

"The cybers fear *you?*" Julia mocked.

Maddox made a formal bow, sweeping an arm low. "I'm at your service, Grandma Julia. I can help you expand your power, and…I can help you extend your life expectancy."

The five-hundred-year-old woman stared at him. "You're a fool to make such empty promises," she said in a hoarse voice.

"I would be a fool if I was wrong, but I'm not wrong. This little stunt here today should help you see that."

"So, you slew three dreadfangs. I could have done better in a moment." Julia indicated her needler.

"I don't dispute that," Maddox said. "I am merely offering my services as a mercenary. I'm the best at what I do. I can fight in any manner. I suspect that you in the Highlands lack experts at space combat. That is my specialty. With those of Leviathan fast approaching, you may have need of such specialty."

"You say this because you fear the arena."

"Fighting in the arena is a waste of my skills, Grandma Julia. You are in charge here. I don't dispute that. I think those of Leviathan might."

"I'll simply trade you to them for an advantage," Julia said.

"That is your prerogative, of course. You rule here. I doubt that will buy you long-term survival from Leviathan. They sense weakness on Gath, not needing telepaths to do that. I can help you strengthen your defenses and make sure Leviathan weighs the pros and cons for a long time to come before they dare to try to steal your honey."

"You said they came for you."

"Is that the only reason?"

Another of the Old Ones spoke quietly to Grandma Julia.

Maddox kept his feelings and thoughts blank. He was gambling. He had done this openly for a reason: that other Old Ones could hear him and reflect on the dangers of the approaching assault vessels. Those others were surely not on the verge of death like Grandma Julia.

"The fight is over," Julia said. "Guards, take the captain to the waiting cell." She stared at Maddox. "We will speak of this in private."

-42-

Maddox showered, stretched but refused to let his mind relax. He used the Way of the Pilgrim as a shield. He wondered now if eating Gath honey did more than grant longevity. Maybe it opened channels in certain people's minds, creating the conditions needed for sensitives and telepaths.

Was that the real secret to the Highlanders' ability to stave off most legion assaults? Could they predict or read in the tribune minds the attack paths? Did they have telepaths read centurions' thoughts on the ground?

In any case, Maddox protected his thoughts. The attendants hadn't allowed Dravek in the waiting room, and that was probably a plus. The clone would ask too many questions.

After showering, Maddox ate sandwiches and drank plenty of water. He found new clothes, softer and better made than his training garments.

Then, he waited. While doing so, he fell asleep.

"Captain Maddox," a woman said softly.

Maddox sat up, blinking.

The beautiful woman wore little, was red-haired, curvaceous and smiled seductively. "I'm here to please you," she said.

Maddox shook his head. "Thank you, but no."

There was a moment of obvious disappointment on her face. "Oh. Would you like someone else?"

"No. I'm married."

She frowned. "I don't understand."

"I have a wife at home. Surely, you understand the concept of husband and wife."

"I do. But your wife is far away, yes?"

"Yes."

The woman smiled and ran her hands suggestively down her lovely thighs. "I am here, not far. Enjoy me while you are able."

"That isn't possible, as I took vows when I got married."

"What sort of vows?"

"For one, to remain faithful to my wife until death do us part."

"Faithful…you mean you don't sample the fruit from other trees?"

"No."

She peered at him. "That is sad. You must be starving for attention and love. Surely, your wife will never know if you indulge far from home. Besides, have you considered the possibility you might never return home."

"I have."

"Then…?" she said, making ready to slip off her skimpy attire.

Maddox shook his head. "Don't do that. I hold to my vows. I love my wife."

"You don't find me attractive?"

"You're lovely."

"Then why not enjoy me?"

Maddox inhaled through his nostrils, looking away as if bored. The woman was beautiful, and Meta was far away, and he might never return home as the woman suggested. Yet, he'd taken a vow before God. God would know what he did, if nothing else. Besides, this was one of those tests of life and character. Did he wish to enjoy Meta to the fullest? He did indeed. Then he needed to remain faithful and enjoy the wife of his youth. This was his chosen path. He would remain on it despite the temptation in this room.

"Captain Maddox," the woman said, softly touching his shoulder.

Maddox reacted fast, grabbing the wrist and twisting, turning the woman away from him.

"Do you like it rough?" she said. "I'm more than willing."

Maddox pushed her away, so she stumbled. "Go. I'm done with you. Tell Grandma Julia I'm ready to talk."

The woman stared at Maddox. "You really mean it?"

Maddox said nothing, no longer looking at her.

The woman shook her head, clearly perplexed. "You're a strange man, Captain."

"It's been said."

She opened her mouth to say more, but perhaps she saw something in Maddox that stopped her. With a sniff of distain, the woman turned and walked out, slamming the door behind her.

Twenty minutes later, guards escorted Maddox through underground tunnels. The guards changed several times. The first carried hand catapults. The second set had pistols. The last group carried machine pistols, walking with Maddox up a ramp to a waiting armored car outside.

A rear door opened, and Gallant Ophir leaned into view from within. "Join me, Captain."

Maddox slid into the back seat with Ophir. One of the guards outside slammed the door shut. At a word from Ophir, the car slid forward.

Once past the stadium parking lot they traveled on a road with long brick buildings and flowering ferns and fronds along the sides. An occasional, twenty-pound bee buzzed overhead.

Maddox wondered what had happened to Dravek, but he knew better than to ask. That would show interest in Dravek's fate. Doing that might complicate matters and certainly put Dravek's life in danger.

"Where are we headed?"

Ignoring Maddox's question, Ophir said, "That was well played."

Maddox frowned. "You mean in the arena?"

"That, too," Ophir said. "No, I mean Julia's whore. You surprised Grandma. I believe it persuaded her to talk with you."

"She already said that in the arena."

"That was for the crowd's benefit and the other Old Ones."

"They won't be at the meeting?"

"Do you think that's where we're going?"

231

"I don't know," Maddox said.

"…No," Ophir said. "The other Old Ones won't be there."

The car took several turns, so they left the settlement and drove through hilly territory with slave gangs hacking at the ground with mattocks. Guards with electric whips watched them while dreadfangs prowled the working perimeter.

"Is there a reason you personally picked me up?" Maddox asked.

Ophir grinned at him. "Getting nervous, are we?"

Maddox said nothing to that.

Ophir crossed his legs and examined his red-painted fingernails. "Can you truly help Grandma extend her life?"

"There's a chance."

Ophir grinned but in a strained manner. "How would you achieve this miracle?"

Maddox had a feeling Ophir didn't like the possibility. Was he slated to inherit Grandma's position when she died? Did Ophir thus want Grandma out of the way sooner instead of later? Was the man eager to wield real power?

"Were those just words then?" Ophir asked.

Was there the hint of hope in the man's voice? Maddox couldn't tell and his intuitive sense wasn't helping. He peered at the divide that separated them from the driver. "Is Mara on the other side trying to read my mind?"

Ophir frowned. "Getting cute with me is a good way to find yourself bleeding to death in a ditch. Grandma is the head of our clan. I'm her deadly right hand, the enforcer. If I think you're a danger to us, I'll kill you. Are we clear on that?"

"Perfectly," Maddox said.

"Now answer the question. How could you possibly extend Grandma's life?"

"Leviathan possesses longevity treatments. It's possibly those will work on regular humans."

Ophir stared at him, taking his time to think it through. "I've never heard that."

"That may be. Have you traveled extensively then in Leviathan territory?"

"Didn't I warn you about being cute?"

"It was an honest question, Gallant."

Ophir touched one of his ruby rings. "You must know I've never left Gath."

"I suspected as much." Maddox shrugged. "I, on the other hand, have spent far too much time in a Leviathan laboratory. I learned much more about them there then I wanted to know."

"And you found out about the longevity treatments then?"

"That's right," Maddox said.

"The clone, Dravek, will attest to this?"

"That's doubtful."

"Because you're lying?" asked Ophir.

That was true, but Maddox did his best to remain calm and disinterested, as if the question was too droll to bother with an answer.

Ophir leaned forward and knocked on the black-tinted window dividing the back from the front of the car.

The panel slid down to reveal a hollow-eyed Mara sitting on the passenger side. She looked beat up, not with fists but with—

Then it hit Maddox. She must have felt one of the dreadfangs' deaths when he'd slain the beast. It had affected her physically or taken a psychic toll, as she must have been controlling its mind when it died.

"Is he lying about the longevity treatments?" Ophir asked.

Mara stared at Maddox.

He felt a tickle in his mind but no more than that.

"I can't tell," she said.

"Are you lying about better longevity treatments?" Ophir asked practically in Maddox's face.

"No," Maddox said. "I'm telling you the truth. I wouldn't dare do less."

Ophir studied him closely and finally turned to Mara. "Don't you have a premonition one way or the other?"

"He refused Grandma's courtesan—the man's a rock of morality." Mara shook her head. "He must be telling the truth. He's one of those stubborn honest fools."

"Not a fool," Ophir said. "But he is stubborn. Very well," he directed his voice at the driver. "Take us to the Stenholm Tower."

233

-43-

The tower was a graceful and daunting edifice, looking too fragile to stand so high. Maddox rode up in an elevator with Ophir and Mara. There was no guard, unless Ophir was supposed to be his guard. They had exited the armored car in a grand parking area filled with military vehicles and milling soldiers.

That meant something portentous, Maddox was sure.

When the elevator stopped, Ophir had to remove his ruby rings, handing them to a severely dressed woman with a shaved head. She had iron bracelets with wires extending from them to steel caps on her fingertips.

Soon, Ophir led the way down a curving corridor. The endlessly long window on the outer curve showed the countryside from a four-hundred-foot vantage. The stadium was in the distance along with the brick building settlement and boundless fields and groves. The carpet softened their footfalls until they reached large ornate wooden doors.

Several severely dressed women with shaved heads and the same steel bracelets and fingertip caps waited as guards. Without acknowledging any of them, the women opened the doors.

Ophir led the way into a large, packed chamber. An old, withered man wearing a black robe was hunched over what seemed like an imposing judge's bench at the front of the chamber. Closer to them and behind a wooden barrier in rows of padded seats sat many Old Ones and their juniors like Ophir.

Maddox found two of the severely dressed women at his side.

"You'll stay with them," Ophir said.

Maddox nodded, stopping.

Ophir and Mara left him and worked down a row until they sat down beside an impatient Grandma Julia.

The two bald women escorted Maddox past the wooden barrier, leaving the seated Old Ones and their attendants behind. The two women marched him before the imposing bench and the gnarled man seated up there looking down at him. He had a long nose and hate-filled eyes burning with something extra.

A murmur had begun as Maddox approached the bench. That stilled as the wizened old man scanned the assembled throng.

The old man cleared his throat. He looked like a living corpse with pallid, badly wrinkled facial skin. The splotches on his bald head made an ugly spectacle. The eyes, however, were terrifying and far too knowing.

"You are Captain Maddox," the old man said in a raspy though loud voice. He must have speech amplification.

"I am, sir."

The old man shook his head. "I am not sir. I am the Shofet, the Judge of the Highlands. You may refer to me as Shofet Zadoury. I am the authority in this chamber. I have been granted license to make a degree by those you see behind you."

Maddox turned and bowed respectfully before the assembled. This was better than he'd expected from his performance in the arena. He must have guessed right about their lust for extended life beyond what the honey gave them.

There was an old German proverb: *eating builds appetite*. Might that prove true to those granted extended life wanting even more? That was the human cry after all, "More, I want more."

"I'm not going to do the speaking in favor of this proposal," Shofet Zadoury said crossly. "I will do the ruling, though. Grandma Julia, if you please."

From her place in the padded rows, the old dame struggled to her feet. Ophir reached out to help her. She slapped his hands away. He retracted them immediately.

Struggling, Julia worked through the row and hobbled with a gnarled walking stick, moving past the wooden barrier. One of the severe women put a wooden chair with armrests on a dais. Then the two severe women helped Grandma Julia onto the dais and into the chair. The last one handed her a disc of a throat mike, which Julia pasted to her wrinkled throat.

"Can everyone hear me?" Julia asked.

"Fine, fine," Zadoury said. "Now, get on with it. I have an orgy to watch and I'm getting randy just sitting here."

A ripple of polite laughter rose from the assembled.

"Captain Maddox," Julia said. "You spoke in the arena about your expertise. Would you tell the assembled what that is?"

Maddox repeated what he'd told Julia in the arena about his multiple combat experiences and abilities.

"Wait a minute," Zadoury said. "This ruffian thinks he can defeat the Leviathan assault vessels heading to Gath?"

"I can indeed, Shofet," Maddox said.

"How can you perform this military miracle?" Zadoury asked.

"First, I must dig out the ancient weapon hidden in the desert. I mean in a Gath mid-world desert."

A loud murmur began from the assembled.

"Silence if you please." When the murmuring ceased, Zadoury regarded Maddox. "Do you realize that none of us is rash enough to send an expedition into the mid-world desert? We're the Honey Men. Fools and aggrandizers come to us, and we take from them. That has been our way ever since we found the bees."

"That strikes me as understandable," Maddox said. "You have what everyone wants—"

"Enough of this," Zadoury said, his enhanced voice drowning out Maddox. "You're an outlander. You're not here to judge our ways as good or bad. You're a slave, no less, a gladiator. You will refrain from such comments. Grandma

Julia, what is the reason for this nonsense? The man is a fraud. Digging up a mid-world desert weapon indeed."

Julia turned in her armchair and stared up at the Shofet. "It's more than that. He knows how to increase our longevity."

Stunned silence greeted her words. Some of the silent in the assembled seemed worried and upset by the possibility. Those were the younger Old Ones and the juniors like Ophir.

Maddox had an immediate suspicion as to why. The oldest wanted to keep on living, naturally. The younger ones wanted the oldest ones to die so they could climb and gain more authority. He'd just dropped a bombshell into the long-lived Honey Men society. This was even better than he'd hoped.

"Outlander," Zadoury said.

Maddox faced the Shofet.

"Is all this true about extended lifespans?"

"It is," Maddox said.

"Then let us get to the point," Zadoury said in a suddenly hoarse voice. "Tell us how you can increase our already legendary existences."

"I'd like to, Shofet, but I dislike being a slave and a gladiator. It makes everything harder to recall, if you catch my drift?"

Zadoury's rheumy old evil eyes widened with disbelief. "You'll be meat for the dreadfangs unless you speak up quickly, you dolt."

Maddox laughed, shaking his head. "Surely, you jest, Shofet. If I'm dead, how can I tell you my wonderful knowledge and thereby increase your lifespan?"

Zadoury sat back, his breathing labored.

"If anything, you need to insure my conditioned survival," Maddox said.

Several Old Ones in the rows stood up and shouted at Maddox, shaking their fists at him for his insolence. Others yelled for him to divulge the secret this instant or face dire repercussions.

Maddox held out imploring hands to Zadoury. "Shofet, surely you realize that owning such a secret as this, I desire compensation for revealing it. Is that not fair practice?"

Zadoury leaned over the bench to glare down at Maddox. "This has nothing to do with fair practice, you cunning deceiver. This has everything to do with power and pain. You will receive more pain than you can bear until you're screaming out what we want to know. Otherwise, I'll believe that you're a fraud, telling us what we want to hear."

Maddox chuckled.

"Shofet Zadoury," Julia said, "I'd like to make a point before we continue."

"Silence!" Zadoury thundered to everyone in the chamber. "Sit down, all of you." He pointed at the standing Old Ones.

They sat down as the room quieted.

Zadoury turned to Julia, nodding.

"Captain Maddox claims he can take his own life with a thought at any moment he chooses," Julia said.

"What arrant nonsense is this?" Zadoury said.

"I'm inclined to disagree that he speaks nonsense," Julia said. "Given everything else we've learned of him, I believe he is capable of the feat."

"Are you serious?" Zadoury asked.

Julia nodded solemnly.

Zadoury glared at Maddox. "You expect us to believe such drivel?"

"Believe what you want," Maddox said indifferently. "I'm tired of this existence. After I die, I'll be reborn in a better position, having learned from this one."

"What?" Zadoury said.

"You've surely heard of reincarnation in this backwater planet of yours, have you not?"

Zadoury stared at Maddox.

Maddox kept himself serene, knowing this was the knife-edge moment. He didn't believe in reincarnation. But he did believe in using whatever tool was at hand to achieve his goal. In this instance, he lied freely to the treacherous Highland Old Ones. It was all he had left in his arsenal for a battle for his life.

"Suppose I agree you know this secret knowledge," Zadoury said slowly. "And that you can take your life with a whimsical thought. How can we induce you to tell us about the extended life treatments?"

"This is all about trust, Shofet."

"Don't tell me—" Zadoury forced himself to quit talking. The old man looked away, working to compose himself, no doubt. He pasted a fake smile onto his withered face as he regarded Maddox anew. "Yes, this is about trust," he said in a brittle voice.

"I feel the best way is to show you the evidence at the proper time," Maddox said.

"Meaning what?"

"We retrieve the ancient weapon from the desert—"

"Impossible," Zadoury exploded, his face turning red.

Maddox shook his head, waiting for the old man to calm down. What would happen if the Shofet had a heart attack and died? That might complicate matters.

Finally, though, the pallid color returned to Zadoury's wrinkled face as he breathed evenly again. He nodded for Maddox to continue.

"We retrieve the weapon from the desert and ready it to face the assault vessels," Maddox said. "Once we board the remaining vessel, I will instruct whoever you like in Leviathan's longevity art, using a cyber as illustration."

"You think we'll let you board an orbital assault vessel?"

"If you desire to learn the knowledge, I do."

Zadoury looked at Julia. "What's your opinion about this?"

"We take the risk," Julia said. "The prize is worth it."

Zadoury opened his mouth and then closed it with a snap.

Maddox supposed the Shofet had been about to say, "If he's telling the truth."

"Why will you trust us to act fairly while you're in the last Leviathan assault vessel?" Zadoury asked.

Maddox shrugged. "I'll have my people with me, and you'll have yours. I imagine you'll also have planetary missiles ready to launch at me if I renege on the deal. I'm going to trust you then that joy at greater extended life will still any ill actions against me."

"Who are your people?" Zadoury asked.

"Those who will help me to recover the weapon in the desert. I'll take my clone and Primus Hern, and a few others I plan to pick from your latest batch of field workers."

"You want gelded ones to go with you into the desert?" Zadoury asked in surprise.

Maddox nodded. There was no one else he might conceivably trust among the Honey Men Highlanders.

"Why would you come back to us from the desert?" Zadoury asked.

"For the obvious reason that I imagine you'll send people with me into the mid-world desert that would make it difficult to do otherwise. Besides, I desire a spaceship for travel, one I command. Leviathan possessed the vessels and I suspect I'll need your assistance gaining one."

Zadoury sat back, pondering as he plucked at his lower lip. He looked down at Grandma Julia. "Would you agree to this?"

"I would and do," she said.

There it was, Maddox knew. Her desperation for longer life was clouding her judgment. Shofet Zadoury must want longer life as well. Their greed for more, their fear of death—heightened by their long lives—would weigh against their logic. Would it be enough, though?

Zadoury gazed at the Old Ones in the padded seats. What did he see from them? Likely the same desperate desire to live even longer from the oldest. Soon, Zadoury began to nod. "If you think to flee without telling us your secret, Captain—"

"Play fair with me," Maddox said, interrupting, "and I'll play fair with you."

Zadoury's rheumy eyes burned with hatred. He choked it down, though. "Grandma, I want to discuss this with you in private."

Julia struggled up, the two bald women helping her down from the dais.

Then Julia and Zadoury retired to the room behind the bench, leaving everyone else waiting for their verdict.

-44-

It was obvious Julia and Zadoury wanted greater life extension. All the eldest among the Old Ones must feel this way. They were all likely reaching the age limit that the unique honey had provided them. Thus, they agreed to Maddox's plan with a few provisions.

He could take four men with him as his people. His team would drive its own hover-car once they reached the mid-world desert. The expedition would leave in two days. They would travel by dirigible, two being collected from the latest failed legion raid.

Two companies of Highland soldiers would join the expedition, meaning two hundred in all. One third of those would be Grandma Julia's men. One third would be Shofet Zadoury's men and the last third would be a collection of several other clan leaders. Gallant Ophir would command, taking Mara and several other telepaths along.

Grandma Julia informed Maddox that ballistic missile sensor arrays would always watch them. If he successfully practiced treachery, the missiles would launch, and nuclear detonations would annihilate his pretentions.

"Gallant Ophir would die in the blasts with me," Maddox pointed out.

"If you got that far through treachery, Ophir would already be dead."

"How can you talk like that about your grandson?"

Julia sneered. "Ophir is my great-great-great grandson. Those before him all proved deceitful and paid the ultimate price for it. I loathe deceit, Captain. I have maintained my position as clan leader because I can sniff out liars and protect what is mine with ruthless efficiency."

They spoke in a private chamber in her palace. Maddox had already picked his team, instructing them and listening to their advice.

"This is a small risk on my part," Julia said from behind a huge desk. She aimed a needler at him the entire time. "I realize you could be lying about these things. The possibility you're telling the truth, however, opens vistas I hadn't believed existed. Even if only the desert-hidden weapon exists, this will be worth it. However, if you're lying and prove false about the extended life, I will take great pleasure in personally torturing you before you leave this life. I will also destroy everyone you consider your friend."

"Please, Grandma," Maddox said in a bored voice. "Your threats are tiresome and tedious."

"No matter. You will hear me out."

Maddox sat back, stretched out his legs, crossing them at the ankles, and folded his arms, staring at her.

"If this is an act on our part," she said, "it's a marvelous one. I will add this, however: my desire to kill you is nearly overwhelming. Why do you think this is so?"

Maddox uncrossed his arms, faked a yawn and then examined his fingernails.

Julia clicked the needler to a higher setting.

Maddox looked up, with his eyebrows raised.

"Do you think me incapable of killing?" Julia asked. "Is that why you appear bored?"

"I know you're a killer, having no doubt about that."

Julia lowered the needler, frowning at him, obviously thinking. Finally, "I imagine this is all about the assault vessel. You need it. You said as much to Zadoury."

"To return to the Orion Spiral Arm I need a spaceship. The assault vessels are fast approaching. I don't see a better opportunity to acquiring one."

"How will you cross thousands of light-years in an ordinary assault vessel?"

"I take one problem at a time. As you may have noticed, I have unparalleled concentration and ability. I trust myself to see a way through the next problem after the one I'm dealing with is conquered."

"You're a supremely arrogant man."

"Or a very competent one," Maddox said. "For you, that's a plus. When I'm done here, you'll have the chance to live another few centuries. Instead of berating me about trivia, you should be on the floor kissing my feet."

Julia squinted at him.

"You know it's true," Maddox said. "Your pride keeps you from making the proper gestures of gratitude."

"Enough of your buffoonery," Julia said hoarsely. "Yes, I want another few centuries of life. I admit that. If I gain it, your coming will have been fortuitous. If you're a charlatan, I will gain from having believed extended life possible. It is a glittering prospect. Now, though, get out. I've had more of your company than I can stand."

Maddox stood and bowed at the waist. "It's been a pleasure, Grandma. I hope to see you again within the week."

"That soon?"

"The assault vessels are fast approaching. They lend a certain stimulus to all this."

Julia frowned again, nodding slowly.

Maddox turned and started for the door.

"Captain."

Maddox faced her.

"Good luck."

Maddox nodded and then exited the chamber.

-45-

Two monstrous dirigibles floated upward from near the stadium where Maddox had defeated the dreadfangs.

Maddox found the airships incredible. Each silvery behemoth had been constructed in the north using lightweight composites. Each stretched a little over one thousand feet or three hundred and five meters in length. That was three times the length of a fully-grown blue whale. Each had a diameter of three hundred feet or ninety-one meters. The shape was what he would have expected, like an enormous cigar.

The dirigibles were lined with flexible solar panels. That helped power many onboard systems and would recharge the batteries.

No wonder the legions used these to cross from one pole to the other. They traveled high enough that sunlight shined all day. The batteries saw them through the night.

Inside the airship's envelope were many cells filled with lighter-than-air helium. The cells increased safety, as all would have to pop simultaneously to cause the airship to crash catastrophically.

Under the envelope was the elongated gondola. It housed the cargo, crew quarters, and control cabin.

For maneuvering, the dirigible used electrically driven propellers. They were attached to the envelope rather than the gondola. That provided a wider base, allowing greater control of movement.

The desert hover cars were in the first dirigible. Most of the people were in the second. That included two crew quarters assigned to Maddox and his men.

He kept one cabin for Dravek and him. The other held Primus Hern, Centurion Gricks and Sub-Centurion Eddings.

Hern had been surprised that Maddox had picked him. The Primus found it difficult to show gratitude and had acted surly most of the time.

"You're a man," Maddox had said before they entered the dirigible. "You're tough and don't give up. I admire those traits."

"I'm not going to kiss your ass because you chose me," Hern said.

"I don't want that. I want a man I can trust. But if you love the Honey Men more—"

"Screw them! I hate their guts. They castrated my men. If I could cut their stomachs and yank out their—"

"Let me give you a piece of advice," Maddox said, clutching one of Hern's muscled arms, interrupting the tirade. "Telepaths are joining the expedition. Try to keep your hate of the Honey Men to a minimum. The telepaths will pick that up and it might cause trouble we don't need."

Hern twisted his arm free of Maddox and sneered. "You love the Honey Men for giving you this chance?"

"I'd rather be hunting for the ancient weapon than fighting dreadfangs in the arena."

Hern glared at Maddox until he nodded, grumbling under his breath. He added, "Why did you choose Gricks and Eddings? They let the Honey Men cut off their balls."

"For all that, they're still men."

"Cowed and beaten things wearing the guise of men," Hern said.

It was true that Gricks didn't have his former bluster. He'd lost weight as well and could no longer look Maddox in the eye. It was worse with Eddings. Both Gricks and Eddings would flinch if he said something too loudly. Maybe he'd made a mistake picking them, but it was too late to change his mind now. Could he restore some of their pride? He'd have to wait

245

and see. Hern was too belligerent to trust. But the Primus would fight. Events had proven that.

At first, Maddox kept to the cabin. He couldn't believe they were no longer in the Highlands. Still, the airship was full of Honey Men soldiers. Ophir would always watch him closely, using Mara and the other telepaths to help keep track of him.

"What's the plan anyway?" Dravek asked when Maddox woke from a long nap.

Maddox sat up on his cot. "We must remember how to reach the ancient weapon site. The one that you found on the *Moray's* computer."

"You told them about that?"

"How do you think I got them to agree to the dirigibles and letting us go along?"

"Why did you do it?"

Maddox raised his eyebrows. "You want to stay in the Highlands, fighting in the arena?"

"Hell no," Dravek said.

"Neither do I. The Highlanders fear Leviathan and need a weapon against the assault vessels. We need a weapon against them to remain free."

"We don't know what the weapon does. Are you sure it will help against the assault vessels?"

"There's only one way to find out, right?"

"I guess so," Dravek said.

"Do you remember what the computer said about its exact location?"

Dravek thought about it, and they compared notes.

"That's a little different from what I told Grandma Julia," Maddox said. "I'm going to the control cabin to tell Ophir."

"Want me to come along?"

"I want you to watch Gricks and Eddings."

"You think they'll come out of their cabin long enough for that?" Dravek asked.

"If they do, I want you to help restore their confidence in themselves. We might need them later."

"How am I supposed to do that?" Dravek asked.

Maddox slapped his chest. "I could do it. And if I could, you should be able to, right?"

246

"Sure," Dravek said.

Maddox stared at him. "It could mean the difference later."

"Right," Dravek said, staring at him. "I understand."

With that, Maddox strapped a holster and heavy caliber pistol to his hip. He had the monofilament blade again, hidden in a sheath in his right boot top. He wore a uniform and jacket, and military hat. They were of legion make and design. He certainly didn't want to wear Highlander gear. He had the others dress the same, figuring it might help his team's morale.

After leaving his quarters, Maddox strode down a narrow corridor, passing endless cabin doors, each made of lightweight material. He was back on a ship, this one an airship on a world. It turned out the Honey Men Highlanders had parks upon parks of captured legion equipment.

The three Leviathan assault vessels were still coming fast for Gath, as least as far as he knew. Finding the ancient weapon site—how hard could it be? He needed to learn everything he could about the deep desert. The Highlanders wouldn't want to tell him, so he would need to trick the information out of them. His best bet was Gallant Ophir.

As he headed to the control cabin, Maddox practiced his serenity. He was surprised he'd gotten this far already with his duplicity. This mission was more hair-trigger than most, as he worked from such a lowly position. He also lacked his usual help. If he could have had Galyan, Ludendorff and Valerie with him, most of his problems would have already been solved. If *Victory* were here, he'd just destroy the assault vessels.

Maddox cracked his knuckles. He had what he had. He was supposed to be the *di-far*. It was time to make the trait work for him out here.

One problem at a time: that was what he'd said earlier. He needed information about the deep desert. How could he get Ophir to give him what he wanted?

Maddox quickened his pace. It was time to find out.

-46-

Maddox was in the control cabin. It felt much like being in a spaceship, except land and drifting clouds were far below.

The dirigibles flew high indeed. It wasn't at the limit of their lighter-than-air altitude, but it was getting pretty damn close.

Gallant Ophir sat in the captain's swivel chair in the center of the bridge. He wore his red robes, ruby rings and red eye shadow. Mara stood at his elbow.

Around him at various controls stood the bridge crew. None of them had seats.

Maddox wouldn't have designed the bridge that way, but those of the north had.

Before them and lower down than Maddox had anticipated was a huge almost yawning window. It offered a panoramic view of the world below.

Presently, the world showed endless sand. Far off in the distance was a low-level jungle. Maddox spied an even farther-away river. That river must feed the jungle, allowing it to grow in the dreadful heat of mid-planet.

"Gallant," an officer said.

Ophir looked up and saw the direction of the officer's gaze. He swiveled the seat toward Maddox.

"What brings you to the bridge?" Ophir asked.

"I've refined the location of the ancient weapon site," Maddox said.

Ophir looked at Mara.

She remained silent.

"I forgot," Ophir said. "You can't read his thoughts. You're a troublesome fellow, Maddox. Come stand over here."

Maddox dipped his head and did just that.

"Quite the view, eh?" asked Ophir.

"It's breathtaking," Maddox agreed.

"I've only done this one other time," Ophir said. "I don't see how the legions dare to cross a world in this, but I see the allure of it."

"Should I give the new coordinates to your chief officer?" Maddox asked.

"I don't understand," Ophir said. "You're acting almost meekly. That isn't in character, is it, Mara?"

"No, Gallant," she said.

"Why are you doing that?" Ophir asked.

"Trying to get along," Maddox said.

Ophir snorted. "The way you spoke to Shofet Zadoury at council—I got the feeling you enjoy being a prick. You're certainly a natural at it."

"As are you," Maddox said.

Ophir frowned. "Mara, get my guard. Tell Felix to send three of my best to the bridge."

Mara hurried away.

"Tit for tat," Maddox said softly.

"I'll tat your tit," Ophir muttered. "I'll only accept so much cheek from you. Then," he made a slicing motion across his throat.

"You don't want Grandma living too long, eh?" asked Maddox.

Ophir's red-painted eyes seemed to glitter with malice. "You play a dangerous game, Captain."

"Only the one I'm forced to play."

"Are you crying about your state? I didn't think you capable of that. Do you resent the Honey Men?"

"I do."

"Because of what we did to Gricks and Eddings?" asked Ophir.

"Partly, yes."

Ophir nodded. "We don't waste flesh in the Highlands, even that of our defeated enemies. It's an old way but a good one. The legions send raiders. We defeat them and turn the men into hard workers. It's an elegant system. The gelding ensures they're gentled for proper use."

Maddox said nothing.

"About the new heading," Ophir said. "Tell me about it."

Maddox did.

Ophir snapped his fingers. The chief bridge officer hurried to him. Ophir discussed the new heading with him. Soon, Ophir dismissed Maddox, not allowing him the opportunity to learn about the mid-world people or lack thereof.

Maddox returned to his quarters and spoke with Dravek. Then, he went next door and spoke with the others.

Hern was absent. Gricks said the Primus had gone to exercise.

Eddings lay in bed with the covers completely over him. When Maddox called his name, Eddings lowered the covers enough to reveal the top of his head and eyes.

"What do you know about the mid-world deserts?" Maddox asked.

Eddings pulled the covers back over his eyes and head. "Nothing," he said in a dull voice.

Maddox glanced at Gricks. Gricks looked away.

"Come with me, Centurion," Maddox said.

"Is that an order?" Gricks asked.

"Yes."

The two walked out of the cabin into the narrow corridor.

Gricks kept his hands in his pockets and looked down, with his head hunched as if he'd aged fifty years.

Maddox walked beside him.

Gricks said nothing, just dutifully went where Maddox did.

This is one of the men I'm counting on, Maddox asked himself. Gricks was afraid of his own shadow. The Highlanders had broken his spirit. Why hadn't he seen this before? It was probably because he hadn't wanted to see it.

"Centurion—"

Gricks hunched his shoulders more.

Maddox noticed. Maybe it was time to grab the bull by the horns. "Don't you want me calling you centurion?"

"Call me what you like," Gricks muttered.

"Centurion Gricks is what I want to call you."

Gricks said nothing to that.

"Does the old title bother you?" Maddox asked.

"Maybe, as I'm no longer a centurion."

"Because the Honey Men defeated your cohort?" asked Maddox.

"Partly, but more…" Gricks squeezed his eyes closed.

The Honey Men had gelded the men only a short time ago. The incident must have burned in Gricks' mind, seared his spirit. If the Honey Men meant to break legionnaires by it, they'd picked an effective practice.

"What if they'd hacked off one of your hands instead?" Maddox asked suddenly.

Gricks shook his head.

"Would that make you less than a man?" Maddox asked.

Gricks raised a hand, looking at it, nodding afterward.

"I read about a one-armed admiral once who won one of the greatest sea battles in history," Maddox said. "His name was Lord Nelson. He won more than the Battle of Trafalgar. He died on his warship *Victory* that day. My starship was named after his sailing ship. Lord Nelson inspired his captains and sailors. His lack of an arm didn't hinder him from greatness."

"Losing his testicles might have done that," Gricks whispered.

"Maybe," Maddox said. "Except, I remember reading once about a general named Narses. He was a eunuch, had been castrated in his youth. He defeated barbarian Gothic warriors at the Battle of Taginae. It was a turning point battle fought with swords, bows and lances. Narses' genius and military ability is what helped the Byzantines take back Italy from the German barbarians."

Gricks looked up at Maddox. "You're making that up."

"Not in the least," Maddox said. "Look, you suffered a traumatic event. I'm not going to sugarcoat it. The Honey Men did it in the most demeaning way they could. They did that for

251

a reason. They meant to break all your spirits, making you docile slaves. Yes, it was evil and vilely done. I imagine they mocked you during the procedure, and I imagine the work guards with the electric whips have driven the lesson home."

Gricks barely nodded, his eyes staring almost as if he was on the verge of tears.

Maddox clapped Gricks on the shoulder.

The centurion flinched and whimpered.

"You were a centurion, Gricks. Your men fought hard. I admit the ordeal you underwent would have shaken me to the core. It would do more than sting. It would strike at the core of my manhood. That's a critical concept to a man. But because the Honey Men did that, it didn't change you from a man into a thing. You're still Centurion Gricks. You can let this destroy you, and in a way, I can hardly blame you for it. Or—are you listening to me?"

Gricks barely nodded.

"Look at me, Centurion."

Gricks did, his eyes immediately darting away.

Maddox clapped him on the shoulder for a second time. For a second time, Gricks trembled and whimpered.

"This is the hardest blow you've ever taken," Maddox said. "It's likely you're never taken a worse hit. You can go down in your heart and admit defeat forever. Eddings is doing that. He's given up completely. Or you can crawl your way back to manhood and resolve. You can work to regain your dignity. You can fight against the Honey Men who did this to you. It will take time. It will take resolve. Mostly, it will take desire. Don't mark yourself in your heart by the gelding."

Gricks' head whipped about until he stared at Maddox.

"Yes. I said it. I named it. I suggest you say it."

Gricks swallowed hard.

"Say it and you'll know your foe," Maddox said.

Gricks mouthed the word, "Gelding."

"Good work," Maddox said, clapping Gricks on the shoulder for the third time.

Gricks flinched, but he didn't whimper this time.

"I need a soldier, Centurion Gricks. I need a man who can hold a gun or rifle and shoot straight enough to kill."

252

Gricks was staring at him.

"I need someone who can hold his ground even if terror shakes him. If you need, think of what happened and determine in your heart to die fighting this time. I call it a second chance. I'm giving you a second chance. Do you want to at least try?"

Gricks swallowed again, and he nodded.

"I need to hear you say it, Centurion."

"Yes," Gricks whispered. "I want a second chance."

"Good, excellent," Maddox said.

Gricks stopped and looked at Maddox. Gricks' eyes darted away, but the centurion forced them back until he stared Maddox in the eye. It didn't last.

"There you go," Maddox said. "The training has started. I expect Centurion Gricks to show up when I need him in the desert."

"A second chance?" asked Gricks.

"It's yours for the taking. Let's see what happens, eh?'

"Yes," Gricks whispered. "Yes."

-47-

A day later, the dirigibles battled against strong upper winds, causing shaking now and again. Despite that, the dirigibles continued toward the heading Maddox had given.

Meanwhile, Maddox walked the corridors, stretching his legs. When he returned to his cabin, he noticed the other door was open a crack. He ignored it, reaching for the handle to his quarters.

The other door opened and Gricks stepped out. "Captain, sir, Eddings said he's ready to talk to you. If you'll come in, sir, the lights are low. Eddings doesn't like it bright. He doesn't want to see too much. I know that might not make much sense—"

"That's fine," Maddox said, interrupting.

Gricks nodded. "Hern is out exercising. He hates Eddings, bullying him most of the time. I stood up for Eddings this morning and Hern backed off. I couldn't believe it. Maybe you're right. Maybe you are right."

Gricks must have realized he was clutching Maddox's hand and babbling. Gricks let go as if electricity had surged from Maddox.

"I'm sorry, sir."

"Not at all," Maddox said. "It's good to see you're recovering. I knew it was in you."

Gricks stood a little taller, and he ushered Maddox into the room.

Eddings' covers had been down, revealing the sub-centurion's head. Upon seeing Maddox, Eddings whipped the covers back over his head.

"Eddings, it's Captain Maddox," Gricks said. "It's okay."

"Okay?" Eddings said in a defeated voice.

"I told him you were willing to tell him what you knew about the desert, what you'd learned."

"I thought I could do this," Eddings whimpered. "But I can't."

"Sir," Gricks told Maddox, "Eddings was an assistant in the main library at the spaceport. He worked for the off-worlders. He read some of the secret accounts of the worst legion disasters."

"Sounds interesting," Maddox said. "Eddings, if you care to tell me I'd appreciate it, but it's up to you."

"I don't want to talk about it." Eddings said. "It's too hard to talk to you. You're not like us."

"Now, now," Maddox said, "we're in the same boat, the same airship. You're one of mine, as I'm your commanding officer. That's the only difference that counts. The rest is meaningless."

The covers came down and Eddings looked at Maddox before whipping the covers back up. "Do you mean that, sir?"

"I do. On my honor," Maddox said.

"All right," Eddings said, with the covers still over his head. "I'll tell you, but I think there's only one disaster that fits what you want to know. Gricks says you want to know about the desert people, right?"

"Yes," Maddox said, moving closer. On inspiration, he sat down against Eddings' cot. "Talk when you're ready. I'm all ears. I can wait."

Maddox folded his hands and closed his eyes, leaning back against the cot.

Ten minutes passed, with Gricks clearing his throat three different times.

Finally, Eddings began talking about a legion disaster as the dirigibles headed south. A storm had blown three dirigibles off course, so they used a different route. All legion dirigibles used a proscribed route—for reasons Eddings hadn't learned.

These three had used the Marin Lowland Equatorial Bridge, crossing a highly radiated region.

"One dirigible went down from engine failure," Eddings said. "Some suspect that was from the radiation. Two were hit with rocket fire. One dirigible exploded midair but the other made an emergency landing on the equatorial desert bridge. I know because there were three survivors from it. The survivors told of the deep desert tribes, Metamorphs with horrible leathery skin and tusks growing out of their mouths. The Metamorphs caught most of the legionnaires, taking them underground during the day, only moving at night.

"The radiation is bad there," Eddings continued. "Maybe the ozone isn't as thick in the equatorial regions. The sun blazes hellishly, the temperature reaching one hundred and fifty degrees. The sun scorches the desert as fierce winds howl all day long. Sun and wind turn each grain of sand hard like diamonds. Some of the grains scintillate in the sunlight, causing monochromic colors to shine. Storms and lightning surge across the land at other times. Everything hunkers down then. The few plants are low, often hidden in shadows. Lizards come out at night, and insects, some larger than you would expect. They all scavenge. Anything that dies in the desert has its bones bleached white by the terrible sun and howling wind."

"The legion captives," Maddox said softly. "You were speaking about them?"

"Yes. The Metamorphs caught them. I guess you'd call the Metamorphs cannibals. They must have been human once, but they're not like you and me anymore. They're huge and powerful, more like Hern, but even more so, and taller than you, Captain. Not as tall as the giants that, that—"

Eddings sobbed silently.

Maddox waited, knowing the sobs were therapeutic.

Eventually, Eddings began to talk again. "The Metamorphs brought the legionnaires into their subterranean larders. They strapped the men onto boards and shoved feeding tubes down their throats. They poured an oily feed into them until over the months the captives became grotesquely fat. The Metamorphs cooked the unfortunates in their own fat, feasting upon the flesh."

Maddox scowled.

"The deep deserts are horrible, Captain. I think some Metamorphs live closer to the Highlands. Some of those have tasted the honey. Some of those Metamorphs are longer-lived than average. Others have developed a telepathic gestalt power. At least that was what one special report I read said. I wasn't supposed to have read it. You won't tell on me, will you, sir?"

"Your secret is safe with me."

"Thank you, sir. I appreciate that. These Metamorphs have learned from their captives. They've learned to steal vehicles and trade with others. There are outposts at the fringes of the pole regions. Some caravans cross to some of the nearer lower jungles. The Metamorph cannibals attack and take captives, increasing their meat herds. If they don't have enough regular people, they feed off their own. They're vicious and ugly."

"What sort of weapons do the Metamorphs possess?"

"Every kind of weapon we have: heavy machine guns to the spring rifles cheap tribunes hand out to their troops."

Eddings suppressed a sniffle. "I suppose the tribunes figure the legions are going to die anyway. Why arm them with superior gear. I was a fool to have come on the raid, wasn't I, Captain?"

"Not a fool," Maddox said. "I'm going to see that you're well compensated for all this."

The covers came down just enough, so Eddings peered at Maddox in the dim lighting. He looked a little longer this time. Then the covers went back up.

"I know you're different, Captain Maddox. Gricks told me what you did to get us out of field labor. You're different from others. But, sir, this ancient weapon site, do you think it's really there?"

"I do," Maddox said.

Eddings was silent, until… "I think the mind fusion Metamorphs search for these weapons, too. They might even have some powerful armaments. Those Metamorphs might be deadly and might try to bring us down if we fly over their territory."

"What else can you tell me about the Metamorphs?"

"There's not much more, sir. They live in a desolate and deadly land. Most everything is done by moonlight. Anyone caught in the searing sun—they say Yellow Tusks survived the sun. He leads the mind fusion Metamorphs."

Maddox became thoughtful. His intuitive sense told him… "You have a touch of psi ability, don't you, Eddings?"

"I had some honey once, sir, just a little. It did something in my mind. I can feel the witches probing and trying to read our thoughts as we speak. I block them a little. I try to fight them. I can't stand the light. It hurts my eyes now. It really hurts."

"All right," Maddox said. "I appreciate what you've told me. You've given me what I need. Is there anything else out in the desert we don't know about?"

"Yes," Eddings said. "Rare gems. They're worth a fortune. Some call them singing gems. They have unique properties. They entertain and do something else I can't remember. There are very few gems for sale, but those that are bring a fortune. Sometimes the Metamorphs have them, and that seems to increase the gestalt mind power. But that's all I know, sir. Not too many people know that. I wasn't supposed to have read what I did. I think the off-worlders that run the library discovered what I read. That's why they sent me on the raid. Now that I look back, I didn't volunteer. I was bullied into it. Sir, can I ever stop people from bullying me?"

"You've gone through a horrible experience," Maddox said. "You know the worst life can give you. Now it's time to take the broken pieces and reassemble them so you're the man you want to be."

"A man, sir? I can't be a man anymore. I mean, not when I lost—"

"It's not just balls that make a man, though they certainly help," Maddox said. "You lost something precious to a man. But you were born a man, a man you are, and a man you shall remain, unless you become a coward who utterly runs. I picked you for a reason. Do you know that Eddings?"

"I'm beginning to understand that sir."

"Good. You hang in there. You keep recouping. When I ask for you to do a tough thing, you do it. That will go a long way to rebuilding the confidence that was shattered."

258

"Yes, sir. Thank you, sir."

Maddox got up. He looked at Eddings hidden under the covers. "You hang in there, son. It's going to be okay."

"You think so?"

"I do, thanks for what you told me. It's going to help."

"I'm going to keep back the witches for now, sir. They're excited over what I just said. But I don't think they're going to remember as much as they think."

"You holler if they give you any guff," said Maddox.

"Yes, sir."

Maddox pointed at Gricks, nodding his thanks.

Gricks grinned.

Maddox stepped into the corridor. That was useful information. Now he needed to think about it and see what kind of plan he could get out of it.

-48-

It was during dusk as the bright sun-star sank below the horizon that Maddox received a summons from Ophir.

Maddox left Dravek and the others in their quarters as he hurried down the long corridor. He wore the heavy pistol in its holster and the monofilament blade in his boot.

As Maddox neared the forward control cabin, he sensed an intuitive…warning. There was danger ahead, he couldn't tell from what, though. Maddox inhaled, trying to calm himself. It didn't work as it usually did. The sense of danger increased.

Maddox came to a halt in the corridor.

He felt the dirigible's steady thrum, a sign that the propellers continued to twirl. In some ways, it was like a spaceship's thrum during space travel.

Thinking of space, Maddox missed Galyan, Valerie, Ludendorff and Riker. Should he have brought Dravek along with him tonight? Would an extra gun avert his death if Ophir meant to assassinate him here? Ophir might try assassination to keep Julia from living longer. If Maddox wasn't alive to trade his secret, Julia might soon die of old age. In such a case, Ophir could conceivably take her position as head of the clan.

Maddox chewed on his lower lip. The sense of danger built into a nearly overwhelming pressure within.

I'm being a fool, Maddox realized even as the sense of danger almost drove him to his knees.

Maddox roved outward with his Balron-trained senses, seeing if he could pinpoint the danger. Vaguely, he was aware the danger came from far below in the desert. That meant Ophir had no part in the danger. Below was the desert, Metamorphs and a possible telepathic gestalt power.

Abruptly, Maddox raised intuitive defenses like a mind shield. He felt then a questing mind seeking souls to devour.

Was that the right way to think of it?

Maddox had no idea. This mind felt like a Ska or a Yon Soth.

He shuddered, finding both concepts horrible.

Firming his resolve, seeking a serenity that wasn't coming, Maddox continued down the corridor until he sought permission to enter the bridge.

Ophir swiveled around in his seat, granting permission.

Maddox walked into the control chamber, the dirigible bridge. The lights were dim. The consoles around the room glowed red and blue. The distant desert floor through the low wide window in front glowed with an eerie silver color. Motes of prismatic colors shimmered on the desert surface. Two moons glided in the dark sky, surrounded by stars that were just beginning to glitter.

"A remarkable sight, eh?" asked Ophir.

Maddox nodded mutely as the sense of threat grew worse. It felt as if missiles were ready to launch at the airship.

Mara groaned, shivering, as she stood near Ophir.

It was only then Maddox grew aware that two men held Mara up, one on either side of her. Sweat dotted her forehead. Her brown hair hung limply from her head as she continued to shiver.

Ophir cast a nervous glance at her. Abruptly, Ophir stood. "Follow me," he told Maddox.

In his red robes, Ophir swirled through a hatch into a ready room. He went to a small desk, sitting behind it.

The two guards brought Mara, setting her onto a chair before the desk.

Maddox stepped through the hatch, standing to the side.

"Care for a drink?" asked Ophir.

"No thanks," Maddox said.

Ophir snapped his fingers at one of the guards. The man hurried to a wet bar, mixing a drink and bringing it to Ophir.

He took it, sipping gingerly.

Mara groaned again. Her eyes were screwed shut and she shivered constantly.

"Close the door," Ophir said.

Maddox did.

"Sit," Ophir said, indicating another chair.

Maddox went there, sitting, ill at ease.

Ophir leaned back in his chair, staring at Mara and sipping his drink.

The guard had retreated to Mara, standing behind her with the other guard. Both men wore red uniforms and had holsters on their black belts.

"What's happening to her?" Ophir asked Maddox.

"How should I know?"

"I suspect you of planning this." Ophir said. "You spoke to the wretch who lies in his bed with the covers pulled over his head. He knew much more than I understood. Mara has been probing his mind from afar. The fool knows about a Metamorph mind fusion in this part of the world. They name themselves the Yun People."

Maddox shook his head.

"Don't lie to me, Maddox," Ophir said. "Tell me what you know about the Yun People."

Maddox didn't know if he should keep his eyes on the guards or Ophir. Was this all an excuse to shoot him?

Ophir must have divined his thoughts. "Wait outside."

The two guards hurried out as if they were glad to leave.

Maddox frowned.

"You're too nervous about all this," Ophir said. "I'm beginning to believe this isn't your doing."

Maddox remained silent.

"How old do think I am?"

"Thirty, thirty-five," Maddox said.

Ophir barked laughter. "I'm one hundred and twelve. Does that surprise you?"

"Very."

"I've made a study of people, their physical reactions, what they unknowingly give away about themselves. You're good at hiding your intentions, but not perfect."

"Meaning what?" Maddox asked.

"I know you're afraid whereas before you showed courage. Did you know about the Metamorph mind fusion community?"

"Not until Sub-Centurion Eddings told me about it."

"What do you fear?"

Maddox stared at Ophir.

"What has you worried?" Ophir amended.

"You don't want your grandma to survive much longer."

"Ah. You think I plan to assassinate you in order to forestall her continued rule?"

"It's a possibility," Maddox said.

"Why should you care? I thought you didn't want to live anymore."

"Not as a slave to a depraved people."

"You refer to us Highlanders as being depraved?"

"Most assuredly," Maddox said.

"This is interesting. You've suddenly dropped your pretenses. Why is that?"

From her chair, Mara groaned once more.

"What's wrong with her?" Maddox asked.

"I want you to tell me."

Maddox shook his head. "I don't know."

"Yet you've sensed something to cause you to fear."

"That isn't how I'd say it," Maddox replied.

Mara's eyes snapped open. She raised her head and turned to look at Maddox and then Ophir.

"Her eyes," Ophir said, finishing his drink in a gulp.

Light or brightness shined from Mara's eyes. At the same time, a terrible sense of wrongness filled the ready room. It radiated from Mara, but Maddox was sure it didn't originate from her.

Mara opened her mouth.

Maddox found that his right hand was on the handle of his holstered pistol. He yearned to draw the gun and shoot Mara. He looked at Ophir. The man had clenched his right fist, aiming the ruby rings at her. He must feel the same thing from her.

Maddox scowled, and then understanding hit him. "What are you?"

263

Mara stared at him.

"You're using the woman," Maddox said. "Well, you have our attention. Tell us what you want and then leave her mind."

Mara began to laugh with a dreadful sound.

-49-

Maddox understood what Ophir had said a moment ago about Mara's eyes. They'd become shiny with a luminance, as if an inner fire burned in her.

Mara's laughter continued.

It must have become too much for Ophir. Red rays from his rubies shined upon Mara. The rays stopped the barest fraction before touching her.

"No!" Mara, or the thing controlling Mara, said abruptly. She raised an arm and pointed at Ophir.

An eerie power struck Ophir, stopped by his personal force field.

Mara scowled. "How is that possible?"

"I'm wondering the same thing about you stopping my rings," Ophir said.

"Perhaps we could get down to basics," Maddox said. "Let's cease attacking each other, at least for the moment, and talk it over."

"Well?" Mara said in an impossibly deep voice as she stared at Ophir.

"Agreed," said Ophir.

Mara lowered her arm. At least she was no longer laughing. "Who is in charge here?"

"I am," Ophir said.

"You have ordered the…?" Mara frowned. Was the mental power that controlled her rifling through her memories? "You have ordered the airships over my territory?"

"By territory, you mean the desert below?" Ophir asked.

"And the air over the territory," Mara said.

"Before we continue our talk," Maddox said, "it might be a good idea if we introduce ourselves. I'm Captain Maddox. That is Gallant Ophir. What should we call you?"

"Mara."

"No," Maddox said. "You're an outside mental force originating from elsewhere. Mara's voice is being used, but she isn't the one speaking to us."

"Since you insist, I am the Yun."

"As in the Yun People?" asked Ophir.

Mara turned to him. "I am speaking for the Yun."

"Ophir and I are individual entities," Maddox said. "Are you the combined gestalt power of the Yun People?"

"I have named myself," Mara said. "That is enough. I have come seeking the leader of the...airships. I understand very well that you are individuals. And yet, you act for a greater whole. Whom shall I address here?"

"That would still be me," Ophir said.

"Why does he speak then?" Mara asked, pointing at Maddox.

Ophir made to sip from an empty glass, then set it down, annoyed. "Maddox is an advisor. He is helping me."

"I comprehend," Mara said. "Now, I will know your intentions. Do you plan to land in my territory?"

"That depends where it lies," Ophir said. "Are you claiming the entire desert?"

"This is the equatorial belt. I do claim it."

"We had planned on touching down for a few hours," Ophir said. "Can we come to an accommodation?"

"Possibly," Mara said. "Tell me where exactly you wish to land."

"I'd tell the Yun People exactly where we plan to land," Maddox said. "No tricks or dissembling."

Ophir studied the captain until he nodded. He gave the precise coordinates for the weapon site.

"You seek an ancient thing," Mara said. "Why do you seek it?"

266

"We're historians," Maddox said. "We seek to learn about the past."

Mara's eyes brightened with power. "You are a practiced deceiver. That was a lie. You seek a weapon. I know. I see it plainly in the woman's mind."

"Do you mind if we take the weapon?" Maddox asked.

"I would want an extraction fee for it."

"Money?" asked Maddox.

"People," Mara said. "I would demand…" She touched her fingers as if silently counting. "I would demand one hundred and fifty people."

"For what reason?" asked Ophir.

"For my larder," Mara said.

Ophir glanced at Maddox. "What's it talking about?"

"The Yun Metamorphs eat humans," Maddox said.

"We eat all meat," Mara said.

Ophir blanched.

Maddox expected Ophir to tell the Yun People to go to hell.

Instead, Ophir said, "Make it seventy people and you have a deal."

"I have stated one hundred and fifty," Mara said. "I am not a merchant to bicker about the price. It is final. How do you say? Take it or leave it."

"I'm not authorized to hand over one hundred and fifty Honey Men," Ophir said smoothly.

"Then I forbid you to land," Mara said.

"How will you stop us?" Ophir asked.

"I can stop you any time I wish."

"Through missiles?" asked Maddox.

"Or beams," Mara said. "I have grown more sophisticated since the people of Eddings' tale."

"Was the tale true?" asked Maddox.

Ophir pressed a switch on his desk.

"Yes, Gallant," a woman said over the desk comm.

"Take the airships higher," Ophir said, "tell the weapons team to keep a strict watch for missiles launching from the desert. They're to intercept them as soon as possible."

"I understand, Gallant," the woman said over the desk comm.

Mara was shaking her head. "That won't help you."

"We're going to turn around," Ophir said. "You can keep your ancient weapon. We don't need it that badly."

"I'm going to insist upon the bargain," Mara said. "If you don't agree and land, I will launch the missiles. You carry much feast meat. I desire it. Thus, before you leave my range, I will force your airships down. It is either that or you must make a bargain with me."

"One hundred and fifty men aren't that many," Maddox told Ophir.

"I'll give the desert people three of yours," Ophir said.

"Done," Maddox said.

Ophir frowned.

Maddox tried to signal him on the sly.

Suddenly, Ophir's eyebrows lifted. "Yes. I agree. We will land—"

"You are attempting to deceive me," Mara said. "I am the Yun People. I refuse to accept such deception. Prepare to die."

"Why?" asked Maddox. "We're going to land, and you'll receive one hundred and fifty prime humans. You can fatten them for weeks or months. If you attack with missiles, much of your feast meat will perish in the explosions."

"Your airships are attempting to climb out of range," Mara said.

A light on Ophir's desk began to blink. He clicked a switch.

"Sir," a woman said over the desk comm, "missiles are launching from the desert. They're heading straight up for us."

"Are the counter-batteries aligned?" asked Ophir.

"They are, Gallant."

Mara groaned, her eyes blinking as the glow from them ceased. At the same time, she slid bonelessly from the chair to the deck.

Alarms rang in the airship. They were under attack.

-50-

Maddox raced out of the ready room with Ophir onto the bridge. The lighting was still dim here. That allowed Maddox to view the pinprick dots on the silvery desert surface far below. Those must be the missile launches.

Maddox sidled to a weapons console. On the screen, he saw the rising missiles heading for the dirigibles. Counter-missiles were heading down. They were crude missiles and counter-rockets as compared to those on *Victory,* but they would do the job just the same.

Maddox didn't like the idea of resting his fate on the counter-missiles. The airship wasn't like an armored starship with an electromagnetic shield. Here, thin material held the helium-filled cells.

Maddox stepped quietly until he spoke to a guard near the exit hatch. "What are the procedures in case the airship is hit?"

The guard shrugged, either not knowing or caring.

Maddox stepped to a bridge officer, asking the same thing.

The man shrugged. "We jump and hope our parachute works. Unfortunately, it's death to land on the desert."

"Why is that?"

"The sun kills at one hundred and fifty degrees during the middle of the day."

Maddox didn't tell the man it wouldn't do that at night: the time to make things happen. He needed to get back to his team.

Ophir must have noticed him heading toward the exit. "Captain Maddox, come stand here and advise me."

269

Maddox didn't believe the airship was going to survive the missile assault. Thus, he nodded and waited a moment, remaining where he was.

Ophir turned away to answer a woman officer.

Maddox immediately moved for the exit.

"Captain," Ophir said.

Maddox ignored Ophir and walked out.

"Guards," Ophir shouted.

Maddox broke into a run, shouldering a person heading for the bridge out of the way. The man stumbled from Maddox and crashed against a bulkhead. Maddox didn't see what happened next. He was running full tilt, moving fast, blowing past astonished people. He kept waiting for a loudspeaker to announce that he was under arrest. That didn't happen.

It was a long way to his quarters, however. The airship shook as more and more counter-missile left. How much time was left for them?

A grim intuitive sense gripped Maddox. A missile was heading straight for the airship. He wasn't going to make it back to his quarters in time.

Maddox glanced about, spotting an emergency sign. He raced that way. Would it matter if he survived the airship? Metamorphs were surely heading this way on the ground to pick up any surviving meat.

"You," a guard shouted. "Halt!"

Maddox twisted his head.

Several armed guards raced after him.

Maddox drew the heavy pistol, swiveled his torso and fired twice.

Two of the guards crumbled onto the deck.

"Don't fire," one of the fallen said. "Ophir wants him alive."

Maddox fired again, killing all three. It was unsporting to fight like that, but he was all alone again. He doubted any of his team was going to survive this. For Meta and Jewel's sakes, he needed to survive, even if he needed to play dirty in order to do it. Besides, was it dirty to use an enemy's restrictions against him?

"No," Maddox said.

There was a horrific explosion. The deck shook as the airship shuddered. More explosions sounded from outside. The deck tipped one way and then another.

Maddox hurled himself against a closed hatch. It exploded open against his weight and velocity. Soldiers turned to stare at him.

"Arrest him," one said. "Gallant Ophir wants him alive."

Once more, Maddox drew the pistol, firing and killing. He speed-loaded, fired again, used the handle like a club, and practiced savate kicks against the last few.

Soon, no soldier survived the attack. Maddox looked around for survival gear that he'd need on the desert surface. There were none he could find. This was a screw up. The damned Yun was doing this.

Maddox did find a parachute and donned it. He found breathing gear. They were high up in the thin air. He'd need this for what he planned to do.

The airship sagged. Maddox felt his feet leave the deck. They were going down. With the parachute pack on his back, the mask on his face, and his gun holstered, Maddox yanked a lever on a bulkhead.

A hatch blew out. Cold desert air flooded within. The rush of it pushed Maddox back within.

"Meta," he said into the howling wind. "Jewel. I'm coming home."

One step at a time, Maddox fought his way to the hatch. He didn't know he'd survive the desert. But he certainly wouldn't survive in a deflated airship going down.

At last, he gripped the edge of the hatch and hauled himself hard and fast. He catapulted out of the falling dirigible, as it was no longer lighter-than-air.

In the air outside, Maddox held himself in such a way as to slide and fly away from the deflating mass. The desert floor glowed silvery far below. He looked around and didn't spy the second airship anywhere.

It didn't matter. Would Dravek or the others have escaped the doomed vessel? He had no idea, but he doubted Gricks or Eddings had done so.

Maddox breathed deeply through the mask. He could sense the Yun gestalt intelligence all around him. He hated it. The mass mind fusion might have destroyed his chances of ever seeing his family again.

Maddox put that out of his mind as he worked on doing this right. It was far too soon to pull the ripcord. He saw a few others making it from the falling and doomed airship.

He had an idea that if anyone could do this, it would be Dravek. The man was his clone. Well, Maddox would wait to see. If Dravek was going to die—

Maddox shook his head. He needed to concentrate on himself for the moment.

Thus, after a short interval, he pulled the ripcord. The parachute exploded out and soon he drifted toward the nighttime desert. This could be a longer and more painful death than perishing in the airship when it hit.

"At least it isn't daylight yet."

Then, the ground seemed to rush up. Maddox judged it just right. He hit and rolled. He'd made it. Now, what was he going to do?

-51-

The first thing he did was gather his parachute and lines, pushing them into the pack. He didn't want to advertise his position to others, even though he planned to be long gone before the sun rose.

Afterward, he studied the starlit sky. No more missiles rose. No more counter-missiles came down. He didn't see either airship, not in the dark sky or on the silvery ground with its scintillating motes of light.

It was surprisingly cool on the ground, given that it had likely been one hundred and fifty this afternoon. It had to be a balmy eighty-five or so.

He shrugged off his pack. He had water and food, but no desert gear other than a pair of sunglasses. That likely wouldn't be enough protection from the sun during the day. The sun would blind him, particularly as the sunlight reflected off the sand. Given what he'd seen in the moonlight, daylight would be unbearable.

He studied the stars. They were so different from anything on Earth. There was nothing familiar. A pang of homesickness struck. His only consolation was that he likely wasn't going to be alive much longer to worry about it.

He sought for any sign of the Metamorph mind fusion. There was something in the ether, but nothing he could pinpoint.

What now?

With a shrug, Maddox pulled out a compass and checked the heading. He might as well march north. That at least gave the semblance that he was trying to survive.

He began to trudge over the sand, which crunched underfoot. There was the occasional hoot and then screech. Should he worry about the sounds?

He came upon a dead Honey Man. He checked the corpse but found nothing of use. Then, on the wind, he heard the faintest of cries. It almost sounded familiar.

Maddox stood and looked in all directions. There was nothing—

He heard the sound again. It was a shout from a great distance. Could he be sensing his wife calling for him? Did Meta sense his approaching death?

"Maddox," he heard very faintly.

Maddox scowled. Was he losing it here at the end? He didn't want to think so.

The call came again. It almost sounded as if he called himself. He smiled. Maybe Dravek called him.

Maddox's eyes widened. He tried to pinpoint the direction of the call. It came from the south.

Maddox headed that way, walking fast.

Soon, the call was easily audible. Dravek did call him.

"Dravek," Maddox shouted.

He peered south and thought to see a man waving his arms in the moonlight.

Maddox began to trot.

Soon, he could easily make out Dravek. The man had a giant pair of binoculars and seemed to be watching him.

Soon enough, the two men greeted each other on the silvery surface of Gath.

"You old son of a gun," Dravek said, hugging Maddox and slapping him on the back. "You made it."

"So did you," Maddox said, clapping Dravek on the back in turn. "Did you jump from the airship?"

"What else?"

Maddox noticed a huge set of bags at Dravek's feet. "What are in those?"

"I'm guessing you didn't have time to grab any desert gear."

Maddox shook his head.

"I did have time. One of the bags is for you."

Maddox opened it and found stout desert boots and a suit of wind-resistant nu-fiber. There was headgear with a tight-fitting wind-cap and sun-goggles, together with blast flaps.

"I'm beginning to think we can do this," Maddox said, his morale rising. He began to don the gear.

"Glad you think so. I'm not as sanguine. It must be three thousand kilometers or more to any settlement in the north. Plus, there must be hordes of Metamorphs between looking for meat to eat, meaning us."

"We won't survive this by jawing," Maddox said. "Do you have any weapons?"

Dravek showed him a sub-machine gun. "I also have a few grenades. You have a hefty pistol it looks like. You serious about marching to the north?"

"We might as well start now." Maddox didn't want to tell Dravek about Grandma Julia's threat of launching nuclear-tipped missiles. Maybe she would hold back on that. The Leviathan assault vessels were still coming as well. What did he have for time regarding that? Maybe a week and a half at best.

"It sure would have been good if the Eye of Helion had put us at the North Pole spaceport," Dravek said. "We don't even have this ancient weapon we started seeking. How far do you reckon it is from here?"

"That's a good question." Maddox checked his compass and a small slate. He used the stars and triangulated. "The weapon site is about two hundred and fifty kilometers from here."

"Closer than three thousand kilometers to the North Pole," Dravek said.

"Any reason why you think we should try for the weapon site?" Maddox asked.

"Plain cussedness," Dravek said. "Why do you ask?"

As they trekked by the light of two small moons, Maddox told Dravek what had happened in the ready room with Mara and the Yun People mind fusion.

"Shit," Dravek said more than once.

"Any thoughts about all this?" asked Maddox when he was done.

"We're never getting to the North Pole, at least not on foot. We need an edge. I don't think the mind fusion liked the idea of us getting near that ancient weapon site. Maybe there's a good reason for that."

Maddox finally told Dravek about Grandma Julia's nuclear missile threat.

"The Honey Men are pricks to the end," Dravek said. "Too bad we couldn't nuke them."

"I'd rather go home."

"And live a few more years," Dravek said. "We keep marching then?"

"For as long as we're able," Maddox said.

"How many hours to sunrise?"

"Less than six," Maddox said.

"So, let's truck while the trucking's good. We'll sleep while it's hot."

"If we can sleep in such heat," Maddox said.

With that, they trekked in silence, marveling at the beauty of the Gath desert at night.

-52-

As Maddox and Dravek trekked through the moonlit wasteland, the captain was surprised to find more life than he'd expected. There were giant insects weighing two pounds each, with hard shells. They looked like rocks until the "jitterbugs" chirped like insane crickets. When Maddox stepped too near one, twenty exploded into the air with their glossy wings a-blur. A few brushed against Maddox's face. He batted about, hitting one, knocking it down and squishing it with his boot. The buzzing and clicking intensified until the flying bugs disappeared into the night.

Later, a lizard the length of Maddox's arm lunged, revealing itself, and gulped one of the rock-like bugs, audibly crunching it as goo ran down its jaws.

"Damned reptiles," Dravek muttered.

There were alien bats, big suckers, who often circled them before flying elsewhere as they made clicking noises. Maybe the weirdest things were long worms with sharp teeth. A few boiled up out of the sand when Dravek tossed a rock to the side. Three of the worms lunged and gnawed at the rock before leaving it alone. Dravek swore he saw one grin at him, with moonlight shining off its tiny piranha-like teeth.

"The worms must be scavengers," Dravek said.

Maddox shrugged. The desert at night was eerily beautiful but far too deadly for his tastes. What would it be like during the day?

"Do you hear that?" Dravek asked suddenly.

Maddox looked at him.

"It sounds like gunfire."

Maddox listened. It did sound like gunfire far in the distance. "Who's firing at who?"

"Should we try to find out?" Dravek asked.

"Yeah," Maddox said.

A half hour later, they came upon a crashed pod, a thin metallic capsule the size of a small car. It had four crash-seats and torn restraints within, with a huge parachute held by fiber lines outside. The chute rippled in the soft desert breeze.

"That must have come from the dirigible," Dravek said. "It's a way to insert troops without having to land the airship."

"This drop pod is empty," Maddox said.

Dravek had a flashlight, shining it within. There were blood and bullet holes everywhere.

"Hey, look at that," Dravek said.

He shined the light on a grotesque, leathery hand twice the size of Maddox's. It lay behind a seat and had black lacquered fingernails.

"Is that a Metamorph's hand?" asked Maddox.

"It was severed," Dravek said. "Look at the wrist. A blast tore it off. From a grenade, I bet. There should be bodies in here. What happened to them?"

Maddox thought about that. "I think I understand."

"Care to tell me?"

"The Metamorphs are cannibals. The drop pod carried men. Some of the Honey Men must have gotten into this before the airship disintegrated or folded in on itself. The pod floated down and landed, and some Metamorphs arrived and killed the men. Or worse, the Metamorphs captured the men alive."

"Why would that be worse?" Dravek asked.

"Didn't you hear me? The Metamorphs are cannibals. Eddings said the Metamorphs take survivors into a subterranean larder and fatten them for however long it takes. Then, they roast them in their own fat and eat the regular humans at a feast."

"That's disgusting. Should we do something about it?"

"Sure," Maddox said. "Let's call the cavalry. Oh, wait. What cavalry? We're it."

Dravek wasn't listening. He scanned the night sky. "Do the Metamorphs have air sleds? I guess what I'm asking is how are they maneuvering?"

"An excellent point," Maddox said. "Let's walk around the pod in a widening circle and see if we can find anything."

Soon, they found wide tire marks in the sand.

Maddox thought about that. "They must use balloon-tired vehicles. The balloon tires make sure the vehicles don't bog down in loose sand."

"Okay, okay. Do you think the Metamorphs are searching for more drop pods?"

"Without a doubt," Maddox said. "The gunfire we heard means some of the people have enough time to collect their arms and fight, however much good it does or did them."

Maddox could have said more on the subject. He decided to wait. He sensed the Yun mind fusion roving or sweeping the silvery landscape for prey. It was an eerie, fantastical sensation.

"Look over there," Dravek said.

Maddox looked where Dravek pointed. There were bright flashes in the distance. He heard the distinctive sound of gunfire, lots of it.

The two looked at each other.

"What do we do?" Dravek asked.

"We need others if we hope to survive the desert," Maddox said. "Let's see if those others can use some help against the Metamorphs. There's another thing: the more we know about this place, without getting captured, the better for us. We need to investigate this."

The two began to trot, using a long-legged lope that was Maddox's trademark. For once, he was with a man who could match him stride for stride. Dravek was not only as fast and long-legged as Maddox, but had his endurance, perhaps a little more. They covered the silvery landscape quickly even as they began to perspire.

Soon, they perceived four, no, five black shapes: big, almost square shapes but with rounded contours. They were enclosed vehicles or vans with huge balloon tires. The black vehicles had parked. From the top of one, through a hatch perhaps, was a Metamorph firing a long-barreled heavy machine gun on a swivel mount. The machine gun must have produced the flashes they'd seen earlier.

Both men dropped to the sand and lay prone. Dravek dug out a night scope, examining the vehicles through it.

"Yep, Metamorphs are killing regular people. Three drop pods landed together in a group."

An electric bullhorn powered up. A Metamorph shouted through it. Perhaps he was telling the men to lay down their weapons and surrender.

Almost as soon as Maddox thought that Dravek announced, "The men are coming out of the drop pods. They're pitching their weapons onto the sand and standing in a file. Doesn't that strike you as weird?"

Maddox realized why he'd just thought about surrender now. The mind fusion was focused on the men. It must have found them and now mentally worked against them. Thus, they were foolishly surrendering. A trickle of the focused enemy thought must have seeped to him.

Maddox wanted to jump up and run to them, telling the men to fight to the death. Instead, he kept lying there as Dravek told him how the Metamorphs drove forward and loaded the limp survivors into the vehicles.

Abruptly, the vehicles sped backward, turned around and gunned it. Maddox heard the engines roar. The Metamorphs drove away into the night like cops responding to a call.

"What was that about?" Maddox asked.

"They're going somewhere important in a hurry."

"Let's check the drop pods for weapons."

"Good thinking," Dravek said.

They got up and headed to them. Inside the pods were smears of blood and machine gun-riddled corpses.

"Must have been an important call if the Metamorphs didn't bother to collect the freshly killed meat," Maddox said.

"Hey," Dravek said, "look at this." He held up a big machine gun.

They found more weapons, loading up with the extra gear.

Maddox now had a heavy assault rifle. It was as big as he dared carry together with the extra ammo. He had a gut feeling they'd be in a firefight tonight. If they were lucky, they'd gain

280

a vehicle through it. Thus, he was willing to carry more than he would otherwise.

"I'm hearing something," Maddox said. "See anything interesting with those night vision binoculars of yours?"

Dravek climbed up the least damaged pod and scanned the darkness.

"Yeah, maybe five clicks away is a bonfire of something. I see at least a dozen drop pods and a landed air vehicle. Hey, the air vehicle is firing shells at the Metamorph vehicles, making some explode and burn. Other black vans are farther away. Maddox, the air vehicle looks like the front part of the gondola, the former control cabin of the dirigible."

Maddox thought about that. Would the legions have designed an airship for fast escape? The control cabin could detach and become an air-mobile vehicle. Had it glided? Could it stay airborne for a time? Was that why Ophir had called for him to stay, to tell him the control room was the safest place on the dirigible?

"We should head there," Maddox said. He hadn't forgotten the mind fusion that could tip the scales in the Metamorphs' favor. "If we're going to survive, we need transportation. Hoofing it on foot, especially once the sun shines—this may be our best chance for getting off Gath."

"Right," Dravek said. "I'm with you."

They secured their gear, cinching every buckle tight. They clutched the heavy weaponry and ammo, loading up with as much as they dared carry. Then the two set out at a stiff pace, seeing if they could reach the firefight in time to be of service.

-53-

Maddox could feel the play of the Yun mind fusion the closer they came to the firefight. There were burning, balloon-tired vans, some closer to the grounded pods and air vehicle. The cannon from the grounded air vehicle must have destroyed most of the Metamorph vans. The trouble was that the Metamorphs offloaded from their surviving vehicles, running individually across the sand, dropping down and crawling like Wild West Indians to outcroppings or rocks. From there the Metamorphs fired rifles, grenade launchers and heavy machine guns.

"I wonder if Gallant Ophir is there," Maddox said. "If he is, would he call down a nuclear strike on top of his head, killing everyone?"

"From what I've seen of the Honey Men," Dravek said, "they don't want to die any time soon. They want to live forever."

"Good point," Maddox said. "If anything, Ophir is calling home for reinforcements."

"Reinforcements from the Honey Men would be days away."

"Maybe," Maddox said. "Grandma Julia might have planned for mishaps and sent other dirigibles as backup. Anyway, how much longer until dawn?"

"Four hours tops," Dravek said.

The firefight out there was still some distance from them.

282

They'd stopped to drink water and eat. Then, the two men in desert gear continued their swift approach to the adversary. The Honey Men had been their enemies, but that had changed with the arrival of the Metamorphs, and the Yun People mind fusion.

The landed air vehicle used its cannon sparingly. Maybe it was running out of munitions. Men behind the pods and lying on the sand traded fire with the circling, crawling Metamorphs.

The Metamorphs were going to lose a lot more of their tusked soldiers doing it this way.

As Maddox contemplated this, sprinting toward the firefight, he felt a dreadful force approaching. It wasn't a physical thing but mental, telepathic. The awareness of it grew in Maddox until he realized—

"Hit the ground, Dravek!"

Maddox dove onto the glittering silvery sand. He felt Dravek thud beside him. Then Maddox did something most unconventional: he crawled atop Dravek and used his hands to clutch his companion's head.

"Don't move," Maddox hissed. "I'm gonna have to protect us both."

How did Maddox know this? It was an intuitive thing, something trained by Balron the Traveler many years ago.

Maddox concentrated with every particle of his being as an intense telepathic force swept over the area. It reverberated with the forceful command of surrender: *Lay down your weaponry. You are defeated. You cannot stand. You are on our territory. You are food. You are meat.*

The telepathic force beat like a heart. It was living. It was a terrifying thing.

Dravek cried out, "We're doomed! We're doomed!" He repeated that over and over, adding, "Let me go. I must surrender."

Maddox clutched Dravek's head even harder. "Listen," he hissed into the clone's ear. "We're not doomed. Fight it. Concentrate. Believe we can win. We can always find a way. We are Captain Maddox. We always find a way to defeat the foe. We never surrender. We fight until the last breath, and

283

then we still find a way to fight. Do you hear me, Dravek? Fight it. Do not concede defeat."

"No defeat," Dravek said in a hoarse voice.

"Right, that's right. Hold on, brother. Hold on."

As the intensity of the telepathic—would one call it a mind bomb? A silent explosion blasted the desert ahead of them. The force bloomed outward in an explosive circumference.

When it hit them, Dravek cried out and likely fell unconscious.

Maddox barely held on to consciousness. That was most likely due to the Erill spiritual energy he'd absorbed long ago. By degrees, he shook off the debilitating mind blast and struggled up to his feet.

"Come on, Dravek."

The clone didn't respond.

Maddox dragged Dravek upright by main force of strength. He slapped Dravek across the face once, twice.

"Okay," Dravek said groggily, "I'm awake. Let's go—but where do we go?"

Maddox pointed at the enemy.

"That's crazy."

"Is it?" Maddox asked. "The Yun People used a mind-fusion blast. I suspect it took them time to gather it. I also suspect it has used up their mental energy for a time. If ever there's a moment where our presence can do wonders, I bet this is it."

"Is this more of your intuitive reasoning?"

"Probably," Maddox said. "I've learned to trust it. Come on, Dravek. Pick up your weapons. Let's go."

Now the two men ran. They ran through the night like cheetahs chasing prey. And unlike cheetahs, these two had the vitality and wind to run for a kilometer at high speed.

They watched as black, balloon-tired vans inched toward the pods and the grounded air vehicle. Metamorphs staggered out of the vehicles, seemingly hurt or wounded by the mind blast—an unexpected and perplexing result.

"We don't know how all this operates," Maddox said.

"What? Huh?" Dravek said. "What in the hell are you talking about? I don't understand what's going on. How are you even breathing?"

They'd stopped and were observing the enemy less than a quarter kilometer from them as they crouched behind a dune.

"They're dragging bodies from near the pods," Maddox said. "The mind blast must have knocked the men out cold."

"I don't see how anything we do is going to help. This is madness."

Maddox turned to stare at Dravek. "I agree. It is madness. And it's our only chance at this point. We must grasp madness with both hands and go for it to the nth degree. Because the mind fusion is in play. Because there's no other way that we're gonna win."

Dravek studied Maddox, perhaps grasping the other's earnestness. "Yeah, sure, we'll do it your way. I'm certainly out of ideas."

Maddox stood, picking up his heavy assault rifle, watching Dravek stand and clutch his.

"All right," Maddox said, "we walk there and observe as carefully as we can. When I say go, start killing Metamorphs and if you can, blow up their vehicles, as many as you can."

"We should have taken a grenade launcher with us," Dravek said.

"Would-a, could-a, should-a. We have what we have. Now let's do it."

"All right, Captain, I'm right behind you."

-54-

It was weird watching the Metamorphs stagger like puppets that had lost their strings. They were jerky, slow and supremely ugly-looking. In the moonlight and in the lamplight of some of the surviving balloon-tired vans, the Metamorphs were shown to be huge, as Eddings had suggested.

Each was larger than Primus Hern, boasting a broad shoulder span and deep chest, their mouths bristling with yellow, curling tusks. Most were bald and naked except for a human skull to cover his genitalia, desert boots, a long human-skin cape and an almost sword-like knife strapped to his side while he cradled a heavy gun.

The Metamorphs carried soldiers of the Honey Men, those who were still alive but frozen into immobility by the mind-blast bomb. The Metamorphs carried the soldiers as husbands would their wives across the threshold: with ease and a grotesque eagerness. You could almost hear the Metamorphs salivating over all this feast meat they were carrying. They had captured a haul of live people.

Other Honey Men were dead. The Metamorphs had laid the corpses in rows. Vehicles moved backward toward them. Smaller Metamorphs carried the corpses by limp arms and legs, tossing them in as if the vehicle was a meat wagon, which indeed it was.

None of the Metamorphs seemed alert, but like drunkards who had been roused from a deep sleep. The Metamorphs were seemingly at the limit of their endurance. Still, the mind fusion must be forcing them to work.

"Let's spread apart a little," Maddox said.

Dravek didn't need any more prodding than that.

The two men stood in the moonlight, unobserved by the Metamorphs. Each gripped a heavy assault rifle.

"Now," Maddox said.

Like angels of death, the two opened fire. They didn't simply spray the enemy with bullets indiscriminately. They used three bullet bursts, tumbling Metamorphs, blowing up the vans, as they quickly discovered which the right places to shoot were. It helped that they used vehicle-destroying rounds.

The two slaughtered stunned Metamorphs. Finally, a few of the enemy bellowed and stumbled away. A few pulled out their weapons but hardly seemed to know what to do with them.

As Maddox and Dravek switched magazines, slapping them in, pulling back the bolts and continuing their slaughter, they advanced at a walking pace toward the camp.

Maddox and Dravek were alert, their luck seemingly holding.

Then, two other people joined the killing. A lean man in red robes and a woman staggered out of the grounded air vehicle, each picking up a gun and opening fire.

"Mara and Ophir." Maddox turned to Dravek. "Come on, this way."

The two men moved at an oblique angle toward the other two.

Fires raged as the Metamorph vans burned intensely. The gasoline fuel and occasional internal explosions sent shrapnel flying in all directions. Dead and dying Metamorphs lay everywhere.

There was an impotent rage in the air. Maddox believed it was the sluggish, Yun mind fusion trying to act. It couldn't, not yet anyway. It was too weak after using its mind blast earlier.

Mara saw Maddox, and she seemed to sense what had happened. She moved to sleeping people, kneeling and touching their heads. With some, she had to do that for longer.

A few woke up, rising to their feet and grabbing weapons. Gallant Ophir gave them orders.

Soon five Honey Men soldiers attacked Metamorphs still trying to react.

The mind-fusion attack had started out as a Metamorph advantage. Now, with Maddox and Dravek throwing a monkey wrench into it, and with Mara's help, it had upset the Yun People's equilibrium.

Mara's telepathic "witchery" had shielded or revived men.

Thus, a few hours before sunrise, the handful of survivors from the dirigible disaster slaughtered the remaining Metamorphs. There were hundreds of dead, if one included everyone.

As the last Metamorphs fell, Maddox ran to Gallant Ophir, greeting him on the desert floor.

"You're alive," Ophir said.

"I didn't think you were either."

"You saved our asses. I'm grateful and won't forget that."

"That's good to hear," Maddox said. "Now what happens?"

"We need to decide," Ophir said. "Grandma Julia is eager to send nukes. You were right about ballistic missiles. So far, I've told her you're unconscious and can't speak to her. She demands to see you, as she doesn't believe I still have you. But if I could have you talk to her, that might delay her launching the nukes, as she'll believe she can live a few more centuries through your efforts."

"Let's get to it," Maddox said.

Ophir escorted Maddox with Dravek covering his back into the grounded air vehicle that lay bullet-riddled in the desert.

-55-

Gallant Ophir stood before a comm screen in what had once been the control cabin for the dirigible, now repurposed as an air vehicle. Mara sat to the side, working the comm controls. There was dim lighting in here, which flickered at times.

Ophir aimed his ruby rings at Maddox, while two Honey Men gripped the captain's arms.

Dravek was behind them, watching, with his assault rifle in hand.

The screen flickered. A screen blizzard appeared, gradually clearing to reveal a face. Grandma Julia with her wrinkled skin and dot-like black eyes stared accusingly at Maddox.

"You see, Grandma," Ophir said with a grin. "I told you I had him."

"What's wrong over there?" Julia asked.

"Rockets rose from the desert," Ophir said. "We used our counter-missiles, but they proved ineffective. It did give us time to load the drop pods, though. It also allowed us to detach the control cabin from the doomed dirigible."

"You're grounded on the desert?" Julia asked.

"Yes," Ophir said.

"Then it's over. You're all as good as dead. I should launch the missiles."

Ophir laughed, shaking his head.

"Are you addled because you know you're meat for the Metamorphs?" Julia asked.

"We just won a tactical victory," Ophir said. "The Metamorphs attacked us in force, using a telepathic mind assault against us. It hurt their own people, though. With Mara and the others' help, we regrouped and hit the Metamorphs from several directions. We've taken control of the situation."

"Don't be a fool," Julia said. "Dawn is fast approaching. You'll all cook in the heat."

"We've found Metamorph holes to use as temporary shelter," Maddox said.

Julia glared at Ophir, as if angry he'd let Maddox speak. Finally, Julia responded, saying, "How could that possibly help you?"

"To survive the heat, the day," Maddox said. "You need to send reinforcements, if nothing else to pick us up once we acquire the ancient weapon."

"You can't think you'll survive the Yun for several days while on the ground," Julia said in disbelief.

"Of course, we can survive," Maddox said. "We've learned the value of our telepaths. They're instrumental in defending ourselves against the mind fusion."

Julia stared at Maddox.

"I'm alive," Maddox said. "And we can still acquire the ancient weapon we need to fight the incoming Leviathan assault vessels. That will allow me to teach you their longevity treatments."

Ancient Julia shook her head. "You lost both dirigibles. You're stranded in the mid-world desert. It's over for you. I'm going to launch the nukes and teach the Yun People a lesson they'll never forget."

"Do that," Maddox said, "and you lose any chance of increasing your longevity. Surely, you can wait a day or two to launch the ballistic missiles."

"Are you begging, Captain?" Julia asked with a sneer.

"Grandma," Ophir said. "We're in a seriously bad situation. We all recognize that. We're not meat for the Metamorphs yet, though. We have the equipment we need, and we plan to use the Metamorphs' own desert vehicles against them."

"It's over I tell you," Julia said.

Ophir glanced at Maddox and then looked at Julia on the screen. "I'm not too proud to beg. I most certainly want to live. We can still do this. We need reinforcements, though."

"So, the Yun People can destroy two more dirigibles?" Julia asked.

"You have the wrong perspective to all this," Maddox said. "We're much closer to victory than anyone realizes. The Yun mind fusion is sluggish due to its recent activity. This is the moment to strike. We're going to attempt just that. You can win all that you've desired. Or you can sulk and throw it all away by ordering the ballistic missile strike."

"You dare to insult me?" Julia asked.

Maddox shrugged. "I didn't realize you were such a fool as to throw away an opportunity for more life."

"Enough," Ophir said harshly, using the back of one of his ringed hands to slap Maddox across the face. "You will address my grandmother with respect or learn the reason why you should have."

Maddox drew himself to his full height. "Don't dare strike me again or you'll lose the opportunity to Leviathan longevity."

Julia's cackle echoed over the comm. "You just earned the right to a chance at more life, Gallant," she told Ophir. "If Maddox had begged—never mind. You lost the dirigibles. Can you gather more soldiers who might have landed through using drop pods?"

"We're going to look," Ophir said. "A few more pods might have survived. Right now, though, we're going to strike for the ancient weapon site. Maddox and Mara both think the Yun mind fusion seeks the same weapon. It could be a hard fight. But that's better than letting them capture us. We have plenty of small-arms weapons. Whether that's enough—I plan to find out."

"I'm sending three dirigibles," Julia said. "They're already halfway to you. The truth is that I expected such an assault from the Yun People and prepared for it ahead of time. This weapon—I want it. I want Maddox alive. More than any of this, reaching the assault vessels and learning Leviathan's secret is critical."

"I'll guard Maddox with my life," Ophir said.

"Good," Julia said. "Because your life depends on his—do I make myself clear?"

"Yes, Grandma," Ophir said.

That was the last of the communication. Possible desert activity or jamming devices caused the screen to show blizzard conditions.

"I lost her," Mara said.

Ophir nodded to the two men. They released Maddox.

He rubbed his cheek where he'd been struck.

"Sorry about that," Ophir said. "Tricking Grandma can be difficult."

Maddox nodded stiffly.

"Sir," a Honey Man soldier said. "We've found people alive in the vans. Some of them are stirring."

"Should we take a look?" Dravek asked Maddox.

Maddox raised an eyebrow.

"Maybe one of ours made it to the drop pods," Dravek said.

"We'll be right back," Maddox told Ophir.

With that, the two men left the grounded air vehicle to see if Eddings, Gricks or Hern might have made it to a pod.

-56-

To Maddox's astonishment, Gricks and Hern were stacked in a Metamorph van, their wrists and ankles shackled.

With his monofilament blade, Maddox freed both men. He got both to open their eyes, but that was it. They stared blankly at nothing, unable or unwilling to speak.

Maddox and Dravek transferred the two to their van. This one lacked a heavy machine gun on top. It had two seats in front, three rows in back and room for equipment behind that.

Dravek sat in the shotgun seat. Maddox drove. Both Gricks and Hern lay on the floor between the rows. The rest of the van was filled with military equipment and gear.

"Too bad we didn't find some mortars," Dravek said.

"We do have grenade launchers now, though," Maddox said.

Six ex-Metamorph vans left the killing ground. Nineteen people rode in them, most as unaware as Gricks and Hern.

After nine kilometers of speeding past dunes, boulders and rocky terrain, the six vans parked in a semi-circle. It was nearly two hours until dawn. Ophir and Mara climbed out of one van, Maddox another. The rest of the drivers remained in theirs.

"Mara can't wake up our living dead," Ophir said.

"Why do you call them that?" Maddox asked.

Ophir indicated that Mara would answer.

She wore desert gear, looking tiny beside Ophir. Her helmet hid her hair while goggles covered her eyes.

"The Yun mind fusion did something to their brains," Mara said. "It's like a shut-off switch was thrown in them. I've tried to reverse that in several men. One went into a seizure and died. The other two—" She shook her head.

"Will the men recover from their brain freeze over time?" Maddox asked.

Mara shrugged.

"You don't care, or you don't know?" Maddox asked.

"Don't know," Mara said.

"That means we have a total of nine people to do this," Maddox said.

"Maybe I should have Grandma launch some nukes after all," Ophir said. "They could land in patterns that ring our general area. That might disrupt the mind fusion or whoever rules it."

Maddox thought about the idea. "That's a possibility, but…"

"What would you suggest?" Ophir said.

"That depends on a few factors," Maddox said. "How badly do you want to go back to the South Pole Highlands?"

"Very," Ophir said.

"Without having acquired the ancient weapon or longevity treatment?" Maddox asked.

Ophir gave him a searching stare. "Are you saying you made all that up to get out of the Highlands?"

"That can't be it," Mara said. "The weapon site is real, as the mind fusion believes in it."

"What about the longevity treatment then?" Ophir asked Maddox.

"It's all real," Maddox said. "Getting the items into Grandma's hands is another story. So let me ask you again: do you want to return to the Highlands if you fail to produce the desired items?"

Ophir appeared to think about it. "Where else would I go if I don't go home?"

"To the North Pole," Maddox said.

"I'd be a pariah there."

"Not if you hired out to the tribunes as a Honey Man specialist."

"Turn traitor to my people?" asked Ophir.

"I'm trying to understand all the options," Maddox said. "I need to know as we're running out of plays down here."

Ophir tugged at his lower lip. "I understand. You fear Grandma's repercussions. You doubt that we can win through even to the weapon site and want to run away to the north."

"I'm trying to decide what gives us the best percentages to surviving," Maddox said. "Is it trying to beat the Yun mind fusion and reach the ancient weapon site? Is it trying to flee to the North Pole region? What?"

"The North Pole is thousands of kilometers from here," Ophir said. "Even if we could achieve such a miracle, how do we defeat the Leviathan assault vessels if we fail to snatch the ancient weapon you promised?"

"Using ballistic missiles and whatever space force the North Pole people have," Maddox said. "Remember, Leviathan is only bringing three assault vessels to Gath."

Ophir spat at the sand. "We're wasting time talking here. We lack fuel to reach the north, so that's out. Likely, Grandma can track us and nuke us at her leisure."

"Cogent points each," Maddox admitted. "Mara, what can you tell us about the mind fusion? I have a feeling you know more about it than any of us."

Mara glanced at Ophir.

He nodded his permission.

Mara breathed deeply. "I don't know much. The mind fusion is dormant now. It has been ever since it launched that mind blast back at the firefight."

"Have you tried to use your telepathy to figure out what it is?" Maddox asked.

Mara shook her head. "I'm afraid to try. It would notice, I think, and come after me in retaliation."

"That makes sense," Maddox said, who'd been playing a hunch that a telepath would know more about the Yun. "Look, it's always better to know one's enemy. The more you know about him or her and the more you know about yourself—as old Sun Tzu said, *Know yourself and know your enemy and you will win every time.* We have to know who and what the mind fusion is if we're going to outwit it, find the weapon site and find out what's going on."

"That makes sense to me," Ophir said. "I want you to try, Mara."

She swallowed audibly. "The other witches are dead. That's what the men call us. The Old Ones say we have the talent. I have the talent stronger than most. Gallant Ophir has always backed me, and I've tried to back him because of my gratitude. What you're asking—I'm frightened to try."

"We need to know," Maddox said. "If ever there was a time to find out, this is it."

Mara stared at him. "You have a touch of the talent yourself, don't you, Captain?"

Ophir looked sharply at Maddox.

"I wouldn't call it a talent," Maddox said. "I have something else."

"What else?" Ophir asked. "Can you read my mind?"

"No, nothing like that," Maddox said. "I judge you by your actions, your words and mannerisms. That gives me more than I need to know you. But none of that matters here. We're allies of the moment. One of the things that I try to do is give the other person what he wants, if I can. That way he'll cooperate with me as much as possible. We're both looking for something. I don't know what you want, Ophir, but if it's in my power, I'll give it to you."

"And in return," Mara said, "you want your freedom. You want to leave Gath."

"Of course, I want to leave," Maddox said. "That's well known."

"Even if you—" Mara gasped.

"What is it?" Ophir asked her.

Mara and Maddox exchanged a glance. What did she read in that moment? The captain sensed she knew too much. But he also hoped—

His right hand fell onto the butt of his holstered pistol. There was another way to end this.

"Maddox feels that the prize is near," Mara told Ophir.

Ophir studied her closely and then nodded.

"Let's get back to the critical issue," Maddox said. "Mara, can you find out what this Yun mind gestalt is exactly? From the little I can tell, now's the time to try."

Mara nodded. She closed her eyes and touched her forehead with her gloved fingertips. She didn't make a sound but stood still as the seconds ticked away. Was she scanning? Was she questing with her mental power? How did her telepathic power operate?

Maddox didn't know. He'd dealt with telepaths in the past, and he imagined they operated on various principles. His was an intuitive gift. Did that mean it was telepathic? Perhaps only in the sense that he'd been able to detect telepathic mind assaults and had been able to protect himself from them.

Abruptly, Mara raised her head. Then her knees unhinged.

Ophir caught her, helping her to remain standing.

"I'm sorry," Mara said, as she straightened.

Ophir brushed himself where she'd touched him.

Mara turned to Maddox. "I have a sense of what's going on. I saw a Metamorph watching us. He's way over there."

She pointed.

They all looked into the night in that direction, seeing nothing unusual.

"He's hiding behind a large dune two kilometers away," Mara said. "I doubt you could see him from here. He has a rifle, a long-range weapon. He's hoping we come in range of him. He...he's grotesque with two brains in his head. They grew side by side. His skull is much different from ours, like two halves pushed together, each half containing a brain. He's normally part of the mind fusion. It reaches far back, for hundreds of kilometers, maybe more. His kind is linked mentally in a way I don't understand. When they're in unity, when they're all awake—that was the mind fusion we dealt with."

"They're all one in a gestalt?" Maddox asked.

"Not quite," Mara said. "I detected a guiding intellect, although I'm not sure where the guiding intellect is. The mind fusion doesn't sense us the way we sense its individual components. It must have sensed the dirigibles, though. The guiding intellect surely is the operative or decision-

297

making…entity. Although the fusion is weak right now, some of the individual pieces watch us. I'm sorry I can't explain it better than that."

"You're doing great," Maddox said. "Did you sense the weapon site?"

"I did, along with radiation sensors. There is a pit maybe a hundred kilometers from here. That's where the excess radiation comes from. It doesn't come from the sun. The pit is a scar, a wound, from some ancient war. There was something else, though."

Mara shuddered, hugging herself. "It was an oily, ancient and evil mind. It was asleep or terribly wounded, lingering. Does any of this make sense, Captain?"

"I'm the one you should be asking," Ophir said.

Mara dipped her head. "You're in charge, Gallant, but Maddox understands these things. He's an explorer and has gone to many strange places." She looked at Maddox with adoration.

Ophir frowned and shifted, perhaps angrily.

Maddox realized the man was jealous, which was odd. He was sure the Honey Men were all decadent and depraved, rutting like dogs with anyone that would unite with them. Why would Ophir care how Mara thought about him?

"You said you detected the weapon site," Maddox said. "How far is it from here?"

"Twenty-two kilometers." Mara moved her gloved index finger back and forth, and then pointed. "That way. There are dangers ahead. I think we must fight our way through."

"What about our sleeping men," Dravek said. "Did you sense anything about that?"

Maddox turned. He hadn't heard Dravek approach. The two men nodded at each other.

Mara looked at Dravek and then Maddox. "You two are remarkably similar. It is uncanny, and yet you are different. You are each unique."

"I'm his clone," Dravek said with an edge to his voice.

Mara stepped up to him and put a gloved hand on Dravek's cheek. "You're more than that."

Ophir grunted, and it wasn't a happy sound.

298

Mara stepped away from Dravek. She lowered her head before Ophir. "We should be leaving, my lord. The sun will be up soon. It would be good to reach the weapon site before the sun shines."

"Is the weapon site underground?" Maddox asked.

"It is," Mara said. "And there are guards. I also think the only way we're getting out of the desert is through there. That was the sense I received from the minds. They're waking up and groping for the fusion linkage. The mind blast severely tested their operative abilities. They're not used to using the gestalt like that. The mind fusion is new and growing. It may be a threat to all Gath. I don't know if the ancient evil underneath is prodding it or what."

For a moment, Maddox pictured a gigantic, oily, whale-sized creature with tentacles, a Yon Soth. Had the Yon Soth reached this spiral arm? Undoubtedly, as they were all over the galaxy. Was he about to face one of the dreaded ancient entities again? It wouldn't surprise him if some of what was going on here had a Yon Soth origin.

"Gallant Ophir," Maddox said, "I suggest you lead the caravan with Mara's aid."

"I'm in charge," Ophir said. "Is that understood? I make the decisions."

"I do understand," Maddox said. "I was only making a suggestion."

"You're coming back with me to the Highlands to show the longevity treatment to Grandma Julia. I'm her cherished grandchild. I won't fail her."

"I'm coming back with you," Maddox said, wondering what that was all about.

They returned to their separate vans, climbing in.

"Did you catch that last part from Ophir?" Dravek asked.

"I did. It's nothing to worry about. We'll take one step at a time, doing what we must at the right moment."

"Sounds good to me," Dravek said.

Maddox started up the van, putting it into gear.

-57-

The caravan of giant, balloon-tired vans raced across the silvery landscape. They startled giant jitterbugs that flew away in swarms. Lizards, some as long as Maddox, scuttled out of the way. One time, a lizard chewed on something so green gore stained its jaws.

The kilometers slipped away one by one, as the caravan headed for the ancient weapon site as recorded in the *Moray's* ship log. There were no more glittering sand particles and the silvery desert color had vanished. The moons had sunk below the horizon. In the darkness above, the stars shined like gems. Soon the sun would rise and heat the landscape, turning it into a burning cauldron that would sizzle even those in the vans.

How was it possible that ordinary humans moved so effortlessly through the heart of the cannibalistic Yun People territory? Was it because of the slaughter that had taken place near the grounded air vehicle and drop pods? The battle had been ferocious. The air-vehicle cannon had exploded many black vans. Anti-personnel weapons had riddled seemingly endless Metamorphs. In truth, the Metamorphs had taken devastating losses tonight, larger than any recorded in legends or oral traditions. The guiding intellect that had moved them as pawns was silent. That hadn't occurred in the memory of the oldest Metamorph.

Most of the remaining Metamorphs slept because the mind fusion usually compelled them to exhausting work. That included increasing the underground tunnels and chambers or digging for treasures that none of them comprehended.

Perhaps a third of the two-brained Metamorphs remained awake. They were different from the ordinary ruck and had tasted of Highlander honey, which had expanded their already overdeveloped brains. They were successful experiments. Primitive cannibals hadn't performed the experiments in the depths of the desert. So, who had?

There were deep laboratories under the sands. There, an alien creature used ancient automatons to run its experiments. Did the creature do this all the time? The answer was it hardly ever did the experiments anymore. The alien creature slumbered for long periods, at times for years on end.

In the legends of the Yun People, the alien was an evil god. When it woke, it demanded so much. The alien experiments had produced the two-brained Metamorphs.

Some of the two-brained watched the passing caravan from behind dunes or boulders. They did not raise their long rifles and fire because no command came for them to do this.

Singly, the two-brained struggled in the desert realm, more primitive in the survival art than the lesser Metamorphs were. But when linked in gestalt with each other they rose to a great intellectual height, having greater analytical ability than any genius on Gath.

They were the servants of the dark god under the sands. Tonight, the god slept. The mind fusion had shattered, the two-brained not yet attempting true linkage with one another. Thus, the caravan of humans continued its way, even Mara unaware that this was a unique opportunity in the desert annals.

***

Maddox drove the van.

He was the *di-far*. Perhaps his ability to take a people's course out of one track and set it on another for a different destiny had something to do with all this. His power worked even here in the Scutum-Centaurus Spiral Arm.

Maddox drove with terrible urgency; certain he needed what was at this ancient weapon site. How could it help against Leviathan attack vessels? Maybe that was the wrong question. What could three Leviathan attack vessels do from Gath orbit? No doubt, they had antimatter-tipped missiles or bombs. Likely, they could send those warheads at precise points on Gath. Realistically, they could give an ultimatum to those on the planet.

"Hand Maddox over to us or we devastate your spaceport. We will devastate all the places you consider important."

Would more attack vessels arrive in the star system and head for Gath? Why had Leviathan waited so long to send any vessels into the Heydell Cloud? Why had Leviathan picked this star system in the Heydell Cloud? Did Leviathan avoid this region due to the vortexes, gravitational distortions, and other spatial anomalies?

Maddox pondered these things as he drove with his hands gripped on the steering wheel.

He didn't believe those things frightened Leviathan. There must be something else about the Heydell Cloud that did.

He stiffened at the sudden realization. For just a moment, he imagined a Yon Soth in the subterranean depths of the planet. Was it a coincidence that the oldsters of the Honey Man society called themselves Old Ones? Did the name reveal a hidden Yon Soth identity on Gath?

If there was a Yon Soth here, it must be slumbering. Maybe its dreams had activated the evil of the Yun mind fusion.

If that were the case, would he, Maddox, have to kill this one too?

Star Watch had always slain a Yon Soth when they found one. Star Watch treated the dreaded Yon Soths as if they were black widow spiders. Humanity had a history of stamping out any poisonous insect, arachnid or snake. One didn't show a rattlesnake mercy, he exterminated it. There was something about poisonous creatures that humanity found loathsome.

Yon Soths weren't poisonous in the chemical sense, but in the mental or spiritual thrust of their intellect. Were they enemies of the Creator? Were they akin to biblical devils?

Maddox shook his head. He didn't know. He was no theologian.

"Meta, Jewel," he whispered, "I'm doing the best I can."

This one was hard because he had so many hands against him and only one true friend, Dravek. Would the clone help to the same extent as Galyan, Valerie or even Ludendorff?

Maddox didn't know the answer.

He drove knowing his destiny waited at the weapon site. Live or die, no, live. He had to succeed and grab the weapon. He had to defeat all comers even if that meant Ophir.

Maddox licked his lips as he stared out of the windshield at the desert. They'd gone sixteen kilometers. The ancient site was fast approaching.

Maddox sensed the stirring of the mind fusion. It quested like an idiot child that didn't know what to do yet, missing what it attempted to grab.

Because of that, the caravan continued its thrust to the ancient weapon site.

Radiation was in the air, but the radiation didn't come from the site. Radiation came from an ancient scar, Mara had said, an ancient battle scar. What type of battle had been fought on Gath? Had it been some kind of space-borne conflict? Was that because a Yon Soth lived here? Had Leviathan once attempted to destroy a Yon Soth the way Star Watch did to protect itself?

Maddox sighed.

"You want me to spell you for a bit?" Dravek asked.

"What?" Maddox said. "Oh. I'm fine. I'm awake."

"What do you think we're going to find at the weapon site?"

"I haven't the foggiest." Maddox glanced at Dravek. "What do you think of Mara?"

"What do you mean?"

"Let me try it again. What do you think of her?"

Dravek shrugged. "She's pretty."

"She could be useful to a man who wanted to become a pirate, trader or star rover."

"A telepath for a partner?" asked Dravek. "Is that what you're suggesting for me?"

It was Maddox's turn to shrug.

"She'd be reading my mind all the time," Dravek said. "She'd know what I'm thinking. Whenever I looked at another girl, she'd be upset."

"Learn how to shield your mind. Learn how to think differently. Marry her."

"Marry her?" Dravek asked, surprised. "You're infatuated with the ancient custom. Me? I don't have all your memories. I know you love Meta. And I know you want to protect Jewel. But you never stay at home. You're always off and running. Do you ever wonder why that is?"

"I have an itch to explore," Maddox said.

"Oh yeah, an itch," said Dravek. "You ever think it might be something else?"

"Maybe it was something I inherited from my dad."

"Oh, so you like your dad now, is that it?"

"Yes," Maddox said in a clipped voice. Once, such a thought would have been anathema to him. But he had learned to respect his father. It was more than that. He'd learned to love the memory of his father, the man who'd sacrificed his life for his mother and him. He hadn't forgotten about the Emperor of the New Men. He hadn't forgotten about the other bastards who had helped kill his father. He was going to get some payback against them one of these days. Maybe, if he got out of this, he should make the payback sooner rather than later. His missions and adventures were getting hairier and more outrageous, not easier with time.

Another kilometer ticked by.

Maddox thought about that, and he decided— "Hey, see if you can wake those two sluggards again. We might need all the firepower we can get."

Dravek got up, moving to a prone Gricks and Hern as the van continued across the alien desert.

-58-

"It's no good," Dravek said. "Their cheeks are red, I've slapped them so much. And I've shaken them so much I'm afraid I'm going to rattle the brains out of their heads. Whatever has them sleeping must have switched them into hibernation mode."

Maddox sat up suddenly at the wheel. The first glimmer of dawn-light peeked over the horizon and struck the windshield, showing an agonizingly bright sun.

He slipped on his desert goggles. He'd have to put on the polarizers next. They'd make him look like some alien insect with a forward thrusting eyepiece. Once the full sunlight hit, though, he'd need the protection even behind the polarized windshield.

What would it be like outside once the sun was shining high in the sky? Why was the sun like this mid-world and not like that at the poles? The answer must have to do with angles, deflection and other space mechanics, and the elevation of the Polar Regions.

However, Maddox hadn't sat up because of the sunlight. Instead, his intuitive sense had pinged loud and clear. It told him they'd better wake up those two no matter how hard it might be. They were going to need every man they could get.

"Take the wheel," Maddox said. "I'm going to switch places with you."

Dravek moved over and slid past Maddox into the driver's seat.

305

Maddox went back, deciding to start with Hern, the tougher of the two.

Maddox concentrated. And as he'd done in the desert to protect Dravek from the attacking mind fusion, he clutched Hern's head. He thought at Hern—*Wake up, you bastard. If you ever wanted to show the universe how tough you are, now's the time.*

As Maddox expended whatever he possessed, he leaned low and whispered into one of the man's ears, "Wake up, Hern. This is the fight of your life. If you can't snap out of it, I'm leaving you behind. This is the moment where every man must carry his own weight. Can you carry yours?"

Hern grunted as his eyes opened.

Maddox kept his hands on Hern's head, staring into his eyes. There was a glimmer of recognition.

"Wake up," Maddox said. "This is it. Are you going to serve Legion Culain? Or are you a coward who's going to run? Do you want your balls snipped off? Is that what you're telling me? If not, then wake up and fight."

Hern grunted again and raised his arms. He tried to push off Maddox's hands but lacked the strength.

Maddox removed his hands.

"What's happening?" Hern said. "Why are you so close to me? Where is this place? The last thing I remember... The dirigible went down."

"Steady now, Primus. I picked you. I want you to fight on my team. Do you understand?"

Hern struggled up to a sitting position, leaning against the seat and touched his forehead. "My head hurts. Everything's splotchy and blurry. Why is that?"

"Drink some water. Eat. Try to stay awake and I'll explain after I wake up Gricks."

Sliding over, Maddox started a similar procedure with Gricks. It took longer and it took more furious whispering. Maybe Maddox didn't have the same force as before. Perhaps the usage of his mental strength was draining it.

Despite that, as he clutched Gricks' head, Maddox tried to pour his force of will into the man. "Wake up. We need you, Gricks. You said you wanted a second chance. This is your second chance to fight to the end. I need another shooter. I need a man to watch my back. Centurion Gricks, wake the hell up."

Gricks opened his eyes as he whimpered. That wasn't a good sign. Then Gricks stared at Maddox. "What happened? Have the Honey Men captured us again?"

"Sit up, Centurion. Listen to your orders."

Gricks struggled to a sitting position.

Maddox told him to get some water and grub.

Gricks did, as the items were beside him. He chowed down, glancing at Hern.

"Listen up," Maddox said. "We're in the desert in Indian country. Things are moving fast and hairy. We're almost to the ancient weapon site. When we reach it, you're coming with me locked and loaded. You also need to don desert gear. We're going to go underground. You probably know, Gricks, what that means because you listened to Eddings. By the way, what happened to Eddings?"

"He didn't want to leave his bed, sir," Gricks said. "I tried to get him up and join me. He refused."

"We'll remember him fondly because he gave us warning of what to expect out here. Because of him, we may have a chance. So, he died a man."

"A man?" Hern asked with scorn.

Maddox pointed a finger in Hern's face. "Did you hear what I just said? That's how you'll address Eddings if you speak about him."

What did Hern see in Maddox's eyes, in the cast of his jaw? Whatever it was, Hern said, "You're the captain. You're in charge."

"Don't forget it," Maddox said.

"So, what's going on again?" Hern asked.

Maddox outlined the situation as best as he understood it, even as the sun rose over the horizon.

"Two more kilometers and we're there," Dravek said from the front.

Hern climbed onto a row seat and saw the other balloon-tired vehicles. He looked at Maddox.

307

"We landed in the desert," Maddox said. "We've had to kill a lot of Metamorphs since we got here. They have someone with some kind of mind-control power. He's the one who put you two to sleep."

"You're kidding," Hern said.

"I woke you up," Maddox said. "If I hadn't done that, we'd have had to leave you behind. You would have probably woken up tied to a board with a feeding tube shoved down your throat, feast meat in a Metamorph's larder. If you want to show your gratitude for what I did, fight like crazy when I tell you. Don't turn on me. We live or die as a team. Do you hear?"

"I ain't no traitor," Hern said. "Yeah, I get it. You saw us through. I'll do the same for you."

Something on Gricks' face hardened. It reminded Maddox of the centurion he'd first seen when the Eye of Helion had put them on this godforsaken planet.

"Second chance," Gricks said. "I want a second chance to prove myself."

"That's what I want to hear," Maddox said, "because I want a man who's tough and going to fight."

"I'll fight." Gricks paused. "I'm going to fight, because I don't care if I die. I'm also going to take down every mother-loving bastard there is that did this to me."

"The Honey Men here are our allies for now."

Gricks shook his head. "I don't care about them. The universe—it's a dark universe, Captain. I intend to make everyone in it pay, except for those who help me."

"What I hear is fighting spirit," Maddox said. "You two ready for this?"

Maddox got two yeses.

"How much farther to the site?" Maddox asked.

"Half a kilometer," Dravek said.

"All right, gear up you two. Pick your weapons and then overload. We're going to need a lot of firepower. There's a lot of killing ahead of us. There's something here we need. If we're going to make it, if we're going to survive this desert madness, this is the moment to do it."

"What in the hell is that?" Dravek asked, staring out of the windshield.

They all peered forward, and all saw the vast sinkhole ahead.

-59-

Ophir parked his van and the others parked beside his. The sun had begun to climb over the horizon. It was decidedly bright, the rays already beginning to heat up the landscape and making weird chromatic colors bounce off the sand, at least bounce off some of the particles of it.

The van doors opened. Maddox led his team. The other van doors opened, and it was the few men, together with Mara and Ophir. They hadn't been able to wake any of the others in their vans.

They all looked like humanoid insects with their polarizers and desert gear. They turned around so the blazing sun and giant sinkhole were behind them.

"The Metamorphs are waking up all around us," Mara said. "I'm referring to those that establish the mind fusion link. I don't think we can leave as easily as we got in. Even though they're waking up, I don't believe they fully comprehend our intentions yet."

"We're here," Maddox said. "I see a giant sinkhole ahead of us, a great big hole down into the depths. Now what happens?"

"There may be a way down," Mara said. "It's nearby."

"You sense it?" Maddox asked.

Mara nodded.

"Well, Gallant Ophir," Maddox said. "Let's follow your talent, shall we?"

"Agreed," Ophir said.

Armed with assault rifles, machine guns and grenades, they marched toward the giant sinkhole. It had to be at least a kilometer in diameter and was perfectly round as if made by a monstrous stamping machine. It sank out of sight.

As Maddox approached, a feeling of vertigo struck. What would cause such that? He wasn't afraid of heights. Even so, the others must have felt it too because they began to stagger.

"My head hurts worse than ever," Hern complained. "What's going on?"

"The mind fusion is awakening, beginning to perceive we're here with bad intentions," Mara said. "The first stirring of their working against us has started. Come, I know now the way to get down."

The smallest and physically weakest of them marched in her desert boots, crunching sand. Rainbow colors glittered around Mara as the sun continued to climb into the sky.

They all felt the dreadfully growing heat.

Maddox hurried until he was even with Mara. "You're sure about this?"

"I'm not sure about anything, but I want to live, and I think this is the only way to do it. We've got to grab what they want and bargain with it for our lives."

Maddox had a grim sense that was going to be the thrust of it.

They reached the edge of the great hole. Mara tugged at a rock formation—what seemed like one. Some of the rock moved as if it was heavy cloth. She began to pull a camouflage tarp that hid a sky raft.

"We're supposed to get on that contraption and descend into the sinkhole?" Ophir asked.

"That would be my advice," Mara said hoarsely as she kept tugging at the heavy tarp.

"I agree with that," Maddox said. "Let's get this unveiled so we can do it pronto."

The rest of them helped unroll the tarp and shove it to the side. Afterward, they dragged their heavy equipment aboard. With themselves, there was barely room enough for everything.

"This is spaceliner tech. I know how to fly this." Dravek went to the controls and began to flip switches.

In moments, the engine purred and anti-gravity repellers kicked in. The raft lifted off the sandy ground.

Maddox wondered if the sky raft might be the way to reach the thousands of kilometers they needed to the North Pole. They'd have to do it at night. Otherwise, the sun would cook them.

Dravek guided the raft over the giant sinkhole. Immediately, the engine complained with a sharp whine and the raft sank fast, sliding hard to the left.

One of the men cried out. It wasn't Gricks, Hern or Maddox. It was one of the Honey Men.

Dravek slowed the descent and righted the raft, bringing the engine back to its purr. It was dark in here. The men who had them turned on their flashlights, shining them into the gloom. They shined it down. No one saw the bottom. Maddox liked this even less than before. Even so, at a steady pace, Dravek took them lower and lower.

Although weaker than before, the mind-fusion force started pressuring Maddox. What was it doing to the others?

Hern cried out, clutching his forehead. One of the Honey Men closed his eyes as it threatening to slump asleep.

"Stay close to Mara and me," Maddox said. "We're your only hope."

The others huddled around Mara and Maddox for protection.

Maddox felt increasing pressure. He stretched his arms over those nearest him. That increased the throb against him. He gritted his teeth, determined to reach the bottom with his crew.

The entire time, the sky raft lowered meter-by-meter, heading down the ancient opening.

At a certain point, the mind-fusion attack slackened.

"The mind fusion doesn't like this place," Mara said.

"Can you tell why?" Maddox asked.

"The mind fusion fears it, and there's something else I can't comprehend."

The slackening mind assault was a boon. Maddox would take it, even if it meant entering the lair of something worse.

What had created this vast shaft into the depths? The smooth sides added to the feeling that some giant stamping machine had created the hole in the past. Might this have once been an ancient seabed? Had a vast, alien aquatic race inhabited that ancient ocean?

Maddox sensed that was so and... Had this been one of the primary worlds of the Yon Soths at the beginning of the creation of the universe? What a dreadful thought.

Dravek hadn't altered the rate of descent. He took them slow and steady. The anti-grav repellers hummed and the raft sank lower, lower, lower. They had to be a quarter kilometer below the sandy surface. Still the raft went down.

"I see a bottom," Ophir said.

Maddox looked over the edge. He didn't see any tunnels as the flashlight beams shined on the floor.

The raft descended until they were three-quarters of a kilometer below the desert surface. At that point, the raft gently landed against solid ground.

"We're here," Dravek said, shutting down the engine.

"Where is here, and what does it mean?" Maddox asked.

"Follow me." Mara jumped off the raft, hurrying.

After a moment's hesitation, Maddox and the others did just that, following her.

-60-

With Mara in the lead, they soon discovered a huge, sealed hatch an elephant might have easily walked through, if it were open. The lights from the flashlights washed over the sturdy metal hatch. Maddox traced the sides with his fingertips, his flashlight revealing every detail of the surface. As he finished, his gaze fell on Mara.

"How do we open this?"

Mara shook her head. "I have no idea."

"Are there any other hatches we can try?"

"There may be. But behind this one is the key to our success."

Maddox rapped his knuckles against the metal. It sounded immensely thick. "We have explosives. Let's see if they do the trick."

"They won't work," Mara said. "There has to be another way."

Maddox ran his hands along the sides and then used a flashlight to examine everything closely. He turned to Mara afterward. "You have to do this."

"Why me?"

"It must be some kind of telepathic code or lock, or maybe it has to be opened from the other side. That means you again."

Mara stared at the hatch, nodding slowly. "I'm warning you that the Yun mind fusion is hovering. More are linking to it, increasing its strength. The fusion might interfere with me. There's something else: a grotesque evil far below us. It could

314

be waking, aware that something threatens its existence. I'm not sure about the last, though."

"You mean us as its threat?" asked Maddox.

Mara stared at Maddox in shock. "The ancient evil *hates* you, maybe even dreads you personally."

"Why would it be afraid of *him?*" Ophir asked.

Mara shook her head. "I can't sense that. What I said is an impression only."

Maddox placed his gloved hands against the metal hatch. He looked up at its top and faced Mara. "Despite the various risks, you have to risk using your talent to open this."

"Don't you understand? There's no one to shield me. My sisters in the expedition are all dead. And you, Captain, have no talent to shield me."

Maddox removed one of his gloves and one of Mara's desert gloves. He held her small, fine-boned hand. It was not like Meta's, which was strong and could withstand the pressure if he squeezed forcefully. Maddox felt that if he squeezed Mara's hand like that, he'd break the bones.

"I'm here, Mara," Maddox reassured her. "And I'll do everything I can to protect you. But unless we can unlock the hatch, we're all dead anyway. The mind fusion is gathering and it's probably summoning the rest of the fighting Metamorphs. What more do you have to fear?"

"My talent might awaken the evil below. If it awakens, it might possess me. I would do indescribable and horrid things then."

"I'll shoot you before that happens."

Mara searched Maddox's face. "You promise? You'd truly do that for me?"

"Yes."

Maddox felt Ophir glaring at and hating him, wanting to drill him with the beams from his ruby rings. Surely, Ophir could feel Dravek and Gricks watching him. Even with his personal force shield to protect him, would it be enough if Dravek and Gricks slaughtered the other Honey Men and ran back to the sky raft, lifting off and leaving Ophir down here alone?

"Mara," Ophir said. "I agree with the captain." His voice was ragged and full of insincerity.

Nonetheless, Mara nodded and closed her eyes. She disengaged her hand from Maddox's and put both hands against the huge hatch. In a moment, she rested a cheek against it and groaned. Surely, Mara quested with her talent and sought—

There were loud clicks and tumbling sounds from the hatch.

Maddox grabbed the back of Mara's uniform and pulled her away as the hatch slid open fast.

She was limp, exhausted, looking at Maddox with wide staring eyes.

Maddox pushed Mara into Ophir's arms, a hard, swift motion that left them both startled.

"No!" Ophir shouted. "Don't defile me by her touch."

Maddox hadn't released Mara yet. He pulled her back and shoved her into Dravek's arms.

"Carry her if you must," Maddox said. "Don't let her die. We're going to need her probably more than we need me."

Without looking at Ophir, not understanding the social mores of the Honey Men Highlanders—other than that they were depraved—Maddox led the way. Gricks was hard on his heels. Hern brought up the rear behind the other Honey Men.

Maddox didn't get the feeling Hern hung back out of fear but so he could keep an eye on Ophir. The Primus understood morale and personal interactions. As Legion Culain's chief centurion, he must understand men's motivations better than most.

They hurried through the giant tunnel. Instead of the cold rock one might expect, the sides were of steel or titanium, reminiscent of a spaceship's corridors. Something about it reminded Maddox of a Builder nexus. Maybe it was simply the sense of great age. There weren't any hieroglyphs but smooth sides.

With the flashlights providing light, the party took every twist and turn. Then the corridor headed down as if it were a ramp. This went on for two kilometers at least, the air becoming hotter and thicker.

Finally, a sense of doom filled them. There was something bad ahead.

Maddox looked back.

Dravek carried the slip of a telepath, the talent. He carried Mara as if he cared for her.

This place set Maddox's teeth on edge. He was tired of Metamorphs and sick of Yon Soths and other ancient entities plaguing the younger races. Seeing Dravek carry the telepath stirred a longing in Maddox's heart to see Meta again. He longed to put his arms around his wife and shower her face with kisses. He longed to lift Jewel in the air and throw her high. He wanted to hear her squeal with delight and say, "Daddy's home, Daddy's home. Daddy don't go."

Maddox shook his head. Why did he think the last?

"Please don't go, Daddy," Jewel said in Maddox's imagination.

In his imagination, Maddox caught Jewel and set her down. He wanted to explain that he had to go. This was his job. It was what he did. He was an explorer and soldier. He went out and fought the nasty things of the universe so his family would be safe, so Star Watch could be safe. This was his hour in the cockpit. Who else was going to do these things if he didn't? Someone else would have to do it. Would they be as skilled as he was? Could these others do as good a job as he had done all these years?

Maddox heeded the trumpet's call. He was a fighter, a soldier, and needed to go into the dark lands to kill those that preyed on humanity, would destroy mankind. It was his job. God had given him a family even though he was the scout that went out to find and eliminated these dangers. Or he ran back to the fort of the Commonwealth and told the people in charge about the coming danger and how to prepare for it.

As the darkness of the tunnel on Gath closed around him, Maddox gripped his assault rifle, his only tangible source of protection.

This time, someone had ripped him from the Commonwealth and brought him out here. According to what Dravek had told him, Leviathan was planning an assault on the Commonwealth. Leviathan had made its beginning moves.

This down here was all part of that. He was finding out about the Heydell Cloud. He was finding out why Leviathan didn't want to send its ships into the cloud. Maybe those living in the Heydell Cloud would make good allies of Star Watch. Maybe Star Watch could send an expeditionary fleet here to hold the warships of Leviathan in this spiral arm instead of bringing the war to the Commonwealth in the Orion Spiral Arm.

Maddox grinned, shaking his head. Thoughts of solutions, desires, his family—they were all distractions to keep his mind off what lay ahead.

"There's light ahead," Dravek whispered.

Maddox could see that for himself. Was this the end of the long tunnel? Maddox slowed and looked at the others.

They looked at him, too many with wide, frightened eyes.

"Let's get ready to do what we have to," Maddox said. "Remember, we're a team. We all make it or none of us makes it. We're sticking together and we have each other's back. Is that clear?"

"It's clear," Hern said.

Gricks nodded.

The Honey Men soldiers glanced at Ophir.

"We're all in this together," Ophir said.

"Good," Maddox said. "Let's do this."

-61-

The party slowed because they heard murmuring and machines gurgling ahead.

To Maddox's trained ear, it seemed that there was a large, cavernous area before them. It struck him that the mind-fusion pressure had completely ceased. There had to be more of a reason than what Mara had said earlier.

Maddox looked back.

Dravek yet carried a sleeping Mara with her curly-haired head nestled against his chest.

If Maddox were any judge, he believed Dravek held her closer, more protectively than before.

He and Dravek traded glances.

"I may have to set her down," Dravek said.

"You keep her alive. You're her bodyguard. Do you understand?"

"I do," Dravek said.

Maddox winked.

They were about to possibly fight to the death, but there was no reason for his knees to quake. This was adventure. This was the moment. He'd fought ever since waking up on the spaceliner.

"Come on." Maddox led the way from the tunnel into a lit and vast, cavernous area.

He was shocked to see fifty or more Metamorphs. Some had over-large two-brain heads. Others were tusked, ugly suckers. They all wore white lab coats and held slates or testing equipment. All around were working machines. Some were attached to vast aquariums built along the sides of the incredible chamber. In the aquariums floated bodies attached to lines. Some were naked Metamorphs. Some had three-brained skulls. Others were aquatic creatures like huge octopuses or squids. Could those be baby Yon Soths?

Maddox didn't see any of the mechanical automatons he'd sensed before.

The place was a vast laboratory. Was this where they perfected the desert Metamorphs? Why create a Yun mind fusion? Why did the mind fusion not penetrate this place? It didn't make sense.

Whistles blew from enemy mouths. Some of the Metamorphs dropped their slates and testing equipment. It felt to Maddox as if they were going to run away or maybe grab weapons.

Maddox could have called out. He could have asked to parley. "You give us that and we'll give you this." Instead, he took the stance he had earlier with Dravek. He held the assault rifle with both hands and fired with three bullet bursts. He cut down those attempting to run.

The others fired, too.

"Use controlled fire," Maddox shouted. "Make all your shots count."

He glanced back.

Dravek had set down Mara. He stood over her, firing his assault rifle.

The team cut down Metamorphs by the bushel. They murdered the scientists, shooting the two-brained and burly Metamorphs indiscriminately.

The surviving Metamorphs stopped trying to flee but pulled out scalpels and other sharp technical instruments. They charged the humans.

Maddox, Dravek, Hern and the Honey Men let rip with a barrage of automatic fire. They riddled the charging enemy with heavy caliber bullets. Gricks used a grenade launcher. He was a wizard with it: dropping detonating grenades where they did the most damage, making Metamorphs fly.

It was carnage, pure and simple.

320

This was the right thing to do, Maddox knew. These creatures were evil as far as what they hoped to achieve. They'd created the mind-fusion Yun People. The Yun had originated here. The—

Maddox grunted as pain lanced his brain. The throb of it increased.

He noticed in back. Three of the two-brained Metamorphs clutched hands with each other, pressing their grotesque foreheads together.

Maddox knelt, raised the assault rifle and willed himself to ignore the agony. With each shot, he blew apart one of the two-brained. He killed them. They'd been a link to the greater mind fusion outside.

Maddox now sensed the cavernous chamber was lined with anti-telepathic material. That meant the team should be safe from the Yun until they tried to leave the giant sinkhole. At that point, the mind fusion would smash against them with furious force.

"Dravek, Gricks, you're with me," Maddox shouted. "Hern, you take those two. The rest check that way. Kill everything you find."

They split into the assigned teams. That was often a stupid thing to do in a horror house where great evil lurked. Here, they wiped out the two-brained and Metamorph muscle by slaughtering them.

Maddox was doing what he had to do. This was part of going into the wild lands. Sometimes, you reached a place where the enemy thought he was safe, where he could relax and didn't have to post a guard. When you reached such a place, you didn't parley or show mercy. This was a rattlesnake, a black widow spider. These were poisonous aliens. What did you do to a rattlesnake in your home? What did you do when you found a black widow spider building a web where your child would play? You killed it. You stamped it out.

With barely suppressed fury and the calmness that was his heritage from the New Men, Maddox shot everything in sight. As he marched back after having searched every nook and cranny, he noticed that some of the creatures in the fluid-filled aquariums watched him. That included the tentacled monsters.

"Trade me weapons," Maddox said.

Gricks handed over his grenade launcher, accepting the assault rifle.

Maddox shoved grenades into the launcher and aimed, blowing holes in the aquarium "glass" so the blue fluids drained and swept across the floor. He aimed again and pumped grenades into the tentacled creatures, killing them as they flopped and struggled. He killed the others, too, new Metamorph experiments waiting to plague the people of Gath.

If Maddox could have, he would have done this to all the Highland Old Ones, the deviants who castrated men, stealing their dignity. He abhorred that kind of thing.

Did this killing make him as bad as his enemies? No. He was the soldier who did his duty as a defender of the home front. If there was too much blood on his hands, well, that was one of the sorrows that could happen to a defender. He overdid it at times. He admitted that to himself. If he overdid it today, he'd ask God's forgiveness later. He didn't mean to indulge in any sin he wanted and use God as a ticket puncher. He had to make sure here. If he were going to have any regrets later, it would be for killing too many enemies instead of seeing his own people die because he'd killed too few.

Thus, Maddox destroyed everything he could find in this huge chamber as a matter of deliberate policy.

-62-

They gathered amidst the watery slipperiness of the floor.

Two Honey Men were dead, slain by hidden Metamorphs. The rest had taken minor bruises at most.

"We killed everyone," Ophir said. "Now what happens? Mara's out and I see no super weapon unless these ugly aquatic creatures were it. You killed them. I hadn't realized you were quite so bloodthirsty, Captain."

"This is stage one," Maddox said. "Now we move to stage two."

"What's stage two?" Ophir demanded. "Everything is dead and shot up."

Maddox pointed at the largest shattered aquarium. There was a man-sized hatch in back. The blue-tinted water had covered and hidden it earlier.

"I see," Ophir said. "You're suggesting we open the hatch and get flooded out?"

"We open the hatch and see what happens," Maddox said. "Unless you know about a different path we can take."

"I don't," Ophir said.

"Then that's what we do. It's onward and forward. Check your weapons and make sure they're working. Take what you need from here, if anything. Are there any other questions?"

There was none from any of them. They all were grim-faced. It was time to find the place worse than this den of iniquity laboratory.

Dravek carried Mara and was ready to go.

Without further ado, they approached the targeted aquarium. Maddox and the others shattered jagged glass with their rifle stocks, creating a safer way in. Then, they helped each other to climb into the drained aquarium.

"Watch your step," Maddox said. "It's slippery in here."

They filed past the dead rubbery creatures. Once, a tentacle moved and an eye opened.

Five weapons chattered at once, riddling the giant creature with explosive rounds, killing it for good.

"Enough, enough," Maddox said.

They reached the hatch at the back. It looked to have an ordinary type of handle. Maddox tried and moved it. With a jerk, he swung open the hatch.

Water or fluids didn't gush out to sweep them away. Maddox opened the hatch all the way. He peered into a dry tunnel or corridor. They all had to hunch. It was maybe half the height of a tall man. They crab walked, filing one at a time with Maddox in the lead.

The sense of grimness grew. They were heading deeper into this place and had no reason to expect any kind of mercy if they should falter.

No, Maddox realized. That was the wrong way to think about it. They were here as avengers. They were here to discover what had been going on in Gath. Maybe this was why someone had kidnapped him. It was a stretch. But whatever would give him a little more gumption to see this through, he figured was good.

Therefore, Maddox kept going. He didn't feel anything from his intuitive sense. He didn't feel the mind fusion, except that it was waiting for the chance to pounce. Maddox had the sense that when it did pounce, it would attack with savagery and unrelenting murder lust.

They wound through the tunnel as it went down at a slant. It seemed to go on and on and on, until three kilometers later, they came to another hatch. No alarms had rung; nothing that they could sense. Yet Maddox felt that beyond this hatch lay the real test, and maybe the weapons that they had come to get.

This must be the heart of the Metamorph lands. Here was what made the Metamorphs tick, the mastermind behind them. Did that mean a Yon Soth? It was impossible to know.

"Is Mara awake yet?" Maddox asked softly.

Gently, Dravek shook her.

Mara smacked her lips and opened bloodshot, red-rimmed eyes. "My head hurts." She gasped, and her eyes opened wide. "Captain Maddox," she said in an eerie voice. "You must turn back or die. You have come too far. I know of you now. I know who and what you are."

Dravek shook Mara, but she slid out of his arms. She stood, reaching for a gun. No doubt, she meant to blow Maddox away. Dravek tore the gun from her grip.

Mara raised her finger, pointing at Maddox. "You are doomed. You murderers have slaughtered my progeny. You have slaughtered the gift of my intellect. You are such a foul, God-besotted creature. You do not understand the forces that you play at. You think to defeat me. You think to harm me. I see no battle fleet arrayed against me, ready to rain down hellburners. We know of you, Captain Maddox. We have learned of you, and now you have come into our nest. Oh, open the door. Let me feast upon your flesh. Let me destroy it with telekinetic delight. Dare you come in any further, Captain Maddox?"

Maddox looked at Dravek. "Put her to sleep. I don't think she should have to bear the Yon Soth's thoughts anymore."

Dravek pinched Mara's carotid artery until she slumped unconscious.

Maddox looked at the others, wondering if the force that had spoken through Mara could speak through any of the others. Suddenly, his intuitive sense told him that before the Yon Soth could gather its intellect to do such a heinous act as taking over another's mind and will again, he needed to go on the attack.

"Let's do this." Maddox reached for the handle to the hatch, turned it, and then readied to throw the hatch open.

-63-

Maddox leapt out of the hatch into an even more immense chamber than the one they'd left. In it were all sorts of equipment and machinery. Some were shuttles, others were tanks, missiles, rockets and such. It was a veritable museum of weaponry. He'd never seen any of these models, though he recognized the types of equipment they were.

Bright lights shined in the ceiling, illuminating everything.

From his intuition, Maddox expected a horde of Metamorphs to rush them. Instead, there was nothing, an empty museum.

The others filed in with their weapons ready.

"Where is everyone?" Ophir asked.

As if to answer him, a large hatch opened at the far end and out boiled—

Maddox blanched as a feeling of utter revulsion shook him to his core. The enemy reminded him of the octagonal robots he'd spent so much time together during a horrific trip from the planet Kregen to the edge of its star system. They boiled out. Was it a hundred creatures? They scuttled across the floor, their metal tentacle tips tap, tap, tapping on the floor as they charged as a group.

The creatures were metallic balls the size of a man's torso. From the balls sprouted segmented metal tentacles. None of the automations had a weapon that Maddox could see. They did have shining red lights on the balls, perhaps their optic ports. They scuttled across the chamber fast.

"Grenade launcher," Maddox said. "Start blowing down those things."

With his grenade launcher aimed, Gricks fired—pop, pop, pop. He sent grenades arching slightly in a flattish trajectory. They exploded among the automations. Some grenades did damage. Mostly, the horde of advancing things scuttled all that much faster at them.

"What do we do?" Dravek said. "We need blasters. We have these chemical slug throwers. Are these rifles going to be of any use to us?"

"There's one way to find out." Maddox took his stance and took deliberate shots. Some of the shots downed the advancing machines. Other shots ricocheted off metal.

The interesting thing was the few shots that penetrated the outer ball hulls. From the holes squished brain matter.

Maddox understood. The automatons had brains inside them. Were those human brains? Were they two-brained Metamorphs? The brains looked pinkish, much more pinkish than a human brain would look. It was disgusting. It was revolting, and it struck Maddox as desperate evil.

Now, all of them opened up with their weapons. A fusillade of fire struck the oncoming horde of metallic, octagonal automatons tap, tap, tapping across the floor. These must be the workers of the Yon Soth, if indeed that was what had been talking through Mara.

Had the talking drained it of energy? Maddox didn't know. He slapped another magazine into his assault rifle, and he kept hammering the things.

"Spread out," Maddox shouted. "We have to kill these things. We have to kill them all. If one survives and it dismembers each of us, we've lost."

Gallant Ophir stepped up. He made fists with both hands. He'd discarded his guns. Instead, with concentrated rays from his ruby rings, he beamed the metallic things. His beams were as good as hot lasers. They burned through metal hull plating as he swept many at a time. The others behind kept coming, crawling over those he'd slain.

"Protect Ophir!" Maddox shouted. "On all accounts, protect him. Make a circle around Ophir."

The team circled Ophir. They chattered assault rifles, lobbed grenades and shot machine guns. They stood around Ophir as the mechanical things rushed at him.

Maddox realized that despite everything they were going to lose. There were too many of the metallic crawlies charging them. Bullets and grenades had too little effect on the metal.

Maddox dropped his assault rifle and pulled out his monofilament blade. This was probably his best weapon against them.

Maddox didn't yell, "Cover me." Instead, he launched himself at the things. It seemed like suicidal madness. Yet what had he told Dravek before? Madness was their only way or chance to escape.

One of the tentacled arms lashed him, hitting him across the head, nearly stunning him. Maddox skewered it, the monofilament blade slicing through the metallic skin and into the brain underneath. Then he was among the metallic spider-like creatures. He endured their tentacled slashes and as they grabbed at him, trying to stretch his limbs.

Maddox had already become a madman of fury. He lashed like a berserk Viking of old, moving, ducking, swaying, accepting the hits, accepting the pummeling to his body. He would be black and blue if he survived this. The knife did damage. It opened armored hides and tore pink brain masses.

Maddox felt the hot rays from the ruby beams. He saw the red rays piercing, slashing and exploding metallic ball-hulls.

Still the creatures skittered at them.

Maddox knew that if he faltered, if he gave in to fatigue, it was all over. He slashed a tentacle from his leg. Some severed tentacles were curled around him like giant bracelets. They squeezed, but they didn't squeeze hard enough to stop him or stop the blood flowing to his limbs.

A few tentacles tried to grab his neck. He slashed them all in a blow.

Maddox was stabbing, hacking, and he didn't realize he was yelling, shouting and foaming at the mouth. His eyes were opened wide like a berserker of old. No one had ever seen such fury in Captain Maddox. What else could he do? That was what the situation called for. He endured blows that would

328

have knocked him unconscious at other times. He was in the zone, the fighting zone, the berserker zone. A lust to kill, maim and destroy gripped his mind. These were the Yon Soth's machines. These were like the things that had almost destroyed him in the Kregen System. This was his chance for payback. He bellowed with rage, slashed, cut, hacked and advanced.

He was a prodigy. This was a display of knife fighting probably none would ever see again. Something of legend was taking place, even as Ophir's rings, one by one, began to sputter, having been drained of whatever energy fueled them.

Grenades launched. Men ran up and fired their assault guns against the metal hulls, smashing them open.

The machine creatures slew men, four in all, all Honey Men.

Gricks bled badly from a leg wound. But even now Mara was dressing the wound. Hern had many cuts and bruises, but he had a savage snarl with two machine guns, one in each fist, blazing away.

Hern fired a final burst, cutting down the last moving automaton. He swiveled more, his gaze searching, seeking. Then he turned to Maddox. "We did it, boss."

Maddox looked upon Hern as a demon of destruction might. Was Maddox about to charge and slay Hern? It was quite possible.

Dravek ran up before Maddox, waving his arms. "We're friends. We're friends, Captain Maddox. You did it. It's over. The fight is done."

Maddox stared at Dravek, raising the monofilament blade. It was wet with pink brain mass, whatever had been within the housings of the tentacled things. Maddox cocked his head.

"We're friends Maddox," Dravek said. "It's over. This part of the battle is over. We must move on to stage three."

Maddox blinked. It seemed as if sanity once more shone in his eyes. He didn't speak. Perhaps he couldn't. His shoulders slumped, and the monofilament blade dropped out of his hand. Exhausted from the fierce underground battle, Captain Maddox collapsed. The berserkergang that had gripped him now left him swooning. He hit the floor, unconscious.

-64-

Captain Maddox dreamed. He didn't like his dream and he had a suspicion that his unconscious body was in a bad place. Yet he couldn't wake up.

In the dream was a creature, a vast, tentacled, whale-sized creature. He didn't see it in the dream, but he knew it swam in fluids far below him. It swam in a specially constructed place and swam not as an alert, awakened creature but as a sleeping shark flicking its tail in order to keep its forward momentum. A shark did that so its gills would continue to extract oxygen from the water.

For a shark's gills were not like a fish's that could pump the water. The shark needed to use the forward motion for the water to flow through and past the gills.

In that sense, the great creature swam slumbering. It swam below as dreaming Maddox stood on a dark plain. In the dream, Maddox was vaguely aware that he'd recently fought with berserk fury akin to madness.

The reason for the berserk fury was his internment in a tiny pursuit sled with octagonal robots. The time spent there had driven him nearly mad with desperation. After surviving the robots and pursuit sled, and defeating the Cosmic Computer, Maddox had overcome some of the horrible torment, or so he had believed. In truth, much of the hidden desperation had coiled like a pressed spring, waiting and straining with his fear of enclosed spaces and a hatred of constructs that warred against humanity.

Maddox stirred in his sleep, though it did not disrupt his dream.

He stood upon a dark and spongy plain with a dot in the sky. The dot was red and bled red illumination. He watched as the surface rolled like a wave, as if something gigantic swam underneath. He knew what it was, but he knew he shouldn't name it. Because in naming it he might call or summon it.

He had a feeling the...creature had spoken to him before through Mara as a dream. The evil creature had dreamed, and that dream had repercussions in the real world.

Maddox believed he understood a truth. The telepathic emanations from the sleeping, slowly swimming thing down there had sent powerful mental thoughts and emotions to the societies on Gath. Those vile emanations had provided the impetus for creating the desert Metamorphs and later two-brained creatures to create a gestalt mind fusion. The emanations had also provided the push for Honey Men to castrate their prisoners and the Old Ones to indulge in their worst sexual perversions.

In his dream, Maddox was certain he could burrow through the spongy substance and meet the whale-sized entity with its tentacles. But he had no weapon to slay it, as he had used weapons long ago as Meta had carried him to safety to a portal. Neither did Maddox possess hellburners or screaming asteroids dropped from orbit to destroy the deep dwelling...monster.

Could nuclear-tipped missiles launched from the Highlands reach and destroy the creature? Maddox deemed that as highly unlikely. The thing was protected by too much earth, rock and substance. Hellburners and dropped asteroids could kill it, but they would also destroy every living creature on the planet Gath.

Dream Maddox stood upon the dark plain, contemplating his next move. There was something he'd missed or failed to decipher and understand. As he dreamed, he waited for his unconscious to give him the answer.

Psychologists call that part of the mind the *sub*conscious. Yet that imparted the idea that the subconscious was below or beneath the conscious mind. In truth, the *un*conscious mind roiled with ideas, thoughts and plans that sparkled into life like rare gems, like stars in the sky that shined with brilliance.

It was that part of his mind that Maddox needed to tap into.

Perhaps that was why he was in his dream state. It was not to battle the—

In his dream, Maddox rubbed his hands nervously. He'd almost named the type of creature, possibly summoning it to wakefulness through that.

The vast evil entity, the ancient thing, the poisonous thing—one way or the other, he was going to have to destroy it. But he wouldn't be able to that today.

Today, he had to find the right weapon in the place where he, awake and aware, had gained victory over the metallic enemy.

In the real world, one of the creations of the evil thing below waited above. The Yun mind fusion waited to slay and destroy or subvert and reprogram wills in the service of the evil below.

Maddox grinned. He was the demon slayer. It would be best to think of the thing down there, swimming in its sleep, its tentacles flicking so it would propel the huge body—

Maddox shook his head. He didn't need to think of the demon below. He needed to engage his unconscious, so he gained a rare gem of an idea as a breakthrough to get out of here.

He was dreaming and wasn't sure what to do next. His anger and rage had subsided. Maddox knew he had far too much rage in his heart. It was one of his secrets. Perhaps it was part of his New Man heritage. Could he change his inner heritage?

Maddox frowned. He was on the wrong tangent. This was the weapons site. Dravek had originally discovered the site in the computer files of the Trader Vessel *Moray*.

Instinctively, Maddox knew the fact was important. Why was it important: the knowledge being in the computer banks of the *Moray?* Because, because...the Triad had hired or bought the *Moray* to this star system. They'd guided the vessel here in order to find the weapon site.

Maddox frowned as he observed a spark of light between him and the red dot bleeding light into this gloomy realm. He studied the light and perceived it to be a scintillating gem.

Maddox rubbed his chin until he raised a hand and then his index finger. The Triad of Naxos aboard the *Moray* had wanted to reach the location where his sleeping body lay. The reason the Triad had wished to come here was to pick up a weapon. What kind of weapon would the Triad use?

Maddox squinted at the scintillating crystal in the sky. His mouth opened in surprise. The answer was obvious…as if had bubbled up from his unconscious mind.

Now that he knew the answer, it was time to wake up.

Maddox shouted in his dreamland. "Wake up, Captain. Time is of great urgency."

With that, dream Maddox vanished from the rolling plain of darkness, with the evil one swimming lazily far below.

In the real world where Maddox lay, deep in the weapon museum, his eyes flashed open.

-65-

On the floor with its metallic remnants, with the smell of fired weaponry, exploded grenades, and the stink of pinkish brain matter torn from its metallic shells, Maddox opened his eyes. He saw several of those lying around him. There was Gricks, Hern—

Dravek, sitting on the floor, stroked Mara's back as she too sat up. Ophir stood and looked at his ruby rings. Perhaps he was worried they'd remain power-drained forever.

Ophir noticed Maddox staring at him. "You're awake."

The others glanced at Maddox.

Maddox groaned and slowly sat up. He was tight and stiff. Already, bruises spread across his body. Metallic tentacles had pummeled, squeezed and slashed him like whips. His head throbbed where he'd received heavy blows. He touched his scalp, discovering that some of the hair had been torn from their roots. When he looked at his hand, there was a smear of blood on his fingertips.

"You look like shit," Dravek said.

"I'm beat up," Maddox said in a low voice, "and my mind is sluggish."

He looked around, and he couldn't recall in detail what had happened, just that he'd known fury that had seemed to put a red mist before his eyes. He'd gone berserk, but it hadn't been a hot berserkergang as the old Vikings did. Rather, it had been a cold and calculating berserkergang. That had been more dangerous to the enemy because his intellect still had analyzed and guided his hand.

Maddox remembered the dream then. He remembered it better than the fight. He had something to do. He remembered that, too. Before he did it, he needed to set the stage. Although he ached and his energy was minuscule, it was time to get started. They were running out of time and had to get on with it.

"Good work, Ophir," Maddox said. "Your rings were invaluable. They made all the difference to our winning down here."

"Yes," Ophir said. "Mara and I have been the keys to this. Because of that, I claim first right of choice for whichever weapon I want."

Maddox dipped his head. "Such a right, I freely—"

"You do not grant me anything," Ophir said, interrupting. "I have claimed it as my right."

"Yes, and I recognize your claim as legitimate. You've indeed won it through your battle skill."

"My battle skills were greater than yours," Ophir said.

Maddox made a small gesture. His limbs and muscles couldn't stand any more. He lay back down, breathing heavily. Even his lungs ached, or rather, the muscles that powered his lungs. Every breath brought another pang where a tentacle had snapped, lashed or tried to curl around him.

"Which weapon do you choose?" Maddox asked while lying on the floor.

"I don't know. I must examine each carefully."

"We don't have time for that."

Mara stared at Maddox. "Do you sense the evil below?"

"I do," Maddox said. "I fear it will awaken or its dreams rise closer to consciousness. I will not name it for that reason. We did earlier and that was a mistake. We've bearded its minions in their den. Now, as Ophir said, we must collect what we came for and leave as soon as possible."

"Do you know what you wish to choose?" Ophir asked.

"Maybe," Maddox said.

"I want to know what that is."

Maddox snorted.

"I want to know because I might choose it for myself. Of course, I might trade my choice if you give me what I desire."

Maddox said nothing. Ophir and his ruby rings and Mara with her talent had been instrumental in winning down here. That was worth remembering and honoring. However, now it was time to divide the treasure. This became a new game. Maddox was very aware that his men outnumbered Ophir's men *down here*. Ophir had the personal force field, but his rings had become useless. Maddox didn't want to descend to outlaw or brigand philosophy, yet this was the time to collect the rewards for all their hard effort. Could he let Ophir stand in the way of what he needed? The answer was clear. No.

"What is he thinking?" Ophir asked Mara.

"That you deserve what you've earned," Mara said, even as she glanced at and away from Maddox.

Maddox saw Dravek's arm tighten around her waist, and he saw Mara's arm tighten around Dravek's waist.

Once again, Maddox forced himself to a sitting position. He reached out and prodded Gricks. Gricks must have understood, as he handed the captain a canteen. Maddox unscrewed the cap and slaked his thirst. It should have revived him, but it didn't.

"Do you have any pain pills?" Maddox asked quietly.

"Try these," Gricks said, handing him a pair of pills.

Maddox put the pills on his tongue and drank again, swallowing. He needed every advantage he could get. He had almost expended everything, but he knew this was the moment. He must make the right choice. To keep his honor intact, he also needed to let Ophir chose first.

"What do you want down here?" Ophir asked.

Maddox smiled. "Is that your choice, to know what I want?"

"No. I want to know what you want. You owe that to me."

"Do I?" Maddox asked with an edge. "Do I owe that to you because your people cut the balls off of one of my men?"

Dravek tried to signal Maddox.

Maddox nodded. What was wrong with him? This wasn't the time for that.

336

Ophir had jumped back, clenching his fists, aiming the ruby rings at Maddox.

Maddox sighed inwardly. He'd gone too far with the last comment. "Have a care, Ophir." Maddox pointed at Hern, who stood to the side and the back of Ophir.

Ophir saw Hern's heavy assault gun aimed at him. Perhaps Ophir noticed the Primus's hard stare: a man ready to kill.

"Is this betrayal?" Ophir asked.

"There's no betrayal," Maddox said smoothly. "Make your choice. I will make mine afterward and we'll part in friendship. So, what do you want?"

"Mara, come to me. I need your assistance in this."

"Gallant Ophir," Mara said. "I haven't made you these promises. I've decided to switch allegiances. I'm following Dravek from now on, not you."

"Witch and whore," Ophir shouted, "how dare you turn traitor at this hour? Don't you realize what will happen to you once we reach home?"

"Will you reach home, Gallant Ophir?" Mara asked in a silky voice.

Ophir unclenched his fists and dropped his hands beside him. He nodded once, twice. "I see. I accept your resignation. Grandma was right about you and them. Still, I can choose anything I wish?"

"Of course," Maddox said. "You have first right of choice. I don't gainsay it." *Unless you choose what I want*, Maddox thought to himself.

Ophir went to various items, studying them. He finally came to a large tank-like vehicle with steep angles and a large turret and cannon. It lacked treads or wheels but had what looked like anti-gravity repellers on the bottom. It must have been a heavy grav tank.

"I want this," Ophir said, pointing at the grav tank. "I'll rise to the surface in it and return to the Highlands with it. I'll take my men with me."

"That strikes me as a good choice," Maddox said. "Now, I need to make mine."

"You don't want the grav tank?" Ophir asked.

"I might have picked it, but you had first choice." Maddox struggled to his feet, swaying and looking around at the museum of weapons. Which was the right choice? Then he noticed one of the shuttles. It had familiar lines, or ones he'd seen before, recently, too. This was interesting. It was time to see if his instincts were correct.

-66-

Maddox slid his booted feet across the floor because his legs were too tired to lift them.

"Dravek, if you could help me."

Dravek and Mara got up, holding hands, advancing to Maddox.

"Let me lean on you," Maddox said.

Dravek put his free arm around Maddox's waist and Maddox put an arm over Dravek's shoulders. He began to shuffle with Dravek's help toward one of the shuttles.

The selected shuttle had lines that reminded him of the *Moray*. He believed the shuttle had a connection to Naxos' Triad. The unconscious thought that had bubbled in his dream was that the Triad, which had used the *Moray,* wanted something in the ancient weapon site. What would the Triad seek in such a dangerous place? Why had they sought it so relentlessly? An idea had flickered in his thoughts. Now he needed to test it.

"There's something familiar about that shuttle," Dravek said.

"Oh?" Maddox asked.

Dravek looked at him. "What's more, you know it, too."

Maddox shrugged.

"What are you hiding?"

"Not so loud." Maddox looked across the clone's torso. "Mara, are you truly Dravek's companion?"

She looked up into Dravek's face. "If he will have me."

"You know I will and do." Dravek became thoughtful. "Maddox foresaw us together. Maybe he has an instinct for these things."

"I think he has an instinct for many things," Mara said quietly. "And I think if any man approaches the captain in his abilities, it must be you."

"You mean because I'm his clone?" Dravek asked with an edge.

"You're missing my meaning," Mara said. "You're your own person. That's obvious to anyone who is with you two for any amount of time. But you have his DNA, some of his memories—"

Maddox looked at her sharply.

"I've seen that in your minds," Mara said. "I didn't read your minds to see that, but it's visible to a telepath like me."

Maddox's features closed as he nodded.

"You also have his capabilities," Mara continued. "Maybe you have some of his mindset."

Dravek frowned at her.

Mara squeezed his hand. "You're you, and it's you I want. I have seen something in him, though. Maddox is devoted to his wife and daughter. I want a man to be devoted to me like that. Since you're like him in many ways, maybe you're like him in that."

Maddox laughed, shaking his head.

"What?" Dravek asked.

"Nothing," Maddox said. He recalled what Dravek had said earlier about romantic attachments. Now that Dravek had a woman like Mara, would he find his Meta in her? "I wish the two of you all the luck in the universe."

"All right, all right," Dravek said. "Let's not get ahead of ourselves. Mara, you're a wonderful girl and I want to be with you. But let's see what happens today and tomorrow and the next day after that before we get too excited about all this."

"Yes, Dravek," Mara said.

Maddox wondered if she'd already used her telepathic ability to study his thoughts. Probably, as he knew women and Mara would want such reassurances.

Maddox focused on the shuttle as they neared it. He slid his arm off Dravek's shoulders.

Dravek released Mara's hand and Maddox's waist, and he went to the shuttle hatch. He inspected it without touching anything. He looked back at Maddox.

Maddox had drawn the heavy pistol. "Be careful."

"What could happen?" Dravek asked.

Maddox looked at Mara.

"I...don't sense anything suspicious," she said.

"Is there a switch or something?" Maddox asked.

Dravek stepped closer, pointing at one.

Maddox raised the pistol at the hatch, not having moved closer.

"Oh," Dravek said. "Are you suggesting I open the hatch?"

"I'm ready to fire."

Dravek snorted to himself and slapped the switch.

There was a whine, a squeal, and then the hatch slid up slowly as if in pain.

Dravek had already skipped back out of the way.

When the hatch ceased moving and nothing happened, Maddox shuffled forward, peering into the darkness of the shuttle. It took effort, but he raised a foot, setting it on the shuttle's threshold. With a grunt, he hoisted himself, stumbling farther within.

Dravek followed close behind, clicking on a flashlight, shining the light ahead of Maddox.

Maddox smelled musty dead air. His nape hairs rose. The shuttle felt...haunted, as if spirits would rise and attack for daring to disturb this coffin.

"You must leave the shuttle at once," Mara said from the open hatch, from on the floor outside the shuttle. "This is dangerous. Neither of you should have entered."

"Wrong," Maddox said. "We very much should have entered. The doom you're sensing is the reason why."

"What do you know?" Mara asked. "I cannot read your thoughts. Is the doom why you choose this shuttle?"

"I'm not used to people questioning me about my actions," Maddox said sharply. "Yet." He glanced back at Mara. "In this case, I'll make an exception. I know something useful is here. What makes it useful also makes it deadly."

"You're hedging," Mara said.

"That's enough of that," Maddox said. "Dravek, stay close."

"Wait a sec." Dravek's voice had a catch in it. "Mara has a point. This place…feels like a crypt with a vampire or other undead creature. What if it wakes up and pounces on us, sucking our blood?"

"That's why we're on our guard." Maddox took another step into the shuttle.

Dravek kept shining his flashlight. He unslung the submachine gun he was carrying and held it with his trigger finger ready.

Maddox and Dravek moved throughout the shuttle, the flashlight shining everywhere. The sense of great age, wrongness and doom pervaded throughout, but there were areas where it was colder or less prevalent.

The sense grew stronger as they approached a sealed hatch.

"My heart's hammering," Dravek whispered.

"This is the place all right." With his fingertips, Maddox rubbed sweat out of his eyes.

They looked around the hatch—

"I see it." Dravek shined the light on the switch.

Maddox pressed it. Nothing happened. The hatches had worked elsewhere in the shuttle, often whining with complaint. Here, there was no power at all. The hatch was dead.

Maddox cocked his head as he stood before the sealed entrance. Finally, he holstered his gun and pulled out the monofilament blade. He touched the metal of the hatch, prepared to leap back if needed.

There was no response.

Maddox pushed the edge of the blade against the hatch. The monofilament edge slid in easily, cutting.

There were hurried footsteps from behind. "Dravek, where are you?" Mara shouted.

"Over here," Dravek said.

In a second, she rushed to Dravek, grabbing his torso, putting her face against his chest.

"Easy now," Dravek said, raising his arms, keeping the light on the hatch and his submachine gun ready to fire.

Maddox continued cutting, slicing a section out of the hatch. He used his boot and pushed against it. The section of metal fell inward, crashing upon the deck of the hidden cabin.

A presence of death billowed out.

Mara gasped, releasing Dravek and staggering until she thumped against the far bulkhead. "I can't go any farther," she said breathlessly. "I'll wait here, Dravek. But please, I beg you, don't go."

Dravek looked at Maddox. "I'm not going in there. This one is wrong. Mara feels it and so do I."

"Give me your flashlight then," Maddox said.

Dravek swallowed and handed it over.

Maddox took it, shining the light ahead of him, ducking through the opening in the hatch and entering the room.

It didn't surprise Maddox to see three anciently dried corpses. Each had thin, leathery limbs, a thin torso and curling tusks from its mouth. Each looked what Maddox would expect Naxos and his clones would if dead as long as these. No doubt, the three in here had also been a Triad.

Maddox shined the light about the room and then he saw it at the foot of the bed. It was a dull-looking crystal but otherwise like what the Eye of Helion had looked like.

Maddox approached warily until he reached it and after some effort crouched before it. His muscles protested and skin itched. First holstering the heavy pistol—he'd drawn it again— Maddox put his hands over the crystal. He did it as if he could feel heat or some other emanation rising from it. From the Eye before, he knew it could be dangerous to touch when the crystal didn't glow.

Was this crystal from the planet Helion? Logic dictated yes. A Triad had made it down here and died. The curling tusks in the corpses reminded him of the Metamorphs.

Crouching here, holding his hands over the baseball-sized crystal, Maddox had some questions. Before this Triad had died, had they or the crystal before going inert, sealed this room? Why hadn't the evil below taken the possibly inert Eye? Couldn't the evil below use something like this?

Maddox suspected the Eye of Helion aboard the *Moray* had agreed to teleport Dravek and him here so they could reach this shuttle. But if that were true, why had the Eye placed them in the Highlands before a landing legion?

Maddox hadn't figured that out yet.

He looked at the crystal. He knew he was avoiding the issue of the moment. Dare he touch it? Maddox swallowed, gathered his courage and touched it with an index fingertip.

The crystal shocked him. It wasn't a heavy, explosive shock, but a mild one. Even so, it coursed through his entire body, and once it finished, Maddox collapsed back with a thump.

"Are you okay in there?" Dravek shouted.

Maddox worked a constricted throat.

"Maddox?"

"I'm fine," Maddox said.

"You're sure?"

"Yes," he said with greater volume.

Maddox rocked himself onto his side so his eyes faced the crystal. There was the tiniest glow in the center of it. The crystal was no longer inert. His touch seemed to have turned it on like an electrical device.

Maddox forced himself to sit up and then crouched before it again, holding his hands over it as if to feel heat.

"Listen," Maddox said. "I think you're an Eye of Helion. I don't know exactly what that means, but I have spoken to a different Eye before. My friend outside killed the Triad that had put that Eye under its control. If you loved the dead Triad in here, then this is all for naught and I've guessed wrong. But if I've guessed right—that you hated your enslavement and wish to go back to Helion—I'll help you achieve that if you'll help me."

Maddox stopped talking. It seemed to him that the crystal glowed a little brighter than before.

What he did next was likely foolish. He grabbed the crystal.

A powerful shock surged through him.

It might have killed him, Maddox wasn't sure, but he threw the crystal from him. A second later, he thumped back against the floor.

344

This time Dravek rushed into the room. He grabbed Maddox under his armpits and dragged him out into the corridor.

Mara was there, concentrating deeply as she stared at the open hatch.

"What are you trying to do, kill yourself? What's in there?" Dravek looked hard at Maddox. "Is it one of the damn crystals of Helion?"

"Maybe," Maddox said from the floor.

"What's he talking about?" Mara asked.

Maddox sat up. "What do you sense?"

After a moment, Mara concentrated again. "There's a power in the room. You turned it on. It's angry, confused and hostile. I can't read more. It doesn't think like a flesh and blood creature."

"Can you defend us against it if it asserts itself against us?" Maddox asked.

"I don't know." Mara looked up and gasped.

While sitting, Maddox turned around.

Floating out of the hatch was an Eye of Helion. It floated directly for Maddox.

-67-

Maddox used the bulkhead to struggle up until he stood, leaning against it. "I touched you."

The Eye of Helion stopped in midair. Did it brighten? It was difficult to tell.

"I touched you in order to bring you back into operation," Maddox said.

A pale beam ejected from the crystal, shining against Maddox's forehead. The captain stood there as if dumbfounded.

"Stop that!" Mara shouted, as she raised her hands.

The beam ceased. The Eye seemed to regard her, although it didn't move in any way.

Mara dropped her hands down to her sides.

"Captain Maddox is unharmed," the Eye said in a high-pitched, warbling voice. "I needed a point of reference. Now, after scanning his mentality, I have it. Why shouldn't I destroy you, Maddox? Touching me as you did was illegal in the extreme."

"I met a different Eye of Helion off-planet." Maddox didn't feel any worse for the mind scan, if that was what it had been. "The off-world Eye told me about this place. I believe it told me so I could find and rescue you."

"Why would the other Eye do this?"

"I'm sure you're a better judge of that than me. My guess... So, you could awake enough to return to Helion."

The Eye bobbed up and down in the air. "Helion, sweet crystals of Helion, how I long for thee—it has been ages since I left home."

"The other Eye gave me an image of Helion and its position in this spiral arm," Maddox said. "Later, I'll share that with you so you can find your way home."

"Why should I believe you?"

"Because I need your help," Maddox said. "I'm bargaining for it and am willing to give help to you in return."

"You wish to make a bargain with me?"

"That's what I said."

The Eye hovered in one place again. "The Triad is long dead. They tricked me."

"I thought so," Maddox said. "We slew the Triad that had tricked the off-world Eye."

"I saw that in your mind. May I say, you have a many-layered intellect? That is unusual in a humanoid like you. What accounts for it?"

"We can talk about that later. First, we should seal the bargain."

"If I agree to this, what would be the next step?"

Maddox talked fast, conserving strength by continuing to lean against the bulkhead. This just might work after all. An Eye of Helion could do things others could not. It probably wouldn't be enough to get him home to Earth. It might not be enough to deal with the approaching assault vessels of Leviathan. But maybe it would be enough to get out of this damned sinkhole and the mid-world desert.

"Yes," the Eye said at least. "I will provisionally agree. Let us proceed with the next phase of the operation."

***

Mara carried the Eye of Helion by using her telekinetic power to keep it from touching her flesh. In that way, the Eye didn't have to use any its power to continue to levitate.

"You see," the Eye of Helion said, "too much expenditure on my part, even at this low wattage, might trickle down to the

347

one below. We of Helion are antithetical to those who are below. We were early creations, as far as we have been able to tell, as they were early creations also. They did not like the way of things and started their war against the Creator and creation almost immediately."

"That's interesting of course," Maddox said. "But sticking to the point at hand will be more germane to our mutual survival."

"I suppose you have a point," the Eye said.

They'd been walking as a group, having left the shuttle and now examining the various pieces of equipment in the vast chamber.

The Eye noticed power outlets, indicating them. "Ah, if you could hook up and turn on that generator over there, I could reenergize myself faster and more efficiently."

They hooked up the generator. It had a heavy power cord. And they set the Eye upon it. Dravek threw the switch. The generator shook and whined. Soon, flows of power surged in growing bolts. The generator kept pulsating, increasing its charges. The Eye sucked each electrical discharge into itself. The floating crystal brightened at each intake.

Ophir with his surviving Honey Man approached them. "What you're doing is madness. The Eye is an alien construct and likely means to attack us once it's fully charged."

"Quite the opposite," Maddox said. "It's our only ticket out of here."

"How do you mean?"

"I'll let actions do the talking. Will you trust us in this, Gallant Ophir?"

Ophir blinked repeatedly, his face sweaty and as he bit his lower lip. "Do you swear to allow me the grav tank and its munitions?"

"Absolutely," Maddox said.

"I'll take your word for it, as I hope you're a man of honor."

"Noted and appreciated," Maddox said. "I, too, trust you regarding your given word once we return to the Highlands."

Ophir nodded curtly.

Then they waited, everyone anxious about the outcome. How much time could they afford to waste while the Eye powered up?

A half hour passed.

"My grav tank is full," Ophir informed Maddox. He and his man had been carting items into it. "I'm ready to leave."

"How will you get the tank to the bottom of the sinkhole?" Maddox asked.

Ophir pointed across the chamber. "There's a large cargo hatch in back. I checked. It's open. I'll drive the tank through to wherever it leads."

That seemed reasonable enough. Still—Maddox glanced at the Eye sucking down bolts of energy. He motioned to Dravek and Mara. "Shut down the generator. Bring the Eye to me. It's time to decide our next move."

Dravek did as ordered.

The Eye complained when the generator wound down, saying it needed more.

"The captain would like a word with you," Mara said.

"Oh?" the Eye said. "In that case, will you carry me?"

"With honor," Mara said.

Using her telekinetic power, she brought the Eye to where the others gathered, keeping it hovering just above her outstretched hand.

"Eye of Helion," Maddox said. "Can you teleport us out of here to the surface?"

"Theoretically I can," the Eye said. "However, such a discharge of my power might awaken…it below."

Maddox scowled. "If it awakens, all we've done will be for naught. Gath will be at its mercy. Do you know if Leviathan is connected or allied to those who are like the one below?"

"I do not perceive that to be the case," the Eye said. "I'm sure those of Leviathan fear the ones that is represented by it below."

Maddox found that interesting and hopeful. Maybe instead of having a war against Leviathan, Star Watch should seek an alliance with them predicated against any surviving Yon Soths. He doubted those of Leviathan would think that way, though.

"So, how do we get out of here?" Maddox asked.

349

"Describe the situation in detail," the Eye said. "I may see a solution that has escaped you."

That seemed reasonable. So, each of them in turn told the Eye what they knew. It hovered above Mara's hand, absorbing the knowledge.

"Tell me about the rest of the planet," the Eye said.

Maddox, Ophir, and finally Mara did so.

Afterward, they waited as the Eye pondered the possibilities.

Maddox checked his chronometer. Time was ticking. They needed to get on with it.

"I may have a solution," the Eye said at last. "You spoke about Grandma Julia sending ballistic missiles. Do these missiles have cobalt-enhanced warheads?"

"Thermonuclear warheads," Ophir said.

"That isn't ideal, but it should be enough. Have Grandma launch the missiles at these coordinates." The Eye gave them in terms of Gath latitude and longitude. "Those coordinates will place the detonations around the sinkhole in a wide circumference. The warheads should destroy the effective mind-fusion and fighting Metamorphs. Thus, they will no longer bar our way from here."

"I can't reach Grandma by comm from down here," Ophir said. "Communications with the Highlands have been cut off."

The Eye fell silent until at last it said, "I will show you some equipment that might solve our dilemma."

Soon, Ophir was at an underground comm station as Mara worked the console. On the third try, they reached Highland GHQ. Shortly after that, Grandma Julia appeared on the screen.

There was some fuzziness and crackling. "Ophir, my director tells me this is a strange frequency you're using," Julia said. "What is the cause of that?"

"We're deep underground in the mid-world desert," Ophir said. "We've broken through into the main weapon vault. We've reached the weapon site in other words."

"Then you've succeeded?"

"I have a grav tank," Ophir said.

"That's the super weapon you're bringing home?" Julia asked. "Isn't there anything else you could find better than that?"

"The shuttles down here aren't operative. The grav tank is and it's huge. It has superior armor and cannon, and it has grav-repellers. If we can manufacture these—"

"I'm disappointed in you," Julia said, interrupting. "We expended two dirigibles for a lousy tank?"

"I've studied the legion armories," Ophir said. "They have nothing like this tank. Believe me, it's a game changer for us."

On the screen, Grandma Julia appeared dubious.

"Tell her," Maddox urged from the side.

Ophir stood taller and seemed to gather his resolve. "Grandma, it's doubtful we can leave the sinkhole unless you launch ballistic missiles at precise coordinates?"

Julia scowled and shook her head. "This is a farce then and your tank a joke. You want me to provide the weapon, so you won't have to commit suicide. You lack the courage to take care of this yourself."

"No, no, it's nothing like that," Ophir said. "Our enemies surround the outer sinkhole on the surface. Some of the enemies have created a telepathic mind fusion. They're a growing menace to everyone on the planet. The missiles will wipe out most of them and give us in the Highlands time to prepare for their inevitable resurgence."

"I'm dubious about all of this," Julia said. "If your grav tank is so wonderful, use it to kill these desert marauders. What else could you bring home?"

"I've packed the tank with every interesting weapon I could find."

Julia shrugged with indifference.

From out of sight to Julia on the screen, Maddox yanked off his shirt and whispered to Ophir.

"Grandma," Ophir said, "I've also taken Captain Maddox prisoner."

The last Honey Man clutched Maddox, pushing him before the screen. Black and blue bruises covered his torso. The captain also kept his hands behind his back as if they were manacled.

"My, my," Julia said, "did he attempt treachery against you?"

"He did," Ophir said. "By doing that, he forced me to subdue him. I've taught him several bitter lessons already. Look at me, prisoner."

Maddox would not.

"He's still disobedient," Julia said.

"It only appears that way," Ophir said. "I've driven all pretenses from him. I believe he fears to look upon my greatness or possibly fear of you has bewildered and confused him."

Julia studied a contrite-looking, head-bowed Maddox. "Yes," she said. "You're correct in believing I have a few lessons I wish to give the once haughty captain. For that, you must escape the sinkhole and desert. And who knows, maybe this grav tank will prove useful after all. I'll have my commanders launch the missiles immediately."

"It might be better, Grandma, if you launched in two hours and fifty-two minutes," Ophir said.

"You're coordinating your efforts, are you?" Julia asked.

"Yes, Grandma," Ophir said.

"Very well, so it shall be done." Soon after that, Julia cut the connection.

-68-

Less than an hour later in the Highlands of the South Pole region, the commander of a ballistic missile silo received orders from Grandma Julia. Shofet Zadoury had countersigned the orders, making them official.

The commander checked the codes. They were in order. He had his men input the coordinates into the simulator. Several tests confirmed that the projected flight paths would achieve their function.

The commander now had his men input the coordinates into the actual missiles. The silo team made the adjustments, cleared the launch sites and finally signaled that everything was ready to go.

The commander began to watch the clock. Exactly eighty-nine minutes and forty-two seconds later, the first gigantic booster ignited. The great missile left its silo and lofted toward the cloudy heavens.

These were old-style chemically fueled rockets, using solid fuel propellant.

After the first missile rose into the air, with its fiery tail still visible to those on the ground, the other two rockets launched as well.

All three began the journey that would take them in a parabolic trajectory to the coordinates provided by Grandma Julia. First, they would reach low orbital space before beginning their flight down to the middle planet desert.

Meanwhile, around the mid-desert, kilometer-wide sinkhole, as the sun sank below the horizon, Metamorphs stirred. They came out of their hastily but deeply dug holes. The vast majority were thickly muscled, leathery-skinned fighters with assault rifles, machine guns and crew-served artillery. The rest were two-brained Metamorphs, part of the Yun mind fusion. It had grown stronger during this time as other two-brained gestalt-oriented Metamorphs joined in telepathic linkage. At last, the lines of mind-fusion communication hummed as before the mind blast last night.

As the terrible day's heat began its first slow dissipation, the Yun mind fusion communicated amongst itself. It waited for the enemy to show themselves so they could attack.

The gestalt-fusion intellect knew the sinkhole led to the glorious one, the god of the underworld. It also knew that from the sinkhole arose from time to time new and dangerous thoughts and new two-brained Yun. The new ones were always more powerful than the old.

The Yun gestalt knew its mental strength was growing. It was ready to hit those who had slaughtered so many fighters last night. There had been war in the desert. Far too many Metamorph fighters were dead. But the larders had grown with new meat that had dropped from the sky. Even now, some of the most resistant new meat was strapped to boards as feeding tubes were thrust past their clicking, resisting teeth and down their throats.

The handlers laughed at such vain efforts. The new meat would be fattened with the oily and nutritious gruel. In a month or two, there would be a grand feast. The Yun would come from everywhere. They'd watch the chefs cook the living meat and delight in the hopelessness and despair of the meat.

The despair particularly was a garnish of delight. It oiled the mind-fusion feasters like almost nothing else. As the meat screamed, the Yun would hum a chorus. It was the Song of Conquest detailing Metamorph obstinacy and certainty of victory. They would prevail and spread throughout the rest of the planet.

The Song of Conquest explained that they would no longer be outcasts living in the wretchedly hot deserts or sleeping in

354

holes like beasts. In the days of victory, they would live in the mansions built by those they had eaten. According to the song, they would know great feasting as they took hundreds of thousands, maybe even millions of captives. They would choose the very fattest and start new herds of feast meat. In the days of paradise, they would only take the young and fatten them until they were a delectable delight. The Song of Conquest envisioned a new time for Gath, a time of plenty indeed.

It was all part of the great plan: to spread and grow. The Yun mind fusion realized it would become smarter and more cunning with time and expansion.

Perhaps it flailed about at times, attempting to gain greater coherence. The song told how the gestalt would finally gain the power needed to awaken the great god below that swam in slumber.

The Yun knew, as Maddox and the others could not, that it was not an easy thing to awaken a Yon Soth when it was deep in slumber.

That was the secret reason why the dreaming god propelled them, adding knowledge and insights to the collective Yun fusion.

Maybe they had lost many fighters last night. Stronger and better fighters would replace those. The artificers deep in the sinkhole would no doubt take some of the weapons removed from the meat and study them. Then, the scientists below would give the Yun even better weapons.

The Yun mind fusion was restricted for now. It understood that it lacked the strength to pierce the mental shield of the laboratories below. The Yun didn't know part of the protection was to allow the scientists to work in peace. The other thing was practice. When the mind fusion could finally pierce the telepathic block over the deep labs, it would have gained the strength to awaken the great god that had given it reality.

On that glorious day, the dark god would arise and link with others of its kind in the universe. Then the Yun would grow in power and understanding as it served the new greatness.

355

As the Yun fusion contemplated these things, waiting for the enemy to appear out of the sinkhole, it noticed a glint of light high up in the heavens.

That was interesting and beautiful. Wait. Could that be an enemy rocket? Yes, yes, it was an enemy attack.

At a thought from the Yun fusion, counter batteries fired from hidden sites in the desert. Before, the batteries had brought down two dirigibles.

Rockets also rose from secret desert silos, heading into the heavens.

The Yun fusion wasn't sure the rockets would reach the warhead in time. Maybe it needed to do this directly.

Suiting thought to action, the gestalt cast its mental strength upward, doing so with terrible urgency.

The glittering warhead had become brighter as it came down from the heavens.

Then the Yun understood the threat; that was a capsule, a thermonuclear warhead. The monstrous device was meant to annihilate them down here.

The warhead launched decoys and chaff. The counter rockets would surely fail. Thus, the Yun fusion strove to burn out the main firing mechanism. It used telekinetic force—

Click.

The Yun fusion did it, ruining the firing mechanism and thus disarming the bomb. The warhead came down with furious speed. It slammed against the desert sand, sinking, causing a slight tremor around it and sending up showers of sand, but otherwise not doing a damn thing.

Wait!

Two more warheads were coming down. They did so fast.

The Yun fusion knew what to do now, as it had just done it with the first. The mental power once again raced up and manipulated with telekinesis. Something was different about this switch.

No, no, no, we are panicking, the Yun fusion told itself.

The Yun forced itself into objectivity and calmness. It utilized its mental power. The correct switch clicked.

That warhead also came down, slamming upon the desert sands and not doing shinola.

The Yun fusion strove upon the third warhead. It worked fast.

Click.

The Yun fusion experienced a moment of horror. The click was not it successfully shutting down everything. The click was the switch to a small detonation in the warhead. That detonation began a chain reaction.

In a microsecond, a thermonuclear airburst showed as a new sun. Heat, radiation and EMP swept down near the sinkhole that led to the scientists that led to the great one. The explosion slaughtered Metamorphs around the sinkhole by the thousands. It also destroyed many two-brains, dissolving what remained of the Yun mind fusion.

Many two-brains survived; those outside the immediate blast radius of the bomb. Some of the two-brained and regular Metamorphs looked up. They saw a great flash upon the horizon. Some were so close that the flash burned out their optic nerves. They would be blind until radiation poisoning killed them. Others even farther away saw an intense light that put splotches in their vision, but they would see normally soon enough. Nor would radiation kill them any time soon, as they were far enough away. More than average would grow cancerous tumors, though.

In any case, one thermonuclear warhead had made it to the coordinates. That created a dead zone, and that was what those below in the labs had asked for.

-69-

Gallant Ophir sat in the command chair of the gigantic grav armor unit. It was a heavy grav tank from a time long ago. Unknown aliens had brought the tank to Gath, a relic from the great tank wars, from Cestus 9.

The grav tank worked and was crammed with weapons and those who'd survived the time underground. That included Ophir, a Honey Man soldier, Hern, Gricks, Dravek, Mara and Maddox.

The grav tank negotiated large tunnels until it reached a new chamber with a transport pad. Once on it, the activated pad caused the tank to dematerialize and then materialize at the bottom of the great sinkhole. This was forty-seven minutes after the detonation of the warhead.

At Ophir's command, the Honey Man driver manipulated the controls. The engine revved, giving the gravity repellers enough power for the massive tank to levitate upward. It did so much faster than the sky raft had descended.

"Sir," the driver said. "I detect massive levels of radiation up there."

"Excellent," Ophir said. "That means Grandma was successful." He glanced at the others sitting on the floor of the main tank chamber. "I don't think we need to worry. The tank's armor will keep us safe from radiation while we drive through the radiated zone. Luckily, we don't have to travel all the way to the Highlands. Grandma said dirigibles are on the way, including a transport dirigible. It will pick us up and fly us to the Highlands."

"Good news indeed," Maddox said.

Dravek and Mara sat on the floor near Maddox. Dravek held one of Mara's hands. They had been whispering together. Now Dravek leaned over and whispered so low that Maddox could barely hear him.

"We dare not return to the Highlands. They'll make us eunuchs for sure."

"No doubt, no doubt," Maddox said equally as quietly.

Maddox didn't think the Honey Men would keep their word any more than he would have kept his if Ophir had chosen the wrong item. Fortunately, he had kept his word. In that sense, he sat in moral superiority over the Honey Men—if that was what he needed.

In truth, Maddox thought about Meta, Jewel, and getting home. How could he get home? He didn't think the Eye of Helion would stay long enough to see him to Earth. The crystal had already been contemplating about going back to Helion.

It seemed like every kind of power source—mechanical, biological, whatever—imparted energy to the Eye. As it gained energy, it lost interest in what happened around it. That struck Maddox as odd. Yet perhaps that was the essence of the Eyes of Helion. Maybe that was why they were so antithetical to Yon Soths.

"Captain, are you listening to me?" Dravek whispered.

Maddox nodded, even as he kept watch of Ophir.

"We're almost to the surface," Ophir said.

The engines whined louder. The tank shivered, dipped lower and then rose again.

Everyone waited in anticipation.

Then, the tank made it out of the giant sinkhole, roaring across the radiated surface. Some of the sand had fused into glass, making sheets of it. There were no black, balloon-tired vehicles. No doubt, the thermonuclear warhead had shredded them along with slaying any nearby Metamorphs.

In no time, the grav tank reached the impressive speed of one hundred and ten miles per hour. The ride was smooth, too. This thing was a marvel.

Maddox leaned back where the Eye of Helion lay with its brightness dimmed.

"Eye," Maddox whispered. "Can you hear me?"

"I hear you very well, Captain Maddox," the Eye said so loudly that Ophir whirled around in his command chair.

"I'm sorry, Gallant Ophir," Maddox said. "I'll keep quiet."

"No need, no need," Ophir said, who studied Maddox with speculation.

Ophir had gotten cockier already, but Maddox's people outnumbered his in the tank. Perhaps Ophir trusted in his personal force field. Maddox had also seen a glint or two from the ruby rings. Ophir must have recharged them, at least to a degree. If their roles were reversed and Maddox was at the mercy of Ophir—now that he'd given the Honey Men what they wanted, Maddox didn't believe he could rely upon their good will, especially once they reached Grandma Julia and Shofet Zadoury.

"Captain Maddox," the Eye whispered, "I thought you wanted to converse with me."

"Yes," Maddox whispered. "Dravek, Mara and I rescued you from your internment as an inert nothing. Who knows how long you would have stayed there. Perhaps you would have stayed inert in the underground shuttle until the Yon Soth regenerated or regained its consciousness. Then perhaps it would have used and corrupted you."

"I do not contest your allegation," the Eye whispered. "I am grateful. You must not believe that we of Helion do not understand obligation and debt. Thank you so much for your part in my revival. When I return home, I shall inform those of Helion of your wonderful generosity. I will insist that we always sing your praises when we hum about the glories of the past. Now, however, I'm afraid I don't care for this radiated zone. Some is seeping through the armor. Thus, Captain Maddox, I wish to bid you—"

"Now hold on, hold on," Maddox whispered. "That's not the way to show your gratitude."

"Who are you to tell a crystal of Helion how to show gratitude?" the Eye whispered haughtily.

"What I mean," Maddox said, "is if you're going to make me feel grateful for what I did for you, I should feel grateful for what you did for me in return."

"That would demean your act of altruism, would it not?"

"No, no, no. I purposely came to help you in order to win your help for me."

"Oh," the Eye said. "Your action wasn't purely altruistic?"

"I told you that in the beginning. Surely you cannot have forgotten."

"I suppose not. I'd hoped you'd spoken with hyperbole about all that. Now, I fear you're indeed serious. This is unwelcome news, I assure you. How do you wish me to sully myself? Do you know that those of the Triad always made me sully myself with this material act and that material act. It was most upsetting, most demeaning to my philosophic insights."

Maddox spoke carefully as he was sure the Eye was trying to wriggle out of its obligation. Therefore, it would be best to use precise statements so no ambiguity could seep into the conversation.

"I have two critical problems," Maddox whispered. "If you help me solve them, I'll truly believe you're grateful for what I did for you."

"Go on," said the Eye. "Make your point."

"The first problem regards the Leviathan assault vessels heading for Gath."

"I'm aware of them. I don't believe they present you much of a problem. My advice to you is to avoid the assault vessels."

"Surely, the assault vessels carry antimatter weaponry."

"What of it?" the Eye asked softly.

"I don't want the inhabitants of the planet to turn against me. The Soldiers of Leviathan might well threaten the population unless those of the planet turn me over to them."

"Did you ever think maybe that those of Leviathan came to destroy the Yon Soth?"

"Do they know of its existence," Maddox asked.

"I find that doubtful," the Eye admitted.

"That means your premise is unlikely."

"Are you attempting to chop logic with an eye of Helion? Is this a contest, Captain Maddox? Please tell me if that is so."

361

"No. I admire those of Helion. But I'll admire them even more after you do me these two small deeds out of gratitude."

Maddox glanced at Ophir in his command chair. The man was busy studying their progress. The chair was just far enough away to make this secret talk possible.

"Oh, very well," the Eye whispered. "Let's get on with it. I weary of this gross and demeaning conversation. Why can't you talk of high concepts and interesting propositions?"

"I lack your loftiness," Maddox said.

"I believe you say that in jest. You don't really mean it."

"Does it matter?" asked Maddox.

"It does to me."

"I'll stick to the point then," Maddox said. "How can I destroy the three assault vessels of Leviathan with your help?"

"Really, Captain, I'm not a war-waging artifact. I'm an eye of Helion. I was made to contemplate wonderful things, to teleport here, to teleport—"

"Eye, Eye, Eye," Maddox said. "I wish you'd calm down and help me figure this out."

"Very well. I have noted your first problem. What is the second one?"

"In less than a year, I wish to go from here, Gath, to the Orion Spiral Arm, the edge of it. I desire this so I can go home to my wife and child."

"Oh, is that all? I suppose you want me to teleport you all the way there, too."

"If it's not too much trouble—"

"Yes! It is far too much trouble. It is much too far out of the way for me. And it would take me years of effort to achieve this. I'd have to re-energize constantly. With each teleportation—do you not realize, Captain, that it is a geometric problem? It isn't merely an arithmetical problem. The longer the distance, the greater energy is expended in geometric proportion. Do I make myself clear?"

"Indeed."

"But perhaps if I study star charts and anomalies—this is the Heydell Cloud, is it not?"

"It most certainly is," Maddox said.

"Ah, yes, yes. Then you must take me to an astrophysical station. There, I may study the entirety of the Heydell Cloud, all the anomalies together, and as much as you can show me of the Scutum-Centaurus Spiral Arm. Then, perhaps, I will be able to supply you with a route you could use. I mean with an ordinary ship of this technological level that I detect on the planet."

"Could I make this journey within the year?" Maddox asked.

"It's theoretically possible if there are the needed anomalies I'm supposing. If not, do not expect more from me, Captain Maddox."

Maddox controlled his worry. Maybe it was time to take care of the first problem. "What do we do about the Leviathan assault vessels?"

"You cannot stop worrying about all this, can you? This is really too much. All you did was wake me up and now you expect multiple miracles from me."

"We've already gone over that," Maddox said. "You could have awoken in the tentacle of a Yon Soth after it had suborned you and twisted you to its ends. The Triad did so, why not a Yon Soth?"

"Maybe you're right. Besides, I'm tired of the grav tank, as it has an evil taint. I will, if you don't mind, take us elsewhere from here."

"If you do that, my people need to go with me," Maddox said. "Otherwise, Gallant Ophir will harm them."

"I know who your people are," the Eye said.

"Just to make sure, I want Gricks, Hern, Dravek and Mara, and me."

"Really? This is quite insulting. Do you think I'm a retard that you must be so specific?"

"No, no, the opposite."

"That's it then? That's all you have to say?"

"Yes," Maddox said.

"Very well," the Eye said. "We are gone."

With that, there was a flash within the grav tank.

Ophir whipped around, astonished to find that Maddox and the others, including the Eye, had disappeared.

363

-70-

Maddox and his party appeared at the spaceport in the North Pole region. Soon, with Gricks and Hern advising them, they sold some equipment for currency notes. With the notes, they rented a hotel room and bought supplies. Afterward, they made calculations and awaited events.

During the wait, Maddox went to the library where Sub-Centurion Eddings had worked. Maddox rented a solo computer room, hiding the Eye of Helion in a pocket. Using the computer, Maddox and the Eye learned more about the Heydell Cloud.

The cloud was a large region, spanning many hundreds of light years. Many of the planets were allied in treaties. There were many pirates, spatial and time anomalies, and other dangers. Leviathan seldom sent ships into the Heydell Cloud.

That Leviathan had sent ships here...maybe he'd underestimated the hatred that Leviathan held for him when *Victory* had reached this spiral arm years ago. He'd also thwarted the small, alien Dhows on the planet Kregen. The Dhows had been connected to Leviathan. Could the Dhows have brought a bad report about him to the rulers of Leviathan? It seemed more than possible.

The two days of rest and study were cut short as the assault vessels of Leviathan reached orbital space around Gath. From there, the warships launched several nuclear-tipped missiles. One landed near the spaceport. It wasn't close enough to devastate the city, but it destroyed a giant farm complex the city used.

A similar event took place in the Highlands of the South Pole.

That provoked planetary retaliation. Masses of ballistic missiles rose to do battle against the assault vessels. Alas, the assault vessels of Leviathan proved superior, although one took damage, retreating into deeper space. There, its reactors blew. The vessel exploded in a furious ball of nuclear devastation. This left only two assault vessels in orbit.

The Soldier in charge demanded via communications that those of the planet give up Captain Maddox or Dravek, his clone. If not, the planet would face further bombardment. If that were insufficient motivation, the assault vessels would leave to report to Leviathan so an even greater fleet would arrive at Gath to apply salutary justice.

If there had been a Strategist along, he must have perished in the exploded assault vessel, as the enemy plan didn't seem that complex or cunning.

Still, fearing the worst, Maddox retreated into a dark alley with the Eye of Helion. He'd ducked here after two policemen looked at him keenly, his face just having been on vid screens everywhere.

"It's hit the fan," Maddox told the Eye. "How do we solve this?"

"By leaving Gath, of course," the Eye said.

"I'd need a spaceship for that, one which I don't have."

"You could buy a spaceship."

"I lack the necessary funds," Maddox said.

"You could steal one, although that is highly unethical."

"Let's say I succeeded in the theft. How could I slip past the assault vessels?"

"Must I think of everything for you?"

"So far, you've thought of nothing," Maddox said.

"Oh, very well, we come to the obvious conclusion. Nuclear weapons. You ordered nuclear weapons dropped on the poor desert Metamorphs in order that you could escape from the sinkhole. Are you not disgusted with yourself, Captain Maddox, with all the death and destruction you create?

365

It is a stain upon my being to have been involved in this, and I frankly want no further part of it."

"You promised me aid."

The Eye brightened as if angry. "All right, there's a way I can do this with nuclear weapons, but I have to do it quickly, and I have to do it now."

"What's that?" Maddox asked.

"More killing that will stain me—this time killing Soldiers of Leviathan."

Maddox had been wondering when the Eye would come to the obvious solution. He'd seen it days ago. Maybe he could smooth this for the crystal.

"You should remember that Soldiers of Leviathan are hostile creatures threatening nuclear devastation of a planet. They'll kill many through nuclear bombardment. By stopping them, you're going to save millions of lives."

"I understand your sophistry, and it has a point," the Eye said. "That's what makes it such good sophistry. Still, I'm angry that you are forcing me to this. You should have accepted my gratitude and been done with it. Instead, you have dragged me down to the level of material well-being. Why do you not contemplate and enjoy whatever is given you and take it as a sign of the goodwill of the Creator?"

"You make a good point. I attempt to do that, but I can't let all these people die because of me."

"The easy solution is obvious," the Eye said. "Surrender to Leviathan."

Maddox snorted. "I see what you're doing. You want me to free you of the obligation to help me get back to Earth."

The Eye brightened more. "Your logic chopping is making me even angrier. Very well, let us do it. Then I don't want to hear anything more about the subject. Is that clear, Captain Maddox?"

"Why are you so testy?"

"I've already told you why. Now let us do this."

The Eye blinked, teleporting the two of them to a nuclear weapon station in a legion hall in the North Pole region. There, Maddox picked two large nuclear devices. The Eye teleported the two of them and the first bomb into a storage area in the first assault vessel. Maddox set the timer. The Eye teleported them back to the second nuclear weapon. They then teleported with it into the second assault vessel. In moments, they were back at the spaceport on the planet.

"I feel so soiled and disgusted with myself," the Eye said. "I almost feel that since I've done this, I'm fulfilled all my obligations to help you. You have angered me, Captain Maddox. At first, I thought you were a noble person. But having recognized your bloodthirsty nature and how you wish to dominate your enemies—your solution is always to kill, kill, kill. Can't you think of another way?"

"Not always," Maddox said. "I wish I was more like you."

"That is a flat-out lie. Why do you bother lying to me? Tell me the truth."

"All right, I'm tired. I want to go home. I want to love, but I'm a soldier trying to do his duty."

"As are the Soldiers of Leviathan doing their duty," the Eye said.

As they spoke, brightness flared into existence high in the sky. It was like a new sun, but it only lasted a moment. Almost instantly, a second sun appeared.

The two assault vessels of Leviathan that had escaped the ballistic missiles now exploded mysteriously—mysteriously to the rest of the population of Gath.

Thus, the threat from Leviathan was over for Maddox, at least temporarily. He had reached a place where he could possibly acquire a spaceship, once he found the needed funds to do so.

Until then, he was stuck on Gath, seven to eight thousand light-years from Earth, home and his beloved. He had an angry Eye of Helion, which began to sulk and no longer listened to his entreaties.

Was this then to be his epilogue: freed of everything, but unable to return home? Would he be like Odysseus, ten years away from his loved ones as he wandered from one locale to the next?

No, Maddox thought. There had to be a way to convince the Eye to give him the information he needed. They had to use the collected data about the Heydell Cloud.

Maddox retreated to the hotel room. He also had to figure out how to acquire or book passage on one of the trader ships at the North Pole spaceport.

-71-

Several days passed as the money supply dwindled.

During that time, rumors abounded as to why the attack vessels had detonated. There were rumors of secret defensive systems employed in orbital space. Rumors the Honey Men had developed telepathic methods against alien invaders. There was even a rumor that a team had gone into the mid-world desert and found ancient weaponry and used it against the Leviathan ships. Then there were rumors about this Maddox and his supposed clone.

More days passed and the rumors faded in public interest as other news took the forefront. One item concerned a recruitment drive for a new legion assault to take place in six weeks. Legion Lanarck needed the recruits.

That evening, Dravek, Gricks and Hern accosted Maddox at the public table where they ate. They were in a far corner, away from others. Even so, the men spoke in whispers.

"What are your plans, Captain?" Hern asked.

Maddox worked during the day at the spaceport as part of a loading team. He was earning currency, studying what he could about space passage and listening to everything.

"I'm still gathering intel," Maddox said.

"That's what I thought," Hern said, as he glanced at the others. "You're dithering. Well, I'm thinking about joining Legion Lanarck for its assault against the Honey Men."

Maddox just looked at him.

"What?" Hern said. "I'm a Primus. Legion work is what I do best."

"You barely escaped with everything intact this last time," Maddox said. "Why risk it all over again?"

"It's simple," Hern said. "I know things now. I could sell the information to Tribune Lanarck and maybe use it to gain higher rank in the legion."

"Who's going to believe you?" Maddox asked. "No doubt, you'd have to explain how you got from the mid-world desert to here. Do you think anyone will believe a teleportation story?"

Maddox didn't add that he didn't want Hern talking about teleportation or the Eye of Helion. That should be clear enough. If he had to tell Hern that, he'd probably end up telling Hern he was taking his life into his hands by talking about all this. Maddox might have to silence the man. Hern would understand the latent threat and probably go to Lanarck anyway out of stubborn pride. That would force Maddox to act prematurely against the Primus.

"Believability would be a problem," Hern said, with his big hands on the table. He looked Maddox in the eye. "Unless you came forward, showed people the Eye of Helion and explained the situation. We could change the ways of Gath, set ourselves up as important people."

"Possibly, possibly," Maddox said, who did not intend to do anything of the sort.

He'd been working on the Eye of Helion, trying to get it to commit to getting him home. The truth, Maddox was sick of being stranded on this strange planet, sick of being grounded, and sick of every day that went by he wasn't already on his way home. He'd been gone well over a year, maybe two. Star Watch might consider him dead. What would Jewel be thinking? Had she started kindergarten yet or first grade?

Hern spoke more, slinging various arguments why Maddox should come out about the Eye. None of the arguments stuck, as they were all logically weak.

Dravek finally put a hand on one of Hern's wrists.

The beefy Primus glared at Dravek.

Dravek gave the barest shake of his head.

370

Hern must have gotten the message, as he finally shut up.

"Listen," Dravek said, leaning closer to Maddox, who was across the table from him. "What are your plans? I need to know so I can make mine accordingly."

Maddox sat up. Dravek was a different matter entirely. "Is there anything specific you're thinking?"

Dravek nodded. "I need a spaceship in order to implement my plans. For that, either we storm the spaceport—"

"Wait a minute," Maddox said, interrupting. "Have you studied spaceport security?"

"I have," Dravek said. "And you're right. Security is tight. We'll need the Eye for this."

Now Maddox understood the thrust of Hern's questions. The Primus had been feeling him out for Dravek. The Eye of Helion was in his jacket pocket. It remained there all the time unless Maddox and the Eye argued while they were alone. Then the Eye came out of his pocket.

"You say you want a spaceship, maybe even steal one to get it," Maddox said. "What happens once you have it? I mean, if you steal it from here, you'd have to leave Gath—unless you plan to go to the South Pole with it."

Dravek shook his head. "I don't trust the Honey Men. That means I'd leave Gath. You're right about that."

"To become a pirate?" asked Maddox.

Dravek shrugged. "I'll need to do something to keep life and limb together. I have good crewmembers in those two." He indicated Gricks and Hern.

"Don't forget me," Mara said.

"I haven't," Dravek said with a smile.

"You'll also need someone who knows how to keep engines running," Maddox said.

"I know."

"I've been studying space mechanics," Gricks said. "Unlike Hern, I'm never going back to legion work."

Maddox took a sip from his pot of beer and took another bite from his fish cakes. The others were getting restless from waiting out the days. He couldn't say he blamed them. "Let me think on it. I'll give you an answer later tonight or tomorrow. Is that fair?"

They all agreed it was.

Maddox finished his meal. One way or another, he had to do something. The time for waiting was over. What was his next move?

-72-

As was his way, Maddox strolled alone through the spaceport city's alleyways that evening. There were footpads along the route. So far, none had dared to accost him during his nightly forays. Maybe they sensed something threatening in his tigerish stride, or the thrust of his head or alertness. In any case, they kept away from him.

Maddox reached into a pocket, his hand hovering over the Eye of Helion. He glanced around warily, a cool breeze stirring his hair as the quiet hum of the city echoed around him. He stood atop an older abandoned manufacturing building and didn't sense anyone in proximity.

"Come on out at a dim light setting."

The Eye rose from the pocket as Maddox removed his hand. The crystal drifted near head level.

"We've been spinning our wheels too long here," Maddox said.

"I understand the idiom," the Eye said. "Unfortunately, I'm filled with remorse as I have been contemplating my part in destroying the cybernetic soldiers and their assault vessels. I've also contemplated my part in the thermonuclear destruction of the desert Metamorphs."

"You had no part in the latter."

"I disagree. I connected communications between Grandma Julia and Ophir. That allowed them to plot the Metamorphs' destruction."

"You did do that. But you weren't in the loop about what to do back then. And you were still being grateful for having been raised from your ageless slumber."

"True," the Eye said, in a wistful tone. "Now, I don't know if I should be grateful anymore. There are so many evils, so many harsh things in the universe. Maybe I would be better off inert. I admit the universe was like this when I was awake the first time. Still, I sense the stirring of the one below. I sense others of its kind alive and working in this spiral arm."

"What about the Orion Spiral Arm?" Maddox asked. "How many Yon Soths do you feel working there?"

"That surpasses my range of knowledge," the Eye said.

Maddox waited. The Eye sounded too wistful, too forlorn. He didn't like this.

"I do dream about going back to Helion," the Eye said after a time. "I could take the coordinates of Helion from your mind, even though that might involve an effort. I have found you more resistant the more that I gently probe your mind."

Maddox didn't say that he'd been sensing the probes and hardening his resolve accordingly.

"I also realize I could do you a service, one that you would desire but haven't had the wit to ask about."

"Oh," Maddox said.

"I believe I could tell you who kidnapped you from the bridge when your Starship *Victory* was trapped."

In an instant, Maddox became hyper-alert. "Is *Victory* free now?"

"I have no way of knowing. I do know that the process of trapping *Victory* was a concerted plan. At least you believed so, and so did your crew before you were snatched off the bridge of your starship."

Maddox's heart began to hammer. Was the Eye being deceptive? He didn't think so. "How could you know any of this?"

"Through the impressions and memories that you've suppressed or forgotten. They're much like erased computer files. Those that understand can reconstruct them. Your mind is a deep and layered thing, as I have once said. It is different from those around me, who are open slates, as it were. Dravek

374

has some of your complexity, but it's not the same. What accounts for your difference, Captain Maddox?"

Maddox shrugged as if he was indifferent to the whole thing.

"Was it the Erill creatures you absorbed? Was it Balron the Traveler who trained you and changed the trajectory of your brain?"

"Why do you ask if you already know the answers?" Maddox said.

"Testing, studying, probing, I seek to know more. I find that I do not care to study the dregs around us, the small-minded. I am interested in uniqueness. You are unique, Captain. You have a role to play in the grand scheme of the universe, and I detect you long for your wife. You long to see your daughter, and I almost want to help you."

"You promised to help me."

"It was a promise tricked and ripped from me by your sophistry. I'm not sure that I want to agree to such trickery any longer."

"If you break your word, you'll defame all the crystals of Helion."

"There you go again," the Eye said. "Why do you always resort to these ruses and subtleties?"

Maddox shrugged. Did he resort to ruses as a matter of course? If he did, it was because he lived in a cruel universe. He fought for the spark of life called Humanity, for its place in the universe. He wasn't going to apologize for that in the least.

Maddox rubbed his jaw as he regarded the floating Eye. "Who kidnapped me? And is my starship safe?"

"You seek this from me?"

"Tell me those things and I'll give you the coordinates to your planet without demanding that you show me a quick way home."

"This is a surprise."

"I bargained for two problems solved. I'll go by that even though I long to reach—search my mind freely. I have the coordinates to the planet Helion. I'll trust in your goodness do tell me what I've asked for after you get what you seek."

The Eye projected a beam at Maddox's head that lasted for seconds and then quit.

"This is interesting," the Eye said. "Your coordinates for Helion match mine."

"You already knew the coordinates?"

"Perhaps."

"Was this another test then?"

Maddox hated tests of his character. He was who he was. He hated—he worked to calm himself and breathed deeply. He used the Way of the Pilgrim until he felt at peace with himself.

"You are a remarkable man, Captain. The trick of the breath to bring yourself serenity—I admire that."

Maddox nodded.

"I have detected these bits of data in you. In that sense, I am merely a conduit from you to you," the Eye said, a touch of melancholy in its tone. "Take the Adoks, for instance, those deceitful beings from the refugee planet tricked you, as they feared the one called Galyan. I think the Adoks feared irrationally. In any case, they sent the starship to a locale where another waited. That one practiced deceit. From what I can piece together from your mind, your crew overcame the deceit, the stasis, and other manipulative energies. The starship broke free. As it did, a bug-eyed monster with tentacles appeared on your bridge. It snatched you and disappeared."

"Do you know the name of this one?" Maddox asked.

"You've already named him in your mind, Captain. His name was Grutch. He brought you to those I believe you call Spacers. The Spacers decided to sell you to Leviathan. You arrived at a science station deep in the Scutum-Centaurus Spiral Arm. They cloned Dravek there and used a chronowarp to speed his growth. They transferred many of your memories to him. As far as I can tell, Dravek is the reason you are free. He committed treacherous acts to achieve this and yet he saved you. Why or for what reason—I haven't probed his mind. I am leaving that to Mara."

"Do you have a secret alliance with Mara?"

"Negative," the Eye said. "I believe your starship escaped the trap, but you were not aboard. As to what happened to your starship after that, I don't know."

A sudden chill ran down Maddox's spine, his fists clenching tight. "Grutch," he spat out the name like venom. "He's going to wish he never crossed paths with me."

The Spacers were going to rue the day for interfering with him like this as well.

"Captain Maddox, Captain Maddox, are you still able to comprehend what I'm saying?"

It took Maddox a moment. He nodded. "Go ahead, Eye. You have my attention."

"I'm going to return to Helion. It will take time, but after all these millennia, I believe I can safely reach home. Thank you for what you have done, Captain. I appreciate it and I wish you the best. I am still grateful for what you dared to do deep underground near the evil Yon Soth."

Maddox saluted the Eye. "Good luck. Godspeed and I hope you make it home."

"By the way, Captain, even as we speak, I'm imprinting a certain sequence of events, stars and spatial anomalies in your mind. If you follow those coordinates and can make split-second decisions while traveling from one spatial anomaly to another—do you see it in your mind?"

Maddox realized he did. "Yes. Yes, I do."

"In less than a year, you shall reach the Omicron 9 System. From there I warrant you will be able to reach home rather rapidly. I've decided to gift you with that knowledge as well as certain other key pieces of data regarding what I know of this spiral arm. Beware the Sovereign Hierarchy of Leviathan, Captain. I believe they are well able to send a powerful expeditionary force into your spiral arm. No doubt, the force would handily defeat a Commonwealth-New Men combined fleet."

"What do you suggest we do about that?"

"That is up to you and your people. I have given you fair warning. That is enough. I will grant you this, however. I have added one tiny refinement to your mind. It should allow you to stop anyone from doing what I did to you. I give you this as a parting gift. I am indeed more grateful than you could suppose. Captain Maddox, it has been an honor knowing you, you are a mover and a shaker."

"I've been told I'm a *di-far.*"

"That is a Spacer term. Go with the Creator's blessing. May you reach your family and kiss your daughter and wife for me. Physical longing and yearning are things I do not know. I suppose you will hunt for Grutch and Venna the Spacer spy."

"What? She had a part of this?"

"I let that slip," the Eye said. "I think she convinced the other Spacers to sell you to Leviathan. Leviathan is on the march. I do not think you in the Orion Arm can do much against them. I wish you well despite that."

"I wish you well, Eye."

The baseball-sized crystal from Helion flashed and was gone.

Maddox felt a sudden sting of loneliness. Yet now he had a way of getting home. All he needed was a spaceship.

-73-

While unloading at the spaceport the next day, Maddox studied spaceship security even more closely. He didn't think the five of them could storm onto a trader vessel and lift off. Could they hire on as extra crewmembers and hijack the ship while in space?

That seemed even more doubtful.

A possibility came from an odd direction.

Dravek had been studying the problem of acquiring a spaceship longer than Maddox had. Dravek possessed a mind as keen as Maddox's, honed by his experience as an intelligence officer. He'd wondered about something for some time: Tribune Culain had armed his legion with spring rifles. That had always struck Dravek as odd.

Because of the question as to why, Dravek began a personality profile on the tribune. The tribunes of the North Pole spaceport—the larger city—were some of the highest ranked aristocrats of the region, some of the richest and most influential people. By going to the off-world run library, Dravek learned much about Tribune Culain.

Little hints and ideas gave him the second method to extracting information. That way was Mara, through telepathic probing of his thoughts. It meant getting her near enough the grand villa to reach the man's mind.

After a detailed, two-pronged approach, Dravek discovered that Tribune Culain was a Honey Man bastard from the South Pole. Likely, he was two generations removed. How he'd

379

gained the vast sums to begin a legion was unknown. How he'd earned the tribune status needed to launch raids on the South Pole was also a secret. That implied greater age on his part. That implied honey, the longevity treatment.

Tribune Culain's first raid forty-eight years ago had proven to be a fantastic success, earning him greater funds and status. Since then, he had one of the worst raid records. He also had one of the lowest raid attempts.

By searching through library records, Dravek discovered that several of Culain's legions had been woefully under-armed with weaponry such as spring rifles.

That caused him to risk using Mara even more.

She discovered a dark secret. Culain had alerted the South Pole Honey Men of the raids ahead of time. That had happened with the last raid as well. The Honey Men waited in ambush, collecting the dirigibles, helos and troops—more slaves for working the fields. In return, Culain received large monetary kickbacks.

Mara also learned that Culain was a direct descendant of Grandma Julia, of an earlier generation than Ophir.

Tribune Culain knowingly sent men to their enslavement and castration.

Dravek reported to Maddox all he'd learned.

For Maddox it was grist for the mill of his ideas. A plan had begun to unfold, a mad plan. He needed a dupe, however. Since Tribune Culain was so vile, Maddox decided he would be the target.

This would be dangerous as well as highly risky. But as he'd told Dravek before, "Madness is our only hope. We're not going home without it."

Maddox had more than one reason for getting it done now. *Victory* could be in trouble. He was fiercely homesick. Leviathan might be sending a fleet against the Commonwealth and had certainly already sent spies. Star Watch needed to know this yesterday.

His risky and audacious plan involved a face-to-face visit with Tribune Culain. The tribune was hard to see, though, and suspicious of anyone who tried.

Dravek learned more about him. Culain loved blood sports. There were more than a few at the spaceport, the largest city on Gath. Culain often attended the night exhibitions in The Pit. Culain had some questionable habits as well, another reason he went to the tunnels that held The Pit. The tribune also had an excellent spy service and usually knew when others tracked him.

Dravek thought long and hard about all that, using Mara again to lift a few quirks from Culain's mind.

"He's learned about Captain Maddox," Mara reported. "He's curious about him and has read a report from Grandma about what happened in the South Pole."

"Curious enough to see Maddox one on one?" asked Dravek.

Mara scrunched her eyebrows. "I think Culain needs one more prod for that."

"Like what?"

"Losing money on Maddox in a knife fight in The Pit seems the easiest way to stir him," Mara said.

"You saw something that specific in his mind?" Dravek asked.

Mara nodded.

"Could Culain suspect what we're doing and be setting Maddox up?" Dravek asked.

"You mean does Culain have Honey Men telepathic talent around him?"

"Does he?" Dravek asked.

"Yes," Mara said. "Doing this will be a risk. But no, I don't think this is a setup through me."

Dravek fretted. But in the end, he told Maddox about it, including his fears about a double-cross through Mara.

At work the next day, Maddox talked about The Pit. He discovered it was one of the fastest ways to make currency. There were matches every weekend. He asked about how to get in The Pit against a fighter that would gain a big purse.

"You don't want to do that," said his foreman, a squat man with a booming voice. "They'll slice you up after a few minutes of fancy footwork. There are the main events, the killers, and the pasties they cut up for the crowd's pleasure. Don't be a pasty. Few ever come out alive."

Later, after work, a thin man with shifty eyes told Maddox he knew a way to enter The Pit.

Maddox could feel other eyes watching him. He spotted two gunmen leaning against crates across an alley. Was this a setup? Was Mara double-crossing him or was Culain's talent better than Dravek's?

Maddox trusted his intuition. It didn't say anything negative. So, he figured he'd try this, trusting to his skills to see him through.

That night he went with his shifty eyed friend. He entered a low building that smelled of despair, drugs and prostitution. He met a gangly man wearing a slick black suit and the same two gunmen as before.

"Stick says you want a shot at some fast money," the gangly man said, known as Casimir.

"That depends," Maddox said.

"On what?"

"What I'd have to do?"

"How much are you hoping to make?" Casimir asked.

"A big fat score," Maddox said.

Casimir watched Maddox closely. "You willing to face the Razor in The Pit for a chance at it?"

Mara had planted the suggestion in Casimir's mind earlier. Dravek had discovered these connections.

"What would I make if I did?" Maddox asked.

Casimir pulled out a slip of paper, set it against a crate and wrote on it. He handed the slip of paper to Maddox.

His eyes went wide when he saw the amount. He'd have to work two years at the spaceport to make this much. Then he looked up in concern. "It isn't a death match, is it?"

Casimir's eyes shone with evil delight. "No," he lied. "It's to first cut and the judges decide."

"Sure," Maddox said. "For that amount, I don't mind a few stitches. I need the currency."

"Who doesn't?" Casimir said. "I'll set it up. You show up first night of the weekend. If you fail to show up—" He jerked

382

a thumb at the watching gunmen. "They'll come hunting to kill you."

"There's no need for threats," Maddox said. "I'll be there. You can count on me."

-74-

Maddox went first weekend night. The place was a vast underground maze of tunnels, carved from volcanic lava. It was jammed with dressed-up people, smoke, booze and broads selling their charms. Almost everyone was drunk or high. A few big shots prowled the tunnels with their bodyguards.

Maddox went to The Pit backrooms. He had to change into revealing fighting gear.

"That way the crowd can see you spurt blood," Casimir said.

"One cut, right?" Maddox said.

Casimir smirked.

Maddox pulled off his boots, so he was barefoot. He then put on the loincloth outfit and took out a knife with a nine-inch blade. It was sharp and well balanced for throwing. He'd been practicing with it since agreeing to the match.

Maddox warmed up, shadowboxing before a mirror to get limber and sweaty. Occasionally, through the stone wall, were bloodcurdling screams from the stands around The Pit.

At last, Casimir told Maddox it was time.

Maddox marched down a worn corridor with the two gunmen trailing. He turned a corner and went through swinging doors. He approached the arena, The Pit.

Around The Pit were crowded stands with yelling, drunken people, at least five hundred. It smelled of alcohol, sweat and death. Bright lights shined from the ceiling.

Maddox walked into The Pit, his bare feet stepping on fine sand. He noted covered areas that hid spilled blood. It reminded him of the Highland arena.

Gricks and Hern were in the crowd. Maddox saw thick-faced Culain with massive bodyguards around him. The tribune sat on a front row bench.

The Razor was Culain's man. Everyone knew the tribune bet on his prized fighter.

A hard-faced referee appeared, a man with a holstered sidearm and bloodstained leather shirt. He spoke into a microphone, his voice booming to those in the stands.

As he introduced Maddox, a few boos and catcalls echoed from the crowd.

Soon enough, the Razor loped into The Pit from the other direction Maddox had entered. He was a lean muscular man, shorter than Maddox. His eyes looked dead, and his face was pockmarked. Clearly, he took drugs. There were a few old wounds on his oily torso. He also moved with a jerky quickness. Maddox realized the Razor took enhancers. They surely gave him greater stamina and likely speeded reflexes. The man might not feel pain. He'd be like a snake that wouldn't know when it was dead. Fighting him would be more dangerous than Maddox had anticipated.

Despite that, getting into the spirit of things, Maddox practiced a few slices as the Razor strutted around The Pit, holding up his knives to the crowd. They cheered him, many blowing kisses.

The announcer said it was a fight to the death.

The crowd roared with delight.

Maddox saw Casimir at the bottom entrance to the Pit. The man made an obscene hand gesture at Maddox, laughing at him.

Maddox ignored the promoter. He'd always known it was a death match. He could finally drop the pretense of being a foolhardy individual. Now, he turned, keeping his eye on the strutting Razor.

Mara and Dravek were also in the stands apart from Gricks and Hern. They were all watching for anyone with a dart gun. If Maddox started doing too well, it was possible Culain would have someone dart him with a muscle inhibitor. Someone else might try to shine a light in his eyes and momentarily blind him. Those were all tricks of the trade, ways to help a champion continue his winning streak.

Thus, Maddox had his own trick. The longer the fight lasted, the more time Culain would have to signal a cheating move. Thus, the match needed to be as short as possible.

"Start," said the announcer, as he drew his gun and backed away.

The Razor already faced Maddox. Now, the drug-enhanced knifeman began to stalk Maddox. He practiced slashing with his two knives, grinning, his dead eyes shining with contempt as he approached.

Maddox feigned bewilderment.

The crowd booed when Maddox staggered away.

The Razor spat at the sand.

Maddox noticed the gesture and how the Razor slightly turned his head to the left as he did it. The man dropped his guard in that moment just a bit.

Maddox pretended to gain courage, charging.

The Razor stepped in, slashing in a crisscross move.

Maddox halted and jumped back fast as if terrified again.

The Razor puckered his lips to spit, slightly turned his head once more—

Maddox flipped the knife, grabbed it by the sharp tip and threw smoothly. The knife flashed through the air. The point sank into the Razor's left eye, sliding into the brain and killing the champion.

The Razor stood there for a second with the handle sprouting from his face like an obscene growth. Then he toppled backward.

Maddox raised his long arms into the air and began to strut about The Pit, finally going to the dead champion, reaching down and yanking out his knife.

It was then that the cheers began.

***

At the start of the next workweek, at the spaceport, a man handed Maddox a slip of paper. It told him to report to Culain Palace tomorrow at the fifth hour as Tribune Culain wished to speak with him.

-75-

Maddox went to Culain Palace at the edge of the city. In many ways, it was a miniature of Grandma's Palace at the South Pole.

Maddox didn't have his monofilament blade or pistol. He didn't have anything but his wits, although he'd purchased a few heavy iron rings with odd designs on them. They would serve as brass knuckles if the need arose.

He endured a thorough search and knew chem scanners had sniffed his clothes. Maddox now walked through a narrow corridor. He imagined spy devices scanned him. Then he felt something prick against his mind, feeling disquiet that he blocked the telepathic thrust.

That proved Tribune Culain employed South Pole talent.

Maddox knew this was madness. He was counting on the Honey Man's greed for more. As a man aged, he became more of his essential-core propensity. If he was given to drink, by the time he was old, he was a converted drunkard. If he practiced sexual license, whatever direction that had taken, he would be consumed by the particular lust. If a man always attempted to help others, by the time he was old, he would do it as a matter of course.

The difference was that a Honey Man lived longer than others did. He had the power of youth even when he was old. Thus, he could metastasize into whatever he was to an even greater degree. Given that Tribune Culain had sent legion men into castrated bondage, Maddox assumed that the man was a greed-driven evil force, always looking for opportunities to increase his wealth. Maddox had devised the plan upon that premise.

A heavy stone door opened at the end of the narrow corridor. Maddox stepped into a sumptuous room with silk hangings, erotic posters and weapons on the wall. There was a mammoth desk with small gold statutes on it. Behind the desk sat a large man. Flanked on either side of the desk were genetically enhanced wrestlers. They almost seemed like desert Metamorphs, such was the breadth of their chest and shoulders. They each wore dark garments and heavy bracelets on their massive wrists. They stared at Maddox with baleful expressions.

The man behind the desk had short gray hair, a broad square face and intensely black eyes. He wore a legion uniform and exuded power.

"Sit, Captain, sit.'"

Culain had called him Captain. Things were proceeding to plan.

"Are you surprised I know your name, Captain Maddox? And that I know you're from a different spiral arm than ours?"

"I am," Maddox said, as he sat in a chair.

"Would you have some wine with me before we discuss why you've come to see me?"

"I'd be delighted."

Culain opened a drawer and took out two glasses and a bottle. He uncorked the bottle and poured red wine into each glass. "This was grown on my own estates. It has a rich and exotic taste. I hope you enjoy it."

Culain pushed a glass across the huge desk.

As Maddox leaned forward to take the glass, he noticed the creases on Culain's face. He noticed that Culain's hair was dyed, and his face was painted like a woman's. Both were done for the same reason, to make Culain appear older.

That was a good sign for several reasons. If Culain cared what Maddox thought, that meant he might allow Maddox to leave. More importantly, Culain was likely one hundred and twenty years old but looked thirty or forty normally. Because he'd been around for so long, he tried to look his age.

Maddox sipped the wine as he watched Culain sip his. It was rich and sugary, not to Maddox's taste at all. He swallowed a minute amount. There was a slight taint. It was drugged.

Maddox smiled and set down the glass.

"Don't you like it, Captain?"

"On the contrary," Maddox said. "This is a rare vintage, quite enjoyable. However, I wish to keep my mind clear. You're an important man. I don't wish to waste your time by speaking to you with cluttered thoughts."

"I see." Culain rested his broad hands on his chest, intertwining his fingers. "Do you wonder how I've learned your identity?"

"I imagine you spoke to one of the people with me."

"Do you recognize the name Gricks?"

"You know I do."

"Do you know he offered to sell me information about you?"

"What?" Maddox asked.

"That surprises you?"

"Yes. After all I've done for him, it surprises me a lot."

"It shouldn't. I watched you destroy my knifeman in The Pit. You pretended to be a buffoon but are clearly something else entirely. That means you're a trickster. You surely know that men are venal, grasping for what they don't have. Gricks lacks his manhood, seeking it everywhere. Thus, he sells out his friends like a cheap whore to whatever bidder will pay the price."

Culain made a faint gesture. "In this case, I desired to learn about you. I knew that Gricks had fought in Legion Culain. How did he escape the debacle in the Highlands? Even now, my men are learning the truth from him. What do you think of that, Captain?"

"That you're a careful and suspicious man."

Culain scowled. "You're brash to say that to my face."

It was Maddox's turn to make a suave gesture. "I intend to speak the truth, Tribune. I also wish to sell to whoever meets my price. What I sell, however, isn't cheap, as it can bring you greater wealth and power."

390

Culain stared at Maddox, seeming to pretend haughty indifference. Intuition told Maddox otherwise.

"If you know my name," Maddox said, "you must know I appeared mysteriously as your legion landed in the Highlands. Like Gricks, I managed to escape not only from Grandma Julia, but to have her outfit me. I went into the mid-world desert. There, we descended and attacked Metamorphs."

"I've heard of that. I've also heard that Gallant Ophir left the sinkhole with a grav tank."

Maddox kept his features bland. He sensed a telepathic intrusion and blocked it easier than he'd ever done. Could this be part of the tiny change the Eye of Helion had made to his mind?

"Gallant Ophir left in one direction," Maddox said. "We left in another."

Culain's eyes narrowed. "How did you leave to reach here so quickly? I happen to know a little about the timeframe of all this. It doesn't match normal travel times."

"If you don't mind, I'll keep the how secret for now."

Culain pressed his thumb tips against each other, as he remained silent, staring at his desk. Finally, he looked up. "What can you tell me?"

"Do you know that nuclear warheads ignited mid-desert to slay thousands of Metamorphs?"

"Gricks said as much. He indicated Grandma Julia had something to do with that."

Maddox sat up, becoming earnest, deciding this was the moment to plant the hook. "What I wish to tell you has nothing to do with the mid-world desert or the sinkhole we entered and left."

"Oh?"

"Before reaching Gath, I was on a trader ship that had escaped from the ice moon of the gas giant far across the star system."

"You mean the gas giant Thetis?"

"I do," Maddox said. "On Thetis' ice moon was a computer Entity: a Leviathan project gone awry. The assault vessels were part of a Leviathan group that destroyed the Entity."

391

Culain nodded. "That matches what I've learned elsewhere."

"The Entity mined rich radioactive or fissionable ores on the ice moon. I'm sure much of the mined fissionables are still there. Leviathan hadn't had time to collect the ores before their assault vessels blew up."

"These fissionables are the great wealth you seek to hand me?" asked Culain.

"That's only part of it. There are empty spaceships on the ice moon," Maddox said. "The Entity waylaid these spaceships like a spider does flies. In truth, I escaped the ice moon in one of them. It's why I know they're there."

"The assault vessels surely destroyed the grounded spaceships when they defeated the Entity."

"There's that possibility," Maddox admitted. "Yet, I suggest there's a greater possibility some of the spaceships still exist, waiting for whoever takes the risk to claim them. I doubt the leader of the assault vessels thought they would lose at Gath. Thus, Leviathan would have no reason to have simply destroyed the trader ships."

"You may be right," Culain said. "What does any of that have to do with me?"

"With both of us, sir," Maddox said.

"I have no need of radioactive ores."

"Firstly, the ores are worth much currency. Secondly, what ambitious legion tribune wouldn't like a fleet of his own trader ships? He might start with taking the fissionables to worlds where they would sell for much profit."

An eager brightness appeared in Culain's eyes.

"That is what I'm selling, Tribune: the fissionables and the whereabouts of the trader ships. I'd join the expedition to locate and take control of the lost spaceships. I remember their location on the ice moon. I should add that it's a tricky place. I know the Entity laid traps for the greedy or unwary. I learned about those traps before I escaped."

"That's something that has been bothering me," Culain said. "How did you manage to escape such a desperate situation?"

Maddox nodded. "The Entity learned to trust me. At times, I moved some of the spaceships for it."

"Why would this Entity trust you?"

"Because I did more for it than I said I would. I gave it more than it wanted from me."

Culain's features hardened. "Do you believe me another Entity you can trick and fool? As it is obvious you eventually double-crossed the Entity."

"You aren't as gullible as the Entity. It's also in my interest to do as I say and accept the rewards from you. On the ice moon, the Entity would have eventually slain me, as it was in the computer's nature. Here, I believe you will be grateful for what I'm doing for you."

Culain's nostrils flared. "Why should I give you anything? Clearly, the trader vessels are near the mining operation. It would be a simple matter locating them through their radiation signatures."

"The traps, sir, the traps would destroy your expedition and leave you nothing but wasted currency."

Culain touched his chin. "What do you hope to gain from all this?"

"There are many vessels at the mining site. I want one. You can take the rest."

Culain nodded slowly. "Did you stage the knife fight to gain my interest?"

"You must know I did," Maddox said. "I doubt we would be talking otherwise."

Culain touched his chin again. "You're a dangerous man, Captain. What happens if I decided to take all the spaceships?"

"I don't think you would. There wouldn't be any advantage in it. There will be plenty of ships for all of us."

"Your offer is unusual and interesting," Culain said. "Spaceships, you've actually seen them?"

Maddox nodded.

"Of course, you have," Culain said. "How else could you have escaped in one? How did you reach the South Pole?"

"Through a teleportation device in the ship," Maddox said. "The spaceship was breaking up. As a last-ditch effort for survival, I risked using the device."

393

"You expect me to believe such fool nonsense as teleportation?"

"Tribune Culain, I raced to Gath in order to escape the assault vessels. Since you know my name, you know Leviathan sought me. You know the Soldier demanded my capture before their assault vessels detonated."

Culain became thoughtful. "Yes. How did the vessels detonate? Was this by teleportation again?"

"If so," Maddox said, "it wasn't of my doing."

"I believe you. If it were, you could have used the teleportation in a more inventive way. You intrigue me, Captain. Your tale intrigues me. Perhaps I shall rent an off-world spaceship and gather a crew. You would join the expedition to the ice moon, eh?"

"That is part of the bargain, sir."

Culain drummed his fingers on the desk. "I'd like to have spaceships of my own, no longer having to rely upon the off-worlders. This is an intriguing proposition. Why did you come to me and not someone else?"

"Gricks told me you were an ambitious man of wealth."

"Did he? Did he now?" Culain nodded. "I need time to think about this. I will send a man to meet you in three days. During that time, keep this information to yourself. Are we agreed?"

"I will give you three days to decide, Tribune."

"Now, finish your drink, Captain."

"Sir, if it pleases you, I prefer not to drink."

"A cautious man. Very well, Captain. This once you may escape a draught of the special vintage."

"It has been a pleasure, sir."

Tribune Culain dipped his head. "You may leave the same way you came."

Maddox rose and turned for the exit.

-76-

With Gricks' consent, Mara had mentally prepared him in anticipation of Culain's actions and to endure the tribune's usual interrogation procedures.

Why had Gricks agreed to such humiliation and pain? He hated Tribune Culain for what had occurred in the Highlands. Desperate in his hatred, Gricks yearned to retaliate against the instigator of the raid.

Mara had subdued the hate and temporarily changed facets of his personality. Therefore, Gricks appeared to be what Culain and his talent expected from such a one.

Under interrogation, Gricks pleaded, begged and cried, and gave information. It was slanted enough so Maddox's lies had sounded convincing. Further, Mara, through Dravek's cunning, had conditioned Gricks' mind so he only revealed certain choice items under harsh pain levels. These Gricks shouted out under grim torture and foul drug treatment.

Three days after the interview, Culain's agents brought Maddox to the compound. There, Maddox underwent tests proving he was proficient with spaceships.

Others began to gather for the secret mission to the ice moon. Among them were Mara and Dravek, disguised, and Hern, who was there as himself.

Nine days later, the team drove to spaceport central and entered a trader ship rented from the Off-world Syndicate that ran the library and ships coming to Gath.

Thirty people filed aboard. Some were Syndicate personnel to run the ship. Others were Culain's people, while a handful were Maddox and his team.

During the space trip to the Thetis ice moon, Maddox discovered that Culain, his talent and bruisers had joined the expedition. The reasons seemed clear enough. Culain didn't trust the Syndicate people to play him true. Culain had paid heavily for the privilege of renting an off-world spaceship. That included low-priced stock options in the legion organization. If the spaceship and prizes failed to return to Gath, Culain would be hard put to recoup what would be substantial losses. He was here to make sure things went his way.

It took three weeks of steady travel to near the gas giant Thetis. During that time, Maddox worked as a regular spaceman would. Dravek did the same. Mara endured, using her talent to detour any unwanted advances and protecting the others from Culain's talent.

Mara bumped into Maddox one day as she sashayed down a corridor. Maddox stopped her, leering. There were other spacemen present, Culain people.

Mara and Maddox thus spoke in code.

"He has taken much honey," Mara said. "That means he's old, in the range of two to two hundred and fifty years. He's like a spider, more dangerous than any of us realize. He may have guessed some among us have the ability. He may think you do. I know he suspects me. I cannot attempt any more telepathic probing."

"Understood," Maddox said, as he chucked her under the chin and told her how beautiful she was. Mara swung to slap his face. He caught her hand and spun her around, slapping her ass good and hard, making her yelp and jump.

Several watching spacemen laughed.

"My man will kill you for that," Mara screamed, with her fists clenched.

Maddox shrugged.

Mara left weeping.

It was an interesting situation. The trader ship belonged to the Syndicate. They were jealous of their ships. They didn't want Honey Men or North Pole tribunes to have spaceships of their own. There were thus spy games on the vessel run by the Syndicate, Tribune Culain and Maddox and Dravek.

Maddox figured out which were the off-world Syndicate men and which men belonged body and soul to Culain. All the while, the image of Thetis on the screens grew larger. The wealth of the ice moon's fissionable mines became obvious. Talk increased, and tension grew.

The time of testing would soon arrive. Who would make the first move, and would they surprise the others?

Three days later, the trader ship started to decelerate as they neared the ice moon.

So far, there had been no indications the Entity had survived the assault vessels. That didn't mean the computer intelligence was gone.

Soon now, the next stage of Maddox's desperate ploy was about to begin.

The vessel decelerated again as the gas giant's massive gravitational pull began to tug at it. Like Jupiter in the Solar System, Thetis contained most of the system's planetary mass. Only the system star was bigger.

As Thetis grew on the screens, so did the ice moon. Those on the bridge—Syndicate crew and Culain—watched closely. They sought any indication the Entity or a Leviathan trap was there.

The crew launched a probe and then another. Telemetry data showed that nothing Entity or Leviathan-based reacted to the probes. No missiles rose from the ice moon or elsewhere. No sensor sweep struck the trader vessel. No mines activated or beams stabbed.

The vessel moved more boldly as the Syndicate crew began to murmur among themselves. Maybe this was the time to dump the unwanted legion people. Culain debated if the moment was ripe to disarm those he distrusted, the Syndicate crew his primary suspects. Maddox and company knew they needed to strike first, hard and ruthlessly. Their numbers and position were the smallest and weakest, their plight the most desperate.

An interesting situation developed when Mara saw Culain's talent head toward the exercise room with others.

The telepath, or talent, was tall, imperious, and dark-haired. She wore a long black gown and her hair reached behind her shoulders. She had deep brown eyes that radiated with power.

She may not have been one of Grandma Julia's descendants, but she was certainly from the South Pole Highlands.

The two wrestlers with their black garments and heavy iron bracelets trailed her. What was interesting was that they pulled Gricks along by a leash attached to a collar as if he were a dog. He didn't crawl on all fours but whimpered and stumbled after them.

Mara hurried to Maddox, explaining the situation. He told her to get Dravek.

Soon, Maddox, Dravek and Mara hurried down the corridor to the weight room. Two of Culain's security men stood before the hatch.

"Can't use the weights for a while," one of the security men said. "The room's occupied for now."

Maddox laughed as if they'd told a joke. "There's something on your shoulder." Incredibly, the security man let Maddox touch him as if to brush the something away. Instead, Maddox slammed an elbow into the man's face. Dravek did likewise to the other. Both security men were thus rendered unconscious and laid on the deck.

Maddox looked at the other two. "Ready?"

Dravek nodded sharply. Mara took a fast breath.

Maddox opened the hatch. All three entered the chamber.

Gricks was on the floor, partly crushed by extremely heavy weights on his chest as he fought to breathe. The wrestlers were on either side of him with more weights in their hands.

The talent, the woman, stood at Gricks head. She'd pulled her dress up enough, so she couched over him, her long fingers pressed against his forehead.

"Hey," one wrestler said.

The talent looked up, frowning at the three intruders. "Leave at once," she said.

Maddox smirked at her.

The woman frowned more, perhaps concentrating her talent at Maddox.

Psionic power might have slammed against them, but Mara stepped up. She raised both hands, palms forward, shielding the other two.

The black-haired talent shot to her feet, facing them fully. She raised her hands.

Mara grunted, taking a step back and then holding her spot.

"You're more than a child," the woman said. "Yes. I've sensed you before. You're the one trying to tamper with the Tribune. Kill all three."

Nothing happened.

The woman glared at one of the wrestlers. "You oaf, I said kill them."

Both wrestlers dropped their weights, so they hit the floor hard. Gricks whimpered with fear as he continued to struggle for breath. The two wrestlers were big, thickly muscled and moved athletically. They were dynamos of physical prowess. The first slapped his meaty hands together as if this was a treat, which it probably was for him.

"Stay back," Maddox said, as if frightened of the man.

Idiot grins broke out upon both faces. The nearest wrestler reached for Maddox. It seemed as if the big man was going to twist Maddox into a pretzel.

Maddox moved fast with that unique speed that was his birthright. It was a blur as Maddox swept near and then to the side of the man.

The first wrestler jerked to a halt with a bewildered stare. He looked down at his slashed-open stomach as the entrails gushed out onto the floor.

Maddox had already attacked the second wrestler. The brute had swiped with his big hands. It had been futile against Maddox's speed. The monofilament blade had created a second smile underneath the man's chin. As if synchronized, both wrestlers toppled to the floor together, their heavy bracelets clunking loudly. The one gasped hideously, shuddering as he died. Maddox applied the coup de grace to the other, killing him so he didn't have to suffer.

"You're insane," the tall woman said. "You have no idea what you're playing at. You're all dead unless you release me this instant."

Dravek was behind her, having pulled both arms behind her back.

Mara stepped up.

400

Maddox made a point of cleaning the blood off his knife, using one of the wrestler's black shirts. Then he stepped near the talent, showing her the blade.

"You're going to tell us how Culain plans to disable the Syndicate crew," Maddox said.

The talent had nerve, giving him a cool sneer and slowly shaking her head. "I'll never tell you."

That started fifteen minutes of mental prying from Mara and physical pain inducements from Dravek. The talent gasped in agony more than once, gritting her teeth as she resisted.

"It won't work," Dravek whispered into an ear.

The talent cried out as he applied more pain.

Finally, Mara broke through the talent's weakened mental shield and ripped out of her mind the knowledge they needed.

Meanwhile, Maddox had removed the heavy weights from Gricks' chest. Gricks kept massaging his aching chest as he gulped air.

"I'm done," Mara said.

"What are you going to do to me?" the talent asked. Her cool reserve had vanished as fear shined in her eyes.

Maddox stepped up and pressed a hypogun against her neck. Air injected a knockout drug. Soon, the talent lay unconscious on the floor.

"I'm going to help you," Mara told Gricks.

The centurion looked at her fearfully.

"It's okay," Maddox said. "You're going to feel better soon. We're your friends, remember?"

At last, Gricks nodded.

Mara put her hands on Gricks' head.

He screamed and tried to hit her.

Luckily, Dravek and Maddox had stood behind him. They each grabbed an arm, holding him fast. Gricks bellowed and struggled as tears streamed down his face.

Mara used her psionic abilities to change his mind back to what it had been before. She returned his normal personality to the forefront.

At last, Gricks sagged, breathing deeply. He nodded. "You can release me. I am myself again."

Experimentally, Maddox and Dravek let go.

Gricks massaged his arms where they'd held him. Then he wiped the tears from his face and asked Mara, "What did you learn?"

"We need to get out of here," Mara said.

Gricks didn't pry further but nodded. He went to one of the wrestlers and knelt by him. What did he take?

Maddox was about to ask. Before he got to it, Gricks stood, turned and walked fast to the talent lying unconscious on the floor. He raised a squat little gun, a chemical-fueled slug thrower. He fired three bullets into the telepath, killing her.

Dravek was closest. He ripped the gun out of Gricks' hands. "Why'd you do that?"

"Why?" Gricks asked, his features a mask. "Because they did unspeakable things to me. Because she worked for the monster Culain. You have no idea what he's really like. He's much older than we suspected. Worse, he's a true Honey Man, steeped in evil. I hate him."

"That's understandable," Maddox said crisply. "Mara, what did you learn from her? What's Culain's plan?"

Mara told him.

"Right," Maddox said. "We need to make our move. Luckily Culain has given us the tools we need."

They left the weight room, first dragging the two security guards inside and injecting them with the knockout drug. Then they headed for engineering.

Dravek used the squat black gun, lining the engineers against the back bulkhead.

Maddox and Gricks found the special container placed there at the beginning of the voyage. They connected it and began injecting knockout gas through the venting system. They forced the engineers to breathe the gas.

Maddox recalled the Okos, scavengers who'd tried to pirate an inert *Victory* the first time the starship had arrived in the Scutum-Centaurus Spiral Arm. The plan had almost worked for the Okos, too. In a way, it was fitting using a similar tactic while in this spiral arm.

They had donned breathing masks and set to work to get everything ready for the next phase of the operation. It was almost time to see if they could achieve the near impossible.

-78-

The knockout gas worked to perfection. Every member of the ship, Syndicate, Culain's men, any others, were unconscious in their rooms, on the bridge, engineering, wherever.

They found Culain. That is to say, Gricks did. The others heard several shots from the next room.

"Damn it," Dravek said. "Gricks must have found another gun. We should have been more careful."

"It is a small matter," Maddox said.

Dravek stared at him. "What, you didn't want to dirty your hands with the lowbrow tactic of killing your defenseless enemy? Thus, you allowed Gricks a gun to do it for you?"

"Remember what we asked of Gricks," Maddox said quietly. "Because of that, we owed it to him to make a decision as to how he would deal with it."

Dravek didn't look convinced.

Soon, Gricks showed up. Even behind his breathing mask, he looked worried. "I killed Culain."

"Do you feel better because you did it?" Dravek asked.

Gricks cocked his head. "I do and I don't. He deserved it. His evil can't harm others now. What I did helps those in the North Pole of Gath, as he was a false legion tribune. Yet killing him doesn't change what happened to me. I...I wonder if vengeance killing will change my personality."

"Most assuredly," Mara said.

Gricks stared at the floor. Then he looked up. "So be it. They changed me first. I was just a regular legionnaire, but they changed me by castrating me. I'll continue to see what other changes develop because of what I just did. Do you still want my help, Dravek?"

"Yes," Dravek said.

"Don't fret about what you did," Hern said. They'd revived him from the gas and put a mask on his face. "What's done is done. You're a soldier, and in this instance, you brought retribution against the man who screwed over all our lost comrades. You did well, acting like a true centurion. We may make a primus of you yet."

Gricks stood a little taller.

Shortly after that, they loaded up the main lifeboat with supplies and departed the now drifting trader vessel.

The knockout gas would dissipate in the unconscious people's systems after a time. They would wake up, likely with horrible headaches and dry mouths. That meant those in the lifeboat only had a short time to do this.

Dravek sat in the piloting chair. The massive gas giant was monstrous behind them. The ice moon glittered before them. Maddox watched as Dravek piloted the lifeboat closer, resisting Thetis' gravitational pull. They soon entered the ice moon's orbital space and descended toward the surface.

Were the parked spaceships still down there? Were they intact or all destroyed by assault vessel beams and missiles weeks ago?

The sensor scope on the trader vessel's bridge had shown parked vessels. Maddox didn't believe the parked vessels were a ruse by a hidden Entity, but the possibility existed. Even if the ships were exactly as advertised, it didn't mean they were operational. If the grounded spaceships were a bust, they'd need the lifeboat to return to the drifting trader vessel as quickly as possible.

Given such an unwelcome situation—Maddox didn't have a contingency plan in case the spaceships down here didn't work. Could he just space all the excess people on the drifting trader vessel from Gath? No. That would be murder. Maybe he could land on the ice moon and put them in temporary internment buildings, calling the Gath spaceport and telling the off-worlders their people were stranded out here.

He didn't want to have to do that either.

Dravek piloted the lifeboat, so the frozen surface spread out before them. Maddox felt a sense of deja vu. He spotted the Methane Sea and the radioactive ores clicked as the sensors detected them. Ah. He saw masses of machine-pressed and cubed fissionables neatly stacked and ready for transport. Over there was the row of spaceships. One of them was upright as an old-style ship from Earth that had landed on its fins.

Which ship should he take?

Their time to choose was short, as time was running out for them.

Dravek maneuvered the lifeboat, so it flew low over the greater complex. Most of the domes, shacks and even anti-space launch systems were smashed wreckage. The Leviathan assault vessels must have done this. It didn't look as if there would be anywhere to house extra people. It didn't seem the Entity had survived in any capacity either.

Dravek landed the lifeboat near the row of captured spaceships. They suited up and went through the airlock, inspecting each of the smallish trader vessels. Most were intact and loaded with fuel, ready to go.

That was excellent news. Maddox wanted to leave the Gath Star System yesterday, meaning he wanted to leave as soon as he could.

Because time was at such a premium, they didn't return to the lifeboat but congregated outside the first trader ship, using the short comm in their spacesuits.

"The ships all look good," Dravek said. "Now what do we do?"

"Unless you want that one," Maddox said, pointing at the third ship, "I'll take it. That one strikes me as the easiest for one man to control."

"You're going alone?" Dravek asked, concerned. "What if you're stranded somewhere and never make it home? Or worse, what if something goes wrong with the ship and you're drifting in space for thirty years?"

"What if my arms fall off?" Maddox said. "I'm taking my chances. What do you say?"

"The ship is yours, Captain Maddox." Dravek came to attention on the icy surface of the moon. With Thetis large in the sky, he saluted.

The others stood straight, saluting as well.

"Thanks," Maddox said. "Now listen, I don't know what your plans are. I certainly wish you the best. But you should know I may be returning someday, maybe even someday soon. Leviathan is moving against Star Watch." Maddox's speech petered out as he reconsidered. "Try to keep out of Leviathan's way."

"Of course," Dravek said. "I'm remaining in the Heydell Cloud. But why do you say you might be back?"

"I have my reasons. Look, if I do return, I plan to look you up. Maybe if it's to your benefit, I'll enlist you in the service of Star Watch and you can help mankind here and, in the Commonwealth, as we work together against Leviathan."

"I'll keep that mind," Dravek said.

Maddox stepped forward, shaking gloved hands solemnly with Mara, Gricks, Hern and finally with Dravek.

"My brother," Maddox said, speaking on a private channel. "Thank you for all you've done. I never had a brother until I met you. Now, I hold you in the highest esteem. If ever you need my help, you need but ask."

For a moment, Dravek couldn't speak. Then he slapped Maddox on the suited shoulder. "I'm patterned after you, but I'm my own man. I've taken Mara, as you suggested. Now I'm choosing the best ship. It has armament. I have a few people but plan to recruit more. I'll collect enough here so I have goods to sell. Who knows what I'm going to do after that."

"In many ways, I envy you," Maddox said. "You have a great future ahead of you. It will be exactly what you make out of it. I know my own driving ambition. You have your own driving ambition. I would very much like to see what you've done ten years from now, twenty."

"Thanks for the encouragement," Dravek said.

They shook hands again, and then both men hugged each other, slapping each other on the suited shoulders.

"Goodbye, my brother."

"Goodbye, my brother."

Captain Maddox turned and headed for his chosen vessel. They headed for theirs.

Soon, Maddox's trader ship lifted off, heading into space. The thoughts and information placed by the Eye of Helion in his mind began to surface.

Maddox knew which spatial anomaly he needed to reach first. Thus, inputting the data, the ship headed for deeper space.

This had been a harsh adventure. The planet Gath was a dreadful place, made more dangerous by the Yon Soth asleep deep underground. If Star Watch ever used Gath as headquarters for an expeditionary force sent to the Heydell Cloud, they'd need to kill the Yon Soth first.

Maddox shrugged. That was all in the future. Who knew what was going to happen. First, he had to get home and give Star Watch a warning of what was happening out here.

"Meta," he said, as the ship began to accelerate for the distant spatial anomaly. "Jewel, I'm coming home."

-79-

Captain Maddox left the Gath Star System by plunging at precisely the right moment into an on-again, off-again spatial anomaly. He did so by using his intuitive sense and a little something extra in his mind that said go.

It was the first of many long-distance jumps. This one took him twenty-seven light-years in a bound. He appeared in a combat-blasted star system. There was floating rubble everywhere. After a quick check, Maddox realized the rubble was spread out evenly throughout the former system. That was puzzling and odd.

It took weeks of careful, precise maneuvering to reach the next spatial anomaly. That one propelled him one hundred and ten light-years in a bound.

Thus started his hard, tiring, often mind-numbing task of piloting his ship through space. He ate and worked out alone. His dreams were usually horrific and horrible. He relived his time in the southern Highlands and facing regular Metamorphs or the two-brained. In other dreams, he felt the grim evil of the Yon Soth searching for him throughout the cosmos, knowing that at this moment he was defenseless against it.

Other times, he dreamed of Meta, her beauty, having her almost in his arms. As he reached for her, Meta would dissipate, leaving him. In a different dream, he would hear Jewel calling him. He'd race down dark corridors, shouting, "Jewel, Jewel, I'm here." He'd catch fleeting glimpses of her, and then she would disappear. He'd wake up angry, determined, wanting the trip to go faster.

Another odd feature was that the knowledge of the locations and types of spatial anomalies given from the Eye of Helion as a gift in his mind dissipated a little after each successful jump. These were jumps made with precise timing. Without his intuitive sense and calm from the Way of the Pilgrim, and the mind map given by the Eye, this would have been impossible.

The months ticked by until he reached a dread gulf that he thought he could never cross. He did find a way, but it cost him two months of waiting for a rare anomaly to appear.

He raced after that, reaching to within one hundred and twenty-nine light years from the Omicron 9 System.

There was a terrible accident. A ship system failed, and noxious gases ejected. Maddox barely made it into a spacesuit in time to save his life. Alas, he slumped unconscious, stricken by the gases.

The air inside his helmet and tanks would last for a little while. When that failed, he would die, no longer having to strive against the cruel universe.

However, at that point a strange event took place. It was conceivable that Maddox had a guardian angel of sorts.

There was a wink like a bright star or gem or crystal. That wink sent a faster-than-light message many light years.

At the other end was an AI entity named Galyan, a defied AI of Adok design. He received the data, as he was the only one capable of receiving it.

From that began a chain reaction of events as Galyan spoke to Valerie, who spoke to Maddox's grandmother Mary O'Hara, who spoke to the Lord High Admiral, and he spoke again to Galyan.

In a relatively short time from first receiving the message from deep space, Galyan appeared to Meta in her house near Carson City, Nevada Sector.

"Meta," Galyan said in the living room.

Meta was a beautiful, blonde-haired, voluptuous woman who yet grieved for her lost husband. She sat in an easy chair watching a mindless sitcom.

"Meta," Galyan said again.

Meta finally looked up, frowning. "What are you doing in my house? You're not supposed to do this, Galyan."

"Quickly, Meta, you must retrieve Jewel from school. A shuttle is already being sent down for the two of you."

"Why? What has happened?"

"Hurry, Meta. We think we have found the captain."

"No," Meta said. "You mean Maddox, my husband?"

"Hurry, Meta, please. I do not want him to have died because he did so much to try to bring me together with the living Adoks. This has all been my fault and now I must help him."

"Enough of this," Meta said, as hope transformed her into a raving beauty indeed. "We must hurry."

She dashed to the air car outside. Maddox had bought it for her some time ago. She flew to the local elementary school, rushing into the classroom and picking up her daughter.

"Do you have a pass?" the teacher asked.

Meta ran out without saying a word. One person tried to interfere. He crashed onto his back as Meta ran over him as she clutched Jewel against her.

Within the hour, with everyone aboard, Starship *Victory* used the Builder nexus, the one between Earth and its moon. The starship made a hyper-spatial jump to the Omicron 9 System. At the Omicron 9 Builder nexus, in conjunction with the Builder scanner in Pluto giving the precise coordinates, *Victory* used another hyper-spatial tube. The starship catapulted the one hundred and twenty-nine light-years, popping out of the tube. Galyan, Andros and Ludendorff scanned the star system, searching.

"There it is," Galyan said, "I see it. Do you see the little ship? Can Captain Maddox be aboard it?"

Galyan disappeared before anyone could answer him. The little Adok holoimage reappeared on the bridge almost instantly. His eyes were huge and staring. "It is Captain Maddox. His air is almost gone. We must go to him. We must hurry."

Lieutenant Commander Valerie Noonan gave a smooth command.

Victory used its star drive to make a short jump. Moments later, Keith was aboard a shuttle, leaving through a hangar bay hatch. Faster than anyone else could, Keith docked with the alien trader vessel. Then he, Professor Ludendorff and others in spacesuits rushed into the ship. They took Captain Maddox's inert space-suited form. Keith added an emergency breathing pack to the suit.

Maddox shuddered and shuddered again. He opened his eyes, seeing helmets with dark visors staring down at him. They looked so familiar, though. He remembered the time he'd woken up in a cryo unit on an alien spaceliner. Was he beginning this adventure all over again? Had he had an awful dream?

"Captain, Captain Maddox," Keith said, "Are you awake?"

"Keith Maker?" Maddox said weakly. "Is that you?"

They all cheered.

Then Maddox saw Galyan watching. "Oh. I take it you found me."

"Yes, sir," Galyan said, "You are going to be home on *Victory* shortly. Your wife and daughter are there waiting for you."

"Oh," Maddox said. He struggled to sit up.

"No, no, you're too weak," Keith said. "We're going to take you to the shuttle. Then we're going to take you to your wife and daughter."

"How long have I been gone?" Maddox said.

"Over three years," Keith said. His voice was choked with emotion, as if he were on the verge of tears.

"It's good to see you, old son," Ludendorff said in a gruff voice. "What did you do? How did you disappear off the bridge? The last thing we remember was Grutch grabbing you. Did you kill him?"

"Not yet," Maddox said.

They carried the captain aboard the shuttle. Keith piloted him to *Victory*. There, in the hangar bay, tired, exhausted, but oh, so intensely happy Captain Maddox staggered out. He no longer wore the spacesuit.

"Maddox, Maddox, Maddox!" Meta called out, rushing to him. She would have knocked him down, but she clutched him

411

so hard that she kept that from happening. It was a bone-crushing grip.

Maddox found it hard to breathe. That breathing became even harder as Meta showered his face with wet kisses. Finally, he laughed and kissed her back on the mouth.

"Oh, Daddy, Daddy," Jewel said.

Released by Meta, Maddox knelt beside Jewel. He hugged his little baby girl. She'd gotten so big. It was amazing. "I missed you, honey. I missed you so much. I love you."

"I love you, too, Daddy. Don't ever leave me again. Please, Daddy, don't ever leave me again."

Maddox tousled the hair on her head. She was so beautiful. Jewel so looked like Meta. He lifted her in his arm and then clutched Meta in his other arm. "It's so good to be home. It's so good to be among my family and friends. I've missed you all."

"We've missed you," Meta said.

Everyone cheered again.

The captain was back. Everything was going to be okay.

THE END

LOST STARSHIP SERIES:

The Lost Starship
The Lost Command
The Lost Destroyer
The Lost Colony
The Lost Patrol
The Lost Planet
The Lost Earth
The Lost Artifactt
The Lost Star Gate
The Lost Supernova
The Lost Swarm
The Lost Intelligence
The Lost Tech
The Lost Secret
The Lost Barrier
The Lost Nebula
The Lost Relic
The Lost Task Force
The Lost Clone

Visit VaughnHeppner.com for more information

Printed in Great Britain
by Amazon

29720160R00235